A MATTER OF REVENGE

A JOHN APPARITE NOVEL

A MATTER OF REVENGE

I. MICHAEL KOONTZ

FIVE STAR

A part of Gale, Cengage Learning

Detroit • New York • San Francisco • New Haven, Conn • Waterville, Maine • London

GALE
CENGAGE Learning·

Copyright © 2008 by I. Michael Koontz.
Five Star Publishing, a part of Gale, Cengage Learning.

Set in 11 pt. Plantin.
Printed on permanent paper.

LIBRARY OF CONGRESS CATALOGING-IN-PUBLICATION DATA

Koontz, I. Michael, 1963–
    A matter of revenge : a John Apparite novel / I. Michael Koontz. — 1st ed.
    p. cm.
    ISBN-13: 978-1-59414-674-9 (alk. paper)
    ISBN-10: 1-59414-674-8 (alk. paper)
    1. Berlin (Germany)—Fiction. 2. Germany—History—1945–1990—Fiction. I. Title.
    PS3611.0625M38 2008
    813'.6—dc22
                            2008019930

First Edition. First Printing: September 2008.
Published in 2008 in conjunction with Tekno Books and Ed Gorman.

Printed in the United States of America
1 2 3 4 5 6 7 12 11 10 09 08

For the men and women of U.S. Intelligence who bravely
served in the city of Berlin during the Cold War

The world is large when weary leagues
two loving hearts divide,
But the world is small when your enemy
is loose on the other side.

John Boyle O'Reilly, 1844–1890

Distance

INTRODUCTION

In the half-century following World War Two, the epicenter of the Cold War was the German city of Berlin. Pre-war Berlin was a marvel, perhaps the most beautiful and sophisticated city in the world, but as the capital and spiritual heart of the Third Reich it had also been uniquely fated for destruction in the war that followed. For over three years Allied bombing razed countless blocks of it into the ground, and then, in the spring of 1945 in the great, last battle of the European theater, Russian *katyushas* and T-34 tanks leveled much of the remainder, building by building and block by block. By the end of the war, Berlin was, to most observers, no longer a city but one giant, smoking pile of rubble. In fact, one-seventh of all rubble in post-war Germany would belong to its former, glorious capital.

But to the Russians, who had suffered most from the evil aims of Hitler's armies and to whom the city eventually would fall, the destruction of Berlin was to be more than simply a mechanical dismantling of its defenses or its buildings. To Stalin, the Soviet conquering of Berlin was meant to be a thorough humbling, even debasing of an arrogant people and city; a complete pay-back, *with interest,* for the terror Hitler had inflicted upon "Mother Russia" since 1941.

This, perhaps, explains the rapes; the thousands and thousands of rapes when the Red Army swept through the city. This, perhaps, explains the suicides; the wave of suicides, especially among the women, that came with the city's fall.

7

Introduction

This, perhaps, explains the tortures and decade-long imprisonments of German POWs captured in the battle; and this, perhaps, explains the blockade of 1948–49, when the Soviets attempted to starve the western half of Berlin into capitulation. This, perhaps, explains why no other city suffered as much under Soviet occupation.

Per the terms of the Potsdam Agreement, post-war Berlin was split into four sectors—French, British, American, and Soviet—but in practical terms, the split had actually been in two: there was Soviet East Berlin, where the people lived austerely and often in fear, and Free West Berlin, where the people lived better but in dread of the Soviets, who held the lands surrounding their small island of freedom. If one might have said that the face of Berlin had been split into two sides, one also might have noted, a decade after war's end, how little each side of that face still resembled the other.

And as Berlin tried to heal itself after the war, and the German people tried to come to grips with what they had wrought the decade before, the Cold War played itself out in intense miniature on the streets of Germany's former capital. It was estimated that thousands—not dozens, not hundreds, but *thousands*—of intelligence agents and personnel were operating in Berlin, each doing their part in the spying, kidnapping, and even killing that was occurring in the name of their various causes and nations. It became, as sometimes it was put, a "swamp of spies," where friends might be exposed as enemies, enemies might become one's friends, and the man sitting next to you might kidnap or kill you if you were inattentive.

It is therefore not surprising that one day John Apparite would find himself in this city of spies, working in his capacity as a "Superagent" in the most covert and powerful espionage program in United States history. Much has been uncovered about Berlin since the Wall fell in 1989, but in the great tales of spies and dupes and defectors and assassins the name "John Apparite" remains hidden, just as his superior, the mysterious man he called the "Director," would have wished. And yet to those few who knew him, John Apparite's Berlin adventures are thought to be, perhaps, the greatest in his legendary career as a Superagent, although it must be said that in other ways, meaning those on a personal, human level, they were also certainly among the worst.

What follows is another part of his seemingly implausible, impossible, and unbelievable tale—it begins and ends in Belgium, though most of it takes place in the morass of intrigue that was Cold War Berlin—but how implausible, impossible, and unbelievable will be left for the reader to decide. Suffice it to say that John Apparite's name does not appear in any government file or computer data bank. Suffice it to say that no one I have spoken with in the official United States Government has ever heard of a "Superagent," or of anyone who might have been known as the "Director."

Suffice it to say that if such a spy and such an agency ever *had* indeed existed, would any reasonable person have expected anything different?

ONE:
A DEATH IN BELGIUM

The panicked American GI ran down the snow-covered dirt road as fast as his tired legs could propel him, but it was a damned tough slog: the ground had been turned into a muddy quagmire under the pressure of heavy armored vehicles and tanks, and he was carrying over thirty pounds of equipment, including a bazooka and M1 rifle. This man, who was a private in the U.S. Army, was literally running for his life. He had been separated from his company after a skirmish near the town of Malmédy, Belgium, and German Panzers and armored assault vehicles were less than a quarter-mile behind him. He could hear the metallic grinding of their tank treads and the spinning of truck wheels in the increasing mud-bath that slowed all who encountered it.

The Germans were members of the 1ˢᵗ SS Panzer Division, an elite fighting force whose reputation was bolstered by the fact that they were also known as the "Adolf Hitler Division," a point of intense pride for the men who served in it. They were notorious for their ruthlessness and ferocity, and as an essential part of Hitler's grand December offensive (their being on the northern edge of the salient into Belgium), they were thirsting for action. Since the *Führer* had launched his surprise attack the day before, December 16ᵗʰ, 1944, the 1ˢᵗ SS Panzers had sent countless American units scattering, and killed hundreds of GIs.

If all went well, it was hoped this incursion into the American lines would reach the vital port of Antwerp, and the U.S. and British offensive toward Germany would be halted. The commander of the lead group of tanks and armored vehicles, SS Captain Wilhelm Heydrich, was especially zealous in his pursuit of the fleeing Americans. If his unit was the first to reach Antwerp, he would surely receive the "Iron Cross" as his reward—to be pinned on by the *Führer* himself, he surmised. A fanatical Nazi (as was his commander, SS Lieutenant-Colonel Joachim Peiper, an uncompromising man whom Heydrich worshipped with extreme devotion), he knew that this event was woven into the fabric of the future, as was the eventual victory of the Third Reich. He would let nothing stand in his way.

The GI ran toward a small café, which was a short distance from a road intersection known to the native Belgians as the "Baugnez Crossroads," but the Americans, who never could pronounce any foreign words the way they were designed, had simply renamed it "Five Points." The lone GI knew that if he held out but another few hours, or perhaps a day at the most, his unit would eventually reform at this intersection, and when their numbers became great enough they would launch a counter-attack against the advancing Germans.

But that was in a very uncertain future. At present, he was most concerned with the increasing sound of armored vehicles coming in his direction, and the lack of places for him to hide. The café in question was the only building in the immediate area, and though it would be in an exposed position as the enemy came down the road, the GI figured he could at least gather his thoughts inside it. Surprisingly it had been left untouched by the fighting, and despite its boarded windows still looked rather warm and inviting.

The GI burst into the small, two-story wooden building. He fully expected it to be empty, given that a frantic battle was raging in the surrounding countryside, but to his surprise two men dressed in native Belgian clothing were seated at a small round table in the corner of the room, sipping coffee as they pored over some documents. One of the men, who appeared to be about forty years of age despite the deep skin creases around his eyes, expertly whipped out an American military service revolver and pointed it directly at the GI's chest.

"Who are you, soldier?" he demanded. "What are you doing here?"

"I'm lost; my unit was scattered when we came under fire near Five Points."

"Where're you from? What's your hometown?"

"*What?*" the GI answered with incredulity: he did not understand why he was being asked such an irrelevant question with German Panzer tanks rolling down the road toward them. Even from inside the café he could hear the rumbling of their treads as they approached.

"Your hometown!" the man repeated. He cocked his revolver to add emphasis to the query.

"Eckhart Springs, Maryland. Came as a replacement a month ago: the Two Ninety-first Combat Engineers."

"You a baseball fan?"

This was getting ridiculous, the GI thought. *Baseball*—at a time like this? Still, the man had him at gunpoint, so he was not about to argue.

"Sure," he answered. "Big Senators fan, though most people where I'm from are for the Pirates."

"Who is 'Big Poison'?"

" 'Big Poison'? Paul Waner; Pirates outfielder. Why're you ask—?"

"And who is his brother?"

"His brother? Lloyd Waner—they call him 'Little Poison.' 'Big Poison,' 'Little Poison.' "

The man lowered his pistol; he smiled grimly and spoke.

"There are German SS disguised as Americans. They speak English and can be very convincing, so I had to be sure." The sound of an artillery round exploding nearby caused the three men to simultaneously turn their heads in the direction of the road outside.

"How close are they?" the man asked.

"About a quarter-mile away. They'll be here in less than ten minutes."

"Their strength?"

"More than the three of us can handle. They got tanks, armored troop carriers—everything. We're running out of time—we gotta get the hell out of here!" he exclaimed, losing patience.

Despite the GI's outburst the man remained calm, answering him in a calculated, even manner.

"I need to tell you about me, and make you understand the situation, Private. Have you heard of the OSS, the Office of Strategic Services?"

"Yeah, it's where our spies are from."

"I am going to tell you something you can never repeat. I am an OSS operative. I escaped across the German border with a case of scientific documents and samples that might change the course of the war. My companion," he said, gesturing with the barrel of the pistol toward an older, silver-haired man with a kind face, "is the owner of this café and my contact on the border. If captured by the Germans, we would both be treated as spies. Do you understand what that would mean?"

The GI nodded: they would be shot on sight, or tortured for information and killed.

"We cannot be taken. If it comes to it, the last two bullets in this revolver are meant for ourselves."

"The Krauts are gonna be here in two minutes—what're we gonna do?" the GI asked.

The Belgian man spoke.

"Under this floor is a secret room; it can accommodate two. There is food for three days, and perhaps, by then, the American Army will have returned. But it must be concealed from the outside, you know—otherwise it might fit all of us."

The GI thought for a second and spoke.

"Okay, I see what has to be done. You two get inside the room—I'll make sure the entrance is hidden and hold off the Krauts. Just before you crawl in, put a round in the bazooka and I'll try and hit their lead tank."

The OSS man nodded, answering him in a grave tone.

"If we make it, I won't forget you, Private."

The sound of the German tanks increased in intensity; they had rounded a turn in the road, coming clear of the woods, and were now less than two hundred yards away. The silver-haired Belgian rolled back the rug from under the heavy table, revealing the dusty, worn wooden floor. He tapped in a few places and then removed a small knife from his pocket. He lifted the edge of a hidden trap-door with the blade, and pulled it open.

"After we are inside, you must disguise the edge of the door with dirt, and then rearrange the rug and table," he said.

The GI nodded. He was frightened but also knew that he was doing something important, for once, and that tempered his fear. For so long he had done so *little* of importance, it seemed: back home he was only an insurance salesman, and not a very successful one, at that. He'd spent most of his time traveling the Atlantic Coast trying to get people to insure their meager lives and possessions, but usually ended up coming home with very little in his pocket to show for it. His wife, he hated to admit, made more money than he at her job as a schoolteacher, and his young son, only fourteen years of age, was practically a stranger to him. About all they did together (and only when he was home from his travels) was hunt, and follow their favorite ball-club, the Washington Senators. Was that enough to truly be called a father? Sometimes, he just didn't know.

So he had volunteered for the Army to prove to them, and also to himself, that he could do something noble, that he could show his worth and mettle by aiding his nation in its time of need. He was nearly rejected by the Army right out of the blocks—he was approaching forty and had feet perched on the edge of flatness—but they had taken him in their need to supply the vast numbers of men for the big push into Germany.

And now he *was* doing something important! *Vitally* important—just as the mysterious OSS man had said! When he got back home after the war, he thought, I'll finally have something to tell my family that will make them proud.

He peeked through the cracks of the boarded-up window and saw them coming: there were at least five German tanks plus a couple of troop carriers. Despite the rumblings of the Panzers he could hear the *tramp-tramp-tramp* of the rows of infantry marching behind.

The OSS man was standing behind him, holding the bazooka-round in his hands. The GI grabbed one of the small boards covering the window and gave it a firm tug; with a jolt, it came off in his hands. He broke the glass with the barrel of the bazooka, knelt on one knee, and steadied himself.

"When I say 'now,' put the round in and tap me on the shoulder when it is seated. Then jump down the trap-door and I'll do the rest. If I make it back to our lines, I'll send someone for you."

The Germans were now less than one hundred yards away. The GI could not only hear them but could *smell* them; the fumes and acrid smoke from their tanks wafted with the breeze into the little café. He knew he would only get one shot—hell, he only *had* one shot—so if he was to slow them, he'd have to hit that first Panzer on the nose. Complicating matters was the fact that he'd never fired a bazooka before, but he did have a buddy that once showed him how to do it, and perhaps, he hoped, his prior hunting experience would take care of the rest. A tank *is* a bigger target than a buck, he thought.

The lead Panzer on the narrow road closed to within fifty yards. The windows of the café rattled madly and the chandelier began to sway from the vibration of the oncoming tanks. The GI knew it was time. He steadied himself, aimed the bazooka just under the lead tank's turret, and shouted, "Now!"

The OSS man shoved the round into the bazooka. Feeling it seat inside it, he tapped the GI on the shoulder and disappeared into the hidden room. The trap-door shut with a hollow thud.

The GI fired the bazooka, although the kick from the weapon was much stronger than he had expected and it nearly knocked him over from his kneeling position. And yet the round hit home. The front of the Panzer exploded in a red and black flash; even from his position inside the café the GI felt the concussion from the blast. The tank spun slightly in the road, blocking it, its gun pointing at a thirty-degree angle to the ground.

The GI dove under the heavy table and quickly covered the crack of the trap-door with dirt and crumbs until it was invisible. He heard the sound of tanks straining to move down the road and guessed the Germans were trying to push the disabled Panzer into the ditch. He frantically replaced the rug, covering the trap-door, and began to place chairs around the table when he heard an unusual sound.

It was not a *bang*, nor was it a *boom;* rather, it was the *woosh* of air being moved and parted by the firing of a Panzer round, and the moment after the *woosh* was heard the café came down on him—only then did he hear the familiar *boom* of a German tank firing a shell. Fortunately, the GI had ducked under the table at the first hint of an oncoming round, and remained uninjured.

But the damage had been done. There was practically no café *left* anymore; the cold breeze from the unusually harsh Belgian winter rushed in unimpeded by walls or furnishings. Although the GI had been stunned but a little from the concussion of the blast, he knew it was useless to fight any longer. He was exhausted; his M1 rifle lay buried under ten thousand pounds of destroyed café; German tanks and infantry were only forty yards distant; and he was alone.

He did not wish the Krauts to investigate the ruins of the café, so he decided to give himself up down the road. Before crawling out from the wreckage, however, he wanted to make sure the two hidden men were still okay. He thought he'd tap on the door as a signal, thinking that if he used the old "Shave and a haircut: two bits!" tap, then the men in the small cellar might feel safe in answering him.

"*Tap, tap, tap-tap, tap* . . ." Pause.

"*Tap, tap,*" came the muffled answer in perfect rhythm.

Satisfied that he had done all he could, the GI worked his way through the wreckage, stood up with his hands behind his head, and walked onto the muddy road in front of the café. He was about to be captured and taken to a prison-camp, but as far as he was concerned it was the proudest day of his life.

An hour later, the GI was standing in the middle of a field with scores of other captured Americans. He saw a few men from his own unit, but there appeared to be many men from many units, which he knew was a bad sign: it meant that the Germans had disrupted the American lines along a very wide front. Despite the presence of well over one hundred U.S. soldiers, the field was absolutely silent: shortly after they had gathered here, the Germans shot and killed a GI who had spoken harshly to the

SS captain in command. The message had immediately hit home: *We are not fooling around today, Americans.*

It was cold and the ground was covered in snow; the sight of these grown men all shivering and blowing into their hands to keep warm might have been comical if not for the severity of their situation. But the German commander, SS Captain Wilhelm Heydrich, did not find *anything* amusing about it: he did *not* want to waste valuable time herding freezing prisoners around. This was delaying the inevitable! These stupid, *captured* Americans were holding up his triumphant drive to the Meuse River and then to Antwerp! He had been ordered to wait for reinforcements to take these GIs off his hands, but they had not come, nor did he have anywhere to securely sequester these men. For now, he and they were stuck in this snowy field on the edge of the woods, waiting in the cold.

Suddenly, a shot rang out from a German *Schmeisser MP43.* It was unclear to witnesses whether this had been ordered by Heydrich or whether a German infantryman had decided to permanently silence an unruly American, but all heads turned the same direction, and the GIs saw, for the second time that day, one of their own hit the ground: dead. There was a tense two seconds of silence, and then the Germans let them have it: countless *Schmeissers* and *Mauser MP42* machine-guns opened up on the American prisoners. The GIs scattered and ran.

Some got as far as the woods before they were gunned-down; others were cut almost in half as they stood, too stunned to move their near-frozen legs; and some, the fortunate ones, escaped into the cold. The GI who had been captured at the café took off for the woods with the speed of a startled deer, and had almost reached them when a shot hit him in the leg, and then the left flank, and he was down. He was not to be among the fortunate.

His face was partly buried in the snow and his breathing was heavy, and yet his wounds hardly hurt at all. His body's natural opiates were coursing through him, and the resulting sensation was almost pleasant, in a way—only the labor of breathing disturbed the peacefulness he felt. After a minute of silence, he heard the sound of scattered and yet deliberate-sounding gunshots: *Crack! Crack!* Pause. *Crack! Crack-crack!* And he guessed what they meant: the Germans were shooting the wounded. He heard nearby footsteps and knew that his time, too, had come.

But though the end of his life was imminent, the GI felt no fear. He had done his duty, and he had done his family proud. He thought of his son back in Maryland, praying that the boy would someday learn what his daddy had done on December 17th, 1944, in what later became known as "the Battle of the Bulge." The GI was not a terribly religious man, but thought that if, indeed, there was an Almighty, then somehow it would happen. Somehow, it *had* to happen.

"Frank," the GI said aloud, speaking his boy's name. "My Frankie." And then a shot rang out. And then he was dead.

It was mid-January, 1945, and the American 30th Division had stumbled upon a massacre: in a snow-covered field were the frozen bodies of over eighty GIs. Some had been wounded in the back; others had been shot in the buttocks or the rear of the thigh; and the implication was clear: they were fleeing and had been shot from behind. But an even more disturbing sign was present to the careful observer, for many of the bodies had bullet-holes in the backs of their skulls, indicating a deliberate, calculated execution of the wounded.

A short distance away, in the town of Malmédy, an OSS man was told of the massacre. He had been searching for a GI from Maryland who had saved him and a colleague in a nearby café, but all he had discovered was that the soldier had been listed as

"Missing in Action." He wondered if the GI had somehow fallen-in with the murdered American prisoners in the field, but he hoped to God not. The man was a hero; he did not deserve to die like that.

He hopped into a jeep and his adjutant drove him to the location of the massacre. The sight of it was a horror: there were dozens of frozen bodies, some in grotesque positions—arms at odd angles, legs splayed in all directions—with dark maroon stains of coagulated and frozen blood surrounding each dead man. Numbered tags had been attached to each corpse for the purpose of identification, and Army photographers, carefully stepping between the bodies, took pictures for war-crimes documentation.

The OSS man paused at each body. Some were easily identifiable but others had been mutilated; probably by scavengers, he guessed. But when he reached the woods, he saw an untouched, familiar face partly buried in the snow: it was the GI from Maryland. The man bent over and gently took the dog-tags from the dead soldier's neck, slipping them into his own pocket. He removed the GI's leather wallet and opened it. Inside it were a few dollars, a photograph of the GI (dressed in a suit) standing next to an attractive woman and a young boy, and, oddly, an old tobacco card of famous Washington Senators pitcher Walter Johnson, which he had found inside a folded sheet of paper.

The OSS man gingerly held the small card between his thumb and forefinger: "Piedmont: The Cigarette of Quality" it said on the back. Though the card was at least three decades old, it was in surprisingly good condition (just a little wear at the corners was all it had suffered over the years). The care with which the GI had preserved the card betrayed its status as a prized possession.

The sight of this card had an unusual effect on the OSS man.

Despite his sadness at learning of the heroic GI's tragic fate, he allowed a slight smile to cross his face: unbeknownst to nearly everyone at the OSS, he and Hall of Fame pitcher Walter Johnson had long been the closest of friends.

The coincidence struck him in a way that little else had in his very serious, ordered, and regimented life. The OSS man was known to be one of the most talented but mysterious and dour characters in all of the American intelligence community; even his superior, the legendary "Wild Bill" Donovan, was in awe of the man's competence and inscrutable demeanor. But there was something in the discovery of this card that brought the OSS man out of his usual mind-set: he had been *meant* to find it, he believed. Despite the admittedly illogical nature of the thought, he knew that this baseball card was more than just a reminder of home to the dead GI and to himself. It was a signal, a sign of *kismet* that he could not ignore.

He looked at the boy in the photograph, then back at the tobacco card, and knew what he would do. When he returned to the States, he would discreetly take the card to his old friend Walter Johnson to have it autographed, and then send it anonymously to the young boy's mother, the dead GI's widow. The OSS man decided to pass the card onto them just as mysteriously as it seemingly had been passed onto him, and the thought of the boy's expression of delight when his mother inevitably gave it to him made the OSS man smile again.

He took another look at the child in the photograph. The boy appeared somewhat smallish but had an expression of unusual sensitivity and intelligence on his face, and though this was just a snap-shot, the briefest of moments from this boy's life, the OSS man felt he knew him. This child, he decided, deserved to know what his father did for his country; he would write the letter of condolence himself and send it to him. As the OSS man covered up the face of the dead GI with a blanket, he had a very strange but definite feeling that someday he and the dead man's young son would meet, a feeling he could not shake.

Curiously, he would be proved correct.

Two:
Jack Dempsey's Broadway Restaurant

A young man sat at a small table in Jack Dempsey's Broadway Restaurant; it was mid-April of 1956 and he was alone. By the word "alone," it is not only meant that there was no one sitting with him at the small table (upon which a half-empty glass of Knickerbocker beer was resting next to a squat, lit candle), but also that he was by himself, for all intents and purposes, in the whole of the world. He had no living relatives, and no friends to call his own at this point of his life. He lived alone, dined alone, and definitely slept alone, and even if there had been others to share his time with at this moment, or at his table, they would not have known, really, with whom they were dining, anyway. The young man's driver's license said his name was "Stanley Harris," but that was untrue: the name was an alias, provided by his supervisor. His "real" name, which had also been given to him by his supervisor, and was used in public only outside of the United States, was John Apparite.

And behind the name "John Apparite" was another, even more convoluted tale: *that* name had only belonged to the young man since July 2nd, 1955, when the then twenty-five-year-old ex-FBI agent and CIA trainee had joined the most clandestine and powerful of United States espionage agencies. If his old life no longer existed since he had "died" in the staged wreck of his Studebaker that July day, then his new life existed only a hair's breadth beyond one who actually *was* dead. He was essentially a nameless, faceless presence in this and every town, biding his time in the public world like it was a sort of purgatory to be suffered until his next mission—and he hated it.

Apparite took a sip of the Knickerbocker. It was a decent beer, he thought—even better than National Bohemian, the beer he had drank in D.C. in his old life—and although it was his sixth of the evening, it tasted just about as good as the first. He took another bite of the sirloin steak he had ordered (a Jack Dempsey's specialty) and washed it down with a sip of the bubbly, golden liquid. Fidgeting in the green-and-white-striped chair, he tried to get a kink out of his back; finding success, he wiped his mouth with a cloth napkin and smiled. His head, he was pleased to note, was swimming with *just* the right amount of alcohol-induced buzzing; not too much as to appear grossly intoxicated, and yet enough to briefly forget his troubles. But it would not last. Peace from his troubles had never lasted long enough and would not this night, either; even now, though he tried and tried to avoid it as he drained his glass, his troubles began pushing through his pleasant, beery haze.

His troubles. He had served in his present agency for less than nine months but had accumulated enough troubles, he believed, to last a lifetime. Just a few months earlier he had returned from his last mission in London and was still reeling from its effects. His supervisor (whom Apparite called the "Director," since the man's true name was unknown and he had no formal title), had told him the mission had been a success, but Apparite knew better. Sure, he'd assassinated a vital Soviet rocket scientist with *Ricinus* poison; had thwarted a SMERSH plot to obtain missile-fuel secrets; had killed two KGB agents while held captive; had exposed and eliminated an English traitor from the British MI6 agency; and had foiled an assassination plot to kill the Queen of England—but none of that seemed to matter to Apparite. Those events might have been placed in the plus column for the mission, but it was the minus column that was overwhelming him.

That column held three entries. Number one was the escape of the Soviet SMERSH assassin Viktor. Apparite had a chance to kill him, but instead chose to save the life of a young boy, a bystander whose throat Viktor had cut. It was a decision that continued to haunt him. He knew it had been his duty to leave the boy to die and pursue his enemy, and in that he had failed.

Number two was that Apparite's closest and practically only friend, the Director's field liaison, a man called "J," had died in the mission; had died because Apparite had not eliminated the SMERSH threat when he had the chance. J's death crushed him as agonizingly as that of his own parents' had back in the forties, and he was seldom very far from being reminded of it: prior to his fateful mission, Apparite rarely remembered his dreams, but after returning to the States they had become unusually vivid and life-like, and his dead friend always was in them. Nowadays, when he would awaken, he usually did so with tears in his eyes, as his unconscious mourned for his friend even as the conscious mind of John Apparite seemingly could not.

And number three was his poisoning and near-death at the hands of SMERSH while boarding the *Queen Elizabeth* liner on his way home. Against all odds Apparite had survived the attempt, and after his recovery had pledged to avenge his dead friend. But that had not yet occurred, nor was there any immediate sign of it occurring, so here it was, six months later, and Apparite was no closer to killing Viktor than he would have been to walking on the moon.

He ordered another beer. It would be his seventh of the evening but probably *not* his last. Apparite had always liked the taste of a cold beer, but in his continued misery had begun to appreciate the alcohol in it even more. As an elite "Super-agent"—there were only two in the entire world, and their powers had no limit—he knew that the Director would frown on such drinking. Still, as long as he did not make any trouble, or reveal the existence of their ultra-secret agency to anyone, Apparite thought it was no one's God damn business what he did in New York City when he was "off-duty."

Besides, he figured, the Director was assuredly back in D.C. (the mysterious man seldom left the area, he had once told him), which seemed a million miles away from where Apparite was sitting at the moment. He decided that only when the Director contacted him with a new mission would he have to quit drinking Knickerbockers at Dempsey's—until then, he thought in his irritation, who the hell really cared?

He heard a commotion nearby. Turning his head, he saw a small party of swarthy-appearing men being seated at one of the larger tables. They looked drunk; they were talking loudly and one of them had already knocked over a water glass, spilling ice onto the table and floor. Oddly, although three of the men were over six feet tall, the toughest-looking of the four, and loudest and most intoxicated of them, was only about an inch taller than Apparite, who himself was barely five feet six inches in height.

The man looked familiar, and when Apparite had a chance to make a closer inspection of the group on his way to the restroom he recognized him: it was Johnny "Kid" Leonard, the welterweight prize-fighter. Boxers and sports-writers often congregated at Jack Dempsey's, but this was the most well-known fighter Apparite had ever seen in the place (and he had been there many, many times since his arrival in New York). Leonard was unique among most of his pugilist colleagues in that his nose had never been broken and his face bore no scars—he was so unusually quick on his feet that his opponents rarely got a clean shot at him—but though his mug remained unmarred despite the disfiguring nature of his profession, it was *not* one that would be called handsome. If anyone's face defined the word "thug," then it was his.

Apparite returned to his seat. After another sip of beer, he looked over at Leonard once again. Unlike many in the restaurant who were making the effort to meet the boxer and ask for an autograph, Apparite just sat and glared at him. Just three weeks ago the Kid had beaten Apparite's favorite fighter, Carmen Basilio (the "Canastota Clouter") to take the welterweight championship in a vicious fight at Madison Square Garden. It had been a close fifteen-round decision, and as Apparite believed the Kid had fought dirty that night—kidney punches, low-blows, and "accidental" head-butts being a staple for him—he had no wish to increase the boxer's feeling of celebrity by joining in the adulation by the others at Dempsey's. He took another large swig of beer.

Well, he said to himself, *even if Basilio got beat, at least baseball's starting and I'll have that to occupy my time. And maybe if the "Nats"* (as Apparite and many die-hard fans of the Washington Senators referred to the team) *come out of the blocks well this season, it'll improve my mood.*

Apparite had always relied on his ballclub to occupy his emotions and bury the pain of his past, even when they were well under five hundred—which was about always. And then there had been that strange coincidence with the Director: not only was he a fellow Senators fan, but Apparite discovered that he had once actually *played* for the team. This mutual affection for the Nats had helped bring the two men together, forming a connection between them that Apparite would have previously thought impossible.

In fact, the only continuing personal relationship in Apparite's life was between himself and the enigmatic Director, which, at one point, had become almost as close as that of father and son. Thinking of his supervisor in this intimate and affectionate light briefly brought a smile to Apparite's face, but it did not stay long: he had not spoken to the Director in many weeks, and the last time he had, he had been told in no uncertain terms to stay in New York until further notice. It had not been a pleasant call.

When Apparite hung up the phone that day, he had cursed the man and his unnamed secret agency, realizing that he would not be allowed to seek out Viktor and avenge his friend's death. There had been tension between them in that last conversation, and tension involving the Director, Apparite knew, could be dangerous to one's health. Apparite's only human connection in the world might be with that man, but that would never stop the Director from doing what it took to protect the security of his agency if he felt it was threatened—even by one of his own. Even by John Apparite.

Aw, to hell with him, Apparite said to himself; *he's not here in New York, so why am I so worried about him? And where's that waitress?* Apparite had drained his beer and wanted his next one: thinking of the Director had riled him considerably. A quick search for the waitress found her at Leonard's table: the men were grabbing at her dress and she looked harried and upset. She took their sizeable drink order and walked briskly to the oval, brass-rimmed bar in the middle of the crowded room, wiping tears from the corners of her eyes.

God damn punks, Apparite said to himself. He had a particular hatred for people who abused wait-staff—*especially* wait-staff who were supposed to be bringing him another beer! He ate the last bite of his steak, took a sip from his water glass (all of the ice had melted and it tasted like cardboard), and cracked his knuckles. He took a few deep breaths and made an *Isshin-Ryu* karate fist—a vertical fist with the thumb on top—wondering how long he would be forced to wait here in New York before he could be a secret agent again; before he could use all that he had learned again. The previous summer he had put in eight back-breaking weeks of combat training in a run-down D.C. warehouse, becoming expert in three of the deadliest hand-to-hand combat arts in the world, and for what? To sit in Jack Dempsey's alone and get drunk night after night? To idly bide his time while Viktor roamed the world at will doing God-knows-what evil deeds in the name of the Soviet hard-liners back in Moscow?

From somewhere in the crowded restaurant he heard the song "Happy Birthday." Turning his somewhat unsteady head, he saw a group of men and women singing to a bashful young man who was hiding his face behind a napkin. Hearing the song reminded Apparite of the date, which he had hardly paid attention to (each boring, frustrating day seemingly melding into the next), for in addition to the young man at Dempsey's birthday, it was Apparite's dead father's as well.

Rather than looking on the day with nostalgic fondness, this discovery only served to place him into an even more irritable mood. He missed his father, sure, but trying to figure out exactly *what* he missed about him was what bothered him. He could hardly come up with anything to remember him *for,* as no defining characteristics or events sprang to mind on which he could anchor his remembrances.

His father had been nice enough, Apparite admitted; had never beaten him, and rarely shouted in anger. But that was partly because he was so seldom *around;* seldom at their little two-bedroom home in Eckhart Springs, Maryland. Apparite was raised mainly by his mother (his father always seemed to be off trying to sell insurance), and he and his dad had shared little over the years: a few hunting expeditions, some trips to D.C., and a love of the Senators were about it.

Was that enough, Apparite asked himself, *to call a man "my father"?* And then just when Apparite was approaching adulthood, when it looked as if he might finally be able to forge some relationship with him, his father had volunteered for the Army, *out of the blue!* Apparite and his mother had tried to talk him out of it, but his father seemed to have found a sudden passion for the idea of fighting for the United States. In fact, he had seemed almost cheerful when, after a final leave, he'd boarded the train at the Cumberland B & O station to take him to his embarkation point, smiling and waving as the train carriage slipped over the horizon. After his father left, and for the first time in many years, the young Apparite sincerely *missed* him; truly wished that he would come back the next day so they could have a game of catch, or hunt squirrels, or sit and do nothing at all, but to do it together.

But it was not to be. His father had been reported "Missing in Action" in late December 1944, and then in January the crushing but inevitable news had finally come: he was dead. He would be buried in Belgium with the usual honors and rituals, and his personal effects would be returned sometime later in 1945. But little that had belonged to his father ever made it back to Eckhart Springs: a set of dog-tags arrived in February, and an official letter of condolence followed in March, but that was it.

Apparite had been the one to go to the post office to get them, but as they only reminded him of his loss and pain he threw them away: the dog-tags ended up on the rubbish pile, and the letter, unopened and unread, in the fireplace. Ever since that day, Apparite had done his best to repress his memories of his father—that is, when he acknowledged having any memories of him at all.

Only one thing had happened in 1945 that had been any good: a signed Walter Johnson tobacco card had been mysteriously sent to his mother, and she had given it to Apparite for his birthday. He treasured that card above any other single possession he had ever had, and the fact that it had arrived so soon after his father's death caused him to clutch it ever more tightly to his chest in times of sadness or doubt.

Its charm was enhanced by the fact that he'd never discovered where it had come from; Apparite recalled that his father often carried one in his wallet, but it was not signed and almost certainly had been lost in the war along with his other personal effects. Hardly a day went by that Apparite did not wonder about that card's origin, sometimes asking it, *"Where did you come from?"* as he held it gently in his hand, but no answers were ever forthcoming. Nevertheless, he had a funny feeling that someday he would know the story of its journey to him— probably, he mused, on the one day he hadn't thought about it.

But today is not going to be that day, he said to himself, as "Happy Birthday" concluded with laughter and cheering.

In their attempts to talk over the song, which much of the restaurant had joined in singing, Leonard's table had become increasingly noisy and boisterous. Jack Dempsey himself had come out and shook their hands, as he often did when boxers came to his joint, but even his gentle remonstrations had not settled the group into a lasting civility, and they continued to loudly needle their waitress. Apparite could see her through the little circular window in the swinging aluminum door that led to the kitchen: she was crying; a sympathetic member of the wait-staff was consoling her. Leonard's voice suddenly rose above the din of his companions. Apparite did not like what he heard.

"Hey, where's that little toots that was waitin' on us? I forgot her tip—tell her I got somethin' under the table *just for her!*" His companions laughed freely at the crude remark and added a few of their own; none of them clean enough to make even the most "blue" of Vegas acts.

Apparite had had enough. Whether it was the six Knickerbockers, or his frustration with the Director, or his inability to get over J's death, or the sight of the tearful waitress in the kitchen, Apparite had suddenly become very angry. He felt compelled to do something about the Kid and he was going to do it right now.

As he stood up, he left a pile of bills on the table. It was going to be the biggest tip the waitress ever had, but as the money had come directly from the U.S. Treasury via the Director, he figured no one would ever miss it. He walked a tad unsteadily toward Leonard's table, but the four men crowded around it remained oblivious to his presence; at least, until Apparite took a nearby glass of water and dumped it down the back of Leonard's shirt.

"Hey! What the hell're you *doin'?*" the muscular welterweight shouted.

Every head in the room turned toward him, and the restaurant got as quiet as a church on a Monday. Nothing like this had ever happened before in Dempsey's—certainly not to one of the toughest boxers in the world.

"Just getting your attention," Apparite answered. "I noticed you need to learn some manners, and I'm here to teach 'em to you."

One of Leonard's companions spoke.

"You gotta be *joking!* Buddy, how much you hadda drink?"

"This doesn't concern you," replied Apparite in a calm voice. "It's between the Kid and me."

The men at Leonard's table burst into riotous laughter in response to Apparite's remark: the idea that a guy Apparite's size was calling out the man who had just beaten the Welterweight Champion of the World seemed as funny to them as Milton Berle in drag. But Apparite was *not* amused; the expression on his face remained as serious as ever.

Leonard noted the unusual intensity in Apparite's eyes, and

although the boxer's three table-mates continued to laugh, he did not. He wondered about this audacious little man, seeing in him the same efficient and cold expression as he had in war-hero Audie Murphy, whom he had met after the Basilio fight. It was an expression that seemed to say, *There's a reason I got balls big enough to call you out, mister,* and it took Leonard aback. But after a moment, a grin formed on his face as he realized the obvious absurdity of this man picking a fight with *him,* the new welterweight champ, the man who the papers said had "cut into Basilio like a butcher," and he laughed and laughed.

"Go home and eat your Wheaties, pal! Get the f--- outta here before ya get hurt."

Apparite continued to glare at him until the laughter died down, and when it had, the unusual quiet that had greeted his appearance at Leonard's table soon returned. The suspense in the large dining room was palpable: every head in the restaurant was turned his way, the only sound the muffled clinks and clanks of trays and plates knocking together in the kitchen. Even Dempsey had been captivated by the confrontation: the ex-heavyweight champ was watching the proceedings from behind the bar, mesmerized like the rest by this incredibly unlikely scene.

"I'll be waiting for you outside, Kid," said Apparite. "I'm gonna teach you a lesson you'll never forget."

Leonard raised his hand, his forefinger in the air. "Bring me the f-----g check. And then anyone who wants to watch me pound this guy like a cheap steak can come outside."

Apparite walked toward the exit, having become as steady and measured as a clock; albeit one whose alarm was about to go off. Just before he reached the door, someone grabbed his arm. It was the waitress.

"You don't have to do this. I get guys like him all the time— I'll be okay." She managed a weak smile but her trembling showed her anxiety. "He could *kill* you," she added in an urgent whisper. "Please don't. *Please.*" Her face had gone pale; her eyes misted over with tears.

Apparite looked at her sympathetically. "When the fight starts, just go ahead and call an ambulance." He walked out of the restaurant with the waitress close on his heels.

"An ambulance? My God, how bad do you think he'll hurt you?"

"Oh, the ambulance isn't for me," said Apparite. When Leonard appeared outside on the walk, Apparite jerked his thumb in the welterweight's direction.

"It's for him."

THREE:
A LESSON IN MANNERS

The Kid followed Apparite outside. The boxer had already taken off his shirt, displaying the lean though muscular physique of a welterweight, and began dancing around, throwing flurries of extremely rapid punches into the air. Apparite motioned to Leonard to follow him a short way down the street to a deserted alley where they could fight, cracking his knuckles and stretching his arms as he walked, focusing on what he was going to do to the brash young prize-fighter. A few people followed, but not nearly as many as Apparite thought might do so; apparently, the patrons at Dempsey's did *not* want to watch the Welterweight Champion of the World dismantle someone who, in a fit of drunkenness (what other explanation could there be?), had unwisely challenged the boxer to a brawl.

"No knives, agreed?" said Apparite.

"I won't need 'em," Leonard answered. "I'll leave them for the docs that'll have ta fix your face."

The boxer's three companions stood at the entrance to the alley, looking out for the cops or anyone else who might wish to stop the fight. They seemed to be making a pretty good time of it, laughing and joking as they waited for the fight to begin. Apparite turned toward the alley's entrance to face his opponent, smiling at what he saw: in the background was the massive form of Madison Square Garden. The Garden's bright lights shone down the alley, illuminating much of it almost as if it were day, though its far reaches remained in darkness.

This is probably as close as I'll ever get to fighting in the Garden, but it should be a memorable battle regardless, he thought.

Just then, the waitress burst into the alley. She grabbed Apparite by both arms and looked earnestly into his face.

"Don't do it—don't! I'll get Mr. Dempsey to pick up your tab—you can just walk away."

"I'll be fine," he said in reassurance. "It's not my first time at the dance, you know."

The waitress was not assuaged by Apparite's confident tone or demeanor. In frustration, she turned and walked out of the alley to find a telephone to call an ambulance and the police. If she couldn't stop this fight from happening, maybe someone else could.

"You throw the first punch," said Apparite. "I don't want anyone saying I jumped you."

The Kid let out a loud guffaw, as did his cronies.

"Man, you're somethin' else!" the boxer said.

Leonard came at Apparite, dancing nimbly about the alley. He threw a few quick jabs with his left, but the darting Apparite easily ducked or weaved his head to the left and right to avoid them, and they were misses. Leonard shot a body-blow at Apparite's sternum, grunting with the exertion of the punch, and Apparite saw his opening. With lightning speed, he blocked the blow with his left forearm, knocking Leonard's punch off-target. In one rapid motion, Apparite brought his right foot around into the boxer's exposed flank; hard.

"*Ooof!*" went the Kid, grasping his side. His companions stopped laughing and the alley went silent.

"Hey! I thought this was a *boxin'* match!" one of Leonard's cronies cried out.

"Shut the hell up!" Leonard yelled through his gasping. "I don't need any help. It was a lucky shot."

Leonard was sweating and he labored to breathe; Apparite's

kick had bruised the boxer's ribs, bringing sharp pain with every movement of his injured torso. He came at Apparite again, dancing, dancing, dancing, and then he threw a flurry of blows that were almost blurs in their speed: three lefts and rights and then a vicious left hook. One of the rights grazed Apparite's jaw and the hook caught him in the temple, but it was only a glancing blow and neither hurt nor stunned him.

But the hook proved to be a mistake for Leonard. As the Kid turned slightly with the punch, he left his mid-section open and Apparite thrust an *Isshin-Ryu* karate fist into the boxer's sternum. The air practically exploded out of the welterweight's lungs and he dropped involuntarily into a three-point crouch; one hand on the ground, the other in the air in a "wait a minute" gesture as he slowly, painfully regained his breath.

"Who *is* this guy?" muttered one of the Kid's pals. The utterance seemed to bring Leonard back to life.

"Don't worry! He's goin' *down*—just like Basilio!"

Leonard rushed at Apparite, but instead of throwing a rapid sequence of left jabs and then a right-cross—which is what he used to floor Basilio in the fourth round two weeks earlier—he threw a few quick jabs and then aimed a kick at Apparite's groin. But Apparite saw the kick coming a mile away: Leonard was untrained in karate, and the manner in which he had suddenly planted his left foot told Apparite that the right one was coming as clearly as if it had been announced by a neon sign in Times Square. As Leonard's leg shot up toward Apparite's groin, Apparite nimbly leapt back a step, grabbed Leonard's foot as it reached the zenith of its upward motion, and pushed it ever higher until Leonard fell over backwards and hit his head on the pavement.

"I'll stop now if you go back and apologize to that waitress," Apparite said. "I'd suggest you do it."

"Go to hell!" Leonard rose unsteadily and spat onto the

ground. He walked to his three buddies, whispered, and turned to face Apparite. "It's time to finish this." He assumed his boxing stance.

"I couldn't agree more," replied Apparite.

But instead of only Leonard coming at Apparite, all *four* men raced down the alley toward him. Leonard reached him first and tried to tackle him, but Apparite side-slipped him and cracked a karate thrust flush into the left side of Leonard's jaw; a bloody tooth flew out of the welterweight's mouth and landed on the pavement. Leonard hit the ground with a crash and spat out a mouthful of blood and saliva.

The next two goons were on Apparite a second later. He slammed a kick into the flank of the first, breaking two ribs; turning, he ducked a wild punch from the second. As the man passed him, Apparite grabbed him by the wrist. He broke the arm at the elbow with a vicious karate thrust, followed by another blow to the side of the head. The man staggered a few steps and held up his injured limb: the forearm dangled sickeningly in the direction of the ground. His face went pale at the sight and he collapsed hard onto the pavement.

The last thug took one step toward Apparite but then paused, seemingly thinking things out—the fight was obviously not going as his boss had planned, and he wasn't so sure he wanted to be involved in it anymore. He looked at his fallen companions, thought the better of what he was about to do, and took off running down Broadway like demons were after him.

But Apparite could not make chase. Leonard was on him once more; he'd shaken most of the cobwebs out of his head and was ready to continue the fight. He danced toward Apparite as best he now could, and threw a rapid succession of lefts and rights. Apparite kept weaving and backing up, weaving and backing up. When his back was against the wall of the alley, he grabbed one of Leonard's jabs, and, using the boxer's own momentum, threw the welterweight into the bricks, turning him around. Apparite then crushed the welterweight's nose with a single, electric current-quick karate thrust, the boxer's face exploding into a red, liquid pulp like a ripe tomato crushed under a tire. Leonard fell to the ground and disappeared into the shadows, spitting-up ever-increasing amounts of blood and mucus, moaning like an animal in its death throes.

A garbage can struck Apparite from behind; the thug with the broken ribs had somehow found the courage to continue the battle, but given his injuries had not been able to put much force into the blow, and Apparite had not been damaged by it. The can's lid hit the ground with a *clang* near Apparite, who deftly kicked it up into his hand. With a rapid turning motion he brought it around and into the man's head, knocking the man off his feet and onto the unyielding pavement with a thud, unconscious. The Superagent then stood back and admired his handiwork.

Aside from a few curious rats watching the scene from underneath a wooden pallet, the alley was deserted and strangely quiet. All of the bystanders had fled when the melee reached full force, leaving only the soft sound of the groans, labored breaths, and spitting and retching of Apparite's wounded opponents. Apparite walked to the end of the alley and made an announcement to his fallen foes.

"End of lesson," he said, tossing the garbage can lid onto the ground with a *clang*. He heard the sound of approaching sirens, and, knowing he could not be caught at such a scene, sped on foot down the street toward his apartment safe-house. John Apparite had indeed taught Kid Leonard the lesson he deserved, but now that the battle was over, anxiety began to hit him.

What if the police had gotten involved? What if the Director finds out about the brawl? Why did I have to make such a stupid scene in a crowded, public place? Why did I have to drink so much? Apparite

40

realized he'd made a bunch of mistakes that night; he'd been careless and foolish, and had nothing to be proud of, even if he'd just KO'd the Welterweight Champion of the World.

Apparite ran all the way to his apartment. He opened the door with trepidation, half-expecting to see the Director sitting in a chair with his Beretta 1951 pointed at him, but there was no one. He sat down in the lime-green upholstered chair next to his bed and closed his eyes. The six Knickerbockers were affecting him once again and he had become fatigued beyond measure. In a moment, he was asleep.

Two blocks away, the Dempsey's waitress was leading the police and medics to the site of the brawl.

"They were going to fight right down here," she said, accelerating her pace. But upon entering the alley she stopped, her mouth agape. Two injured men were visible on the ground; one was clearly unconscious and the other was moaning, his arm crooked at a horrifying and unnatural angle.

The form of a third man appeared from the shadows. The waitress rushed to him, thinking it was her defender from the restaurant, but when his face came into the light she gasped audibly.

It was Kid Leonard, and his face was like so much red mush. He stood unsteadily and looked at her with unfocused eyes.

"*You!*" she shouted. She reared back and unleashed a wicked right hook into the angle of Leonard's jaw, dropping him back onto the pavement, dumb to the world. "How do ya like *your* tip?" she said in triumph.

The man with the broken arm raised his head unsteadily and took in for a moment the unlikely carnage Apparite had wreaked in the alley. In spite of the excruciating discomfort of his fracture, he glanced up at the medics and attendants coming to aid him, managing one last statement before passing out from pain and shock.

"Who *was* that little guy?"

Apparite awoke the next morning, still sitting in the chair next to his bed. His mouth was parched and he had a typical hangover headache, a painful pounding that increased with every little sound, making him want to crawl under the covers and sleep for a week. He rubbed his red and tired eyes, pushed his mussed hair out of his face, and sat up. Only then did he open his eyes, to be greeted by this disturbing sight: a middle-aged man with graying hair was sitting on the end of the bed, pointing a Beretta 1951 semi-automatic pistol at him. It was, of course, the Director, and he did not look happy.

"Busy night?" the Director said.

Apparite did not want to answer. He assumed, correctly, that the Director was aware of what happened at Jack Dempsey's (the Director *always* knew such things) and Apparite guessed he must be mighty displeased. The emotionless tone of the Director's voice made his statement even more menacing than a display of anger would have—similar to the fear instilled by the slow growl of a cornered dog as opposed to one who barks madly—and every response that came to Apparite's mind seemed woefully inadequate or a potential provocation.

He did not have to answer, however, for the Director continued speaking before Apparite could come up with anything to help his case.

"I brought you the papers. There's a story on page one that might interest you."

The Director handed Apparite a copy of the *New York Herald Tribune* with his left hand while still holding the Beretta in his right. On the front page, although below the fold, was the following headline: *"Boxing Champ in Hospital After Brutal Attack."*

"Read it," said the Director. "Read it aloud, please."

Apparite sat up rigidly in his chair. He cleared his throat and began to read, albeit slowly and tentatively.

"Recently crowned welterweight champion Johnny 'Kid' Leonard and two companions were hospitalized late last evening after a violent altercation near Madison Square Garden, site of the boxer's most recent fight. Witnesses state the men were dining in Jack Dempsey's restaurant when they were lured outside by a fair complected, brown-eyed man, described as being twenty to thirty years of age and approximately five feet six inches tall and 140 pounds. According to Leonard's statement, the man led them into an alley where he and his companions were ambushed by a gang of six men waiting in the shadows. 'I knocked three of them down but there were too many for us to handle,' the Kid told authorities. 'When they heard the sirens, they took off down the street. It was lucky for them the cops came. We were starting to get in some pretty good shots.' "

Apparite paused. Despite his discomfort with reading the news story in front of the Director, Leonard's last statement struck him as being irrepressibly amusing given the true events of the night, and a grin formed on his face. He looked over at the Director to see if *he* had found it as funny, but no, there had been no change in his stony visage: it was as rigid and immovable as the Rock of Gibraltar. In a flash, Apparite's grin was gone.

"Continue, please," the Director said in his official monotone.

"Leonard, who took the welterweight championship belt from Carmen Basilio last month in an unforgettable and wild fight at The Garden, suffered a severely broken nose, hairline fracture of the jaw, and concussion while defending himself and his companions against their attackers. His next fight, a fifteen round contest with Sugar Ray Robinson scheduled for September, has been indefinitely postponed. Police are still gathering information on the gang that attacked the men. At press time no suspects had been declared. Doctors at St. Clare's Hospital are unable to state if and when the Kid can resume his promising boxing career given the nature of his facial injuries."

Apparite stopped talking.

"Did crushing Leonard's nose make you feel better?" the Director asked. "Did drinking all those Knickerbockers at Jack Dempsey's bring back J?"

Apparite shook his head: *no* and *no* were the answers to both questions.

"I can't have you losing control in public places, Apparite. I can't have descriptions of you published in the *Herald Tribune*."

"I know," answered Apparite in a barely audible voice. "I know."

If he had had an "L-pill" at hand he might have taken it, so lowly had he been brought down by the Director's arrival and obvious disgust—the man's LASER-like stare was powered full-blast, and Apparite felt as if it was burning a hole right through him.

"There's a reason why I brought this pistol, and you know what it is." The Director leaned forward nearer Apparite, keeping the barrel of the Beretta pointed at the young agent's chest.

"If you can't stay out of trouble, if you can't stay out of sight, I will not hesitate to use it," he continued. "Don't make me do that. I have invested much time and energy in you—more than you can know—and I do not wish to waste it. What happened in London has to *remain* in London: there is nothing you can do to bring back J, and for the time being at least, there is nothing you can do to kill Viktor. That opportunity might present itself someday, but until then, you have to figure out a way to keep your nose clean. You are making my job very difficult."

"I understand; I have no excuses. I would not fault you if you pulled that trigger."

The Director smiled and his gaze dropped in temperature from scalding to merely uncomfortably warm.

"I'm not going to do that—*yet*. Despite your faults, you are still a valuable commodity, even if you need some tinkering and adjusting from time to time. What I can offer you is this: you will remain in New York for one more day, keeping yourself out of hot water the entire time, and then I will send you on your next mission."

"Thank you." Apparite relaxed his posture in relief.

"Business will be the best therapy for you, I believe, and I have plenty of it lined up in the next few weeks. You have sat idle much too long for someone with so much on his mind, and I am willing to accept responsibility for that. Sometimes idleness is desired, but at other times it is a detriment. In your case, I made the wrong decision. But despite recent events, some things have gone well for you, I believe. Have you had any more panics, for instance?"

"No," answered Apparite; he'd almost forgotten the anxiety attacks that plagued him shortly after joining the Director's agency. His last one had been six months ago, when the Director told him that Senators owner Clark Griffith had died and his favorite ballclub might leave D.C., but since then, he had been fine in that regard. Perhaps his subconscious *was* making some beneficial adjustments to his emotional rheostat.

"You know, I might even be able to fly on a plane again," Apparite added, recalling his episode of panic during the take-off of his flight to London the previous autumn.

"Good. Airplanes are a helluva lot faster than ocean liners, and probably less hazardous to one's health. People hardly *ever* get fatally poisoned on them," the Director said, referencing Apparite's near-demise on the liner *Queen Elizabeth*.

The Director started chuckling and Apparite joined in. The Director displayed his morbid sense of humor so rarely that even the smallest attempt at a joke made Apparite laugh out loud.

"As long as SMERSH isn't on the same flight, I'd have to agree," Apparite answered.

"Good. Your flight to London takes off on Saturday and I think I can guarantee you a SMERSH-free cabin. For now, I have obtained a prescription for something to bolster your mood. As you no doubt are aware, the Senators are in town to play the Yankees, and I have obtained a ticket for tomorrow's game. I hope a box seat behind their dugout is satisfactory to you?" He handed Apparite a small envelope.

Apparite opened it slowly, carefully, like he had been given a rare and ancient papyrus, which, if handled too roughly, might disintegrate into oblivion. He held the ticket up to the light and gazed at it in disbelief, much as a parched and weary Knight Templar might do if unexpectedly handed the Grail. It was an impossibly wonderful gift, causing Apparite to ask himself: *Was the ticket he was holding in his hand actually there? Was this wondrous event truly happening, or would he awaken in an instant, only to find himself back in that D.C. warehouse having just returned from a most fantastic and unlikely dream?*

"Yes, the ticket is genuine," the Director said, divining the meaning of Apparite's glowing but quizzical facial expression, "and when you present it to the ticket-takers at Yankee Stadium, they *will* let you in. I could never let you see the Nats in D.C. for security reasons, of course, but I've decided to give in this one time in New York. All I ask is that you stay out of trouble and lie low: do *not* get noticed; do *not* make a nuisance of yourself rooting for the visitors; and for God's sake, don't do anything as foolish as wear a Senators cap."

"I will—I mean, I won't. I mean—thanks," said Apparite, his joy apparent in the unusually musical tone in his voice and the decline of his composure and sentence structure.

"And *God damn it,* don't beat up any more boxers. I had a

ticket to the Ray Robinson fight that got called off because of you!"

Apparite laughed. Given the Director's obsession with secrecy, he sincerely doubted the man would ever go to a public athletic event, not to mention one of the most anticipated prizefights of the year. But then again, with a guy like the Director almost anything seemed possible (at one time, after all, Apparite had discovered he'd been best friends with Senators Hall of Fame pitcher Walter Johnson!). The Director walked toward the door but paused to make one last statement.

"Oh, and by the way, if anyone at Yankee Stadium recognizes you, you'll have to kill them."

He opened the apartment door and stepped into the hallway before Apparite could ask whether that last statement was said in jest. Given his past experience with the man, Apparite admitted he couldn't quite be sure. . . .

Four:
Damn Yankees

Apparite spent the next day in extreme excitement at the prospect of seeing his beloved Nats, and as it was an early evening twilight game, the wait until he left for the ballpark seemed interminable. He spent most of the day in his apartment doing calisthenics and stretching exercises, and then, in an attempt to lose even more of his nervous energy, he took a long walk to Times Square. He would soon be leaving New York and had suddenly gotten nostalgic for it.

When he reached the famous intersection, he took a look around him. There were thousands of New Yorkers packed into the area; some strode with purposeful, focused looks on their faces, but others merely wanted, like him, to be *there* as opposed to anywhere else. To be at Times Square was to be in a place where important and memorable things were happening, even if they were not happening to you.

He looked up at the square's famous billboard—"Chevrolet" on top, "Canadian Club" and "Admiral Television Appliances" in the middle, and "Pepsi-Cola" on the bottom—and though the gaseous neon in the sign was not particularly bright in daylight, the sight had an electric charge to it nonetheless: this was what a *real* city was like! D.C. had those important government buildings, sure, but they were too stuffed with bureaucrats and pencil-pushers to make up a city; there was no pulse to it, no *throb* of life's rhythm to Washington D.C. The difference was an obvious one: in New York, one knew that one was alive; in

D.C., one knew that one was going to *die* (and then be taxed for it).

And, as some say, much as a pet and its master begin to look and act alike over the years, so it also was with a city's ballclub and the town from which it sprang. Take the Red Sox, for instance. They were as moneyed and privileged as an old Massachusetts patriarch, but hadn't won a World Series since 1918. It was almost as if the team somehow thought to do so would be *rude,* would upset the natural order of things, and that simply wasn't done by a true and proud New Englander.

And the Washington Senators were like many District of Columbians: perennially hopeful though always under-funded and left grasping; never getting quite enough to actually get the job done, like a politician who has high hopes for his constituency as Congress goes into session but who always seems to leave with an unused pen and unfulfilled mission. Like all of those tax-dollars that go to Washington never to be seen again, so it was, so often, with its ballplayers, too.

But then there were the Yankees, the "Bronx Bombers," who played in the most exciting city and the most famous stadium in the world. Five straight World Series titles from 1949–1953! Caretakers of the greatest and most successful winning legacy in all of sport, with a roster of stars that could not be matched by a combination of any *three* teams in American League history: Ruth, Gehrig, DiMaggio, Mantle, Dickey, Berra, Rizzuto, Lazzeri, Gomez, Ford. When they won, they won big, and when they lost—which was never very often, or for long—they lost small. The team was a microcosm of their city: big, bold, brash, and unapologetically arrogant, and Lord, how Apparite *hated* them! They even referred to their winning habits and style as "The Yankee Way," as if God himself had come down from the heavens and anointed them: *This will be "The Yankee Way"; follow it, and you shall not be defeated; follow it, and the World Series, the most famous title in sport, shall be yours.*

But wait! In 1955, the Brooklyn Dodgers had finally stolen a Series from the Yanks—stolen being the way Yankees fans seemed most comfortable in referring to the manner in which it was lost—and perhaps this was evidence of a weakness in "The Yankee Way." Mickey Mantle was formidable, but he had injury problems; Ford was an exceptional pitcher, but the rest of the starters could be roughed-up on occasion. And it had been two long years since the Bombers had won a World Series, so who knows—anything could happen, right? Could this be the year the Nats get back into the Series for the first time since 1933? Or possibly even win it, which they had done only once, way, way back in 1924?

Apparite said goodbye to Times Square and took the subway to the Yankee Stadium stop at 161st Street and River Avenue. It was crowded with Yanks fans, and their confidence was obvious: they did not simply wonder *if* Mantle would hit a homer at today's game, they wondered *how many*, and how far? Apparite admitted the possibility of a big day for the "Mick": on the mound for the Senators was Chuck Stobbs, the pitcher who had served up the longest home run in American League history to Mantle back in 1953; a 565-foot rocket-blast in Griffith Stadium that was still spoken of with awe. And, to Apparite's displeasure, on the mound for the Yanks was Johnny Kucks, a very good hurler who had already beaten the Nats in the second game of the young season. By the time Apparite had reached the stadium, his hopes had been shattered.

But when he stepped out of the subway car, he immediately felt better: the sight of proud Yankee Stadium, its pennants flying and its banks of lights illuminated, had dispelled any worries. Whether Washington won or lost didn't matter as much as usual, for today he was going to see a Big League baseball game. Today, he was going to see his Nats.

Yankee Stadium, home though it was of the enemy, looked absolutely glorious. If St. Peter's Basilica was the spiritual home of Christendom, then this immense, brown concrete-jacketed park surely was the spiritual home of baseball; even the most ardent Yankee hater had to admit that. Apparite gave the gate man his ticket—he almost could not watch him tear it, so dear had it become to him—and found his way to the ramp that led to his section. Approaching the end of the tunnel, the grandstand was revealed to him across the way, and then the green patina of the famous copper façade lining the roof inside the stadium came into view, and then all was revealed to him in an eye-opening instant of pleasure: Yankee Stadium, the Mecca of the baseball world was there before him, and he had a prime ticket to the contest it soon would host.

Everything about it exceeded his expectations. Its grass seemed greener than that at Griffith Stadium, and the dirt of its infield looked lighter, finer, and even *browner*, if that were possible. Its green wooden seats looked much more inviting than their thickly painted counterparts in D.C., and the smell of the sizzling "red-hots" was enticing beyond compare. The field was huge and imposing, and the three monuments in the outfield, memorials to Babe Ruth, Miller Huggins, and Lou Gehrig (and which were, amazingly, *in* the field of play!) added a serious, if not somber note to the mood. In fact, some persons, though not Apparite, erroneously believed the three Yankee legends were actually *buried* beneath them, as if the memorials were true tombstones! A ballgame in this impressive setting would naturally seem the most important of the day; the players within it more skilled than those in other, lesser venues.

Apparite slowly walked down the stairs; he was rather early for the game and his section was somewhat empty. Finding his row and seat, he sat down and quietly took in the scene: how much more alive the stadium looked in color than in black and white on television, as he had only seen it before! The Yankees, who were the picture of confidence and competence in their famous pin-stripe uniforms (especially at home), were warming up across the way, but Apparite's attention was soon drawn to the scene directly in front of him: the Senators had just left the dugout and were throwing the ball around the field.

But unlike the Bronx Bombers, his team did not have the look of a winner. The Yankees' throws seemed to crackle through the air and hit each other's gloves with loud, professional *smacks!*, but those of the Senators seemed to arc lazily toward the sky and land unappreciated with dull thuds in their leather mitts. One did not have to be a baseball expert to guess which team had won over a dozen World Series and which team had won only one: the team with the whiter-than-white uniforms with the pinstripes were plainly leagues above those wearing the drab grays.

The stands had begun to fill up. Apparite's grandstand contained a nice cross-section of New Yorkers, and the expectant look on their faces was obvious—this game is gonna be *fun;* it's gonna be *easy.* And though most of the seats immediately around him remained empty, an elderly, gray-haired gentleman sat down right next to him.

Uh, oh, thought Apparite, this guy better not start talking to me: he was thinking of the Director's stern order not to stand out, not to make a scene. The last thing he needed was some lonesome old man striking up a nine-inning-long conversation with him.

But so far the old man seemed content in filling out his scorecard, and Apparite called out for a hot-dog and beer (a cold Ballantine sounded good) as a means to occupy his immediate time as well as satisfy his increasing hunger. The red-hot was very tasty, as was the beer, which Apparite took care to sip slowly—after the fiasco at Jack Dempsey's, he was *not* going to have more than two. The umpires had come out onto the field and were sweeping off the bases, and as the stands had finally become crowded with fans, almost exclusively of the Yankee persuasion (and all with that same expectant look), he figured the game would start in about ten minutes. And yet, despite the crowded stands in other areas of the park, the bleachers in front of, next to, and behind him remained basically empty. It was still just Apparite and the old man in the immediate vicinity.

He was getting concerned about this situation: *There is no way this old guy is not going to start talking to me. And if he does, there's no way I can act like I'm a fellow Yankees fan.*

Apparite began to sweat, wondering whether he should start a conversation—perhaps if he initiated it, he could better control it. But no, he finally decided, I'm just gonna sit here, keep my trap shut, and wait. Hell, even if this old guy does start jabberin', I'll still be okay as long as no one *else* notices me. Just don't get noticed, he reiterated to himself; just don't make a scene. All he had to do was blend in for the next two hours.

But it was not to be.

"Hey! Are you lost?"

Apparite heard the voice coming from, of all places, down on the field; since he was sitting in the third row and the dugout was just to his right, he had heard it very distinctly. He assumed someone was where they shouldn't be—people were always sitting in the wrong section in stadiums, or wandering too near the field—and he didn't pay it much mind. Apparite knew it couldn't involve him; he was where he was supposed to be.

"Hey you! Are you lost?"

The old man to Apparite's left stirred and tugged on the Superagent's shirt-sleeve.

"I think that man is talkin' to *you*, son."

To his astonishment, Apparite looked in the direction of the voice and saw a Senators player looking right at him, smiling!

"Yeah, *you!* Are you lost? You're supposed to be in D.C.!"

It was utility infielder Bobby Raymond and he was talking *to* *Apparite*. Raymond motioned for him to come down nearer the dugout.

"I think he wants to tell you somethin'," said the old man.

As if bewitched by some spell, Apparite rose from his seat and walked down to the rail overlooking the field, his gait and facial expression similar to that of a zombie in a cheap horror film. He was almost stuporous with disbelief.

Why, in all of creation, is a Washington Senator talking to me?

"Me and the fellas were wonderin' what happened to ya," Raymond said to the stunned Apparite. "Haven't seen ya behind the dugout at Griffith since way last year! Whatcha doin' here in New York?"

Apparite realized the impossible had occurred: the players of the Washington Senators baseball team *knew who he was*—they had always known who he was! He had never met one, had never talked to one, but they knew him all the same!

But after a moment, he realized that this was, perhaps, not such a big surprise. He had gone to over a hundred games since he'd been in D.C., always sitting in the same spot; right where he was now, a little behind the dugout to the left. And it wasn't as if the Nats had drawn large crowds (they had a game a year or two earlier when only 500 people had bothered to come), so of course he might have stuck out to them, sitting alone and always in the same seat near their dugout, as was his habit, day after day after losing day.

And then, of course, he had suddenly disappeared. On June 30th, 1955, he had watched the Nats beat the Red Sox 3–2, but by the time they had played another home game, everything had changed: his old life had ended in a faked automobile wreck (it still riled Apparite that the Director had destroyed his *actual car* in the ruse!); his name had been changed to "John Apparite"; and he had become a Superagent in an unnamed, ultra-secret intelligence program.

But now this young fan had returned to the Senators' flock like the prodigal son, sitting in his usual seat behind their dugout, but in, of all places, Yankee Stadium, home of the enemy! Apparite was just about sick with worry, delight, disgust, and anxiety at this strange and unpredictable twist.

"Hey guys! C'mon over—it's *him!*"

Apparite could see Raymond motioning to other Senators in the dugout, and suddenly half of the starting lineup was standing in front of the rail, waving at him. Waving at *him!*

"Where ya been? The fellas have kinda missed ya," said Raymond. Standing next to the infielder were Roy Sievers, Pete Runnels, Eddie Yost, Mickey Vernon, and Jim Lemon, and they all bore friendly, welcoming grins.

Apparite knew he had to play along and answer Raymond's question, or risk attracting even more attention. But the irony of the scene had begun to set in on him: although he was one of the most fanatic Senators fans in all of America, he was a man who was *officially dead;* who had to remain hidden and anonymous in order to do his duty as a *super-secret spy;* who had an order to *kill anyone* who recognized him in New York—and now the heart of the Washington Senators line-up was standing at the rail, anxiously awaiting him to speak! He broke a smile while working out his predicament: would the Director expect him to eliminate the infield first, and then do-in the outfield? Or should he start by killing the pitchers, and work his way up from there?

He chuckled and addressed Raymond's question.

"Moved to New York—got a job in the diamond business," Apparite answered, using a cover that had worked well for him in the past. "I do a lot of traveling, so I don't get to the ballpark much anymore."

"Too bad: we don't draw like we used to in Griffith, and with the American League the way it is now, we can always use the help."

"Yeah," answered Apparite. "Cleveland looks good again, and even the White Sox are comin' on."

"You ain't kiddin'. But wait 'til you see the guy we got comin' up: name of Killebrew—the kid can really hammer the ball. Needs some seasonin', but he'll be one of the greats."

Apparite would have loved to continue this unlikely conversation but thought it best to cut it off while the going was still good.

"Well, you guys got a game to play. Good luck!"

"Thanks," said Raymond. He pounded his fist into his glove and started to walk back to the dugout. But then he turned toward Apparite as if he'd just thought of something else to ask him.

"Say, some of the guys are goin' to Toots Shor's after the game—why dontcha come down and join us for a few? I know the boys'd like to meet their biggest fan."

Apparite nearly gasped: he had been offered a chance to hang out with the Nats! To drink beer with them; swap stories with them; laugh and joke with them—to become *friends* with them, of all people, when he literally had no other friends in the world! It was an offer that tortured him; an offer so beyond his best and wildest dreams, that it was murdering him inside to say what he knew he must.

"Thanks—I wish I could. But I have to fly out tonight. Maybe I'll catch ya on my next trip to D.C., huh?"

"Sure—see ya at Griffith!"

Raymond ran back into the dugout, leaving Apparite standing at the rail in thought. Of all the occurrences that had ever happened in his life, this seemed to be the most diabolically hilarious of them all, and if he had thought the Director could have arranged it, Apparite would have called it the greatest test of loyalty that had ever been devised.

He pounded the iron rail playfully with his fist in bemusement, turned, and walked back to his seat. He realized, however, that if this was simply one of the Director's tests, it was not yet over: there was still the old man sitting next to him with whom he had to contend. Apparite took a few deep breaths and sat back down in his seat, readying himself for the next onslaught and twist of cruel, cruel fate.

"Say, they seemed to know you," said the old man. "Are you a fan of the Nats, too?"

Apparite knew it was useless to try and hide it now. He would have to admit the truth—or, at least, part of the truth—to the old man.

"Yeah," Apparite answered. "But I don't expect them to do much today."

The old man, who seemed pretty fit despite the extensive sun-damaged skin on his face and his gaunt physique, laughed heartily.

"Me neither! I've followed 'em for years and they never fail to disappoint, but they'll always be my team."

Apparite nodded: he knew exactly how the old man felt.

The game began. Apparite had not expected the Senators' bats to exactly send balls flying all over the field, but his mood sank when they went down with extreme rapidity *one-two-three* to Kucks' well-placed fastballs and a couple of two-strike curves. It sure looked like a long day in the Bronx was in the offing for his favorite team.

Stobbs began the bottom half of the first inning in fine fashion, striking out Yankee lead-off hitter Hank Bauer, but then he walked both McDougald and Mantle, throwing two wild pitches in the process. The old man turned to Apparite.

"Don't know why the outfielder in left is playin' so close. He needs to back up, put some distance between himself and the infield."

Great, Apparite said to himself, *I've got an amateur manager next to me who's gonna talk my ear off all day.* But after Berra grounded into a double-play to end the inning, the old man remained silent, content to sit quietly and eat salted peanuts until the Nats came to bat.

But as in the first inning, Kucks once again sent the Washington batsmen quickly packing; it was obvious that, today, the Yankee hurler had his "good stuff." The hitless Senators trudged back out to retake the field, their slow, funereal-like gaits showing their declining confidence in the game's outcome. After Yankee first-baseman Moose Skowron walked on four straight off-target Stobbs pitches, Collins came to bat and the old man finally spoke again.

"Too bad Martin's not in for the Yanks today. He's one to watch. Full of piss and vinegar, isn't he?"

Apparite nodded dumbly but could see that the old man, who was looking at him expectantly, was waiting for some kind of a response.

"Yeah—reminds me of Stanky or Durocher," said Apparite.

"Or Cobb. He used to sharpen his spikes—did ya know that?" Collins took a pitch for a strike.

"No, I didn't," Apparite said, feigning interest in the conversation. This might be the only baseball game he'd see for years, so an old man's dusty reminiscences weren't about to hold his full attention.

"Yep, I've seen a lot of good players down the years, but no one quite like Cobb. He was a right-ol' son of a bitch, but the greatest player I ever saw."

Apparite nodded dumbly yet again as Collins struck out swinging. The young agent looked toward the field in an attempt to end the stilted conversation he had found himself in, but the old man continued undeterred.

"Slaughter's kinda like Cobb. Aggressive base-runner, never quits on a ball. Reminds me of the forty-six Series—boy, that one was a *hum-dinger.*"

The old man then launched into an account of the famous Cardinals–Red Sox World Series of 1946, which Apparite knew would end with Enos Slaughter's famous "Mad Dash" to home, scoring the go-ahead run for the Cards in the seventh game. The telling of this tale seemingly lasted hours, however: the Yankees finished batting in the second inning and no-hit the Senators in the top of the third while the old man droned on and on, discussing every pitch of the ten-year-old Series game in exacting detail. Apparite found it difficult to believe, but by the time Hank Bauer came up for the Yanks in the fourth inning—following Rookie Lumpe and Johnny Kucks, who had both singled—Slaughter *still* hadn't crossed home plate in the old man's story!

"Umm, excuse me," said Apparite, "but I'm gonna go grab a beer." He'd built up quite a thirst and a cold Ballantine sounded good. "Do you want one?"

The old man stopped talking for a moment to accept his offer.

"Sure—thanks, sonny!"

While Apparite was gone, Hank Bauer got hold of a Stobbs fastball that he drove at least 450 feet into the bleachers, putting the Yanks up by three. Apparite heard the muffled roar of the crowd from the concessions stand and did not hurry back. He knew that whatever had happened, it hadn't been good for the visiting side.

He walked dejectedly back to his seat: when he'd left the score was tied, but when he'd returned the Nats were down. *It always seemed to happen that way.*

"Thanks," the old man said after Apparite handed him the

beer. The man took one sip and then, inspired by Bauer's long homer, launched into a second anecdote—never having finished the tale of Slaughter crossing home plate in the first—beginning with the smashing of a center-field seat in Philadelphia by a Jimmy Foxx round-tripper in the 1930's. Apparite sighed: obviously, he was going to have to humor the old man by listening to his stories, and as the game was in danger of getting out of hand in the Yankees' favor (McDougald walked and Mantle singled him around to third with one out), Apparite decided it might not be such a bad idea after all.

The old man leaned over to put his peanuts on the ground, still talking non-stop (he had moved on to a story of catcher Gabby Street having caught a baseball dropped from the top of the Washington Monument), but just as he sat back up in his seat again, Moose Skowron took a big cut and sent an absolute *rocket* shot toward them; one of those screaming foul-ball liners that jets into the crowd with a blur.

Apparite had momentarily turned his head to look at the ball and strikes count on the scoreboard, but out of the corner of his eye saw the ball coming at them at over ninety miles per hour, and on a direct line for the old man's head. Without thinking, Apparite shot his right hand across his body—a southpaw's glove hand—and snared the liner back-handed mere inches from the old man's face.

Suh-mack! went the ball as it hit Apparite's bare right hand, and as soon as he had secured it he tossed it playfully about a foot into the air and caught it again, *as if it had been the easiest thing in the world.*

But it obviously *hadn't.* To the large and attentive Yankee crowd, which had gasped in collective horror as the missile-shot took a bee-line to the old man's unprotected face, it had been about the most incredible bare-handed catch of a ball in the history of Yankee Stadium! To them, Apparite's hand had shot out in a blur and *whammo!*—a millisecond later it was holding the ball.

"*What* a grab! *What* a grab in the stands!" was what radio listeners heard Mel Allen cry that day, causing them to abruptly sit bolt upright in their living room chairs and sofas. "That was the most spectacular bare-handed stab of a ball I've *ever* seen! Howww about *that!*"

The crowd cheered, and then they stood, and then they cheered and stood, and some close to Apparite even threw their hats in the air in appreciation of what he had done. Spectators rushed down into Apparite's section to congratulate him: they mobbed him and slapped his back; they mussed his hair and shook his hand; and brought him beers, and peanuts, and hot-dogs, and sodas.

The stunned and unassuming Apparite forced a smile, thanking them as profusely as he could, even as he knew that the Director would be absolutely *s---ting* his pants if he had known of the attention the feat had drawn: anonymous super-spies in life-and-death secret agencies did *not* let such things happen! All Apparite wanted to do was come and watch his Nats play in peace, and now, to his horror, he had become the toast of New York. More than anything, he wished he could sneak back to his apartment and listen to the rest of the game on the radio.

When the excitement and cheering finally died down, the old man turned to Apparite and spoke.

"Thanks, son; that was a close call. The New York fans sure appreciate a nice grab though, huh?"

"It was nothing," Apparite replied meekly. "I got lucky."

"Naw, that was a great catch." He paused for a second in thought, and continued. "Ya know, I made a pretty good catch myself, once."

The old man launched into another long anecdote, bringing a sigh from Apparite. After the embarrassing incident with the foul-ball, the last thing he wanted to hear were the rambling tales of this old man for the last half of this insane ballgame, even if the Yanks *were* up three runs. He spent a minute in thought and came up with a plan to pass the rest of the game in relative peace: he would look at the old man and nod periodically in order to give the appearance of listening to his tales, but do so only between pitches. The rest of the time he would keep his eyes glued to the field.

After a few batters, he had found his rhythm: turn, nod, watch the pitch; turn, nod, follow the ball; turn, nod, the batter's out. Apparite began to relax and enjoy the game again, especially when the Senators brought a man home in the fifth. The Yanks scored another run in the seventh and the crowd began to thin as the lazier fans left to head home before traffic got too thick.

But in the eighth inning things started to heat up for the Nats, and some of those Yankee fans heading for the exits turned around and sat back down in their seats: Tettlebach singled and took second on a passed ball, and Pete Runnels got hit by a pitch. Sievers then worked a walk through an epic fifteen-pitch at-bat, consisting mostly of repeated foul-balls, and the Nats had the bases loaded with no outs. All of a sudden the outcome seemed in doubt.

But the Nats were the Nats, of course, and although Apparite felt the tense optimism of one whose team's winning run was coming to the plate, he was also waiting for it to unravel—which it did. Courtney struck out swinging; Olsen grounded right back to Yankee pitcher Kucks, who easily threw out Tettlebach at home for a force-out; and Herzog flied out to Mantle in deep, deep, breath-holding center. Just as quickly as the Nats had filled those bases, the next three batters had emptied them all back into the Senators' dugout with nary a run.

The rest of the game quickly raced by, its conclusion as inevitable as the setting of the sun in the west, which was now casting long shadows over the playing field. By the time the last Senator struck out—a called strike, naturally, as the batsman stood stiff and immobile like he'd been turned into a pillar of salt—the crowd had nearly completely dispersed, the sun had completely set, and the old man had finally reached the conclusion to his story.

"And ya know, people couldn't believe I held onto the ball, but I'll tell you a secret, young man. I really did catch it."

"Oh," Apparite said weakly. "Sure." The game had ended in a loss and all he wanted to do was go back to his apartment.

The old man got up to leave. "Well, it sure was enjoyable having someone to talk to during the game. Too bad we couldn't pull it out there, umm—say, I didn't catch your name."

"Stanley Harris," said Apparite, using his New York alias as instructed by the Director, if asked.

"Well, *that's* a funny thing—I once knew a man named Stanley Harris. But no one ever called him 'Stanley.' We all knew him as 'Bucky.' "

"Oh," was all Apparite said in return. He sensed another long anecdote coming but his patience had come to an end. He was not about to encourage more conversation, nor did he wish to take a chance of being regaled with stories all the way to the subway station, so he decided to stay quietly in his seat until the old man left. And yet there was something about what the man had said that sounded familiar to him: Harris. Stanley Harris. Stanley "Bucky" Harris.

"Well, it was good to meet ya, Stanley. My name's Rice— Edgar Rice—but most folks just call me 'Sam.' See ya 'round!"

The old man turned and walked up the steps. Apparite was still waving good-bye when the revelation struck him.

"Bucky" Harris—of course! "Bucky" Harris had been player-manager of the Washington Senators during the greatest years of their long history; no *wonder* the name had sounded so familiar! And as for the name "Edgar 'Sam' Rice," *that* had belonged to a Hall of Fame outfielder who had played for the Senators in the early years of the century!

Holy s--t! Apparite thought, I've been sitting next to one of the most famous ballplayers in Senators history for over two hours and I didn't even know it! And his shock was compounded when he recalled the feat for which Edgar "Sam" Rice was most remembered: the Hall of Famer had made a miraculous diving catch into the stands to save the fifth game of the 1925 World Series for the Senators; a catch so outrageously impossible that it had been debated for years and years as to whether he had actually held on to the ball. Since that day, whenever he had been asked about it, Rice had always smiled and said, "The umpires called it an out," and reaffirmed that he would never say anything more about it as long as he was alive.

But now he *had!* Whether it was because Apparite was (seemingly) listening to his stories and Rice liked him, or whether he had done so in appreciation of Apparite's own miraculous grab, he had finally unbuttoned his puss and told everything, just this once. But what had Rice said about it? How had the story ended?

Apparite laughed out loud: *He couldn't remember!* He racked and racked his brain, but couldn't recall whether Rice said he had or hadn't legally caught the ball. Apparite laughed for a full five minutes at the absurdity of it all, laughed until tears collected in the corners of his eyes, but even when the irony and humor of the situation had begun to die down, he started up all over again, for he'd finally realized what it had all been about; what the whole crazy *day* had been about. The Director, who had given Apparite the ticket to the ballgame in the first place, had *purposefully* sat him next to an old friend, Hall of Famer Sam Rice, because he had thought that Apparite needed cheering, and who better than a famous Washington Senator ballplayer to sit with to guarantee it?

And thinking of how the Director's plan had turned out in the end made him laugh even harder: Apparite had discovered that the Washington Senators baseball team *knew* him. They had even invited him out for drinks! He had then performed his foul ball miracle-catch—possibly saving Hall of Famer Sam Rice's face, if not his life—and had been cheered by thousands of Yankee fans *in* Yankee Stadium! But it was the astonishing and surprising denouement of Rice's long story that had brought him to the brink of apoplexy: Sam Rice had told him the biggest secret in all of baseball history and he couldn't remember what the hell it was!

As he left the stadium, he realized he was still holding the baseball he had caught. He looked at it for a moment, smiled inwardly, and tossed it to a boy of about ten who was eating an ice cream in the parking lot.

"Thanks, Mistuh!" the boy said in a thick Bronx accent. A grin formed on his ice cream–smeared face.

"My pleasure," said Apparite. A distant memory found its way into his mind, released by their brief interaction. It was a damp April afternoon in his hometown of Eckhart Springs; the sound of the Senators' opening day game of 1938 was coming from a radio playing on the porch of his family's house. Apparite was eight years old; he was in their small backyard fielding grounders thrown by his father.

They laughed and talked for hours as they listened to the Nats drub the Athletics 12–8 that April day, and though it seemed like nothing special at the time, as the years passed it would be one of the few memories of his father that would stick in Apparite's head, remaining as pure and vivid and joyful—on those rare occasions when he thought of it—as the day it had happened.

Apparite looked over at the boy: he was still standing nearby, grinning and holding up the ball, eyes scrunched as he examined the spot where Skowron's bat had made contact with it. Apparite had one last thing to say to him before leaving.

"Hey kid—when ya get home, throw it around with your dad, okay?"

The boy shook his head excitedly in the affirmative and ran to his friends, waving his prize in the air. Apparite walked in the direction of the subway station but with more spring to his step than he had in months: the absurd events of the day had been so unbelievable, so wildly weird and wonderful, that despite the Nats' 4–1 loss it would be the Senators game Apparite would treasure above all others in his entire life. And though the Director's aim in sending him to Yankee Stadium had been more than accomplished, Apparite knew that if his boss had seen all that had happened that day, the cautious and secretive man would have probably had a stroke—no doubt about it.

Apparite returned to his small apartment. After the events at the ballgame he fully expected to find the Director sitting by the bed, holding a Beretta, but on opening the door no one awaited him. Apparite had just begun to wonder when his next instructions would reach him when he noticed a folded piece of notebook paper on the bed. He assumed it was a message from the Director, most likely in the form of a "one-time pad," which was reserved for communications of a confidential nature.

He unfolded the paper and confirmed it was indeed this type of communiqué. Reaching into his wallet, he removed the message's "mate," which contained the other half of the code (a code which was, for security purposes, never used but once—hence the name "one-time pad"). He looked at the encoded grid on the paper he had found, and then back at his own. Working out the pattern, he soon decoded the message, writing it deliberately letter by letter onto the back of a piece of scrap paper:

"RV Dr. H, London, Red Lion. Tix Idlewild as JJ."

Plain enough for a trained eye: he was to pick up his airline tickets using his Joseph Judge identification at Idlewild Airport and fly to London. After arrival, he would rendezvous with Dr. Hoevenaers—the Belgian who had provided medical care and a safe-house for the injured Apparite after his last mission—at the Red Lion pub. There were at least half-a-dozen Red Lion pubs in the city, but he knew which one the Director meant, for Apparite and J had once met an English agent at a pub of that name near Covent Garden. He felt confident that when he arrived, Hoevenaers would be waiting for him at a booth in the back of the ancient pub, a pint of bitter at the ready.

Still, he felt a twinge of sadness rush through him at the thought. Apparite had quite enjoyed nearly all of his six-week stay in London the year before, but those memories had been tainted by his confrontation with the SMERSH agent Viktor, and the eventual deaths of J and English MI5 agent Clive Hitch at the conclusion of that mission. He knew that going back to that city, and returning to the Red Lion pub in particular, would only intensify those feelings, especially his unrelieved sense of blame for his colleague and friend J's death, and his shame in not having exacted revenge on Viktor.

But other than killing the elusive Viktor (and knowing the opportunity to do so at present was slim), he had drawn a frustrating blank on how he might calm his tumultuous emotions. Apparite, who had always prided himself on his competence, his ability to work his way out of any jam, had found nothing he could do to actively deal with these traumas from his past. He felt helpless as a kitten; useless as a broken gear.

And yet despite it, he felt an inexplicable glimmer of hope. It came from a place beyond the reach of logic, in defiance of explanation by any rational-thinking being, but he could not shake a strange sensation that everything was going to be okay, if only he could keep his head together for just another month or two. If there was any comfort to be found, it was in this tiny, illogical little glimmer, and he would force himself to believe in it; to *grab* onto it and hang on tight.

He made a mental note: *somehow, the world* will *be a better place for me by Memorial Day. If only I can make it until then.*

He took a match, struck it, and burned the pieces of paper, dropping the smoldering black ashes into an empty stainless-steel wastebasket. Turning to leave the apartment, he saw a small note tacked to the inside of the front door. It contained only two words and was written in block letters to disguise the handwriting, but was revealing and surprising enough to dispel his somber mood and make him laugh out loud:

"NICE CATCH."

FIVE:
RETURN TO THE RED LION

The journey to London was an unexpected pleasure for Apparite. Unlike his anxiety-ridden Pan American flight the year before, this one actually served to calm him, to rest his troubled mind. Perhaps the urgent excesses of the past year's traumas had dispelled any worries of airplanes plummeting from the sky, or perhaps the maturing Apparite was simply outgrowing his fear of flying, but when the airplane landed he did not sigh in relief nor feel an urge to kiss the ground in thanks as he stepped onto English soil. And though it was only after the plane had touched down that Apparite fully realized how peaceful and relaxing the trip had been, the knowledge of it was a significant comfort. At least he was making progress in one area.

If there *had* been any anxiety regarding the trip, it was only in the possibility that he might see the pretty Pan-Am stewardess from his flight the year before, a woman named Peggy Stokes, with whom he'd briefly bonded during his trip back to the States aboard the *Queen Elizabeth* liner (before his near-fatal poisoning, that is). But when his stewardess on this latest trip to London turned out to be an unexpectedly homely woman named Ramona, and since Apparite guessed the Director would certainly avoid putting him on a flight that Peggy Stokes would be working (and yes, he admitted to himself, the Director *would* be that thorough!), he knew that any reunion with the attractive chestnut-haired stewardess was to be postponed for the present, and likely indefinitely, under any circumstance.

He took a cab from London-Heathrow's new Oceanic terminal directly to the Red Lion, telling the driver to wait for him outside with his two bags. It was nearly noon and Apparite was quite fatigued from the nearly ten-hour overnight flight, but his anticipation in reuniting with the kindly Belgian doctor kept him not only awake but alert and anxious. As Apparite eagerly approached the pub by foot—it was located at the confluence of two short alleys, so the taxi could not drop him off at the door—he reflected on his prior interaction with the mysterious Belgian doctor.

Last autumn, Hoevenaers had hinted at some connection between himself, the Director, and Apparite, but what on earth could it possibly be? Apparite surmised that the Doctor had been involved in the Belgian resistance in the war, and afterwards aided the Director's agency as some sort of foreign liaison, but just as obviously the silver-haired, empathetic and good-humored doctor could not *possibly* be a working espionage agent. The idea of this gentle man killing spies in cold blood was as antithetical as a lamb living in a den of starving lions.

It seemed to Apparite that Hoevenaers was most likely some sort of "professional friend" to the Director, a man whose various talents were called upon at need, whether it was binding a wound, passing on secret and valuable intelligence, or hearing the tale of a troubled heart and offering comfort and advice. Though Hoevenaers' previous contact with Apparite had been for but a few hours the previous year, he had made a lasting impression on the young Superagent. Everything he'd said to Apparite that day seemed as wise as the advice of a king's counselor, and his demeanor had served to remove Apparite's anxieties and doubts through its gentle warmth and confidence. If the Director had become a sort of father figure to Apparite, then Hoevenaers was serving the role of kindly grandfather.

Apparite walked into the pub. It was smoky but not terribly

crowded (at noon, the lunch-time throng had not yet fully appeared), and he had no trouble finding his way to the place he knew he was to meet the Belgian: the very same booth in the back of the pub where he, J, and English MI5 agent Clive Hitch had finalized that last, fateful mission the prior autumn.

He ordered a beer from the bar, sat down in the wooden booth, and waited: five minutes, then ten minutes passed, but Hoevenaers did not show. People came and went from the dark, wood-paneled tavern—students, cabbies on lunch, construction workers, and office employees, among others—but no elderly Belgian doctors were among them. After twenty minutes, he rose from his seat and headed toward the door, planning to collect his bags from the cabbie and dismiss him. He caught the bartender's eye as he neared the exit.

"Were you sitting in the booth in the back corner?"

"Yes—why do you ask?" responded Apparite.

"Is your name Joseph Judge?"

"Yes," Apparite said curtly, startled to hear the bartender, a *civilian* in this deadly game, speak his present alias aloud.

"I've a message for you, sir."

Apparite walked over and took a brown, wax-sealed envelope from the barkeep's hand. The sight of the red wax seal (Hoevenaers' old fashioned idea of a security device) caused Apparite to chuckle, but when he opened the envelope and read the cryptic note written in the Doctor's flowery script, his face became grave with concern.

"Followed. Could not rendezvous. Return 2100. H."

"Thank you," Apparite said quietly to the bartender. "If anyone asks, you have never seen me." He handed the man a ten-pound note.

"Thank you, sir. You can count on me to keep a secret."

"See that you do," Apparite said. He exited the pub, walked rapidly down the short alley to the waiting cab, and climbed in.

"Take me to a quiet out-of-the-way hotel, please. There's an extra ten pounds in it if you can insure I'm not followed."

The driver, a thin, jovial East Londoner, smiled broadly and put the car into gear.

"Yes, sir!" he said. "Anything you say." He rapidly drove Apparite through a maze of little side-streets on a circuitous, confusing course through Covent Garden and into Bloomsbury. He eventually stopped at a little two-story wisp of a hotel, The Yorkshire Rose.

"Are you certain we haven't been followed?" Apparite asked.

"Oh yes, sir," the cabbie answered. "Quite sure, sir: no one can drive like me through these here streets, sir."

Apparite handed him thirty pounds. He had not only found confidence and trust in the man's driving, but had taken a bit of a liking to him as well.

"Be back here at twenty forty-five and I'll double this for you."

The driver could not stifle a laugh of surprise and joy.

"Ha-ha! Oh yes, sir!" He took Apparite's luggage out of the boot and escorted him to the front door of the tiny hotel. "Twenty forty-five it is, sir! I'll be here."

Apparite checked into a small room situated around the back of the hotel, and carefully and securely locked and barred the door. Exhausted as much from worry about Hoevenaers as he was from a near-sleepless flight, he fast fell asleep—as much asleep, that is, as a man whose danger-sense buzzed like a hive of angry bees could get. The mission had started badly: Dr. Hoevenaers had not made the rendezvous and in that there was ominous significance. There was always significance when one of the Director's plans went awry.

The taxi arrived precisely as ordered at 2045 that evening. Apparite was in a worried state, so he found the cabbie's bright mood and enthusiasm quite welcome.

"Where to, sir?" The cabbie opened the taxi's rear door for Apparite. "For what you're offering, I'll take ya anyplace ya fancy!"

"Back to the Red Lion, please," Apparite answered. "I have some rather serious business to transact there. I'll need you to wait outside for me."

"No worries, mate! What line of work you in, guv'nor—high finance?"

"Something like that."

The cab pulled away from the small hotel and turned in the direction of the Red Lion. Apparite had reflected on the day's events since he'd awakened from his short sleep, but had not yet been able to pull them into any semblance of understanding. Why was Hoevenaers being followed? It must be the Soviets, of course, but did it have anything to do with his own recent arrival in England? Then again, didn't the Russians believe Apparite had died last year on the *Queen Elizabeth*? If so, why were they tailing an elderly Belgian doctor all over London?

He thought only two people might have answers for him: the Director, who in all likelihood was hundreds of miles away, and the Doctor himself. But then he saw there was someone else who would surely know what was going on: the Russians, of course; *they* knew why they were following the Doctor. They must have had *some* reason to do so; after all, Hoevenaers was admittedly a minor player in this game—almost a diversion from the game itself.

Yet the Soviets' persistence in pursuing the Doctor told Apparite something quite important: they, too, had not forgotten what happened last year in London; perhaps it was haunting *them* as much as it was haunting *him*. And if that were so, he guessed that the very life of the Doctor was in danger. For all he knew, it might already have been lost.

"Here we are, sir," said the cabbie. He pulled up to the alley that led to the Red Lion. "I'll wait here for you, then?"

"Yes. Wait as long as it takes." Apparite took three ten-pound notes from his wallet. "I'll give you the rest when I return, but you must promise never to mention a word of what you see or hear tonight to anyone."

The cabbie's face assumed a look of fear and bewilderment.

"Oh—oh yes, sir. Not a word. On my honor, sir." The cabbie's voice was strained, his confidence and enthusiasm lessening with each word.

"Don't worry: it's just a precaution," Apparite said, reassuring him. "High finance, you know." He smiled at the cabbie and handed him the notes; the man seemed newly convinced that nothing illegal or dangerous was likely to occur and grinned back at Apparite, putting the money promptly into his fare box.

"Good luck on your deal, sir. I'll be waiting for you."

Apparite turned and walked toward the Red Lion. Unlike his previous visits, which had been in daylight, his present one seemed enveloped in mystery and darkness, and a foreboding came upon him as he neared the pub. The noises coming from it had taken on singular significance, as if everyone in the establishment was talking about him, whispering about him, and the faces he saw in it as he approached looked as if they concealed dark secrets. He was unsure if the penetrating dark of the moonless night or the lack of illumination in the old pub was the cause of it, but there seemed to be more shadows and hidden corners in the Red Lion than Apparite had remembered, lending the little tavern a sinister air. Although he had been there just eight hours earlier, it didn't feel like the same place at all.

That was part of the problem. It seemed exceedingly unwise for Hoevenaers to make Apparite come back to the pub a second time that day, for this was one place he feared the Russians would now be watching closely. He walked through the crowded pub, half-expecting to be stabbed in the back (or would it be a poison-cane pellet into the leg?) at any second by an unseen, unheard enemy, but his trip to the back booth was uneventful. And when he got there, he saw a sight that had seemed terribly unlikely a minute ago: sitting in the booth was the good Doctor, smoking a pipe in utter contentment! A glass of straw-colored lager rested on the table in front of him, and on his face was a broad and welcoming smile.

"Mr. Appar—um, Mr. Judge! So good to see you!" He rose and shook Apparite's hand with vigor. "I hope my little message did not frighten you excessively?"

Apparite sat in the booth across from Hoevenaers. If the man had been worried or in danger earlier in the day, he certainly wasn't showing it now.

"Actually, it did bother me," Apparite answered. He lowered his voice. "Aren't you concerned about the Russians? Weren't they following you?"

Hoevenaers laughed, blowing out a mouthful of pipe smoke.

"Oh yes; they're always following me—I see them as plain as day. Sometimes, they're drunk! But they never bother me."

"Why are they following *you?* Is it because I'm here?"

"No," he answered. "They think you died of their poison—but they believe I may lead them to others involved in what happened. I have been made to change houses twice, but they keep finding me. So, I act like I don't care. To them, I say *feh!*" He laughed heartily and took a sip of beer.

"We need to get you out of London," Apparite told him. "You don't know when they'll tire of you and simply decide to get rid of you."

"Your supervisor tells me the same all of the time, but I never listen! And I love England in the spring, with all of the flowers, walking around the garden. Maybe I'll go back to Belgium in the autumn. But not now—not in the *spring!*"

Apparite smiled inwardly. Hoevenaers was a sweet old man who had no clue what danger he was in by being around men like the Director and Apparite. The young Superagent envied the elderly Belgian's ignorance, the simple pleasures the good Doctor could find in the midst of this secret, uncompromising war.

"I will get another drink and then I'll tell you what you need to know," the Doctor told Apparite. "Have some beer and relax—nothing exciting is going to happen tonight." He put a warm, confident hand on Apparite's shoulder and walked over to the bar.

But Apparite's danger-sense was rising: there was a presence in this traditional, old English pub that did not belong here. He looked around in quiet alarm but noted nothing, and no one, that seemed out of the ordinary. What had he heard, or felt, or saw, that might have alerted him? He closed his eyes to concentrate; to listen all around him. And then it hit him.

An accent; his ears were picking up a Russian accent. And unlike the dull sound a full pint makes when it is placed on the bar, or on a table, or even when two Imperial pint glasses knock together, he had picked up another noise that stuck out as distinctly foreign in a three hundred-year-old English pub: the sound of a shot glass being slammed onto a firm surface after its owner had drained its contents. A shot glass full of vodka, he guessed.

He rose and walked purposefully in Hoevenaers' direction. Although he did not wish to make a scene, Apparite knew he had to get the Doctor out of there as soon as possible. But then he saw another person also walking toward the Belgian: a dark-complected man with jet-black hair and beard; he was holding a cane out in front of him. Apparite's breath came in halts and his pulse rose—he knew what was going to happen.

"Doctor, look out!" he yelled urgently at Hoevenaers. The Doctor turned at the sound of Apparite's voice; he was holding a pint of bitter and another glass of lager, smiling without a care.

"What did you say?" he asked.

Apparite pulled his pistol and forced his way through the crowd in the direction of the bar. He had nearly reached the Doctor but the Russian was closer still, holding his cane farther and farther in front of him. Apparite raised his pistol but cursed in frustration at his lack of a clear shot. He was frantically pushing as many patrons out of the way as he could to open a line of fire, but the crowd seemed to be closing in on the bar in front of him. Though he was but a few feet from Hoevenaers and the Russian, it might as well have been a league.

"Oh! *Qu'est-ce que c'est?*" *What is that?* the Doctor said, slipping into his native French.

Apparite pushed his way to Hoevenaers; the Doctor was leaning down and rubbing his left calf. Apparite looked in the direction of where he had last seen the Russian, but the man had disappeared, apparently having fled the pub. But the whereabouts of the Russian had ceased to be a concern to Apparite, for he knew that Hoevenaers had been poisoned and would be dead in minutes, if not seconds, if nothing was done.

"Don't rub it!" Apparite said in alarm. He slipped his pistol back into his suit-coat. "Don't use that leg!"

Apparite lifted the Doctor and carried him toward the exit.

"Out of the way, please!" he cried. "Please move, I must get through!" Precious seconds passed as he forced his way through the crowded pub and out into the alley. Spying a nearby streetlamp, he placed the wounded Doctor on the ground beneath it.

"What did he do to me?" Hoevenaers asked. "Why did he prod me with his cane?"

"He was trying to kill you. I need to see the wound—I pray

to God it's not too late."

Apparite thrust up Hoevenaers' left pant-leg and peered closely at the area where he guessed the cane had made contact. There was a small puncture wound in the fleshy part of the calf.

"It looks different than my wound did," said Apparite. "More of a needle-puncture than a pellet."

Hoevenaers smiled and spoke in so calm and deferential a manner that it seemed like he was trying to comfort Apparite, as if the Superagent had been the one to be poisoned.

"Do not worry—you were not to blame. I guess I underestimated their patience with me, heh?"

"We've got to do something!" said Apparite. "I'll take you to a hospital." He guessed that this poison was designed to kill in ten to twenty minutes, to give the assassin time to flee the scene. He bent over to pick up the Doctor, knowing full well that the man would be dead by the time they reached even the closest emergency room.

But then Hoevenaers did something very odd, given the circumstances: he laughed.

"Oh—the answer is quite obvious, you know," he said. "Give me your tie."

Apparite undid his necktie and handed it to Hoevenaers.

"You must place it around my thigh as tight as you can to prevent the poison from spreading."

"No—you'll lose your leg!" Apparite cried out in horror.

Hoevenaers smiled grimly. "I'm afraid it's the only way. I've had good use of this leg for sixty-five years and I'll be sorry to lose it—but I do not want it to *kill* me! Do it quickly, before it is too late."

Apparite took his switch-blade and cut Hoevenaers' pant-leg wide open. He wrapped the tie very tightly around the Doctor's thigh a short distance above the knee.

"Do you have a pocket comb?" the Doctor asked.

"Yes."

"Place it under the tourniquet. Twist it until it is quite tight, and then secure it in place with the ends of the tie. Once you have done this, no matter what else may happen, you cannot loosen it or I will have an embolus."

Apparite nodded and complied with the request, causing Hoevenaers to wince in pain.

"There," the Doctor said calmly, though sweat poured down his face in discomfort, "it is done. You may take me to the hospital now."

Apparite gently lifted him, carrying him to the cab. Although Hoevenaers remained silent, his deep, measured breaths and the anguished look on his face betrayed the increasing agony of his leg.

"What happened to him?" the cabbie asked. He opened the door and Apparite laid the Doctor in the back seat.

"He injured his leg. I've had to tie a tourniquet. Take us to a surgical hospital as fast as you can."

"Yes—of course." But the cabbie was now shaking and nauseated, and his driving much less steady than before as he drove them down the short, twisting streets that led to University College Hospital in nearby Bloomsbury. But traffic became unusually heavy and the going painfully slow—at this pace, it would take at least half an hour to get there. After many minutes of anxious silence, Apparite spoke.

"Does it hurt much? Is there anything I can do?"

The Doctor smiled at him. "At first the pain was quite exquisite, but now, no—it has become almost completely numb. That is one of the signs the leg is dying, you know."

Apparite reflexively glanced down at the man's exposed leg; it had assumed a strange, unnatural shade of purple from thigh to ankle. The sight sickened him, especially since this grotesque, dying limb belonged to such a gentle soul as Hoevenaers. The

Belgian saw the pained look on Apparite's face and addressed him in a firm voice.

"Once I am inside the hospital you cannot see me, you cannot inquire about me—for your own safety."

Apparite nodded and his eyes began to mist over in sympathy of his friend's plight. Hoevenaers leaned toward Apparite and spoke in an urgent whisper.

"You are to go to France. SMERSH operatives are using an ex-SS commander to expose West German agents; his name is Wilhelm Heydrich. Your supervisor told me you must find this man and kill him. He lives in Rhinbourg—south of Saverne—in a small cottage one mile west of the *rue de Saint Germain,* at the end of a cart-road marked by a white stone wall. I am told that his death should be mysterious, but attract the attention of the public as a warning to others."

"When will I rendezvous with D?" Apparite asked, speaking of the Director's new liaison, who would normally coordinate his actions in the field. "Where should I meet him?"

"It is unfortunate, but you may be on your own for a time. Your supervisor and D were urgently needed in Hungary: there are rumors of an uprising against the Soviets. Make your way to Berlin after Heydrich is dead—that is where his supervisors are heading—and D will find you there. But I beg you to be cautious. Heydrich is dangerous, and SMERSH agents may be with him."

"Why is Heydrich working with the Russians?" asked Apparite. "Why would a German living in the West be on their side?"

"Heydrich was convicted for war-crimes—in the battle you Americans call 'the Bulge.' " He paused as a last spasm of pain flashed across his face. "Have you heard of the Malmédy Massacre?"

Apparite shook his head *no.*

"Heydrich commanded men that shot Allied prisoners in

cold blood. After his trial he had found a hatred for his fellow Germans, but especially for the Americans who had put him in prison. He has been living in France since his release last year, working for SMERSH for money—and for revenge."

"My father was killed in the Bulge," Apparite said softly. "But I never found out how he died."

"It was a very great battle. I was there from the first day, you know. Your supervisor and I were trapped behind German lines; we had information and would have been shot as spies if captured."

Apparite leaned further toward Hoevenaers to take in all that he was saying. The idea that the Director and this Belgian doctor had been in such a famous battle was compelling.

"What happened?" he asked.

"An American soldier saved us; he hid us in the cellar of my family's café and then held off the Germans until he was captured and killed. I never knew his name, but I have never forgotten him; I never will forget him." He paused in thought, closed his eyes for a moment, and resumed speaking in an unusually quiet voice. "I remember the look on his face when he closed the hidden door: he was afraid but *proud;* very proud to be helping us. I often think of him."

The cabbie interrupted the hushed conversation in the rear of the cab.

"Hang on, mates. It's taken a bloody age, but we're almost there."

"Park on a side-street around the corner from the hospital," Apparite ordered. The driver nodded in frightened agreement.

"There is one last thing you must do for me," Hoevenaers said to Apparite.

"What? Anything—I'll do anything."

"They must see a reason for the tourniquet—don't you agree?"

Apparite immediately understood. He could hardly drop off the Doctor at the emergency door with a tourniquet tightly wrapped around an apparently uninjured leg. It would not only look suspicious, but the true reason for it could never be revealed, even if the surgeon might actually have believed it.

"What do you want me to do?" Apparite asked.

"You must shoot me in the leg with your pistol."

Apparite recoiled in dismay.

"I don't want to do that."

"Don't worry; the leg is quite numb now," Hoevenaers reassured him. "I will hardly feel anything at all. It's the only way," he added.

The cab halted and Apparite handed the driver thirty pounds more, giving him a strong admonition to forget everything that had occurred (which was unnecessary: the terrified driver wanted nothing more than to go drain half-a-dozen pints of bitter to obscure the events of the evening).

Apparite lifted the Doctor from the vehicle, closed the cab door, and laid the stricken man at the curb. After the taxi disappeared around the corner, he took his silencer-tipped, custom-made Colt Super Automatic pistol from his coat, and placed it in the depression behind the Doctor's knee. He turned his face away from the dark, discolored limb, as if by averting his eyes the deed might be made less painful for him, and pulled the trigger.

The sound of the bullet tearing through the flesh and bone of the Doctor's knee at point-blank range was one Apparite had never heard before, like the smashing of an over-ripe melon through a measure of balsa wood. He blanched when he raised his gun and saw the barrel, silencer, and even his hand covered with blood, tissue, and fragments of shiny white bone.

"I will see you again, I am sure," Hoevenaers said in a surprisingly unaffected voice. "Removing a leg is quite simple. When I have recovered, I will be in Brussels with my family. Please call on me."

Apparite held the man in his arms, ashamed at what had become of their reunion, ashamed that he had been unable to protect him.

"I'm so sorry," he whispered. "I'm so sorry."

Releasing the Belgian from his embrace, Apparite helped him to his feet and gingerly carried him to the threshold of the hospital.

"Brussels—do not forget!" said Hoevenaers as Apparite briskly walked away. Afraid to look back as the injured man limped inside the hospital, Apparite quickly turned the corner, slipped behind a nearby tall shrub, and vomited.

Six:
Rhinbourg

It was when Apparite returned to his hotel that he fully realized the serious nature of his situation: he was alone and had no means to contact either the Director or D; he had to travel to France to kill a dangerous ex-SS officer working for SMERSH; and he had to do it without any weapons other than those he had brought to England. Most importantly, he would have to complete his mission without any further intelligence regarding his target or the place he was to go, a place he had never been before, to kill a man he had never seen. He had no way of predicting what he would find there, no plan on how to complete his task, and, most frustrating of all, there was nothing he could do about it. If there could be any less promising a start, Apparite could not imagine it.

Oh—and he had to get out of England as soon as possible. He was unsure if the Russian assassin had taken notice of him at the Red Lion, but if so, he might assume Apparite was an operative of some sort and would now be searching for him. Every moment Apparite remained in London therefore put his agency and his life in danger, and he made a hasty though vital decision: he would immediately pack his bags and take a night-train to Paris, and then journey on to Saverne and Rhinbourg.

But once he had settled into his immediate plan, he saw that all was not quite so dire. He took an inventory of his possessions, finding renewed confidence as he held his nine-shot Colt Super Automatic. It was an extremely accurate weapon and had been specially modified for a silencer and riflescope, and though it might not be the first choice of an assassin to kill from a distance, he thought it would do the job. His confidence building, he opened a false-bottomed container of Burma-Shave shaving cream. He removed from its hidden compartment the two lethal poisons he had been issued, plus a sophisticated rubber bullet that could be used to deliver them.

He also had an assortment of throwing-knives (including an advanced switch-blade model suitable for slashing or stabbing), a couple of easily concealed garrotes, plus a miniaturized version of the famous Colt M1911 semi-automatic pistol, which fired seven tiny (but lethal) six-millimeter hollow-tipped bullets. Small enough to be strapped to an arm or a leg, it could prove quite handy in a pinch. In the final reckoning, he decided there were more than enough weapons to complete his mission, regardless of what he found awaiting him in France.

After the events in London, he thought it no longer safe to travel as Joseph Judge—the name might mean something to any Soviets he met along the way—but hidden in the lining of his bag were complete sets of documents that allowed him to assume the identity of a Frenchman (Louis Arnoux), German (Hans Müller), American (Charles Harris), or even Russian (Ivan Rossovich). As Apparite was fluent in the native language of each of his potential aliases, he thought it would be no problem if he had to become one of them for a time. But if there was one trump card he would be able to use in his favor, it was one known and respected the world over: *money.* He had plenty of it hidden in his bag: tens of thousands of American dollars, British pounds, French francs, and German West-marks, plus some thin sheets of pure gold. At the least, he might be able to buy himself out of a jam.

Apparite reordered and packed his bags and left for France. The trip to Dover by train and then to Calais by ferry seemed hectic in its rushed, disorganized genesis, but by the time Apparite arrived in Paris he felt relaxed and even looked forward to the rest of his journey. Traveling by train had always relaxed him: to Apparite, it felt more natural to let one's self lapse into unconsciousness with the *click-clack* of the rails and the gentle swaying of the cars than to remain in the real world. And so, as unlikely as it seemed earlier in the evening, the fatigued Super-agent slept soundly through Nancy and into Saverne, awakening only with the quiet urgings of the sleeping-car's attendant after dawn the next morning.

"*Monsieur* Müller—*reveillez-vous!* Wake-up! You must go— *nous sommes arrivé, Monsieur! Nous sommes à Saverne!* We are here!"

Apparite poked his head out of his berth. The French attendant did not speak German (the native tongue of "Hans Müller"), so Apparite had learned to communicate with him in a combination of German and Teutonic-derived Pidgin-English. It had worked well so far during his journey, serving not only as a means of communication but also of selling Apparite's new identity of a West Berliner on holiday.

"*Danke,*" Apparite said. "*Vielen Dank,* for your kindness," he added in German-accented English. "*Auf Wiedersehen, Monsieur!*" He tipped the attendant a handful of francs and stepped off the train.

Saverne was a pretty town, the home of an imposing chateau as well as a few very beautiful churches, but the most impressive sight to Apparite as he left the station was that of the forest-covered Vosges mountain-range to the immediate south: its steep green slopes towered over the area, reminding him of the Alleghenies back home in western Maryland. After a scenic thirty-minute taxi ride, Apparite reached his destination of Rhinbourg, a small town nestled into a break in the mountains, the forest wrapping around it like a thick green over-coat of timber. The taxi driver drove a few blocks into the small town and let Apparite off at *l'Hôtel Paradis.*

The hotel was one of those quaint but efficient little French hostelries one finds in every Alsatian town like Rhinbourg: two centuries old, half-timbered and with about fifteen small yet tidy rooms, such inns were always blessed with an ultra-attentive concierge who could be counted upon for every help—every *discreet* help—if one slipped her a full roll of francs. Apparite had never stayed in France before, but he had seen these sorts of places in the movies and had a pretty good idea of what to do.

"Fräulein?" he said, getting the concierge's attention. She was a forty-ish though not-unattractive brunette woman with a broad face and hips (in the States, she would have been described as "curvy" and probably drawn wolf-calls walking down the streets of New York). Apparite noted that she was not wearing a wedding band.

"I need a room for tonight, and probably tomorrow night as well," Apparite said in perfect German.

"Je ne parle pas Allemand," she said. *I don't speak German.*

"Do you speak English?" Apparite asked in his faux-German accent.

"Ah, *oui*—yes; *un peu*—a little," she said, smiling. "We find common—um, common earth!"

Apparite laughed. *"Ground,* I think, is the word! But you speak well. For myself, I learned as a boy from *Amerikanische Soldaten* in my town. My name is Müller—Hans Müller. I am a naturalist—for the plants. I need to search for specimens. This area is good for?"

"Ah, *oui.* Rhinbourg is *très jolie*—beautiful, at the foot of the mountains. Much to see; many plants."

"But I may be—what is the English word—*trespassing?"*

The concierge's face assumed a vacant expression: "trespassing" was one term she had not picked up from the GIs who had visited Rhinbourg during the war ("booze" or "dames" were another thing entirely: she had plenty of expertise in the use of those words, although she pegged an intelligent, sophisticated-appearing man like Apparite as not requiring help in either of *those* areas).

"Trespassing," continued Apparite, "is to go on the land of another man; to sneak around. Do you understand? I may need to do to get moss samples for my research. Can I count on your, um, *discretion?* To keep quiet, yes?" He winked at her broadly and passed her a thick handful of francs.

She took the notes and laughed.

"Ahh, *oui, monsieur!* I will keep moss a secret! I keep *good* moss secrets for you and your trespassing!"

Apparite had grown up in a family of meager means and as a result always had an unusually healthy respect for money, but this brief exchange was the first time he had truly appreciated the power of it to get things done: in the span of two minutes, with the aid of about one hundred francs, he had made a trusted ally and essentially been given license to come and go from the hotel as he pleased without suspicion.

After being shown to his room by the flirtatious concierge (who had begun to address him as *"Mon cher"*), Apparite outfitted himself in the guise of a naturalist (over-coat, sturdy wool pants and sweater, leather case, and high-tech custom-made Zeiss binoculars hanging on a strap around his neck) and readied himself for his search for SS-Captain-turned-SMERSH-operative Wilhelm Heydrich. Doctor Hoevenaers' directions to Heydrich's house were rather vague—one mile west of the *rue de St. Germain* and down a cart-path by a white stone wall was all he had been told—but Apparite was unfazed. All it would take was a little perseverance and luck and he would have his man.

Perseverance would be no problem—*that* he could manufacture himself—and after the events at the Red Lion in London he felt he was due for a change in luck, so when he left the hotel and walked down the street to the *rue de St. Germain,* his spirits were high. He thought that as long as he remained entirely focused on the task then nothing would go wrong, and although some might have termed this as being overly "cocky," in some ways it was a necessity. Confidence was almost as important to a Superagent as competence. Apparite would not allow himself to lapse in either.

He reached the *rue de St. Germain.* After walking a mile or more down it, he discovered a narrow dirt road trailing off to the west, flanked on both sides by a weathered, four-foot-high white stone wall. Even without Hoevenaers' directions, Apparite would have guessed this was the route to take: after about one hundred yards the road took a sharp bend, disappearing into a thick wood of tall trees; it seemed to him the perfect place to conceal a small house. Apparite walked down the road until he reached this bend, and ventured into the woods. He kept his course parallel to the road as it plunged into an ever-increasing density of trees—the beeches, larches, and especially firs common with the rise in elevation of the Vosges—remaining vigilant for anyone who might detect his presence.

After a mile or two of tough going through the thick woods, he heard a noise that seemed distinctly unnatural compared to the usual sounds of the forest; a low hum like an engine running at a leisurely pace, not unlike like that of an idling car. Apparite crouched lower to the ground. Although he could not see the origin of the sound, he felt it was only a few hundred yards further down the road and he did not wish to take any chances of discovery.

He moved the undergrowth aside—the pungent, rotting leaves, dirt, moss, and twigs that carpet every forest—and began to dig. When he had unearthed a small, loose pile of damp earth, he smeared it on his face and neck. Not as good as burnt cork, perhaps, but he thought it would provide camouflage enough for his task, particularly after the sun sank in the evening. He then searched out some small end-branches from a nearby beech. Removing his wool over-coat, he stuck these through the weave of his dark green wool sweater, providing him with another avenue of disguise. Only after he was satisfied that he looked more like a pile of leaves than a human being did he begin to crawl, slowly and deliberately, toward the place where he guessed the unnatural sound had its origin.

And when he got there, he was glad for his efforts. From his vantage point behind a fallen fir tree, the crouching Apparite could see a stone-walled cottage in a clearing at the end of the over-grown road. It was topped by what seemed to be a primitive, if not rotting, wooden roof, giving the small house a rather neglected look. On the front stoop was a man peering intently through a pair of binoculars. He, too, had detected an unnatural sound, and was scanning the area around the cottage with interest. Apparite's eyesight was acute enough to see that the man was fair-complected and had light-brown hair; he looked rather Slavic. Apparite guessed he was about thirty years of age—far too young to be Heydrich.

But the man's hyper-vigilant behavior and intense demeanor betrayed him as an agent of some sort. A bird-watcher scanned the trees or the skies, but this man was looking nearer to ground level—to *human* level. He had not spied out Apparite, but his danger-sense had heard, seen, or perhaps only felt that something was amiss, and he had gone outside to investigate. Apparite crouched even lower behind the fallen tree but cleared a line of sight to the man through a pile of branches. And yet he did not feel exposed in the least; if anything, he thought himself invisible and safe, as if no matter how carefully the man looked for him, his eyes could not possibly find him.

After ten minutes of searching, the man put down his binoculars and went back into the house, reappearing in the doorway a few minutes later. He made a face of annoyance and walked over to the source of the sound Apparite had heard earlier: a generator. Seeing it, Apparite surmised the cottage had no outside electrical source. If that was the case, it was also most likely heated by fireplace, and almost certainly did not have running water. Heydrich had apparently decided, in the interest of secrecy, to live in as primitive a manner as possible.

The man walked to the generator and made a few adjustments with a wrench. The hum turned into a whine and then a loud clatter. A second later, the generator ceased working altogether, emitting a puff of thick black smoke.

"Yebat' kopat'!" Clumsy f----r! the man said in an explosion of disgust and alarm, and as soon as Apparite heard it he knew he was in the right place: this was Heydrich's SMERSH protector, and hearing the livid Russian curse caused Apparite to break into a grin. Nothing betrays a secret identity like an expletive foolishly spoken in anger.

Apparite carefully crawled around the perimeter of the clearing, keeping himself about forty yards from the cottage at all times. He stopped when he found something he suspected would be present: an outdoor privy, the kind they called an "out-house" back in the States. And as soon as Apparite saw it, he knew he had them: everyone, no matter how suspicious or cautious, had to have a bowel movement *sometime* (the two men might urinate in a chamber-pot, but in that cramped little cottage they'd *never* chance a stool!), and sooner or later, one of them would put themselves in an exposed position—so to speak.

He had found his quarry and he had found the perfect way to trap it, and though Apparite still had the actual killings to perform, he only had one worry: he hoped to God that neither of the men suffered from constipation. He sure as hell didn't want to wait out in the cold all week until they finally had to go.

Apparite hid his leather case and over-coat under some nearby leaves, and then, taking his binoculars in hand, waited as the day was put-paid. The hours passed slowly, but other than one more expletive-laden episode when the SMERSH agent eventually fixed the ailing generator, Apparite heard and saw nothing but what one expected in the forest: the sound of birds overhead, deer wandering by in search of tender shoots or berries, squirrels jumping from tree to tree, and the rustling of branches and leaves in the breeze that rushed down from the towering Vosges. After a time, Apparite felt the immediate onset of sleep overtake him, but did not resist it. He wanted to be well rested when it came time to do the killings, and decided to allow himself one brief nap to restore his mind and body.

An hour later, Apparite's danger-sense brought him around in a flash: the random sounds of the forest had been replaced by the rhythmic *crunch-crunch* of footsteps; and the unnaturalness of rhythm—which implied purpose, which implied *intelligence*—had aroused him. He was well hidden behind another fallen tree (this one a larch) and nearly enveloped by leaves and falling branches, but he now felt anything but invisible. He had a sense of being exposed, his lapse in vigilance giving him this uncomfortable feeling of nakedness.

The steps came closer and the tempo of the rhythm slowed: *crunch*—pause—*crunch*—pause—*crunch,* telling Apparite that a man was taking a step and looking, taking a step and looking. The situation worried him considerably, for he had not yet prepared his full complement of weapons. All he had at hand was the switch-blade hidden in his belt and the two small all-metal throwing knives in his shoes. But the sound of the steps continued to come nearer. Apparite held his breath in anticipation, fearing that any movement or noise would give him away.

The steps got unbearably close, just a couple of feet away on the other side of the fallen tree, when Apparite heard an unlikely sound: the striking of a match! A few moments later, the fallen tree was jarred by the force of someone sitting upon it, followed by the smell of cigar smoke—jarringly malodorous cigar smoke—and the sound of a man muttering expletives to himself in Russian.

As Apparite realized the significance of what was happening, he relaxed and exhaled. The Russian hadn't left the little house to look for him, after all. He was sitting here only because Heydrich forced him to smoke his offensive, acrid cigars *outside* the cottage!

For a moment, the picture of the ex-SS man kicking the protesting SMERSH agent out of the little house to smoke cigars humanized the two of them, made them seem like real people to Apparite and not simply targets in the hunt. But Apparite knew that to do so was to risk failure: they were *not* men, he told himself; they did not have families, or laugh, or cry, or argue, or smoke bad cigars, or do anything human at all. They were simply enemies to be ruthlessly murdered so they could not murder others. Apparite's duty was to look on them as animals and nothing more. They were to be treated as game that never went out of season, and no limits had been set on how many he was allowed to "bag."

After fifteen minutes, the puffing and swearing ceased, the fallen tree shook again as the SMERSH agent stood to leave, and the *crunch-crunch* of footsteps told Apparite the man was walking back to the stone cottage. When Apparite heard the front door open and close, he snuck a peek in the direction of the little house and breathed a sigh of relief: his presence had remained undetected. He crawled over to his concealed bag of stores and opened it. The sun was almost down and if anyone else decided to drop by his hiding place, he would not be caught unawares a second time.

Besides, he said to himself, *there is killing to do.*

SEVEN:
THE NATURE OF REVENGE

Apparite pored through his satchel, formulating his plan to kill Heydrich and the cigar-smoking SMERSH agent. His first priority would be getting rid of the Russian, the logic being that if one eliminates the target's protector, it becomes easier to eliminate the target. But Apparite had to kill the SMERSH agent in near-silence and do it quickly enough so Heydrich would not be warned of the danger. Not an easy task to perform under any circumstance.

He removed his pistol from the leather bag and threaded a silencer onto its specially modified tip. He then moved on to his binoculars. An advanced and adaptable model, they not only had an infra-red, night-time capability, but could be taken apart and transformed into a riflescope, which could then be attached to his pistol. In just a few minutes Apparite had made the conversion, and he was pleased with the result: his nine-shot pistol had been turned into a mini sniper's-rifle with scope and silencer. With his exceptional eyesight (20:10 in the left eye; 20:8 in the right), he was confident he could hit his target from his hiding place forty yards away.

But he could not use a standard bullet at this range. While Apparite's aim was as expert as any man's, the unusual nature of his weapon provided no guarantee of instantly killing his enemy with a single shot. Instead, Apparite had devised another means that would provide for a quicker and surer death; one that would not require pin-point accuracy or luck.

He took what appeared to be a bullet from a small case in the satchel, but unlike the metallic appearance of most rounds, this one was uniformly jet-black and did not appear to be made of metal—which it was not. Weighing but eighty-two grains, this non-lethal projectile was designed so that it would not completely penetrate the skin, though it did have one potentially lethal characteristic: in its tip was a small well that could accommodate a poison. This poison would be injected into the victim through a tiny needle that would protrude from the bullet's tip on impact. The victim would receive a slight bruise and a microscopic puncture mark but have no evidence of a conventional bullet wound.

But the choice of poison was critical. It had to work rapidly and completely; the victim could not be afforded the opportunity to cry out in pain, or stagger even more than a few steps. Apparite had two poisons at his disposal. The first was *Ricinus,* a castor bean derivative he had used during his last mission, and which was quite useful when the means of death must remain a mystery. In this situation, however, it was unsuitable: Apparite could not wait the three days it took for *Ricinus* to kill.

Instead, he removed from his case a vial of another poison, a chemical known as "tetrodotoxin." Using a syringe, he carefully transferred as much of it as he could into the well of the rubber bullet. Tetrodotoxin, he had been told by the Director, was perhaps the most lethal neurotoxin on earth, having recently been isolated in 1950 by the Japanese from the deadly Puffer Fish.

But the Director's scientist friends had gone the Japanese one further, obtaining, purifying, and intensifying the toxin from another sea creature, the beautiful but deadly Australian Blue-Ringed Octopus. As a result of their efforts, they had created perhaps the most dangerous poison ever devised. With the amount of toxin Apparite had placed into the well of the bullet, paralysis would come nearly instantaneously; death would follow within seconds. Best of all for an assassin, there was no treatment or antidote that might save the unfortunate victim.

He placed the rubber bullet into the first position on the clip, filling the other eight with standard rounds. Slowly and quietly, he seated the clip into his modified Super Automatic. Now it was just a matter of waiting until the Russian made his way to the privy. One shot to the torso and it would be done.

After the Russian was dead, he would then enter the cottage and corner Heydrich. There was much he could learn from him about Soviet operations in Berlin—the names and locations of his handlers, or the secret operations that were underway in the German capital, for example—and he wanted to interrogate the German before killing him. After that, a single pistol shot to Heydrich's heart would be sufficient to complete the mission, followed by a fire inside the tiny stone cottage to destroy any evidence of foul play or of Apparite's visit.

While waiting for the appearance of his target, Apparite thought of the tragic circumstances that brought him to France. If there had been any danger of Apparite becoming uneasy with the killing of the Russian and Heydrich in so cold of blood, his reflections on what SMERSH had done to Dr. Hoevenaers and his friend and colleague J would have removed it. It was SMERSH that had poisoned the doctor at the cost of his leg, if not his life; and it was a SMERSH agent who had caused J's death. No, the killing of two men to fulfill this mission was not going to be a problem. In fact, though he knew it was wrong to think such things, he even wondered if he might not enjoy it.

One hour after dark, the door to the small cottage opened: it was the SMERSH agent. Whatever the two men had eaten for supper was disagreeing with him and he rushed to the privy, holding his abdomen and making a face of discomfort. In his hurry, he had thrown a coat over his shoulders but had not buttoned it, leaving a wide, inviting target. Apparite steadied the barrel of his Super Automatic on a thick branch as he peered through the infra-red scope, waiting for the optimal time to fire.

The man walked hurriedly, his steps increasing in frequency—Apparite was afraid he might vomit and arouse Heydrich—when all of a sudden he slowed and began to take very measured and deliberate steps. It was quite a curious display until Apparite figured it out: *the Russian's afraid he's going to s--t his pants!* The situation could not have been more ideal for Apparite's purpose, and he did not waste the opportunity. Putting the cross-hairs over the SMERSH agent's heart, he squeezed the trigger just as his slow-moving target reached the privy.

"Pheewt!" went the silenced pistol. The SMERSH agent made a slight sound of pain as the soft rubber bullet struck him in the chest.

Immediately, the Russian's facial expression changed: it went from one of impending alarm from the impact of the rubber bullet to essentially *no expression at all.* His eyelids slowly closed, his mouth fell open, and his chin sank to his chest. He took one slow step before his knees buckled and he crumpled to the ground in front of the privy. Apparite placed the Colt back into his satchel, clambered out from his hiding place behind the fallen tree, and walked toward the Russian. He stopped about five feet away from him.

The SMERSH agent was unmoving, but looking at his face Apparite could tell he still lived. His eyelids had opened when he'd hit the ground and the eyes behind them remained bright and alive. Slowly, in a steady but almost imperceptible movement, the Russian's eyes looked upwards toward Apparite—it seemed to take an almost inhuman effort for the stricken man to do so—until he had the American in his sights. The Russian's eyes seemed to focus on Apparite, taking him in for a moment, until the brightness seemed to dissipate from them, the lids closed, and he was dead.

Apparite walked the last couple of steps to where the Russian lay, noting with disgust that, due to the rapid paralysis from the poison, the SMERSH agent had soiled his pants with stool. He felt for the Russian's pulse; finding none, he checked him for weapons. A bulge in the Soviet's over-coat caught his eye. He reached in and pulled a Makarov pistol from an inside pocket. Holding the Russian's pistol out in front of him, he crept in silence to the front porch's stone steps. The cottage was dark except for a pale, flickering light that seemed to emanate from one corner of the room. Given the trouble with their generator, Apparite felt it safe to assume that the two men were using kerosene lamps to conserve power. After a moment of listening for footsteps, and hearing none, he pulled himself onto the porch.

He crawled to the front door and listened again, but heard only one sound: the turning of pages in a book. This told Apparite that Heydrich remained unsuspecting of an intruder, and, importantly, that there was a source of light near his target. Steadying his nerves with two deep breaths, Apparite pulled open the unlatched door and leapt into the cottage's small, single room.

The next three seconds seemed to occur in slow-motion, as so often did the violent, desperate acts he had to perform. Heydrich was lying in bed in the far right corner of the room, reading a book with the light of a kerosene lamp, as expected. He turned his head toward the open door—to berate his Russian colleague for having left it ajar—but when he saw Apparite leap into the room, he brought his hand to his mouth in surprise and let fall the book he was reading.

Apparite heard the book land on the floor. A pistol appeared in its former place in Heydrich's lap; an eight-shot semi-automatic Walther PPK. Heydrich fired but Apparite had already dropped to the ground, letting fly with a shot of his own as he tumbled past the German's bed. Heydrich's shot missed Apparite by a foot, the bullet ricocheting off one of the stone walls and embedding itself in the cottage's pantry, but Apparite's shot went true and hit Heydrich in his gun hand. Blood splattered onto the German's face and bedclothes, and his PPK fell to the floor with a thud. Apparite rose and walked to the end of the bed, coolly aiming the Makarov at Heydrich's chest.

"Keine Bewegung!" *Don't move!* Apparite cried out. *"Hände hoch, bitte!"* *Hands up, please!*

The German raised his hands in a gesture of surrender. To Apparite, Heydrich looked to be in his mid-forties, as evidenced by the streaks of gray hair at his temples; his face was angular and hard. His blue eyes were bright but cold, like a stream that had iced-over in an Alpine winter. They betrayed no fear. It was clear that this was one man who had never known fear, but whose presence had indeed caused fear in others.

"You are American, yes?" he calmly asked Apparite in German-accented English.

Apparite could not conceal a look of surprise: how could Heydrich possibly know he was American? He had spoken only in German, was holding a Soviet pistol, and had taken care to wear garments that would not have told his identity or origin.

"Nein," answered Apparite. *"Ich bin ein Deutscher."* *No, I am a German.*

Heydrich smiled knowingly.

"You cannot fool me; you do not need to pretend for my benefit. I know the Americans would find me someday—for revenge, *ja?"*

Apparite thought on this for a moment. He wondered if he might not get more information by playing up to Heydrich and engaging him in conversation. He decided to answer in English, without his German affectation.

"Yes, I am an American. Why do you think I'm here for revenge?"

"It is quite obvious: because of Malmédy; because of the prisoners my men killed."

"In the Bulge, you mean," said Apparite. "I've heard of it, but that's not why I'm here, *Herr* Heydrich. I'm here because of your work for SMERSH." He paused to add emphasis to his next statement. "Because of your work for Viktor."

"Yes, everyone knows of Viktor." Heydrich's emotions rose as he spoke. "You in the West fear him; you believe him to be the very devil! But he understands his duty and purpose. He is a great man; I only wish there were more like him. Too many Russians know *nothing* of sacrifice or of duty, unlike the men I commanded!" he added with disdain.

"Was killing POWs a part of your duty?" asked Apparite in anger. "And my father was killed in the Bulge, so let me assure you that *I* know something of sacrifice, you arrogant son of a bitch!"

"*Humph!* You ask of duty? It was my duty to kill the enemy. It mattered not if they were prisoners—they were enemies all the same. And did you not know that the Americans killed German prisoners also? Maybe not so many, and not so obvious, but it was done. How many of your GIs were tried at Dachau for such killing, as I was?"

Apparite looked at him in disgust.

"We didn't start the war—you did. We didn't invade France; we didn't kill millions of Jews. Men like you, and Hitler, and Bormann and Goring and Himmler; you've all only gotten what you deserved. At Nuremberg *all* the Nazis said they were just doing their duty—that's the excuse of a coward."

"And what about *you?*" Heydrich had posed the question quietly, almost thoughtfully. "How often have you used it, heh?

Will you use it to excuse killing a wounded, unarmed man in his bed?"

Apparite did not answer. Heydrich's last query had puzzled him; stopped his thought in its tracks. But he came around a moment later, seeing a key point he had been ignoring: his mission did *not* include debating the nature of duty with men like Heydrich. It only included the killing of them.

"I won't need any excuses. There's plenty of reasons to kill a man like you. I'm here because of your work for Viktor and SMERSH, but I'd be happy to kill you in revenge for Malmédy, too. Or even for being a traitor to Germany."

The reference to his native land sent Heydrich into a near-rage.

"Oh, please do not kill me for Germany—no! *Deutschland, Deutschland, über alles!*" he sang in a derisive, sarcastic tone. "Only the *Führer* understood, at the end, how undeserving the German people were to keep the Fatherland. They were weak—they *are* weak—and the weak deserve to die. Much as you think you take revenge on me, I took revenge on *them,* by exposing their pathetic agents. But as you see, I am *not* weak."

Heydrich smiled, revealing a small capsule held between his teeth. He'd slipped it into his mouth as soon as he'd seen an intruder leap into the room. Apparite assumed it contained cyanide.

"Spit that out and let's talk," Apparite said. He hoped to get a little more information before Heydrich bit down on the lethal capsule. "I could get you immunity; get you back to the States and freedom. All you have to do is answer a few questions."

Heydrich laughed; an experienced man such as he instantly saw through Apparite's weak ruse.

"Questions? I am going to die tonight no matter what I say. Do not think me a fool! You will learn nothing about my operations. I trust you know that. But there is one thing I will tell you before I die."

Apparite nodded. "Go right ahead." He re-aimed his pistol at Heydrich's heart, affirming the finality of what the ex-Nazi was about to say.

"You do your duty as I did mine, with emotion and purpose. We are more alike than you may wish to admit. And as I die at your hands for my deeds, I am sure that you will die at others' hands for yours. But ask yourself this: can you take revenge on a man who was only doing his duty? Revenge is a *personal* act—it has nothing to do with duty. Do not give significance, my young American, to what you now do by thinking it is *revenge*." He stopped speaking for a moment but then continued in a firm voice, his pride unbent, his face showing no trace of fear.

"Not that it matters. Not you, or those who sent you, will have their revenge on *me*."

Before Apparite could fire his pistol, Heydrich bit down on the capsule and a faint odor of almonds scented the air. The ex-SS man smiled wanly, uttered a choking sound and retched. His expression turned into one of alarm—he had not expected a death-struggle and for the first time in his life knew the feeling of fear—which was followed by an immediate, violent seizure that threw him onto the floor. He convulsed for a full thirty seconds, all the while gasping and choking as his face turned pale white, then red, and then blue, fading finally into gray. At long last his agonizing spasms ceased and the fearful look on his face was removed. One last, slow exhalation of breath, and he was still.

Apparite felt for a pulse at the German's neck; detecting none, he lifted him back into bed, placing the PPK into the dead man's right hand. He went outside and dragged the SMERSH agent's corpse into the cabin. With some effort, he carefully laid him in bed next to Heydrich, placing the Makarov pistol at his side. Apparite grabbed the kerosene lamp sitting on the kitchen table and emptied its contents onto the cottage's wooden floor. He walked to the night-stand next to the bed and picked up the lit kerosene lamp that Heydrich had been using to read. Taking a few steps toward the door, he tossed it into the air.

Apparite walked briskly out of the cottage and shut the door firmly behind him. He ran a short distance from the cottage and turned to face it. Even from that distance he could hear the sound of the fire spreading within the little house; a sort of *woosh* as the floor, blankets, curtains, and then the clothes of the dead men caught on fire. Smoke began to pour from the chimney and the cracks around the windows when there was a sudden explosion.

The glass blew out of the cottage's windows, the ferocity and volume of the blast startling Apparite. With the fire now free to consume as much oxygen as it wanted—and it seemed an unusually ravenous fire—flames shot out of the windows twenty-five feet into the air; a dancing, red silhouette of living destruction set against the impenetrable indigo of the moonless sky. The pungent smell of burning flesh reached Apparite, and repulsed by it he turned and plunged into the woods to retrieve his gear and make his way back to the hotel. He retraced his steps to Rhinbourg, stopping only briefly at a stream to wash the black dirt from his face and dispose of his tree-branch–pierced sweater. When he reached the *rue de St. Germain,* he turned around once more. Gazing back down the dirt road he noted a faint, dancing glow in the sky above the trees, against which rose a veil of smoke.

He knew that by morning, almost nothing would be left of the little cottage except the kiln-baked ceramic plates, the pistols, and the smoldering bones of the two dead men. Soon, the only remaining physical evidence of Apparite's visit would also disappear. The rubber bullet he had used to kill the Russian was designed to degrade in a few days when exposed to the elements, leaving only a few millimeters of steel needle and release mechanism as a reminder of what had happened. And no one, figured Apparite, would ever find *that* needle in this particular Alsatian haystack.

Apparite walked back to the hotel where he found the concierge awaiting him. To his discomfort, she was wearing rather provocative dress—a black, low-cut evening gown with pronounced décolletage—and was holding a bottle of Moët *et* Chandon champagne. She rushed to him and firmly grabbed his arm. With an effort, she directed him to a small café table in the corner of the little foyer.

"Oh, *Monsieur* Müller—how was your exploring? Have you been out looking for your fungus all this time?"

"Moss," Apparite answered in his German-inflected voice. "I was looking for moss; but yes, I found some *excellent* samples near Gottenhouse."

"Ah, *trés bien;* I am glad you found what you wanted. I thought you might wish to share a bottle of champagne with me when you returned."

Without waiting for an answer, she popped the cork. It shot into the air, striking the ceiling above them as bubbling yellow liquid poured from the bottle in a Vesuvial-like eruption.

"Vielen Dank, Fräulein. . . ." Thank you much, muttered the discomforted Superagent, suddenly at a loss for words: the danger of having a drink with this woman seemed almost as great as that in killing Heydrich, and the reward considerably less. But as he had no easy route of escape, he took a small sip of the champagne to be polite.

"That's fantastic!" he blurted out, nearly forgetting to use his German accent. "I've never had finer champagne—not even in Berlin." And he meant it, for it was the best he'd ever tasted.

"I *knew* you'd find it pleasing." She put down her empty

glass and filled it expertly to its very top with more of the effervescent liquid. "Where did you explore, *Monsieur* Müller? And how does one find moss in the dark? It must be very difficult!"

Apparite saw his peril, for he could ill-afford to discuss his whereabouts with her. He was savvy enough to recognize, however, that as long as he stayed in her good graces, she was unlikely to suspect there was anything unusual about him, or to betray his strange behavior to the authorities. And then there was the champagne. It was so refreshing and exquisite that he did not wish to leave without another glass. Staying for another drink or two perhaps would be best.

"Oh, let's not talk about my work," Apparite said. "Moss would only bore you. Let us just sit in quiet and think about the lovely chance that brought you and I and this wonderful bottle of champagne together tonight." He picked up the bottle and refilled his glass, raising it to her in salute.

She raised her glass as well and tapped it against his. Unknowingly, she spilled champagne down the front of her gown, but would not have cared, anyway: she was beaming in joy; she felt as light and radiant as a feather that floated in the breeze that rushed down from the mountains. Apparite reached out and took her hand, holding it gently in his. After another few sips of champagne, he spoke.

"I am afraid I must leave you. I must catalogue and prepare my specimens for their voyage home. The champagne was wonderful, but even more pleasing was your company tonight while drinking it."

"Do you really have to go? Please, stay and sit with me awhile."

"Unfortunately, I must," answered Apparite. "But there is one last thing I must beg of you. If anyone asks of me, you must say you do not know me."

"Why is that?"

Apparite softly caressed her hand.

"This is so difficult to say. I have a girl back in Heidelberg; we are engaged. I should not have had champagne with you tonight, but I could not resist. *Please* forgive me," he added, with as much sincerity as he could muster.

"I understand." The concierge's face was downcast though her strong voice betrayed an inner pride in the evening's events. It had been years since she'd been so flattered by another man's attentions—going all the way back to her beloved Henri, who'd run off with that hussy from the *Café d'Or* in 1953—and at the moment, she would have done nearly anything for the (apparently) dashing German naturalist. "Your secret is safe with me," she said in reassurance.

"Danke, Fräulein, danke." He grabbed his satchel and walked quickly up the stairs to his room. He had once escaped from two armed KGB agents after being tied up naked in a locked room, but at the moment, his escape from the lovelorn concierge seemed the more impressive feat (and fortunately, unlike the two KGB men, Apparite would not be forced to kill *her*). Lying on his bed, still fully clothed and with his mind softened considerably by the champagne, he rested his head on the pillow and soon fell asleep. He remembered no dreams that night, as was his usual, but as so many of his dreams were vivid self-incriminations of his friend J's death, he did not miss them.

Apparite came down from his room early the next morning.

"Bonjour, Monsieur Müller," the concierge said. But her countenance had changed from the night before: she was no longer smiling and gay. She motioned him to come nearer. "Did you hear about the tragedy?" she whispered. "The dead men? *C'est une mystére*—such a mystery, and *very* sad."

"No—what happened?"

"There was *un feu trés grand*—a big fire. Two men were killed, just a few miles away. Some people are saying one was a German war criminal—a Nazi!—but the other, no one knows. Just think: a Nazi criminal only down the road!"

"Terrible." Apparite adopted a look of sadness. "Even for a Nazi criminal to die like that. What was he doing in France, I wonder?"

"Some say he was hiding from his enemies; many have not forgotten the war, *Monsieur* Müller. It is strange, but they found guns by the men. Why would they have guns, I ask myself?"

"Maybe they were for hunting. Or for protection—if he was in hiding, as you say."

She leaned unusually close to Apparite's ear, whispering softly into it as if in fear of being overheard.

"Do you know what I think, *Monsieur* Müller?"

Apparite shook his head *no*. He hoped she was not shrewder than he had guessed.

"I think the two men were lovers, and left this world—which could not understand such a love—by their own hand, together."

Apparite held back a laugh. The thought that Heydrich and the SMERSH agent could be thought by *anyone* to be homosexual lovers was patently absurd. He rubbed his eyes to hide the startled amusement in them.

"Really?" he said, nearly choking on the word. "Why do you say that?"

"Oh, I saw them together once—they had such sensitive faces; such a *handsome,* charming couple. I could not believe it when I heard the German was a Nazi!"

Apparite felt sorry for her: the woman was such a hopeless romantic that she sought love wherever it might be found, seeing it even in the tumultuous and decidedly *un*-sexual relationship between a SMERSH agent and a hardened Nazi war-criminal who could not stand each other's presence.

"I see," said Apparite. "Yes, I can see why you would think so. It is so sad when such things happen, regardless of the reason."

"You *will* be staying again tonight, won't you *Monsieur* Müller?" she asked brightly in an abrupt change of subject. "I will make you a delicious custard—what we call *'crème brûlée.'* And I have a wonderful sweet wine from our region to share." She raised her face upwards in a gesture of hope to Apparite, who got the feeling he was in imminent danger of being kissed.

"I'm so sorry—no, I must be going," he said. He took a discreet half step backward. "I have so many samples, and they are so delicate, that I must take them immediately back to the Institute."

The concierge's expression fell like a badly cooked soufflé. Apparite thought he even saw tears in her eyes.

"But I will never forget you and your champagne," he added, comforting her, "and will always remember the true reason this hotel is named *'Paradis.'* "

He kissed her on the cheek and left the hotel to take a taxi back to Saverne, leaving the concierge with the remembrance of the handsome young German naturalist who, although he had spent just one night in her little hotel, had left behind a lifetime of romantic memories for her, and although nearly all of them were complete figments of her vivid and wonderful imagination, to a true romantic the truth is always the most inconsequential part of any love affair, and so it would be with her.

An hour later, Apparite boarded the train in Saverne that would take him to Germany. At one time this train was probably thought to be the height of elegance and comfort, but it had long fallen into disrepair from the combination of passenger over-use and maintenance neglect. Its black, wartime-era paint was peeling from its cars, revealing occasional streaks of the original silver underneath. Stepping inside one if its passenger carriages, he noted the rips in the well-worn red carpet that covered the floor. The faded black leather seat-coverings of the small, four-passenger booths were rough-looking and cracked, and, Apparite suspected, mighty uncomfortable. Anyone trying to recapture the elegance of pre-war rail travel on *this* train was bound to be disappointed, he thought.

Taking a seat in one of the booths in the near-empty carriage, he reflected on his time in Rhinbourg. He had fulfilled his mission in its entirety, doing so with stealth and secrecy, and yet one aspect of it puzzled him. He had expected to feel a sense of vindication, if not elation, after dispatching his enemy—a man who had betrayed Germany to work for SMERSH; a man who had killed American POWs in the battle that had also taken his father's life—and yet he had not. In fact, the sight of the Russian's and especially Heydrich's death had been an unexpected revulsion to him.

He made an effort not to think of it, forcing the image of the German's horrific cyanide reaction and the paralyzed, dying SMERSH agent's eerie stare deep within his mind, out of reach from conscious thought. But no matter how Apparite tried, those memories would not stay buried. There was something in what Heydrich had said that was tearing down Apparite's carefully constructed emotional defenses and allowing them to surface.

And yet Apparite refused to admit it, refused to allow himself the possibility that Heydrich had somehow gotten to him.

After all, why should the ravings of a man about to die mean anything? he asked himself, ignoring the fact that Heydrich's last words had been spoken with complete calm and lucidity.

That's all it was: just the ravings of a man about to die, he repeated. The train noisily *click-clacked* over the Saar River and into Germany. Apparite unfolded a German-language newspaper he had picked up at the station in Saverne. He put his mind to reading it, but paused after skimming only a paragraph of a painfully dull story on labor relations in Stuttgart.

That's all it was, he told himself, *just the ravings of a man about to die.* After saying it another couple of times, he had almost convinced himself that it was true.

EIGHT:
A CHANCE MEETING

After perusing a few more stories in the newspaper (none of them approaching the excitement of labor relations in Stuttgart, which had apparently been the big news story of the day), Apparite put it back down onto his seat. He thought of going to the dining car for supper, but since his hunger had deserted him for some reason, he instead spent the next few hours staring out of the window. This region of Germany, the western Rhineland Pfalz, was particularly scenic and he found its beauty calming, almost hypnotic to him. The train passed through Kaiserslauten, Mannheim, and Frankfurt before he finally turned away from the window and suddenly noticed that he was no longer alone in the booth.

Sitting directly across from him was a young woman, though when she had arrived he could not say. Apparite was at first disturbed that he had not detected her presence until that moment, but realized that if she had posed a threat, he would certainly have been aroused from his previous trance-like state. His eyes might have been occupied with the scenery, but his subconscious rarely relaxed its vigilance.

He glanced across the seat and rapidly took her in. She was wearing an elegant black dress, giving her the appearance of a woman in mourning. On her head was a short, round-topped hat with a broad circular brim. It was tilted slightly and rather fashionably to the right. She stared straight ahead with unfocused eyes, as if picturing some memory in her mind that she did not wish the world around her to disturb. A moment later, she wiped a tear from her face with a rather soiled handkerchief. When she felt Apparite's eyes upon her, she stirred and spoke.

"Oh, I'm so sorry—I should have asked if you minded me sitting with you," she said in German. She dabbed away another tear from her clear blue eyes.

Apparite could tell that at some point earlier in the day, or perhaps the night before, her face had been carefully made-up, but tears had smeared the dark liner around her eyes and removed the rouge from her cheeks, leaving long pale streaks that trailed down the sides of her face. And yet she was quite attractive. She had a rounded, smooth, clean beauty to her—not unlike that of Ingrid Bergman, thought Apparite—and her blonde hair fell in long, natural, graceful curls around her shoulders.

"No, it's not a problem," Apparite answered in German. "I'm glad for the company."

"I saw your newspaper lying on the seat and wondered if you might let me keep it," she said. "You see, my father died last week, and the death notice is . . ." But she could say no more. Tears came and her shoulders shook in unstoppable sobs.

Apparite offered her a clean handkerchief. She took it and wiped away the many tears that cascaded down her face. Glancing down, she noted the black smudge-marks from her eyeliner that discolored the cloth. She held it up for Apparite to see.

"I'm so sorry," she said, but when Apparite laughed at the sight, she did as well.

"You may keep that one!" he told her. "I have others."

"Thank you—you are very kind." She held out a pale and trembling hand. "My name is Christiane Grünbach."

"Hans Müller," said Apparite, shaking her hand. "Please— take my newspaper, and let me express my sympathies." She nodded in thanks, took the newspaper from the seat, and placed it in her handbag.

"I've only just returned from his funeral," she said. "My father lived in Berlin, but wished to be buried in the family plot in Otterberg."

"I see. Where in Berlin do you live? I am going there myself."

"Unfortunately, we were both in the East—in the Soviet sector. My work makes traveling difficult, especially into the West. I had to get special permission to leave. Even my father—a dead man!—had to have the correct forms and stamps and papers. And then passing the border, they—they made us open the casket! It was so, so horrible. . . ."

She began to weep again and Apparite instinctively reached over and patted her hand, comforting her.

Apparite felt an undeniably powerful attraction to her; stronger than he had felt for any woman in years. And he had been genuinely affected by her plight—given his own tragic past, he could certainly empathize with someone who had just lost a parent. But despite these feelings, a part of him had remained all-business and taken notice of something she had said: "My work makes traveling difficult, *especially into the West!*" Apparite guessed that she worked with or for the Soviets, and likely had access to classified information. Slipping into his role as a Superagent he pressed her, albeit gently, for more information.

"It is terrible when even the dead are oppressed," he said. "I am fortunate to live in West Berlin; quite fortunate compared to those of you in the East. Why is it they restrict your travel?"

"Do you promise to keep it a secret? You cannot tell anyone."

Apparite took her hands in his, noting their trembling. Despite her hesitation, he sensed that not only did she want to tell him about her work, but that she *needed* to tell him, to tell someone, in what she was involved.

"Yes—of course," replied Apparite. "I'd never tell a soul." He was lying, naturally, but justified it as a part of his duty. It was John Apparite the Superagent who would betray her trust, not John Apparite the man, and the distinction between the two allowed him to do it without remorse.

"I work in an East Berlin telephone exchange, near what was once St. Antonius Hospital. The Soviets use it for their own purpose now."

Apparite's interest rose sharply, for the old St. Antonius Hospital was known to those in his line of work as "Karlshorst," in reality, the largest KGB base in Germany, if not all of Europe. He could only imagine what secrets this woman might be privy to in the transmissions that emanated from that complex! The espionage agent within him recognized her as a potential gold mine of anti-Soviet intelligence.

"It sounds very dangerous to work for the Russians," he said. "Do you have any reason to fear them?"

"They are very strict, and we are rarely allowed to travel outside East Berlin. Some of us have been followed; others say they are watched. But *some* of the Russians are nice: the older ones are very dashing. They remind me of German Barons or Counts!" She laughed heartily, a low-pitched though musical sound that he felt in his chest as well as his ears. For an instant he had an intense longing to kiss her, but quickly dismissed his thoughts of romance.

"Do you enjoy the work?"

She furrowed her brow.

"No—I *hate* it. It is a dull job and the exchange is hot and stuffy. The pay is poor, and always in worthless East German marks. I have tried to change positions but they won't let me."

"I'm sorry," said Apparite. "I have contacts in Berlin that might help you. Will you honor me by letting me mention your situation? I will not use your true name, of course."

"No!" she said roughly. Her expression softened and she caressed Apparite's hands in worry. "Please, do not involve yourself. I do not wish to place you in danger. I'm sorry—I can see that I've imposed on you. I'll leave you now." She started to rise from her seat.

Apparite reached out and placed his hand on her arm to keep her from departing.

"No—please stay." He knew it was his duty to woo her for her services, to see what she could bring to his agency in the interest of the United States, but as a man his feelings were just as strong: she was so lovely, so attractively soft and vulnerable in her grief, that he could not possibly let her go.

"Please stay," he repeated. "And tell me about your father. Speaking of him will make you feel better."

She retook her seat and gave Apparite a warm look: there was nothing he might have said that would have pleased her more. Soon she was telling Apparite of growing up in Otterberg with her family: their likes (dachshunds and pretzels) and dislikes (mushy *spaetzle* made by her aunt); of sing-alongs by a fire in the shadow of the Vosges Mountains while on holiday; of long walks through the woods in search of wildflowers; and even of her father's nickname for her, *"meine kleine Schneeflocke," my little snow-flake,* which made her laugh audibly though tears coursed down her well-stained cheeks as she said it.

As she told him these tales, he could not help but be reminded of his relationship with his own father: he had been near in Apparite's mind since the events in Rhinbourg, and for the first time in ages he felt like thinking of him. They might not have shared much time in terms of hours and minutes during his father's life, but Apparite's remembrances of the two of them shooting squirrels in the Alleghenies, or swimming in the pools of dammed streams, or sitting on the sofa and listening to the Nats on the radio, his father's arm draped lovingly over his shoulder, seemed more vivid and precious than ever.

And before long, Apparite found himself telling her of his own childhood—transposed into a Germanic version to hide his true origins, of course—and the two of them laughed and cried together as he spoke of it, especially when he told her of the time his father tried to soften shoe polish in the oven, only to set it on fire and fill the house with a choking black smoke.

"You must miss him very much," she said. "Do you, even now?"

"Yes, I do." Apparite was surprised by the automatic nature of his response. "He went off to the war and never returned." He briefly stopped in thought before continuing, but when he did his voice was tainted by bitterness. "But a part of me hates him for it, too—hates him for leaving us and dying, just as I was getting to know him."

"I am sorry to hear that. If only you had more time with him, maybe you would remember him as I remember my father." She wiped away her remaining tears and yawned. "May I sit next to you and rest awhile? I have slept so poorly this past week."

Apparite motioned for her to sit beside him; she did so and laid her head on his shoulder, almost immediately falling into a deep sleep. She breathed in and out in a soft, even rhythm, and feeling the warmth and weight of her head on his shoulder brought a contented look to Apparite's face. There was something so natural about this woman sleeping up against him, about the two of them having shared the past hours in so intimate a fashion that he did not wish to part from her when they arrived in Berlin.

The train stopped abruptly, jarring him back into reality and the realization that he had a significant problem: Apparite did not know where his character "Hans Müller" was supposed to be living in West Berlin, or where he was to go when he got there. Fortunately, he had not been asked by the woman to say exactly where he resided in the former German capital, but sooner or later the subject was bound to come up—and he would have to have some answers for her when it did. Seeking inspiration, he removed his forged German passport from his coat pocket and stared at it:

Now, where would a man like Hans Müller live in such a huge city?

And as soon as he asked himself this question, he knew. In fact, it had been so obvious that he almost burst out laughing in relief, for he had been holding the answer in his hands the entire time! Opening the passport to the photograph and data page, Apparite noted the address of "Hans Müller": *Wittenbergstrasse 48.* Knowing the Director as he did—a more organized and thorough man had not been born—Apparite was confident that not only would the house at this address be unoccupied and ready for him when he arrived, but there would be food and beer in the refrigerator, and a newspaper waiting for him on the doorstep as well.

The door at the end of the car opened. A stern, Russian-looking conductor appeared; he held a flashlight. He methodically began to check the papers of the passengers in the carriage. Christiane had been asleep for only fifteen minutes, but Apparite had to find out what was happening. The sudden stopping of the train and the appearance of the conductor was disconcerting.

"Christiane, wake-up," he said in a whisper. "We've stopped."

She stirred and awoke at the sound of his voice. She straightened herself in the seat and smoothed out the wrinkles in her black dress.

"Oh—we must be at Marienborn; the check-point going into the Eastern sector. I need to get my papers."

She rose, assumed her previous seat across from Apparite,

and took a folio from her handbag. Opening it, she perused her papers; slowly and deliberately at first, but then rapidly and in a rising panic.

"My God—I've misplaced my re-entry permit!" She ruffled through the folio once more, but having no success slumped back into the seat in resignation.

"What does that mean?" asked Apparite. "You live in the East, so why wouldn't they let you back into the Soviet sector?"

"I need a form attesting I did not take sensitive material with me; that I do not need to be interviewed or searched on my return. Once they see I work for Karlshorst, they will have a fit—a *fit.*"

"I thought the Soviets didn't come aboard the trains," Apparite said. "Has something changed?"

"Since they found the American spy tunnel, the Russians have gone *crazy:* new check-points, searches, boarding trains and buses. But whatever they do to me, do not protest or you will be taken off the train."

Apparite knew nothing of the discovery of a spy tunnel, having been in seclusion for the past few days. Still, he thought it unwise to pursue the subject with Christiane at the moment: he did not want to alert her to the possibility that he was an intelligence agent. He assumed that the tunnel in question was somewhere in Berlin, the main hot-spot in the Cold War—that was only logical. No matter. D would catch him up on everything soon enough. Besides, with Christiane's predicament coming to a head, he had more pressing matters to worry about.

The conductor approached the booth in which Apparite and the woman were sitting. A uniformed Soviet soldier bearing a machine-gun followed close behind.

"Your papers," the conductor said in Slavic-accented German to Apparite. He had a severe expression on his pox-scarred face and his breath smelled of stale coffee and cigarettes.

Apparite handed the man his documents, thinking, *well, if there was ever a test of the Director's talent in forged papers, then this is gonna be it.* But all went smoothly with nary a query. The conductor deliberately examined the documents, made a notation in the passport, and handed them back to Apparite.

"Danke," Apparite said. The soldier stepped forward, lifting the bill of his Red Army cap to get a better look at Apparite. He stared deeply into Apparite's face, but seeing nothing that made him suspect an enemy or a deception, he pulled it back down again. He moved on with the conductor to Christiane.

"Your papers, *Fräulein.*"

She handed her folio to the conductor. He perused the many documents inside it but then made a face and frowned. "You require a re-entry permit. Where is it, *Fräulein?*"

Christiane turned pale and her hands and voice began to shake.

"I—I must have misplaced it. But all the others are in order."

The conductor turned to the soldier and the two men exchanged hushed words. The conductor nodded and spoke.

"You will be taken off the train. This must be investigated further."

"Please, *please* don't. I am returning from my father's funeral—I beg you." She began to weep and it took all of Apparite's strength not to come to her aid. He knew that to involve himself in her plight in any way might expose himself to interrogation and a search of his bags. He would have to sit tight, no matter how great his fury or shame in not helping her.

"You must come," the Soviet soldier said in a mechanical version of German. He took her arm by the elbow. Christiane rose but reached to retrieve her handbag before leaving the booth.

"Wait a moment," she said. She took the newspaper from her handbag and gave it to Apparite. "Thank you for lending me your newspaper."

When the conductor and the soldier turned to lead her away, she forced a smile for Apparite's benefit before being hustled off the train. The last five minutes had brought Apparite's emotions to a desperate peak and he suppressed a strong urge to run after her and disable the men leading her away. He relaxed, however, when he opened the newspaper and saw the note she had left for him: *"Café Falke, Alex, 1900."*

She'd written it, he surmised, when she was searching for her papers and realized what was going to happen. But his joy in knowing he would see her again was short-lived: while he was certain she would be interrogated, searched, and then released, he was unsure how rough they would be with her, or whether any advantages would be taken against her wishes. He vowed that if she were violated in any way, he would come back and send the unfeeling conductor on a voyage from which that man could not *possibly* return.

The conductor addressed the passengers in Apparite's carriage. "You must pull the shades!" The train began to move. "They must be left in the down position until we reach Berlin. If anyone lifts the shades at any time, the train will be stopped, and I promise you, there will be a delay that all will regret."

Some passengers in the car—the ones who knew the many bluffs of such communist bureaucrats—ignored the conductor's high-pitched voice in disinterest, but those who had not been exposed to the Russian sense of order and command looked frightened. Their faces were filled with doubt, and they glanced often at the Soviet soldier's machine-gun.

"The present time is twenty-three seventeen," the conductor went on. "We will arrive in Berlin in the early morning as long as everyone cooperates. I advise you not to leave the carriage without permission, but since the dining car is now closed there should be little need of it."

He sat back down in a portable chair near one exit of the carriage, as did the Soviet soldier, who positioned himself at the other. For many hours the train swayed and shook as it rumbled on ill-laid tracks toward Berlin. After a time, as the carriage had assumed an unusual quiet fostered by boredom and fear, Apparite fell asleep. His dreams, as they so often were these days, would be filled with events from his past, re-enacted in gory detail but with absurd, surreal enhancements added by his anxious, burdened subconscious.

He dreamt of British MI5 agent Clive Hitch dying in the British Museum's Reading Room while Apparite helplessly stood nearby, feet held fast to the floor by long rail-spikes; then there was J lying on the sofa in the safe-house in London, his last breath leaving him as knee-high cement hardened around Apparite's legs, immobilizing him; and finally the sight of Viktor slashing the throat of the innocent bystander outside the Reading Room: the SMERSH man slowly drew the blade across the young man's neck as gallons of blood poured from it, creating a river of red that washed Apparite out of the building and into the street. Its force swept him toward an open sewer grate, pulling his legs into the filthy black hole, his torso soon following while his arms clawed helplessly at the pavement.

He awoke with a start, gasping for breath.

It was the first episode of panic that Apparite had had for months. He wiped the sweat from his brow, rearranged his shirt and tie, and took a few deep breaths in an effort to find calm. There was a lurch and he felt the train slow and then stop with a shudder. They had reached the outskirts of Berlin. But though he had slept, he had not found the peace he so desperately needed. In their surreal, vivid grotesqueness, his dreams had not only disturbed him to the brink of an anxiety attack, but had done something of which he could not be so quickly relieved: they had *angered* him. If Viktor indeed showed in

Berlin, Apparite vowed he would stop at nothing until he saw the Russian dead.

NINE:
A CITY DIVIDED

Apparite arrived at *Bahnhof Zoo*—the *Zoologischer garten* rail station—in the early morning, the rest of his train journey blissfully uneventful. He took a taxi from the station, but when the driver let him off on the *Wittenbergstrasse* he wondered if the Director had not made some sort of a mistake. While much of this part of West Berlin had already been rebuilt after the war, noticeably in the area near the *Kurfürstendamm,* the most glamorous shopping area in the West, the address in question on the *Wittenbergstrasse* seemed to have more in common with a bombed-out building than any sort of human dwelling. Five stories tall, it was dotted with boarded-up windows, and gaping cracks and holes littered the walls of the upper floors. Apparite could even see the *sky* through some of them.

He glanced back and forth from his passport to the building in question until he was certain that this was, indeed, the right address. He sighed and walked up to the door marked *"48."*

Apparite took a breath and paused before acting. Would the door be open? Or had the Director hidden a key for him somewhere? He tried the latch but drew another quick breath in frustration and cursed when he found it was securely locked. A rapid search of the immediate area for a key did not produce results, identifying not a single place where one could safely be concealed, so he did the most logical, natural, common-sensical thing possible:

He knocked on the door.

"Just a moment!" said a muffled voice in German. The tone was that of a woman, and surprisingly pleasant.

But hearing it ratcheted-up Apparite's tension even further: who the *hell* was this woman, and what would she think of the young man waiting on her—no wait, *his* doorstep? The door opened and a plump, smiling, gray-haired woman appeared. From her looks and demeanor, he thought her to be the very stereotype of a German *"Oma,"* or what in the States would be called one's "granny."

Before Apparite could open his mouth (and frankly, he wasn't sure what to say, anyway), she embraced him in an affectionate bear-hug and kissed him on both cheeks!

"Welcome home, *Herr* Müller. Everything is ready for you."

"Um—yes, yes, um, thank you," Apparite stammered in German. She let him loose from her vise-like grip and led him into the two-story apartment. The outside might have looked a mess, but the inside was quite pleasing to the eye: there were attractive brightly-colored woolen rugs; a comfortable-appearing sofa with a muted yellow floral pattern; a handsome walnut dining table and chairs; a buffet filled with green-glazed German pottery and dishes; and a well-appointed kitchen with gas-burning stove, oven, ice-box, and sink.

"I take it you'll be staying?" he asked with trepidation.

She laughed aloud.

"Of course! A bachelor like yourself would starve without me!"

"Yes, you might be right—I'm sure I can use the help! But it has been a long night. I think I will retire to bed for a while."

She led him upstairs to a tastefully decorated bedroom.

"I need to go the market," she said, "but I'll return in a few minutes. When I heard you were coming, I ran a bath and prepared some *streusel* cake and coffee for you."

"Thank you. I'll take the bath a bit later. After my nap I'll need to go on a few errands, so don't expect me back for some time." He closed the bedroom door.

Apparite lay on the soft down mattress of the unexpectedly elegant four-poster bed. His tired mind flooded him with questions: *Who on earth is this woman? How much does she know about me? Is she someone I can trust? When will I get my next instructions?*

He closed his eyes to rest, but finding he could not sleep, decided to take a bath while the water was still hot. Afterwards, feeling refreshed, he eagerly disposed of the large piece of *streusel* cake and mug of coffee left for him on the kitchen table. He then returned upstairs, unpacked his bags, and carefully concealed his cache of weapons, false documents, and money under a loose floorboard. Mindful of security, he checked the phones and house fixtures for "bugs" and tested the locks on the windows and doors. A spy's housekeeping done, he sat at the kitchen table in thought.

Now what to do? Obviously, the housekeeper had been summoned here by D or the Director, but if they had known Apparite was coming to the Berlin safe-house, then why weren't either of them here? Were things as critical in Hungary as Hoevenaers had hinted?

But Apparite did not much mind the wait. Although he was desperate to find Viktor, and had an assignation with Christiane in the evening, he knew his tired mind and body could use a day of relaxation to get recharged for what he thought would be an intense time ahead. And if he was going to spend any significant time in Berlin—which was quite large, being almost nine times greater in area than Paris—he also needed to get a feel for the city and its geography. As he had done in London the year before, he would spend his first day exploring and see what he might find. And who knows? Maybe he would get some clue as to Viktor's whereabouts. A lucky break was more likely to present itself walking around the city than sitting in a safe-house eating *streusel* cake.

He donned a conservatively tailored gray suit and hat and exited the apartment. He stood for a time on the front stoop, pondering where to go first. Finding his plan, he turned east toward the Soviet sector and began walking at a brisk pace. Looking around him, he was struck not by the color and grandeur of Berlin (as he had been by the city of London), but by the almost complete *lack* of it: the streets, buildings, cars, and even people all seemed to be in varying shades of black, white, or gray.

As he drew closer to the Soviet sector border, this feeling became so pronounced that he wondered if perhaps he was not in some sort of living black and white movie, set in a near-monochromatic city that had, apparently, been nearly wiped off the face of the earth: on every street were empty lots on which sat huge piles of rubble, and of the buildings left standing many appeared to be in the throes of either collapse or demolition.

He turned north, walking along the *Einemstrasse* in the direction of the *Tiergarten,* the huge park situated in central Berlin, when he heard what appeared to be the sound of distant thunder. Strange, he thought, since the sky overhead was clear. He was at a loss as to its origin when he heard a particularly voluminous thunder-clap from around the corner, and then the mystery was solved.

A cloud of dust appeared down the street followed by German shouts and the sound of heavy machines and jack-hammers. Of course, Apparite realized, it's not thunder at all—it's the sound of demolition charges! So much of this city had been destroyed in the war that, even ten years afterwards, the tearing-down before the building-up had not yet been completed. And though he saw no area untouched by the destruction, and the residual damage was still staggering to behold, among the piles of rubble and half-destroyed buildings there were indeed signs of new growth in the form of clean steel gird-ers and freshly poured cement. Berlin *would* rise from its ashes, if only given the time and freedom to do so.

But the city's buildings had not been the only casualties of war. For every new structure or development, there were also the many shacks and huts of temporary refugee camps to house those who had fled the Eastern sector. And much as the new growth in the West was in contrast with the bare city blocks Apparite could see across the border to the East, so it was with the people of Berlin as well. Those who lived in the West wore tailored, clean clothes and had the contented expressions of the well-fed and hopeful, but those who had either escaped from or lived in the East were dressed in oily, stained, ill-fitting pants and shirts; their faces were gaunt and unsmiling, and fear was in their eyes.

The contrast was so striking, that it seemed to Apparite as if there were two distinct races of Germans: the *Wessis,* or Western-ers, whose lives held the promise of the future as typified by the rebirth of the city around them; and the *Ossis,* or Easterners, whose lives held, perhaps, no future at all—just the suffocating stagnation of oppression. Christiane, he guessed, was treated better than most in the East given her situation with Karlshorst, but her future would likely remain in shades of black and white, even as those in the West would someday begin living theirs fully in color.

Reaching the *Tiergarten,* and cutting across its broad, green lawn, he reached the old *Charlottenburgstrasse,* the street that divided the park along its east-west axis (and which had recently been renamed *Strasse des 17 Juni* after the uprising of 1953). After but a few minutes at a brisk pace he was within a quarter-mile of the famous, imposing Brandenburg Gate; the *Branden-burger Tor* to the Germans; the symbol of Berlin's greatness for over 150 years.

But it was no longer so, Apparite noted with sadness. The glory of the *Quadriga*—the statue of the goddess Viktoria driving her chariot, which had long-crowned the gate—had been replaced by a single red flag, and to anyone who saw it, the message this flag had been raised to deliver was this one:

We are the Soviets, and we are here.

Apparite slowed his pace. He noted, for the first time, the presence of Soviet soldiers in the city. A dozen of them (along with East German *polizei*) were clustered around the Gate, and if pedestrians approached, they accosted them—rudely it seemed, even from Apparite's distant vantage point—and demanded to see their papers. Most of them they let out of (or into) the Soviet sector, but the odd one was berated and turned away after a notation was made into a log-book.

Apparite walked another fifty yards toward the Gate, squinting to better focus on the Soviet soldiers at the crossing. Could Viktor possibly be among them? He scanned their faces, using as much of his unusually sensitive vision as possible, but came up empty: there were no tall, pale men with intense, burning eyes in view. But somehow, he knew it would be so; somehow, he knew that his first sight of Viktor would be felt in his gut even before it registered on his vision. He resumed walking, his eyes still focused on the crossing.

When he reached a point about forty yards from the Gate, he turned to the south and began to circle the *Tiergarten* to make his way back to the safe-house. Tensions between East and West were unusually high, and as he had no reason to pass into the Soviet sector until he was to meet Christiane at 1900, he decided to take no chances of exposure to the enemy. That would be saved for another time.

But though he remained in the West, he stayed vigilant and observant. He noted that road-blocks had been placed at key intersections near the border to allow inspection of vehicles traveling into the West, and at every crossing stood a Soviet sentry or East German policeman carrying a rifle or machine-gun. It did not take a fortune-teller to see into this future: Apparite imagined the day when East was completely separate from West; when the *U-bahn* and *S-bahn* stopped at the border and went no further, and there were no work-passes or compassionate visits or any valid reasons at all for those wishing to go into the West. If it did not come this year then perhaps the next, he figured, and though his guess would prove to be a few years off the mark, for all practical purposes the separation had already begun.

"I hope the *spaetzle* isn't too salty for your taste."

Apparite put a spoonful of the classic German dish into his mouth. Watching his *Oma* (as he had nicknamed the housekeeper) prepare it, he had expected it to be rather bland and tasteless, but was surprised when he began chewing: it was firm but pleasantly yielding in texture, with a tasty, buttery, nut-like flavor.

"It's very good!" Apparite replied in German. "Better even then my mother used to make."

The beaming expression on his *Oma's* face showed her appreciation of the remark. "I like mine with fresh parsley or a little nutmeg," she said. "But even with the blockade over, one cannot find it easily in Berlin."

"It's great the way it is." And then, thinking of his conversation with Christiane on the train, Apparite added, "just so it's not mushy—that's all I care about!"

She put a spoonful of sauerkraut and a thick sausage nearly bursting through its skin onto his plate. "I so love to cook for young people," she said. "They eat quickly, and always with a smile."

Apparite nodded in famished agreement. He devoured the

large, juicy *knockwurst* in mere seconds and then moved on to the pile of kraut.

"So much seems to have changed since I was last here," he said. "I saw many Soviet soldiers out today. Have they closed the border?"

"No—or so they *say*. They say that those in the East can travel to work in the West, but many are followed, and some are no longer allowed to pass the border. And then the kidnappings! I know of people—*important* people—who have disappeared in the night, and though no one talks, everyone knows they are taken into the East." She took a moment to put another thick, juicy *wurst* on his plate.

"Has it really gotten that bad?" asked Apparite. "Do the Soviets search cars crossing the border?"

"Almost every one this past week. They have even begun disrupting the *S-bahn* and *U-bahn;* checking everyone's papers. This is a frightened city, *Herr* Müller; almost as bad as during the uprising."

Apparite recognized the risk Christiane was taking. If it was discovered she was meeting a man from the West, even if Apparite's identity as an espionage operative remained secret, then her life might be in danger.

"If I wanted to visit a friend in the Russian sector tonight, should I expect trouble?"

The woman reached down and grabbed his hands, almost as if she was physically trying to stop him from making such a journey. Looking up at her from the dining room table, Apparite could see that her color had paled, so unnerved had she been by his question.

"Please don't go there. Nothing but trouble can come from it; especially at night when they are suspicious of those coming from the West. But if you must, take your papers and do whatever they tell you."

They: he realized that was at least the third time she had used that word to refer to the Soviets. The Communists had apparently so infested Berlin that they were no longer referred to by name, but by that amorphous and yet more sinister term: *they.*

"Has anyone called for me?" asked Apparite. "I'm expecting a friend."

"No." She placed yet another sausage on Apparite's plate. "But I am only here during the day and for meals, so I might have missed it."

Apparite finished the last of the satisfying and filling sausages and took a sip of *schwarzbier.* Satiated, he pushed the thickly green-glazed plate away with nary a scrap of *spaetzle* or *wurst* left on its surface.

"I must be leaving soon." He finished his beer, stood, and walked in the direction of the stairs.

"Oh, *Herr* Müller—wait!" she cried out to him. She crossed the kitchen to where he was standing, and, reaching into the chest pocket of her blue-checked apron, removed a small gold key. "I will be gone when you return, so here is the spare key for you. But please—if you do go into their sector, *please* be careful!"

Apparite looked at her reassuringly and gave her a hug, kissing her warmly on both cheeks—just as she had done to him earlier in the day.

"You sound like my own *Oma,*" Apparite said. "But I never listened to *her* either!" The woman laughed but quickly reassumed her serious demeanor.

"That is a good joke. But I would rather you be *careful* than funny."

At 1800, Apparite boarded the *U-bahn* from *Wittenbergplatz* station. The train car was initially packed with people going home after a long, hard day's labor, but as it journeyed closer to the

Eastern sector the crowd began to thin. By the time it reached *Potsdamerplatz* station there were only four persons on it: an elderly man who had, Apparite guessed, been visiting someone in the West; two strapping young men in work-clothes with grimy faces and black oil-smeared hands; and Apparite.

Apparite assumed a look of boredom, of routine, figuring that the Soviets would only trouble those who looked nervous or out of place, but when the train finally halted with a loud metallic shriek, he saw immediately that he had been wrong. The station was crawling with Soviet soldiers and *Volkspolizei*—men of the East German police—and they were interrogating all who wished to cross the border.

Holding his dull, tired expression was becoming a chore, but Apparite took his place in the queue of those waiting to pass the check-point. He took his papers from his pocket (a West German identity card, a work-permit, and a permit authorizing him to transport goods across the Soviet zone and into the West), and held them out in front of him like the others in line.

Don't do too much, and don't do too little, he told himself; *only do what the others are doing.* Apparite did not remove his passport from his trouser pocket (no one else was showing theirs, so he did not either), but he adjusted his suit-coat so he could easily reach the hidden switch-blade in his belt—just in case.

"Schnell! Schnell!" Hurry! Hurry! yelled an underweight, thin-mustachioed "Vopo" (as the *Volkspolizei* were called, generally in derision). "Your papers," he said to Apparite in a harsh German monotone.

Apparite held them up for the man to view as he had seen the others do before him.

"Hand them to me!"

Apparite gave them to the man, who took them roughly from his hands. The angry East German was just the kind of arrogant martinet that Apparite wished he could take into a back alley and teach a lesson to (like he had done with Kid Leonard back in New York), but he was soon sent on his way. The Vopo riffled through the material Apparite had given him, returned them with a scowl, and waved him through the check-point.

Apparite boarded the train that would take him to his final destination at the *Alexanderplatz*. Stepping out of the unkempt, cluttered station and onto the street, he was quite taken aback. As bad as parts of the East looked to him at a distance earlier in the day, it had not prepared him for what he now saw up close. To him, the Soviet sector looked more like a prison than a living, breathing city.

The streets were poorly lit by under-powered street-lamps, the skeletal remains of ruined buildings were more numerous than those in good repair, and vast blocks of the Eastern sector sat empty, covered either by tall weeds or huge mountains of rubble. The people shuffled listlessly down the empty streets (it seemed to Apparite that there were an unusual number of war veterans—amputees—hobbling on crutches), and although every so often a chorus of shouts would reach his ears, they would just as quickly disappear as if the perpetrators had been silenced by a powerful unseen force. East Berlin seemed to have been transformed into a sort of purgatory, its people biding their time before they would either be given freedom like those in the West, or, more likely, put in virtual imprisonment like those in the communist USSR. Sooner or later, he thought, the balance would be forced to fully tilt one way or the other.

Apparite walked around the edge of the square (known fondly as *"Alex"* to Berliners) in search of the *Café Falke*. When it became apparent that he would never find it by himself in this maze of rubble, half-standing buildings, and poorly lit storefronts, he was forced to ask for directions.

"Excuse me," he said in German to a middle-aged man walking a few steps to his left, "I'm looking for the *Café Falke*—can you direct me to it?"

The man stopped but did not answer.

"I'm looking for the *Café Falke*—can you tell me where it is?"

The man scanned the area around him, and, satisfied he was not being watched or tricked in some manner, finally answered.

"Yes—go to the northern side of the square and walk east. It will be to your left on the *Hirtenstrasse*. It is the only store-front with a lighted street-lamp in front of it." Without waiting for a *"Danke,"* he turned abruptly and walked away at a quick pace.

"See ya 'round, buddy," Apparite said under his breath. Following the man's directions, he walked to the northern edge of the square and turned right onto the *Karl Liebnechtstrasse*. He noted a group of Vopos walking toward him about a hundred yards down the road; focusing his eyes, he counted five of them. He half-jogged to the crossing of the *Hirtenstrasse,* briskly cut across the intersection, and headed toward the only lit street-lamp in view. One of the Vopos stopped and stared at him, calling out to the others to halt. To his displeasure, Apparite realized he had just jay-walked crossing the street. Guessing they might decide to confront him, he accelerated his steps and ducked into the café, releasing a cloud of smoke and condensation from the opened door.

Glancing around, he took a quick inventory of the old café, though it was plain to see that it had seen better times. Although it was as clean as a good scrubbing and sweeping could make it, there were hastily-patched holes in the walls, a ceiling that was missing more tiles than it had in place, and a bar scarred with marks and chips from Soviet bullets and shrapnel from the war.

Most unfortunately, there were no places to hide in the small room if indeed the nosy Vopo decided to follow him inside it. An attempt to disappear into the crowd would likely prove unsuccessful, for one obvious reason: there *was* no crowd. Only about fifteen patrons were in the establishment, and even these were dispersed at a variety of small round tables. Apparite's only hope was to find a spare seat and somehow blend in as best he could. He spied an unusually amiable-appearing middle-aged woman sitting by herself at a nearby table. He abruptly sat down at it, startling her.

"Good evening, *Fräulein,*" he said in German with a roguish grin. "May I sit with you a moment? I'd be delighted to buy you a drink."

"Thank you!" the woman exclaimed. She had been waiting for her sister, but this rather attractive young man made for a very desirable alternative. "I'll take a brandy."

A beat later, a Vopo poked his head in the door. Apparite saw him glance around the room, but the Vopo's eyes were not as sharp as Apparite's: in the smoky half-light, the East German could barely make out the number of occupants in the bar, not to mention the one who might have illegally crossed the street. Shaking his head in frustration, he closed the door and departed.

Apparite heard a woman speaking with a nearby waiter.

"I'm meeting someone here—has anyone been asking for me? My name is Christiane Grünbach."

Apparite's relief at hearing her voice was palpable, although he had to extricate himself from his present predicament before he could seek her out.

"Forgive me," he said to the middle-aged woman, "but my wife has arrived—and if she sees me with you, it'll be the sofa for the rest of the week! Have a brandy on me." He handed the woman a ten-mark note and abruptly fled the table, leaving her with a confused and disappointed look on her face (although the cash, fortunately, would buy her enough drinks to more than adequately cushion the blow).

Apparite saw Christiane sit down at a table near the bar. He walked over and took a seat across from her. "It's so good to see you," he said in German. "I'm so relieved you're all right." She was sharply dressed in a long, blue skirt and loose yellow blouse—she seemed to be the only person wearing color in all of East Berlin—and her face was radiant and beautiful.

"I'm fine. I just arrived an hour ago; I was fortunate to catch a special early train today."

"What did they do to you at the check-point?" Apparite asked. He hoped she hadn't sensed his anxiety in the question.

She laughed.

"Nothing—just a bunch of shouting about rule-breaking and carelessness. When they get like that, it makes me laugh. It's when they're quiet that I fear them."

"Really? You were crying when you left the train."

"Oh, I get that way sometimes. But that didn't last long—I'm not as weak as you think!"

No, you're certainly not. Looking at her proud face, he sensed an inner core of steel so strong that though she might be buffeted or battered on the outside, her foundation would never bend or yield to any force. And he was glad to perceive it: for what he was planning, that inner strength of hers would not only be helpful, it would be essential.

"I never thought you were weak—just that you needed some aid," he said. "I was worried for you."

"I know. My father always worried about me, too." She looked at Apparite very directly with unusual feeling in her round, blue eyes. The intimacy of her expression was strangely uncomfortable to him, like he was being forced to undress in public, but he could not look away or speak, so strong was he held by it.

"It's good to have someone worry about me again," she added. She placed her hand on his, which had been resting on the table. A waiter arrived and broke the rising, amorous tension.

"How may I serve you two tonight?"

He had spoken quite formally and with pride, like Apparite

and Christiane were sitting at a sidewalk café table on the majestic *Unter den Linden* during Berlin's pre-war glory years. His worn, scuffed shoes and ratty, black woolen uniform with torn cuffs told a different tale.

"Christiane?" said Apparite.

"I'd like a *Berliner Weisse: grün,* of course," she said with a laugh. She'd ordered one of Berlin's famous sour wheat beers with green (*grün*) woodruff syrup, but when it became apparent that Apparite had not gotten her jest, she sighed.

"*Berliner Grün,*" she emphasized. "*Grünbach—grün?*"

The waiter was the first to laugh in understanding.

"Oh, the young lady's name is *Grünbach!* And I suppose *your* name," he said to Apparite, "is *Rotmann,*" making a play on the German word for "red."

Christiane laughed, as did Apparite, although he had no idea what the hell he was laughing *at.* He was quite fluent in German, of course, but no one at the CI language school had had the foresight to instruct him on puns involving *Berliner Weisse* beer and the potential surnames of his dates.

"My name is Müller," Apparite said, affecting a laugh, "but I'll have the same as her!"

"Very good—two *Berliner Grün!*" The waiter bowed his head smartly and hurried to the bar to fill their order.

"When I was a child," said Christiane, "my father used to tell me that *Berliner Grün* was brewed specially for us—and I *believed* him! I remember when he first let me taste it. Oh, it was like lemon-flavored cough medicine—it was *horrible!* But now, it's my favorite. It reminds me of him."

"This might sound foolish," Apparite said, "but my father used to take me hunting, and even now, if I am served venison, I pretend we hunted it together and are hosting a big party to celebrate." It might have been made-up, but somehow saying it aloud (even in German) made it seem almost real to him.

Christiane's eyes began to moisten. "Now that my father is gone, I have no one anymore. I hate living in the East, but what can I do?"

"There are many in your position—look around you," Apparite said, motioning at the other patrons of the café. "Until the Soviets are gone, everyone here is trapped in some way." He was planting a seed in her mind for the future—and with another night or two like this, he hoped, it just might begin to germinate.

"Yes—I've thought of leaving the East. But won't they follow—"

"*Berliner Grün!*" cried the waiter. He placed two large glass goblets on the table; the liquid inside them was a bright, almost phosphorescent green. It was certainly the oddest-looking beer Apparite had ever been served.

"*Prost!*" said Christiane heartily. She raised her glass. "To our fathers."

"And better days ahead," added Apparite.

He took a sip of the headless beer, but was unprepared for the explosion of tartness that smacked him flush in the mouth: the comparison to lemon-flavored cough medicine did not give the sourness of this brew its due. He had to take a second bracing sip, and then another, before he began to note the refreshing nature of the drink. It was sour, yes, but there were also pleasing hints of citrus and even sweet-smelling flowers to it.

He thought it wise to feign a lifetime of *Berliner Weisse* appreciation to lend authenticity to his German alias. "This is *very* good," he said. "Much better than what they make in the West."

They drank the rest of their beers in silence, during which Apparite's brown eyes and Christiane's deep blues did not break contact. They were locked together in their mutual attraction and desire for each other; in what they had in common—the deaths of their fathers and a pressing need for companionship—

but also in what they had not, for "Hans Müller" lived in the Free West of this city, and Christiane Grünbach in the increasingly oppressed East. Whatever the reasons or motivations either of them had for wanting to change that fact, they both began to formulate their own plans to do so. One of them, however, would not be what they seemed to the other.

TEN:
Meine Kleine Schneeflocke

After another couple of drinks, including a round of *Berliner Rot* (one of the sour wheat beers with red raspberry syrup), Christiane and Apparite left the café. As they walked down the street, her hand slipped into his as naturally as if he had been born holding it. After fifteen minutes of walking in silent contentment, they reached her apartment near the *Immanuelkirche*.

"Let me go inside and make certain no one will see us," said Christiane. "If anyone knows I am bringing a man back to my room, it will start a rumor."

Apparite nodded in agreement. He took a few deep breaths to relax and in a few seconds she reappeared.

"Come with me."

She placed her hand again in his, and Apparite could feel it trembling. Her apartment building was poorly illuminated inside, but even in the dim light he noted evidence of its dilapidation. The stair-rail was incomplete, the wall-plaster had many holes, and all around him was the dank, musty smell of mold. She told him her room was just up on the second floor a short distance away, but as they left the stairwell Apparite found he could not wait a moment longer. He took her in his arms and embraced her.

She seemed to melt as they touched, conforming to his body as if she had been made liquid and poured onto him. Their arms enveloped each other and then their lips met, and Apparite wondered in his pleasure if there could be anything as satisfying or unique as a kiss: the feel of her warm, yielding flesh, followed by wetness after the opening of their mouths and the playing and dancing of the tips of their tongues. There was nothing else like it in the world.

It seemed so long ago since he had last felt that sensation; in fact, it had been way back in the autumn of 1953, when he was with Margaret, his steady while at the FBI. The Terps were playing Alabama in the last game of the football season, and when the clock ran out to give Maryland a win to secure the National Championship, the two of them had embraced in celebration. But the next week they had fought, and the week after, she had tearfully told him it was over, and for more than two years he had not experienced the wonder of a kiss; in some ways, he thought, the most personal of contacts between a man and a woman.

In its subtle intimacy, kissing brought forth more visceral, *human* feelings than did heavy petting or probably even sex—Apparite had heard it said that whores would let you screw them for money but would not let you kiss them for anything. But Christiane was a master of this gentle art, and as their embrace deepened and their hands began to explore the contours of the other's body, Apparite knew this was but a hint of what was to come.

They finally separated and she led him down another corridor and into her apartment. She did not bother to turn on the light, and after closing the door behind her, led Apparite to her bed in the shadows of the semi-darkness, drawing him into the soft down of her pillows and blankets. They kissed again and again, but Apparite felt liquid on his cheeks, and then some hesitancy in the breath from Christiane's mouth, and he pulled away from her. She was crying.

"What's the matter?" he asked. He tenderly ran his forefinger up and down the side of her face.

"It has been so long since I have been with a man. I was once married, long ago; I was very young and so was he, but we loved each other. He died in the fall of the city—he was only eighteen."

"I'm sorry," said Apparite. He grasped her in his arms. "I'm so sorry."

He held her as she sobbed, and when he released her saw that a lock of her soft, blonde hair had fallen over her left eye, like a Germanic version of Veronica Lake, and he swept it back again, uncovering her tear-stained face; and as she laughed in embarrassment she brought him down onto her, and they kissed and kissed and reveled in the touch of each other's arms and legs and back and chest in their caresses; and then they removed each other's clothing, and then they made love long into the ever-darkening quiet East Berlin night, and the joy each took in the presence of the other was like the relief of a drowning man whose gasps suddenly draw in air when his head is finally thrust above the waves.

When the sun poked through the sheets covering her windows (neither she, nor most East Berliners could afford purpose-made drapes) Apparite stirred and awoke, though he did not feel well-rested. His disturbing dreams had returned in all of their grotesque glory, and in the last of them he had been subjected to the sight of Viktor once again drawing his blade across the throat of young Edward Humphreys. He wiped the sweat from his brow and glanced at his wrist-watch. It was already nine in the morning; time to go back to the safe-house and see if there was any word from D. He rose from the warm comfort of Christiane's bed and began to dress.

He did so with unusual stealth, but nevertheless that natural instinct of women to know when a man was leaving them in the morning kicked in, and Christiane's eyes opened. She quickly searched him out.

"Where are you going? Stay here with me, Hans," she said with an enticing, promising purr. "Come back to bed." Her hair was mussed and her make-up had smeared under her eyes, but she looked as lovely as ever and her offer was tempting. Apparite sat back down on the bed; he kissed her and stroked her hair.

"I wish I could, but I need to go home—I'm expecting someone this morning. Why don't we meet again tonight?"

She smiled, and with a smooth wave of her hand pulled behind her head the long curls of blonde hair that had begun to cover her face once again. It had been a simple, unconscious gesture, but was unbearably sexy to behold.

"Let's meet at the café again—alright?" she said.

Apparite leaned over the bed and kissed her deeply, running those soft, blonde curls through his fingers.

"How about ten in the evening this time?" he said when their kiss had ended.

She nodded in the affirmative. "I'm going to miss you, you know."

"So will I," said Apparite, taking her hand. "So will I."

In the early morning rush of commuters, Apparite's return journey was routine. There were too many workers passing into the West to do detailed checks on all of them, so he got back to the *Wittenbergstrasse* before 0930. After a quick trip around the block to insure he hadn't been followed, he went to number forty-eight and removed his safe-house key from a hidden compartment in one of his shoes. He opened the door and quickly stepped inside.

"For Christ's sake, Apparite, where the *bloody hell* have you been?"

Sitting in a chair in the front hall was D. He had always struck

Apparite as the personification of urbanity and intelligence, reminding him of an erudite English professor he once had at the University of Maryland, but the liaison's face was now locked into an unfamiliar scowl, and his English-accented voice had been clipped and harsh. The book sitting in his lap and the turned-out newspapers next to his chair told Apparite that he had been waiting for some time. Looking more closely, Apparite smiled when he noted the title of the book D had been reading: it was the lurid best-seller, *Peyton Place.*

"And wipe that grin off your face," D continued. "I nearly shot you when you burst through that door." He took his hand out from under the book; it held a Beretta semi-automatic pistol.

"I'm sorry. I spent the night in East Berlin. How could I know you wanted me to stay here?"

"Didn't the housekeeper tell you not to go into the East?"

"Yes," answered Apparite rather sheepishly. He felt like a child who'd been caught stealing a sucker from the Five and Dime. "Where did she go?"

"Her husband is ill so I sent her away. You're stuck with me now, whether you like it or not."

Apparite shrugged. Though D's comments initially worried him, he now recognized them as but a harmless manifestation of the liaison's anxiety.

"It's good to know that no matter what happens, we'll always have each other," Apparite jested.

D stood and walked to Apparite. He put his arm around him and led him into the kitchen. "You know," he said in his soft, cultured accent, "I nearly had to call your Shadow."

So it *had* been serious, Apparite realized; no wonder D had been upset at his absence. For Apparite knew that a Shadow-agent was only called to action in the event of an emergency, such as the suspected disappearance of a Superagent. The Shadow's duty would be to find the missing man but *not* necessarily to bring him to safety: in the event the Superagent had been captured or the program significantly exposed, the Shadow's duty would be to *kill* him.

"How much longer did I have?" asked Apparite.

"I would have contacted him tonight if we had not heard from you. I know you've been operating under unusual circumstances, but you'd still better have a good explanation."

Apparite told D everything that had happened since he'd landed in London: of Hoevenaers' near-assassination; of the killing of the SMERSH agent and Heydrich in Rhinbourg; and of his chance meeting with Christiane on the train. At the conclusion of the tale, D cleared his throat and abruptly sat down at the kitchen table. Something about Apparite's relationship with the lovely Christiane Grünbach was bothering him.

"How do you know she isn't working for *them?*" he said. He took a pipe from his jacket and lit it, a nervous habit that sometimes spoke more than words. "Isn't it a little convenient to have met her, a beautiful woman who just happens to work at Karlshorst, and struck up so close a relationship in a matter of hours?" He took a quick puff on the pipe to get it going.

Apparite became defensive. "She's on the level, D. Believe me; I can tell when I'm being taken."

"*Can* you? How do you know it's not a honey-trap? How do you know she's not calling her superiors at Karlshorst right this minute and telling them about the nice West Berliner that wants to help her? The nice West Berliner that has *connections?*"

"Don't be ridiculous," said Apparite, his voice rising. "But here's the deal—if she *is* a 'swallow' and the mission blows up in my face, you can kill me."

D laughed at the Superagent's naïveté.

"Apparite, if the mission blows up in your face, we might have to kill you *anyway!*" He stopped speaking and sat quietly for a moment in thought, smoking his pipe.

"Listen," he then went on, "don't reveal too much until I have a chance to get her vetted. The last thing we need is for you to be caught in a Soviet scheme. But if she *is* telling the truth," he said softly, though with increasing emphasis, "do you understand what this means? If we can get her to work on our side, just think of the information she could give us! And with the discovery of 'Operation Gold' we need as much information as we can get."

" 'Operation Gold'?" said Apparite. "Is that the spy tunnel? I heard about it from Christiane, of all people."

"Oh—did it hurt your bloody great ego to be told about it by your *'kleine Schneeflocke,'* Apparite?" D said in a kidding tone. "Now that you mention it, I can't do the story justice—maybe you should get the rest from her."

Apparite's face showed his irritation and impatience. "That's real funny stuff, D. Did you do burlesque before you took this job? Just tell me what happened."

"All right, suit yourself. Two years ago, MI6 and CI began a tunnel into the Soviet sector, between Rudow and Alt-Glienick. They secretly tapped into their phone lines—not an easy thing to do without getting caught. The operation was known as 'Stopwatch-Gold': 'Stopwatch' for the British portion of the operation, and 'Gold' for ours. For nearly a year, we intercepted thousands and thousands of Soviet communications. Some were helpful and some were not, but it was brilliant all the same—an amazing feat to have done it.

"Then last week the Soviets found it and dug it up, and the next thing you know it's become Piccadilly Circus! Lord, but it's a laugh. They called in cameras to film the whole thing, telling everyone what arse-holes the Americans are to do this, but the best part is that they're giving tours of the damned place. *Tours!* You can even buy a beer and sausage to take into the tunnel in case you get peckish!

"And everyone is acting like it's a bloody brilliant intelligence coup: the U.S. Government is telling everyone how clever they were to have done it, and the Soviets are playing the innocent victim to gain sympathy. Only the Brits have the brains enough to lay low, and that's just because—and you'll *love* this part— because First Secretary Khrushchev was *in England* when it was discovered! Can you imagine the conversation at dinner *that* night?" He paused and affected a mock-Russian accent. "Would you mind passing the salt, Prime Minister—and what's this I hear about you building a f-----g spy tunnel into our sector?"

Apparite laughed: as serious as the situation was in Berlin, it was good to hear that it could sometimes be exceeded by its absurdity.

"But the Russians aren't daft," D continued. "They're blaming the CIA in the press but not mentioning the British contribution at all. You see, they're trying to drive a wedge between the Western allies. Given time it might work, but what they don't know is that in a few months everyone will be talking about Hungary and this tunnel business will be forgotten." He lowered his voice to lend it a serious tone. "There's going to be a widespread revolt in the autumn. Agent B has been working on the specifics; he's been in Budapest since last year. And everything was going to plan until an old chum of yours showed up."

"Viktor."

"Yes. Heydrich was the western arm of Viktor's operation— which has now been severed, thanks to you—but his eastern arm is in Hungary, and it is strong. His men infiltrated all of our resistance groups and he personally killed three top leaders. We're still going to proceed as best we can—Agent B did good work in holding things together before he finally had to escape the country—but if it's a cock-up we'll have Viktor to blame.

"He's a bloody maniac, Apparite. He might be impulsive and

unpredictable, but he's devastatingly effective. You're one of the few who's seen him in action and survived. Even though he'd been injured in the Reading Room, he knew exactly how to get away; he had you pegged in a second. The bastard cut just enough of that boy's throat to make you think he had a chance if you helped him—and somehow he knew you'd do it, too."

"I need to kill him, D. For that kid, for Hitch—and for J."

"It looks like you'll have your chance; intelligence suggests he's coming here. And I've got a plan to get him into the open."

D stood to make a pot of tea.

"Here's the game, Apparite. The Soviets have been posing as West German agents, intercepting and killing East German defectors before they resettle in the West. We'll set you up as an East Berliner about to defect, and with the background we'll give you, they'll almost certainly try and kill you before you do."

"And instead of them killing me, I'm supposed to kill *them*—correct?"

D ignited a stove burner and placed a pot of water on it.

"Of course—did you think we wanted you to teach them how to make *spaetzle?* Of course you're to kill them, and if Viktor is anywhere near Berlin, I expect he'll be involved—and Bob's your uncle, you'll have your revenge. But even if he isn't, we need to disrupt this scheme before our supply of defectors completely dries up.

"For this mission, your name will be Horst Köller; you are a telecommunications expert—just the kind of bloke the Soviets would *not* want to go to the West. I'm told by our sources that your 'defection' will be arranged for May Day. The timing is good. It's a Communist holiday—and even they don't like to work on a holiday. The Soviets will have extra personnel in town for their parades, but most of them will be busy doing other things. Central Intelligence has been kind enough to arrange the meeting through an East German contact; they tell me he can be trusted, so at least you shouldn't have to worry about that. But you must be cautious: he must only think that you are an agent of CI, and nothing more. Do not break your cover! I need not remind you that no one can learn of the existence of our particular agency. Here are your basic documents." He handed Apparite an envelope filled with identity cards and papers.

"We'll make up others with you in disguise before the event," he continued. "As for your new girlfriend, keep seeing her—discreetly, please—and let me know when you think she might be willing to help us. But be damned careful." He took the now-boiling water off the stove. "Berlin is a veritable swamp of spies; you must assume that everyone you meet could be one. And don't get too emotionally involved with the girl. If we discover she's not with us, you know what you'd have to do."

"I know," Apparite answered. He immediately understood what had gone unspoken: he'd have to kill her. "I always knew."

"I never doubted you did."

Apparite glanced at his new identity card. "When will I meet my East German contact?" D poured steaming water into the tea-pot and covered the lid.

"*Heute, Herr* Köller," he said. *Today, Mr. Köller.* "Say, old boy, how'd you like a first-hand look at that spy tunnel?"

ELEVEN:
THE SWAMP OF SPIES

Apparite crossed into the Eastern sector without incident in the early afternoon. In the interest of international and public relations the Soviets had relaxed the stringency of their checkpoints a bit, which pleased Apparite immensely: every time a Vopo or Soviet checked his papers he had to consciously remind himself not to visibly hold his breath in anticipation. For ease of travel, D had provided him with a typical and authentically battered East Berlin automobile, a 1953 Opel Rekord. It seemed adequate as a means of moving him from place to place, as long as he did not mind the unsightliness of the dented fenders or doors, or the side-view mirror hanging like an eyeball dislodged from its socket, or the numerous areas of chipped and peeling black paint along its sides.

His only worry as he drove through East Berlin was that he might run into Christiane—she could hardly understand how his name had suddenly become "Horst Köller"—but as the Eastern sector of the city had over one million inhabitants, he knew the odds of seeing her were slim. Still, "slim" wasn't "none," and all he could do was pray that their paths would not cross.

He drove south along the *Schönefelder Chausee* as D had directed, and was beginning to wonder when he was going to find the tunnel site when his question was answered. Rounding a gentle curve, he saw dozens of cars haphazardly parked to one side of the road. A crowd of at least one hundred people was gathered around a nearby temporary canvas tent.

Parking his Opel alongside the other automobiles, Apparite walked to a small, white-painted wooden sausage and beer stand that had been erected near the tunnel entrance. He stood in line with a dozen other hungry tunnel-gawkers, and after five minutes had reached the front of it. But unlike the others, Apparite's reason for being in this queue included more than satiating himself with an appetizingly plump *wurst* or stein of beer. Instead, it had been to say these words (in his most authentic German, naturally) to the man behind the counter:

"I find the sausages from Munich to be particularly filling."

The man looked at Apparite and took a puff from an American cigarette. He focused his eyes in concentration, although the grin on his face remained broad and friendly. He was unusually heavy-set for an East Berliner, nearly as plump as the *wurst* he peddled, but his smile was a ready one and he had a full, rosy complexion. To Apparite, he looked like a player in an "oompah" band; so much so, that Apparite half-expected him to produce a sousaphone from behind the counter and start playing a tune from a beer hall.

"I prefer the ones from Bamberg," the man finally said. "They are not as salty."

"Nor as sweet," said Apparite as he had been instructed.

"Try these." The man gave Apparite a plate of thickly sliced sausages on black bread. He daubed a little curry sauce on top. "They're a Berlin specialty. I think you'll find them to your liking."

Apparite took the food in hand and passed the man some East German marks. Examining his plate, he spied a small sliver of paper peeking out from underneath the bread. He surreptitiously slipped it into his pocket.

"Danke," he said to the man. *"Auf Wiedersehen."*

Apparite walked away in a casual manner, chewing on the

hot, tasty sausage slices along with a piece of the pungent black bread. He joined the queue of those waiting to see the tunnel. Given the usually unspoken, hidden world of international espionage, this was indeed quite a spectacle; D's comparing of it to Piccadilly Circus was no exaggeration. In addition to a score of journalists excitedly scribbling notes onto small pads of paper, newspaper photographers clicked away with their Leicas while numerous newsreel cameras whirred noisily to record the scene. Behind all of the above, as if to confirm the officially sanctioned nature of the chaos, Soviet diplomats spoke impassionedly to the crowd through microphones attached to loudspeakers.

Apparite reached the head of this line, having already eaten the sausages and bread in his hunger. He took out the ticket he had been given by D to gain entrance to the tunnel, and handed it to the attendant. Since the ticket stated that Apparite was a journalist, he took a small note-pad and pencil from his coat. He began writing madly as the real newspapermen were doing.

The attendant inspected the ticket. *"Danke,"* he said robotically. He pointed to a wooden ladder that led into the dimly lit tunnel, and motioned for Apparite to climb down.

Apparite descended into the tunnel, pen and note-pad in hand. The entrance hole was roughly made (the men who had unearthed the tunnel having done sloppy work in their haste) but once he had gained access to the tunnel itself, he was surprised at how clean and tidy it was. Clearly, not just anyone had built it; this was a professional piece of work.

He took a few more steps and saw the reason for the care the tunnel's builders had taken: banks and banks of sophisticated pre-amplifiers were crammed into the small space; countless wires sprung from each one like long tresses of black, rubbery hair. Looking back toward the entrance hole, Apparite could see the tap-wires that led to the Soviet phone lines, as well as the complicated apparatus that had sealed the tap-chamber from the rest of the tunnel. It was obvious that no expense had been spared. Whoever had built it knew precisely what they were doing.

"Please come with me," a Vopo said. Apparite and four other men followed him into the tunnel. As the man led them along, he subjected them to a combination East German–Soviet harangue on the highly illegal and immoral nature of the Americans' dastardly incursion into the Soviet sector. How could the world trust anything the Americans now said? Why should an honorable man like Khrushchev sign any agreement with that gangster Eisenhower—a man with no respect for the sovereignty of those in the East?

After a time, Apparite tuned-out the propaganda and focused on the tunnel itself. Summing up all he saw around him, only one word seemed to do it justice: *ingenious.* It had been constructed by connecting thousands of circular three-inch wide rings in a row, each taller than a man, until almost a quarter-mile of ground had been traversed from the tunnel's origin at a dummy radar station in the American sector at Rudow. This awesome feat of engineering had been done in complete secrecy beneath one of the busiest roads in this part of Berlin, yet no one driving along the *Schönefelder Chausee* would ever have suspected the presence of the moles burrowing into the Soviet sector mere feet beneath them.

But the best was yet to come. Some distance down the tunnel Apparite saw a makeshift sand-bag and barbed-wire barricade, which the Americans had erected in the event the tunnel was discovered. A sign facing the East had been hung over the obstacle, and in typical smart-aleck fashion, these words had been written upon it in German and Russian: *"You are now entering the American Sector."*

Apparite suppressed a laugh. He had heard that the West

Berlin CIA chief was a bit of a "cowboy," carrying ivory-handled pistols at all times and being on occasion a true pain in the ass, but by God he had to give Bill Harvey credit: the guy had a sense of humor. Closing his eyes, Apparite could almost make out the echo of the curses and insults that must have filled "Harvey's Hole" (as it was called by CI) when the Soviets had first seen the barricade and read that facetious sign. He followed the rest of the tour group back out of the tunnel, wishing more than anything he'd had the foresight to bring a camera.

Leaving the tunnel site, he drove to his new safe-house in East Berlin off of the *Leipzigerstrasse,* a short drive west of the *Potsdamerplatz.* If "ingenious" had been the appropriate word to sum-up Apparite's impression of the spy tunnel, then "rat-hole" was the only one to suit this location. As a safe-house, it served its purpose as safe, perhaps, but it barely qualified as a house: it was a one-room, damp, dirty, malodorous basement apartment with a World War Two–era bed and a stained, who-knows-what-era mattress. The room was without windows, chairs, or a table, and for bathroom facilities a bare toilet and bathtub had been crammed into a corner. To provide illumination, there was a tarnished brass floor lamp sitting next to the bed plus one unadorned yellowish light bulb in the middle of the cracked ceiling.

If this was how most *"Ossis"* lived, then Apparite was shocked that any remained in the East at all: the conditions were almost sub-human; a degradation. But he knew that the more realistic his accommodations, the less likely he would be exposed as an agent of the West. Without a second thought he arranged the belongings he had brought with him—an assortment of weapons and forged documents, plus two changes of clothes—and, after turning on the floor lamp, laid down on the bed.

He removed the note he had been slipped by the East German at the sausage stand: *"1900, Friedelstrasse 24."* Memorizing the address, he slipped the note into his mouth and swallowed it. The day had already been a busy one but it was about to get busier. He had to meet the East German at 1900 as Horst Köller and Christiane at 2200 as Hans Müller. The situation was getting complicated: as if being John Apparite wasn't difficult enough, he would now have to play the parts of distinct East *and* West Berliners as well.

He arrived on the *Friedelstrasse* at 1858 and searched for the address in question, number twenty-four, but the task proved to be difficult. This section of town had suffered mightily in the war, and most of the buildings were missing their address numbers or were obviously uninhabited. But after a careful search of every door, cellar entrance, and alley, he finally found what he sought: down a short flight of basement stairs he saw a silver "24" above the steel door of an apparently small apartment, not unlike the one he had been given on the *Leipzigerstrasse*. He put his ear to it and heard the muffled noise of music mixing with loud voices. Inhaling in anticipation, he opened the door and slipped inside.

But this was no basement apartment. What Apparite found was an unexpectedly large beer-hall jammed with people; smoke hung from the ceiling like a curtain of gray, and the sound of a juke-box playing brassy German swing tunes rent the air. The low, wood-beamed ceiling added to the claustrophobic feel of the room, every square foot of which seemed to be packed with heavy, dark-stained (and occupied) wooden tables. Groups of people stood in the small spaces between them, holding large steins of beer.

The sound in the room was indescribable in its complexity. Over the steady layer of German swing tunes were intermingled shouts in German, Russian, English, and French; the booming laughter of very fat men and the bird-like titters of small, wiry women; and every so often one also heard the crash of a stein being broken, or of a plate being dropped, or of someone who had imbibed too much falling with a thud and a cry onto the dirty concrete floor.

A man spoke directly into Apparite's right ear. "Come with me, my friend!" he said in German. Turning, Apparite saw the jolly expression of the heavy-set sausage vendor. The German led Apparite to a vacant table (the man had enough pull with the owner to warrant one all to himself), and placed a large overflowing stein of beer in front of the young agent.

"Welcome!" the East German said gregariously. "I am Fritz Lohmann, *Herr* Köller. Would you like a smoke?"

"Thank you, no," responded Apparite in German. "But I've brought some American cigarettes for you, if you would like them."

Lohmann laughed loudly. "No, thank you—I do not want for anything! Did you enjoy the tunnel?"

"Yes—it was fantastic; unbelievable."

"And the sausages? They were good?"

"Yes—you make good sausages." Apparite was enjoying the playful, informal nature of their conversation.

Lohmann took a swig of beer and laughed.

"*Good!* Never trust a man who makes bad sausages—that is what I believe! I am told you are ready for the meeting at any time. Is that correct?"

Although Lohmann was speaking directly into his face from across the table, Apparite found he had to concentrate and read the man's lips in order to fully discern what was being said over the din.

"Yes," Apparite answered. "How many will there be?" He took a sizeable sip of beer. It went down easily given the stifling heat of the crowded beer-hall.

"Probably three; that is their usual. I have given your name to one of my contacts at Karlshorst. He will pass it along to the Soviets and let me know the final time of the meeting. I'm still assuming it will be May Day."

"Do they suspect anything?"

"No," replied Lohmann. "I gave them documents that should make them *very* interested in stopping you from going to the West. They have no suspicions."

"Have you heard anything of Viktor?"

Lohmann put down his beer to speak, but did not answer. The sound of the SMERSH agent's name seemed to have robbed him of speech.

Apparite thought that Lohmann might not have heard him clearly. "I said, do you know anything about Viktor?"

"Rumor says he is coming." Lohmann was no longer smiling. "Everyone expects trouble. Whenever Viktor is involved there is much fighting, killing, kidnapping. Even at Karlshorst they fear his name."

"Will he be at the meeting?" asked Apparite.

"I believe so. He would not want to miss the torturing of a defector, you know."

Apparite finished his beer and exhaled: Viktor was coming. That's all he needed to know; that's all he wanted to hear. Lohmann took another sip of beer and resumed speaking.

"Meet me here again tomorrow night at twenty hundred; I should have the final details of the meeting by then. But for now, how would you like to meet your competition?" His smile returned and he drained his liter of pils with a frothy flourish.

"What do you mean?" Apparite responded. The beer had begun to hit him and his speech was slowing. The waitress stopped to place another round of beers onto the table. Apparite paid her in the preferred currency of American black-market dollars.

"Konnie!" Lohmann cried in the direction of a man sitting at a nearby table. "Konnie—come here!"

The man in question, whose back was to Apparite a few feet away, turned his head at the sound of his name. Recognizing Lohmann, he waved and rose from his seat.

"Who's he?" asked Apparite.

"KGB—you'll like him!"

Apparite's face froze: was Lohmann *nuts?* Here he was, an apparent CIA agent under deep cover on a mission to kill as many KGB and SMERSH agents as possible, and now Lohmann was calling one of them over to their table?

"I've got to get out of here," Apparite said. He rose from his seat.

Lohmann made a dismissive gesture with his hand.

"Don't worry, *Herr* Köller—he's not Karlshorst KGB. I won't break your cover. You might even learn something!"

Apparite sat back down. As much as he knew he should leave, he did not wish to create a scene or alienate Lohmann at such an early stage of his mission. And besides, perhaps he *could* get some information from the Russian that might prove helpful. He took a few more sips of beer to steady his nerves and told himself not to worry. He'd just have to be careful; *very* careful.

The KGB man reached their table and sat down next to Apparite. He immediately placed his arm around him.

"What will you have, friend?" he said to Apparite in perfect German. "Try the vodka, *please*—not more of this horrible horse-urine you people make!" He laughed heartily and took a gold cigarette lighter from his pocket.

"My mother gave it to me before she died," he continued. He held up the lighter for his companions to see. "If only she had given me the cigarettes as well!"

Apparite took a pack of Lucky Strikes from his suit-coat pocket.

"Horst Köller," he said, introducing himself to the Russian.

"I bought these on the black market from an American GI."

The Russian's face broke into a grin.

"Ah, Lohmann, your friends get better every day! Thank you, *Herr* Köller." The Russian took a cigarette from the pack and deftly lit it. Placing it in his mouth, he took a few long, savored pulls on it.

"I am known as Konstantin Zhdanovich," he said to Apparite, "but you may call me 'Konnie.' I may be KGB, but I am not, as the Americans say, S-O-B." He laughed and warmly shook Apparite's hand.

This outgoing character was *not* what Apparite had expected from a KGB agent. The man's personality was absolutely infectious; one of those guys who makes everyone smile as soon as he enters a room. In some ways, he reminded Apparite quite a lot of J. This Russian might be an enemy, but he was the damned friendliest enemy he had ever met. Apparite finished his beer and the attentive Lohmann ordered two more.

"KGB?" said Apparite. "This business about the spy tunnel must be keeping you hopping."

"Oh that—yes, we are supposed to be angry; *very* angry about it!" Zhdanovich said with mock fury. "It is an outrage!" he yelled theatrically. He smashed his fist into the table, nearly knocking over the steins of beer in front of him. "It has me so upset that I can only drink one bottle of vodka each day and satisfy two women each night! Oh, to feel such pain for the fortunes of Mother Russia, eh, *Herr* Köller?"

He laughed and produced a flask of vodka from within his coat. He winked at his companions and poured a good-sized measure into a small tin cup he had been concealing in his hand.

"We drink, *Herr* Köller!" Zhdanovich said. He passed the cup to Apparite. "We will drink to—"

"To women, vodka, spy tunnels—and Mother Russia!" interrupted Lohmann.

The three men laughed in unison. Apparite tossed the measure of vodka into the back of his mouth with gusto. Lohmann downed the rest of his beer while Zhdanovich took a large sip directly from his flask. The vodka ran down the back of Apparite's throat like liquid heat, settling rather uncomfortably into the bottom of his stomach. If he was to survive the night, he thought he had better stick to beer from now on, if not make a quick escape from his overly social and inebriated companions.

"Spies," said the Russian. "They are *everywhere*—I can show you half-a-dozen in this room alone!" He drunkenly turned and began pointing with a wobbling forefinger. "There, leaning against the wall: he is an *Ossis* working for the Gehlen organization—oh, wait, it's now called 'B-N-D.' It's *so* hard to keep up with such things! Over by the toilet, talking to that blonde girl he should *not* be talking to—he is a Vopo captain, and he drinks much, too much, too much." He winked at Apparite and shook his head in disapproval. "Oh—and his wife is so ugly you could *die*. And over by the waitress bringing another liter of horse-urine—he is American CIA, and he is a terrible driver. *Terrible!* He has wrecked three Volkswagens this year. And over there by the door is a French agent. He likes boys. We have an *extra-large* dossier on him!"

Zhdanovich concluded his remarkable demonstration with another large drink of vodka, though his companions' laughter continued long after it had reached the drunken Russian's stomach. Apparite, too, was feeling the effects of alcohol, for talking had become rather laborious. Not only had he begun to slur his words, but he had to consciously remind himself *not* to slip into English.

"Won't you get in trouble telling us this?" Apparite said slowly and carefully in German.

Zhdanovich shook his head *no*.

"It's not news—I know who *they* are and they know who *I* am. Do you know what we call this place? *Der Geisterkeller.*" *The Ghost-cellar.*

The Russian paused to take another sip from his flask.

"*That* should tell you something," he continued. "The only trouble comes when we fight over the girls or the cigarettes or the liquor!" He laughed again.

"I should be going," said Apparite. "I have to meet a woman tonight."

Lohmann and Zhdanovich both clapped their hands in drunken approval.

"Good for you—do you have enough money to pay her, or would you like a loan?" said Lohmann. He laughed, spilling beer freely from his stein.

"From my perspective, she should be paying *me!*" Apparite said, bringing more laughter and applause from his table-mates.

"*Das Vadanya!*" Apparite said to the Russian. He rose to leave. "*Auf Wiedersehen!*" he said to Lohmann, bowing low.

Apparite walked unsteadily out of the beer-hall and began a hasty search for the nearest café serving strong coffee. He had less than two hours to sober-up, make himself presentable for Christiane, and once again become Hans Müller. He hoped he was up to the task.

Twelve:
A Dangerous Offer

After many cups of thick, black coffee and a long walk around the ruins of East Berlin, Apparite felt nearly himself again when he arrived at the *Café Falke*. Unlike the evening before, however, the café was crowded and noisy and a quick search of it proved unsuccessful in finding Christiane. Apparite was becoming quite worried at her absence until he felt a tug at his sleeve and saw her face looking up at him.

"Let's get out of here," she said. "It's much too noisy for me tonight."

Apparite put his arm around her but felt fear, rather than warmth, coming from her this evening. *Something has happened. Something is wrong.*

They walked a few more blocks in silence when, turning a corner, a cemetery appeared on their right. "Follow me," she said. She pulled him toward it.

They passed through its gates, and she took him behind a tall fence to shield the two of them from sight. Apparite had never much liked cemeteries, especially at night (he had once been dared in college to kiss Baltimore's "Black Aggie" memorial at midnight, and had almost been unable to do it), but this night he'd hardly noticed where she was leading him, so desperate was he to be with her.

She grasped his collar and pulled his face into hers, kissing it with a passion usually reserved for private love-making. When their kiss ended she embraced him, holding him against her.

She whispered into his ear.

"I want to go to the West."

She released her embrace and looked into Apparite's eyes with unusual intensity.

"I want to go to the West," she repeated.

"Why?" answered Apparite. "What's happened?"

She began to cry, softly at first, but when her sobs increased in volume she grabbed Apparite again and held him tight in her arms.

"They took one of us away today," she said. "A girl I knew—we used to eat our lunches together. Her boyfriend defected to the West without her. I think they are going to kill her—or send her to prison."

"Don't worry—I won't let that happen to you," Apparite said. "But are you sure you want to leave? It might be dangerous."

"I can't live here anymore." She broke their embrace to wipe the tears from her eyes. "And nothing is keeping me here: my father is dead; my friends are disappearing. I can't take it any longer!"

"Aren't you afraid they will follow you?"

"Yes—I am." Her voice lowered in worry. "I think they might kill me if they knew I would not return. But it's the only way for me to be free—and for us to be together."

Apparite assumed his role as a Superagent. "I have friends that might be able to help you. But they will need something first to prove your story. Something the Soviets would not wish to leave Karlshorst."

Christiane thought for a moment and spoke.

"I know. I have access to a confidential telephone directory; I'll bring you a page of it. I can't read any of the names because they're in Cyrillic, but I know it's important—they lock it up every night."

Apparite's emotions pushed the Superagent in him aside.

"Please be careful, Christiane—you cannot let them find out. Take a page from the middle of the directory. One not likely to be used or missed." He could feel her trembling as she leaned up against him.

She turned her face upward again and kissed him. She led him by the hand into a thicket of shrubs and greenery.

"Make love to me, Hans." She placed her hands on his face and kissed him deeply, her touch radiating warmth and affection even as her face showed a combination of terror and strength. She slowly lay down onto the soft ground, drawing him onto her, utterly unknowing of the dagger she had just thrust into her lover's heart.

She had called him *"Hans,"* and as they moved in the synchrony of their sensuous embrace, Apparite could not look into her eyes for the shame he felt in deceiving her.

Apparite opened the door to the West Berlin safe-house on the *Wittenbergstrasse* the next morning.

"Do you know what you're doing with this girl?" said an intimidating, unseen voice. Apparite nearly jumped at the sound. Only one man had a voice like that, and it wasn't D. It was the Director.

Apparite stepped into the house. "What are you doing here?" he asked reflexively.

The Director stood in the front hall, arms crossed. His posture indicated disapproval, although—and it was small consolation to Apparite—he at least was not pointing a loaded pistol at him this time.

"Do you know what you're doing with this girl?" the Director repeated.

Apparite remained silent but responded with a firm nod of his head.

"If you really *did,* I think you'd find the words for it," the Director said in concern. "Fortunately for you, we have investigated her and her story checks out. I don't even want to think of the damage you might have caused if she had been a Soviet 'swallow.' For now, the most important thing is to not allow her to affect your next mission. You can worry about *Fräulein* Grünbach *after* the event tomorrow."

"There's only one thing," Apparite said. "If anything happens to me, I'd like you to take care of her."

"Like I said: don't worry about the girl; don't let her distract you. But yes, if anything happens to you, we'll take care of her—get her into the West. And do you know *why?*"

Apparite did not answer: the tone in the Director's voice had told him not to.

"Let me tell you why. Because she is valuable to our mission. Because she has information that benefits the United States. Because she can cause harm to our enemies. It is *not* because you have asked me to, and it is most definitely not because you may have feelings for her. If you do not understand this, then you might have reason to fear for your life—and not just from the Soviets, Apparite."

The message was clear: *You are crossing a line; you must step back behind it or you risk consequences.*

The Director went on. "Tell me more about the Russian—this Zhdanovich." He led Apparite into the dining room.

"He's not your usual KGB, and he's definitely not SMERSH," Apparite said. He sat down at the sturdy walnut dining table, on which rested a pot of coffee and a half-eaten loaf of bread. "He seems to be here for another reason entirely." He buttered a piece of bread and slowly started chewing.

"It's difficult to tell whose side *any* of them are on," said the Director. "They fight each other as much as they fight us. But this situation gives me concern. Is there a chance he's playing you? Sometimes you make me very nervous—especially when I hear you've been cavorting with the KGB."

"You've got nothing to worry about." Apparite had tried to project confidence in his voice, but wasn't too sure he'd succeeded. "I'm just another East German racketeer to him. If you need to be worried about something, let's talk about the *Geisterkeller*. That place seems like a huge hole in security."

"The *Geisterkeller?* We've known about it for years, Apparite. Think of it as a big club for spies, black marketeers, operators. You might call it a 'pressure release-valve.' More conflicts have been avoided there than ever were created. It's not a problem, as long as people are discreet. You're meeting Lohmann there again tonight, correct? To get the final arrangements for the event?"

"Yes."

"Get there early. Talk to the Russian—alone, if you can—and see what he can tell you. Maybe he'll let you in on something, but I trust that you will use your head and not give anything away. Afterward you'll need to stay in East Berlin until the event is over, but then get back here as soon as you can. The check-points have been relaxed for now, but will re-tighten after they find the bodies. Make sure you take an L-pill with you. If it all goes wrong don't forget to use it."

"Hey, don't get your hopes up!" Apparite said in jest. "I hope to disappoint you by returning alive and well tomorrow night."

"Don't worry—I'm fairly certain we *will* see you again," replied the Director. "Possibly even alive."

Apparite laughed, and the Director continued.

"I have some news about Dr. Hoevenaers, by the way."

"What can you tell me? Is he alright?"

"I am on my way to London. We're going to see about moving him somewhere safer. He lost his leg but suffered only minor effects from the poison."

"Thank God," said Apparite. "I feel terrible about it."

"You did well. By all rights he should be dead. He wanted me to express his gratitude for all you did for him."

All I did? Apparite said to himself. *I nearly got him killed—that's all I did.*

"And don't think it was your fault," added the Director, guessing Apparite's thoughts. "SMERSH had targeted him for elimination. If you hadn't been there, he would have died. Viktor ordered it, by the way. He has decided to eliminate anyone who might have helped you in London. You gave him one of his few defeats last year and he has not forgotten it, even if he thinks you are dead." The Director rose from his chair.

"I'm off to London. Remember what I said about the girl."

He gripped Apparite's shoulder in a spontaneous gesture of affection, and walked out of the front door and onto the *Wittenbergstrasse*. Such displays of warmth and humanity were unusual for the Director, and always got Apparite thinking. He knew the Director treated him differently than his other associates, though Apparite had yet to figure out why, for their relationship went beyond the usual camaraderie of "soldiers," nor could it be explained by their shared passion for the Washington Senators baseball club. Little did Apparite know that he'd been carrying the answer on him for years, tucked into a small hiding place in his wallet.

He buttered another piece of bread, chewed, and wondered.

Apparite entered *Der Geisterkeller* at 1945. It was almost as crowded as before but he found Zhdanovich easily; the Russian was sitting at a table in the far corner of the smoky room with two attractive brunettes. He seemed to be in the midst of telling a joke, and when Apparite got near he heard its riotous conclusion—which, in an unexpected twist, was spoken in broken English:

"So, Ukrainian fighter pilot say, 'No—*these* Fokkers were flying Messerschmitts'!" His table-mates burst into gales of obviously forced laughter, during which the Russian noted Apparite approaching him. He shouted, again in English, "Horst, my friend! Have drink with me!"

Apparite sat down at the table with the amiable Russian.

"I hope you speak English," continued Zhdanovich. "Some nights I like to practice. Drinking makes *easier*, you know!" His companions laughed and the Russian looked over at Apparite with a wry smile on his face. "If only *they* spoke English," he said, nodding in the direction of the women sitting with him, "they might have liked more my joke!"

"It is a good joke," said Apparite, lending his English a German inflection. "But I heard it from the British last year, and the pilot was a Pole."

"Did you come to drink with me, or do you wait for Lohmann?" asked Zhdanovich. The two women at his table got up to move on to more promising and attentive clients. This one, they could tell, had more jokes than money or contraband.

"Lohmann. I have business with him tonight."

The Russian handed Apparite a full stein of beer. "Hmm, I like Lohmann—he makes jokes, and has cigarettes—but I not trust with secrets."

"Why?" asked Apparite. "Is it because he is—how do the Americans say—a 'big operator'?"

"No—I not trust Lohmann because he is *fat!* You have heard of siege of Leningrad?"

Apparite nodded *yes* and took a sip of beer.

"When people are hungry and starve, people are thin," continued Zhdanovich. "Like skeleton. But all stay away from people who are *not* like skeleton. You know why?"

"No—why?"

"Because they kill and *eat* you. They are cannibals, you see, when there is no more food. Lohmann is like that. He is only fat *Ossi* I have seen, and I not trust. He does not eat people, but gets fat in other ways. You understand?"

"I will be careful with Lohmann," answered Apparite. "I have made deal with men like him before.'"

"If so, I feel bad for you. Maybe you need different job!"

Apparite laughed and ordered another two beers.

"Why do you now drink beer?" he asked Zhdanovich. "I thought it was horse-urine, right?"

"Vodka is taken by bosses for May Day party, so it is horse-urine for me tonight. But day *after* May Day, maybe I get vodka from my Vopo friends. They confiscate much tomorrow night! No matter—here is Lohmann. Fritz!"

Lohmann waved at the two men. When he arrived at their table, Zhdanovich rose and offered the East German his seat.

"I hear you have business with *Herr* Köller," he said to Lohmann. He looked at Apparite and added, "Maybe we drink again, my friend."

"That I would like," Apparite responded. "I do not have many Russian friends—you are the first!"

"And I hope not the last," answered the Russian. "*Das Vadanya,* gentlemen," he said to the two men, leaving them. When he was out of ear-shot, Lohmann spoke.

"I hate it when he speaks English," he said in German. "He is a big show-off sometimes. Remember what I said about the sausages?"

Apparite nodded in the affirmative.

"He does not know how to make them—just *blini,* and they are terrible. I would not trust him."

"Tell me about the meeting," said Apparite in an attempt to change the subject. He genuinely liked the Russian and did not want to hear any more of Lohmann's opinions. Something about the East German was beginning to chafe.

"It is tomorrow at twenty-one hundred. It is good that it is at night—it will be much easier for you to get away, and many of the Soviets will be busy with the May Day celebration. Here is the address."

He handed Apparite a small piece of paper from across the table. Apparite took a moment to look at it. Memorizing what had been written, he lit the paper on fire with his lighter and placed it in an ash-receptacle.

"There will be three of them," Lohmann continued. "Four if Viktor comes. The building is abandoned except for a few rooms they use for torture and interrogation. If you kill them quickly, you should get away. If not, then—"

"Then I am in trouble."

"Yes—then you will be in trouble."

Apparite rose from the table. "Thank you for your help," he said, but then, thinking of Christiane's situation, added, "After this, I may have something else for you. Are you interested?"

Lohmann smiled and held up his right hand. He ran his thumb back and forth across his fingers in a "How much?" gesture.

"One thousand—U.S. dollars, of course," said Apparite. "I may need help resettling someone into the West. A girl."

Lohmann's smile turned into a broad grin.

"Meet me here two nights from now and we will talk about it," he said, pleased with what he had been told. "Bring one hundred for a start."

"Fine. I'll see you then."

"I hope so, *Herr* Köller! I sincerely hope so, my friend!"

Apparite walked out into the quiet Berlin night. A thick mist had formed in the air, partly from fog, partly from the dust of nearby demolitions, but somehow the shadowy haze around him seemed to fit what he was thinking: he had been told by D not to trust Christiane, and by Lohmann not to trust Zhdanovich, and by Zhdanovich not to trust Lohmann—and even by the Director seemingly not to trust himself, at least as far as Christiane was concerned.

The picture was pretty damned murky, but it was nothing that a couple of assassinations and defections couldn't clear up, he thought. Of that he was *quite* sure.

Thirteen:
A Long-Awaited Reunion

Apparite spent the next day in quiet contemplation and preparation for the event that evening. At times, his concentration lapsed, however, and he began to think and worry about Christiane (*Has she gotten away with stealing the page from the book? How much danger is she in? What will things be like when I see her again tomorrow?*), but as 2100 approached, his mind naturally and easily narrowed its focus to the mission at hand.

He made a mental list of his plan: Drive unnoticed to the site of the event; park one block away. Conceal his miniature Colt M1911 pistol in his hat; conceal his knives in his shoes and belt. Enter the building while obscuring his face; enter the meeting room prepared for battle at any moment. Assess his opponents and the physical nature of the room; formulate an appropriate plan. Kill everyone in the room; search the hall immediately afterward for guards; kill any that appear. Disable any surveillance devices in the room; exit the building while again obscuring his face. Walk to his car at a brisk pace; drive to the rendezvous point at the West Berlin safe-house to meet D.

After a light supper at a café, Apparite donned his disguise—a broad false moustache held in place by theater glue, and thick, dummy-lensed black glasses—and drove to the site of the event: a neo-classical, gray-bricked five-story building a short distance north of "Museum Island" in Mitte, right in the heart of East Berlin. He circled the building once, on the look-out for anything that might complicate his plan, but saw nothing. The

Communist May Day celebration had taken most people to the *Alexanderplatz* and *Marx-Engels platz* for the parade and festivities, leaving little traffic and few persons on the streets. Good: the fewer eyewitnesses the better in case of a pursuit; the less traffic the better in the event of a mad dash for the border.

He parked his car on a side-street around the corner from the building, which was just off of the *Linienstrasse*. He double-checked his weapons, tilted his hat as far down his face as he could without attracting attention, and began walking down the street in a casual, relaxed manner. As he approached the building, he took a quick survey of the area around it and was relieved that no one was in sight. He figured the Soviets might normally have kept a sentry outside disguised as a beggar, a shopkeeper, or some other innocuous-appearing civilian, but today they had apparently been given a day-off. There was an advantage in having the event on a Communist holiday, he thought.

Apparite entered the building, taking pains to hide his already disguised face by placing his hand to it and feigning a cough. He stepped into the unusually grand foyer, which was open to the other two floors above him, but it was completely deserted. The place reminded him of a university science hall; at any minute he expected to see a rush of students and professors journeying to their classes. He stopped and listened carefully for a moment, but detected no sign of another human within it. It seemed shameful that a handsome building such as this was used for torture and interrogation when it could have served a more noble purpose.

He entered a stairwell to his left and slowly ascended the stairs to the second floor, his steps echoing softly in the apparently unoccupied building. He noiselessly opened the stairwell door and walked into the hall.

It was then he heard the first sound that told him he was not alone: a typewriter clicking as its keys struck the page. *Tap-tap—*

tap-tap-tap—tap-tap-tap-tap—tap-tap—ching! When he neared the source of the sound, an unseen man spoke to him.

"*Herr* Köller—come in, please," he said in German. The voice had come from the half-opened doorway of a small room a few steps down the hall.

Apparite accelerated his pace and entered the room. Three persons were inside it: a dark-complected, black-haired man with a moustache; a tall, blond-haired man with bright blue eyes; and a short, thick-necked and broad-shouldered bald man whose face was unshaven. The black-haired man was seated at a wooden desk in the middle of the room, typing; the other two stood at the sides of the desk, flanking him. Except for an unoccupied chair in front of the desk, the room was empty. Tellingly, it had no windows. Apparite glanced upwards. He noted a ceiling fan rotating madly in an effort to create a breeze, and yet the room was still quite stuffy—well-insulated, he surmised, to hold in the screams and agonies of those tortured within it.

"Your identification, please," said the blue-eyed man. He closed the door to the little room.

Apparite nodded; he removed his hat and placed it on the empty chair in front of the desk. Taking his forged identity card from inside his suit-coat, he handed it to the blue-eyed man.

"Thank you," said the man. He looked closely at Apparite's face and handed the card back to him. "We must also search you."

"Certainly—I understand." Apparite returned the card to his suit-coat, his hand visibly shaking. "I'm sorry," he added in a tremulous voice, "but I'm a little nervous. You know, I've never done anything illegal before." He forced a smile.

"Don't worry—it's but a formality," the blue-eyed man responded. "Your new West German identity documents are almost complete. It's just a matter of putting in the *umlauts*, so to speak."

The short, bald man frisked Apparite very thoroughly, even to the point of cupping Apparite's testicles into his hand to feel the inner thigh. Finding nothing suspicious, he looked up at the dark-complected man seated at the desk.

"There's nothing," he said. He moved to a new spot in the far corner of the room but kept his eyes on Apparite.

"Forgive our precautions," the blue-eyed man said; Apparite assumed he was Russian from the trace of Slavic intonation to his German. "But understand we are very fearful of Soviet infiltration of our little group. Please, have a seat. We need to get some information first, but it won't take long." He smiled in an effort to reassure Apparite that this was but a simple, routine procedure.

Apparite sat in the chair in front of the desk. He picked up his hat and fiddled with it to give the men an impression of anxiety. He figured they would do a gentle interrogation before giving themselves away and going to the hard stuff, so he decided that after the first question he would begin the event. He could not be sure whether Viktor was on his way, or ever had any intention of coming, but it did not matter now—he could not wait for him. His long-sought revenge would have to wait for another day.

The blue-eyed man noticed Apparite's restless demeanor. "You have no cause to be nervous," he said. "We have a few questions to ask, and then we will give you your instructions for resettling into the West. But first, can you tell us more about your work?" He subtly moved to a position behind Apparite. "For example, are there others who might wish to defect to the West? Or have information that might help our cause?"

Apparite squeezed the crown of his brown fedora. The small pistol he had concealed in the hidden compartment in its top fell into his waiting left hand. Fortunately, he had unusually small and dexterous fingers and the weapon was easy for him to grasp in the limited space. He cleared his throat to buy some time and slipped his switch-blade knife from its hiding place in his belt. He engaged it under the hat with a smooth, undetectable gesture of his right hand.

"Um, alright. My work supervisor, who is from Potsdam . . ."

As he spoke, Apparite surveyed his targets to find his opening. He saw the black-haired man typing as he recorded what was being said, and heard the soft shuffle of shoes as the blue-eyed man stepped toward him to better hear his answer. The bald man in the corner of the room took a moment to light a cigarette, briefly breaking his line of sight, and as soon as Apparite saw him do it, he knew it was time.

In mid-sentence, Apparite rapidly brought out the miniature Colt M1911 from underneath his hat and fired one of its six-millimeter hollow-tipped bullets directly into the chest of the man behind the typewriter. The Russian jolted back for the briefest of moments and then his bulky head and neck slammed onto the typewriter, jumbling all of the keys together with a loud *clack!* Apparite threw himself backward in his chair, extending his neck to better see behind him. In that strange sense of slowed-motion he experienced in such moments, he saw the blue-eyed man begin to reach for his weapon.

But the Russian would not get it in time. As Apparite toppled over, his gun-hand fell in line with the blue-eyed man's lower jaw. He aimed an inch beneath it and fired.

The bullet entered just above the Adam's apple and obliterated the man's brain-stem. Blood splattered onto the door behind him like a splash of bright red paint. He jolted back against the door and toppled forward: dead. The bald man in the corner dropped the cigarette from his mouth and pulled his pistol, firing as soon as it had cleared his coat.

But chance was on Apparite's side, for the bullet meant for him struck the falling blue-eyed man instead. The dead man jolted slightly as his body was pushed off the direction of its fall. When it crashed onto the desk, Apparite had already appeared in its former place. He fired a shot into the bald man's heart, slamming him against the corner of the room. The man groaned and fell onto the floor.

Before Apparite could make his way to the door, it burst open, throwing him back against the desk. Another Russian appeared in the doorway. Apparite, though splayed on the desk, kicked his fallen chair up into the man's face. He fired a bullet between the chair legs into his enemy's chest, killing him. The Russian fell back into the hall, his pistol discharging loudly on impact with the floor.

His hopes of sneaking away now dashed, Apparite moved fast to complete the job. He quickly and thoroughly destroyed the typewriter (in which he found a hidden recording device), pulled the fan out of the flimsy plaster ceiling (in which he found a hidden eight-millimeter film camera), and then bolted for the stairs.

A door opened directly in front of him and another Soviet agent stepped into the hall. Apparite brought a karate-kick around into the Russian's flank, knocking the man to the ground. A quick slash across the throat with his knife finished him.

Apparite reached the door to the stairwell, flung it open, and leapt down the stairs. He removed his false moustache and eyeglasses and stuffed them into a pants pocket. He no longer had a hat to shield his face, but had the foresight to conceal a black silk balaclava in his shirt pocket. He slipped it over his head.

He opened the stairwell door and dove into the foyer in a single action, his pistol held in front of him. In mid-air he spied a Russian standing near the front entrance, and though the man had his own weapon ready, the sight of the balaclava-adorned Apparite flying out of the stairwell froze him. Before Apparite hit the ground he had already put two shots into the Russian: one to the heart, one to the forehead. A second later, Apparite was through the door and into the street.

He ran fifty feet, removed the balaclava, and walked to his automobile at a quick pace. Climbing inside it, he was relieved to hear it start—each time he used the Rekord its reliability seemed more in doubt—and, throwing it into gear, pulled the car away from the curb with a squeal.

He figured he had five minutes to pass a check-point before the Soviets and Vopos would close them all down and he would be trapped in the East. With everyone celebrating May Day elsewhere, the streets remained reasonably clear, but behind him in the distance he heard the rising sound of shouts intermingled with sirens. He whipped the car through a couple of left turns to get him pointed south, his foot firmly on the gas pedal.

He was on the *Friedreichstrasse* and passing cars in a frenzy. He swerved right around a KIM-10 and a Moskvich, and then rapidly left around an AWZ. He slammed on his brakes to avoid a rear-end collision when a Volkswagen in front of him made a sudden turn, and then accelerated rapidly, the car's engine straining with each gear-change as he passed another Moskvich at nearly fifty miles per hour.

But then disaster. Passing a BMW, the little Opel shuddered and Apparite heard the ominous sound of grinding gears. Looking in the rear-view mirror, he saw three official-looking black Mercedes pull onto the road behind him, their rear-ends fishtailing in their haste. Apparite mashed the accelerator to the floor. He knew a pursuit when he saw one, though with the passing of each second he drew ever closer to the border and a sure escape on the West Berlin *U-bahn*.

The car lurched as he lost fourth gear. He was forced to down-shift to third as he struggled to maintain enough speed to move around an old Horch. He could only go about forty now, and the way the car was sounding and smoking, he knew it was only a matter of time before third gear was gone and he would have to slow and down-shift to second. But the check-point was just a few hundred yards ahead; fortunately, the only Vopo near the open, temporary crossing-bar appeared to be asleep in a wooden chair. Apparite floored the accelerator, "red-lining" the rev-counter, but the scream of the engine roused the East German from his nap and he leapt to his feet. It would be a frantic race to the finish: Apparite's car closed on the check-point as the Vopo ran to the crossing-bar to disengage it and close the crossing.

Apparite leaned out of the car and fired his pistol into the air. The Vopo ducked, as any man would after hearing a nearby gunshot, delaying his actions. Apparite slipped past the crossing-bar just as the man recovered his wits and lowered it, closing the check-point.

A hundred feet later, the Opel met its maker in a cloud of white smoke from the engine and black from the exhaust. It wrenched itself to a halt, skidding sideways completely out of control with its wheels locked firmly into place. Apparite opened the driver's-side door, climbed out of his newly deceased automobile, and glanced back at the check-point. When the Vopo saw Apparite standing by the car looking at him, he made an obscene gesture at the young American.

Apparite waved at the East German good-naturedly: he had won the race and could afford a moment to gloat. He was just about to make a run for the nearest *U-bahn* station when he heard the three pursuing Mercedes screech to a halt at the crossing. An odd feeling rose in his gut. Something was compelling him to take a look at his pursuers.

The door of the lead Mercedes opened and a man appeared. He took a step and turned to face Apparite.

Apparite picked him out easily: he was tall, pale, thin, and dressed in a long black over-coat. But the feature that made this man's appearance so singular was his eyes—even from a distance they burned with a palpable, unforgettable intensity.

There could be no mistaking him. It was Viktor.

My God! Apparite said aloud. He felt frozen in place by the sight. But astonished as Apparite was to see Viktor, it was no match for what Viktor felt when he recognized the man standing behind the smoking Opel. His eyes widened in shock and he walked slowly toward the barrier, like a man entranced by a supernatural vision or ghostly apparition. Viktor had thought that Apparite was dead, and the sight of him—the man who had almost bested him; the man who had almost *killed* him!—brought him to a rage. He pulled his pistol and fired madly in Apparite's direction. Apparite quickly ducked for cover behind the Opel. When he heard the Russian stop to reload, he tore off running down the street.

He hopped the first *U-bahn* back to the *Wittenbergstrasse*, but even as he entered the relative safety of his home base, he could not remove the picture of his enemy's face from his mind. Viktor was in Berlin, and critically, the SMERSH agent knew that Apparite was as well.

Like they used to say in those old Republic westerns, *This town wasn't big enough for the two of them,* and Apparite knew that one of them would not be leaving it alive.

Fourteen:
An Unwelcome Detour

"Did they photograph you?" asked D. He poured Apparite a cup of coffee from a pot he'd just made.

"I don't think so," Apparite said. "I destroyed a camera hidden in the ceiling and I don't think they caught my face coming or going from the building. They might have had tie or button cameras, but I doubt it. Does it matter? Viktor saw me. He knows I'm here." He picked up the coffee, blowing on it to release the steam.

"As long as your picture isn't posted at every check-point you can go back into the Eastern sector; that's why I'm asking." D took a moment to pour a cup of English tea. He was pleased to have found Twinings, although he had to over-pay for it considerably on the black-market. "You're meeting the girl again tonight?"

"Yes. She's bringing me a page from the Karlshorst central telephone directory."

"Excellent," said D. "If it looks promising, bring her back with you—and with as much of that book as possible. Perhaps your friend Lohmann might be of some help. See what he can offer us. But if it looks like the Soviets are a step ahead of you, don't muck about: leave the girl and get back right away."

Apparite took a sip of the strong coffee but remained silent. He was struggling to accept the fact he might have to leave her behind, though he had known all along that it was a possibility.

"What about Viktor?" continued D. "What are your plans for him?"

Apparite had known from the start what to do about Viktor: he had to flush him out into the open, preferably in the West. He knew, too, exactly who could do that—Christiane. And though Apparite knew his life would not be the same without her, the siren song of his duty and need for revenge called to him, challenging his loyalty and strength. By the time he could have mounted any resistance to it he had already spoken, irrevocably putting his plan into motion.

"We can use Christiane. We use Christiane to bring him out."

"As bait?" D put down his cup of tea to add more milk.

"Yes. We leak that she's going to the West with information. When the Soviets send Viktor after her, I'll kill him. Leave it to me. I won't let Viktor get the better of me a second time."

"About the girl—do you have feelings for her? Will that be a problem?"

Apparite pondered the question: how could he honestly answer it? Damn right he had feelings for her, and he'd be a fool to tell D anything different. He also knew that to succeed in his mission he could not allow them to surface. But how long could he suppress them? *Could* he even suppress them?

"I won't let any feelings get in the way."

"Let's hope not," said D. "We can't miss this opportunity. Get something arranged as soon as possible."

"I'm meeting Lohmann tomorrow; he can tell me what the Soviets know. He can also help us with the girl."

"Good. We'll plan on meeting again when you've brought the girl into the West—bring her here when you've got her. But you've got to get something straight with yourself," said D, his voice and face reflecting the gravity of what he was about to say.

"What's that?" Apparite asked quietly.

"You've *got* to get used to the idea that she is going to get killed. Because no matter how I look at it, I'd give her about a twenty-five percent chance of surviving the week."

Apparite met Christiane at her apartment shortly before midnight. Although the check-points had been especially stringent given the killing of the Russian agents, it appeared that the Soviets had not gotten a good photograph of Apparite's face, for he was allowed to pass into the East after only a brief interrogation: *What business do you have in East Berlin,* Herr *Müller? When will you be leaving? Why are you traveling alone?* Everything had gone smoothly enough, but Apparite could not dispel a feeling that his luck would eventually run out—sooner or later someone from the other side would recognize him as a threat or an enemy. There was only one more trip he wanted to make into the Soviet sector: the one when he would finally bring Christiane into the West.

Compared to their last encounter, Christiane seemed a different woman to him: she was smiling and well made-up, embracing him warmly and with real affection when she opened the door. She led him inside her tiny apartment, and in a manner that seemed as natural as breathing they quickly shed themselves of their clothes and made love on her old, iron-framed bed.

Afterward, Apparite closed his eyes and took a deep breath. He loved the smells of her apartment. He took pleasure in the trace of sweet perfume on her pillows and the unique, musty scent of her worn goose-down comforter that she had wrapped around their naked bodies for warmth. Her skin and hair gave off a fragrance that reminded him of a mixture of salty sweat and rose-water, a pungent scent made all the more alluring after the commingling of their bodies, and he detected a trace of butter and cinnamon in the air from the baking of *strudel* in the morning.

She spoke, bringing him out of his thoughts.

"I brought you a page from their telephone exchange book—just as you asked."

Truth be told, Apparite hadn't planned to broach the subject of her defection until later, fearing that to do so sooner would only make him appear grasping and cold. But he knew that even then it would pain him to do so, pain him to be brought back to his true identity as a Superagent when they could spend hours being nothing but lovers, and with no responsibilities outside of this room.

"Good," he answered. "But let's talk about that later."

Christiane kissed him and ran her fingers through his hair. She looked deeply into his brown eyes.

"I took it from the middle—it was kind of exciting!" she said. She laughed suddenly in a light-hearted manner. "And as soon as I did it, I knew I was going to be free! I *knew* it!"

Apparite did not share her joy.

"There's no going back for you now—not since you took it. Are you sure they won't miss it?"

She shook her head *no*. "It's from a page they never use, right in the middle. I think tomorrow I can take *twenty* at least. I'll get them from the busiest parts this time."

Apparite took her hand in his and caressed it.

"Please be careful," he said. "Come straight here after work and I'll take you over the border. Pack your most important belongings and mail them into the West. Bring nothing with you but the pages from the directory."

"Don't worry—I know you'll take care of me," she told him. "Just like you wanted to do on the train." She paused and cocked her head slightly in a gesture of reflection. "It seems so long ago, doesn't it?"

Yes, it seemed ages: a week ago, Apparite had no one to take care of but himself, and nothing to protect but the integrity of his duty to the United States of America. But she had sat down to read his newspaper on the train to Berlin, and the world had suddenly changed for them both.

Why couldn't they have met at another time, in another place? he asked himself. *Why had fate placed the two of them together only to inevitably break them apart?*

Today they had the freedom to enjoy each other's love, but tomorrow, when his plan went into action, everything would change—*everything*. As soon as he had smuggled her into the West, initiating his diabolical plan to trap Viktor, he knew that the part of John Apparite who loved her would necessarily fade as the duties of the Superagent within him came to the fore. He would need to push his feelings for her into the same deep crevasse where he put all feelings that might harm him, or worse, that might lessen his abilities as an espionage agent. It was true that they sometimes forced themselves out to trouble him anyway, as in the sudden attacks of panic or weeping to which he had been subjected last year, but he had to make the effort all the same.

Their lips met and he embraced her. She gazed up at him and ran her soft hands over his shoulders, back, and legs, and in a moment they were making love once more. And as they moved together in automatic, unconscious rhythm, Apparite opened his eyes to take her all in, to memorize this moment, so that no matter what happened in the next few days it would remain this vivid and pure forever, fully realized and ready to be accessed at any point in the future when he needed to feel human and remember the woman who had once captured his heart.

"*Herr* Köller—how are you, my friend?" said a cheerful voice in German. Apparite had nearly reached the cellar stairs that led to the *Geisterkeller* when Lohmann appeared from a nearby alley and headed him off. "There are people in there that should not see you. Let's walk to a more private spot to talk, heh?"

"Sure," Apparite answered. "I suppose so."

He was still recovering from his earlier parting with Christiane, and his voice was unusually quiet and introspective. Leaving her had been tougher than he'd expected, especially when he realized that this had been, in all likelihood, their last day of freedom together. Even now as he walked with Lohmann his focus and thoughts remained with her, and he hardly registered a word the East German was saying—something about the supply of sausage skins and the price of petrol, nothing really of importance.

Unbeknownst to Apparite, his inattention would put him in jeopardy.

As they turned a corner by an alley, Lohmann made a subtle, nodding gesture with his head. Apparite's innate danger-sense shot up as he realized what was happening, rousing him from the lassitude of his depression, but it was futile: the man summoned by Lohmann was already upon him.

A black-gloved hand holding a damp white handkerchief was thrust over Apparite's mouth and nose before he could react. Apparite tried to reach for his switch-blade, or kick back at his attacker's knee, or back-flip, or grasp a collar to judo-throw his attacker, or do *something* to get away. But somewhere between the thought and the action of doing it the message to his muscles was getting lost, lost in the volatile, medicinal smell of the chemical-infused handkerchief covering his face, and the sleep it was forcing upon him.

The sounds around him became ever more distant, though he was able to discern the voices of men speaking German in hushed tones, followed by the sound of a rapidly approaching automobile. His body was then lifted into the air and he was thrown onto a firm surface, which he recognized as that of the trunk of a car. Just before the world slipped away into an unnatural darkness, one last voice spoke to him. Despite his rising stupor, he recognized it as belonging to Lohmann.

"One thousand is good, but five thousand would have been better! *Auf Wiedersehen, Herr* Köller—though perhaps I should say to you, *good-bye!*"

The East German slammed the old Moskvich-400's trunk door shut, trapping the now unconscious Apparite. Laughing, Lohmann saluted the car and walked back toward the *Geisterkeller* to celebrate his latest triumph. With a screech, the black sedan pulled away from the curb and traveled to the end of the street. Stopping briefly, it made a careful 180-degree turn and went back in the direction from whence it came, albeit slowly and with caution to avoid attracting attention.

It was now traveling due east, and given that the two men inside it were agents of the KGB, the direction the car was going meant only one thing: Karlshorst. John Apparite, it seemed, was going to meet Viktor sooner than he had expected.

FIFTEEN:
ON TO KARLSHORST

Apparite slowly returned to consciousness. In the darkness of the Moskvich's closed trunk his first sensation was not visual as much as olfactory: inhaling, he detected the acrid smell of car exhaust mixed with the pungency of mold on the worn, mildewed carpet that lined the boot of the car. After his eyes had adjusted to the darkness, and with the aid of a trace amount of light that was leaking into the trunk, he was able to make out, minimally, something of his surroundings. Not that there was much to see, or could be seen, he thought at first.

He was soon intrigued, however, by that little bit of light: where was it coming from? He turned his head in all directions and found its source: the base of the trunk had rusted through in a few places. He thought that might prove significant. The effects of the anesthetic had worn off quickly (chloroform, he deduced, from the irritation and burning he felt in his nostrils), and he calculated he was probably but a few city blocks from where he had been kidnapped.

Kidnapped: the word sent a chill through one's spine, for it was well-known that kidnapped spies almost never returned intact, either in mind or body. It was particularly galling that it had been Lohmann who had done it—and for money! The thought sickened him. If he escaped from his predicament, his first order of business would be to even the score with the unprincipled East German, and then some.

But *if* he escaped was not going to be good enough; it had to

189

be *when*. *If* implied there were other options for Apparite to take at the end of this journey, but guessing where the Russians were going, he realized that only one thing awaited him, and that was death. If he had not escaped by the time they had reached Karlshorst and the trunk door was opened, he would have to use his hidden L-pill and end it. Superagent Directive Number One, *Maintenance of Secrecy*, was the most important of the four to follow, and Apparite could not subject himself to interrogation at the hands of an expert like Viktor, or it would be broken. Better to die than betray your agency; better to die than be tortured into madness.

At the rate they were traveling, Apparite figured he had about forty-five minutes to escape. He softly kicked the trunk lid to test the range, and was about to put all of his strength into it when, after a brief period of reflection, he changed his mind. Although forcing open the trunk was the most obvious means of escape, he realized it would do no good: given the speed with which the car was traveling, he was certain to suffer serious injury if he tried jumping out of it as it sped down the road. If he waited for it to stop, the Russians would only chase him down and shoot him, or submit him to physical tortures he would find undesirable. Kicking open the trunk would have to be a last resort; saved until all other possibilities had been exhausted.

Let's call that Plan B, he said to himself, though "Plan B" would have sounded much more promising if he had any idea of what "Plan A" was first.

The light leaking into the trunk started to dim, worrying Apparite further: it was now dusk, and when the sun finally dipped behind the horizon the trunk would progress to a state of complete darkness, making his job even more difficult. He took some deep breaths to maintain his composure and felt around him.

His searching hands found a few papers and pebbles, but just when he thought the trunk was basically empty he found a short length of rubber hose. *Alright,* he said to himself, *it's not exactly a crowbar, but maybe it'll come in handy in some way.* He placed it into a corner, twisted his body around, and probed the rest of the trunk: nothing, nothing, a tin cup, nothing, a few clamps and bolts, nothing, a twisted piece of smooth, rounded metal (brass, he guessed), nothing—but then his hands ran up against something which felt very curious; very curious indeed.

It was a sack filled with small, smooth, irregularly shaped objects. Each was about the size of a potato; they were cold and firm, yet somewhat yielding to the touch. He took one out of the bag and held it to his nose. It was essentially odorless; sniffing it gave him no clue as to its identity. He firmly pushed a finger into its surface. When a small piece of the object broke off in his hand, he brought it up to his mouth and tasted it, letting loose a laugh at his discovery. This large sack of potato-sized objects was filled with—*potatoes!*

He ran an inventory of the contents of the trunk: potatoes, rubber hoses, metal tubing, and a tin cup—all of the parts one would need to outfit a homemade still, including the main ingredient used to make vodka.

How typically Russian! he thought. But how on earth could a man in a moving car's trunk escape using only a sack of potatoes, a length of rubber hose, a brass coil, and a tin cup?

As he rolled a potato around in his hands, an inspiration from his childhood hit him: the old "potato in the exhaust" trick. He remembered how some of the older, more mischievous kids in his hometown would jam a potato firmly into a car's tail-pipe. After the unsuspecting owner started it up, the pressure would build and build until it exploded out of the end with a gunshot-like sound.

He also remembered how one of the victims of the prank had

gotten unusually irate at the perpetrators. He coulda been *killed!* the man had shouted at the youngsters who'd done it. Didn't those punks know how dangerous plugging the exhaust could be? The carbon monoxide could've leaked into the car and gassed him, and he never would've known it! He could've drifted off into sleep and never woke up! Man was he hot, Apparite recalled.

At the time, of course, the neighborhood kids had all laughed and called the man a big sissy and thrown potatoes at him as he drove away, but now Apparite was grateful for the angry lecture. All of fifteen years later, it just might save his life.

He took one of the larger potatoes and rolled over to the part of the trunk that overlooked the exhaust. Peeling back the tattered carpet that lined the car's trunk, he noted the marked thinning of the metal floor from years of rust and decay, just as he'd hoped.

He grabbed the tin cup and started pounding. After a few knocks, a significant hole had formed, through which Apparite could see not only the ground underneath the car whizzing by in a blur, but also, importantly, the end of the tail-pipe just below him. It was expelling gray smoke, but perhaps not as much as he expected—*hmm, that might mean something.*

He held his ear to the hole and took notice of the unusually loud and throaty noise of the motor. Given the sound of the engine, and the apparent decreased exhaust from the pipe, he deduced that the tail-pipe had a sizeable hole in it near the front of the vehicle. It was almost too perfect to be true.

With a potato in hand, he thrust his right arm through the hole. Despite the heat of the exhaust, he felt blindly for the end of the tail-pipe and firmly thrust the potato inside it. He pulled his hand back out of the hole, blowing on it to soothe it (having burned it a bit on the hot metal), and got another potato. He repeated the jamming procedure once more.

He took a quick peek through the hole and was pleased with what he saw: smoke was no longer coming out of the end of the tail-pipe. The noise of the motor had also increased considerably, confirming to Apparite that the exhaust was now being forced out much closer to the passenger compartment. He could only wait and pray that the Russians would not notice it, or stop the car for some other reason on their way to Karlshorst, but if they didn't—well, if they didn't, he just might be in business.

He set about with the rest of his plan. For one thing, he required a source of fresh air; the plugged-up exhaust might kill *him* as easily as the Russians up front. To remedy that, he thought he'd use that length of rubber hose he had found. With his switch-blade, he cut an eight-inch-long piece from it. Threading the measure of hose through the hole in the trunk's floor, he placed the end in his mouth. He inhaled tentatively, unsure as to how much dust or exhaust he would bring in if he took too great a breath, and was relieved when he felt a rush of fresh air flow into his lungs, and nothing else. Holding his switch-blade in his left hand, he took the brass coil in his right—it's not much of a weapon but it'll do in a pinch—and pushed all the other objects in the trunk deep into a corner. And then he waited.

The suspense was terrific. Would enough carbon monoxide leak into the passenger compartment to kill the Russians? And if it did, would the car come to a halt in a fiery crash, killing him anyway, or would it gently slow and stop? And when it stopped, could he get the trunk door open? And if the trunk door opened, where the hell would he be?

There were too many questions for him to answer, or to even make wild guesses. All he knew was that this would end in one of two ways: he would escape or he would die.

He put his ear to the hole to see if he could hear the noises of traffic, but the engine blotted out all other sounds: *brrrrhrrrrrh-*

brrrrrrhrrrrh it droned on, in an increasingly hypnotic rhythm. After uncounted minutes, Apparite was wondering whether anything was going to happen at all, when suddenly something did.

The car swerved sharply to the right and glanced off of a guard-rail. Apparite braced himself for the inevitable crash.

But it never came. With the sound of metal grinding on metal, the car slowed gradually to a halt. Through the hole in the floor, Apparite saw the blur of the moving pavement get clearer and clearer until it came into perfect focus and was still. They had stopped.

He put his ear to the hole but heard nothing. There were neither the sounds of traffic nor noises coming from the front of the car; just the dull drone of the idling engine, telling Apparite that if someone had been pressing on the accelerator a minute earlier, they were pressing on it no longer.

He sharply kicked the trunk's door, but it did not open. He kicked again and again as hard as he could, but still nothing. To have come this close and failed! He had killed two KGB agents using just a couple of potatoes, only to find himself stymied.

Of all the things that might actually work *on this piece of s--t, it would have to be the trunk-latch!*

But then he heard a vehicle in the distance; from the noise of its engine Apparite guessed it was a truck. The changing pitch of the sound told him it was slowing, and after hearing the noise of its (squeaky) brakes being applied, he could tell that it had stopped. A door opened and closed, followed by footsteps.

Apparite frantically kicked the trunk door four times. When he stopped, he heard footsteps run past the tail end of the car. The driver's-side door then opened and a voice cried out in alarm.

"Mein Gott! Mein Gott!"

Apparite kicked the trunk door repeatedly with all of his strength.

The car's engine shut off and there was the cadence of rapid footsteps coming in his direction. He discerned the tinkle unique to the shaking of keys, and the lid of the trunk shuddered and opened, letting in the last few rays of light before sunset.

Facing Apparite was a skinny German man with a broad handle-bar moustache. He wore a bright blue wool cap and gray and blue overalls. His eyes were as wide open in surprise as the human anatomy would allow.

"They're dead!" he shouted to Apparite in German. "They're dead!"

"Good."

"Why were you in there?" the man asked in alarm. He looked as if he were about to burst into tears. "What did they do to you?"

"I was kidnapped." Apparite climbed out of the trunk. "Unfortunately, I need your vehicle."

He showed the man his knife and motioned for him to get in the trunk. He then took a glance up and down the road, but no cars were in sight, just as he'd hoped. From the pastoral look of the countryside, he deduced the KGB had been taking backroads to Karlshorst. That was also in his favor—it would afford him an easier escape.

The German began to weep. "No, please! I only stopped to help!"

"I'm sorry," said Apparite. "I have no choice."

The man climbed into the trunk as commanded. When he was settled inside it, Apparite handed him five hundred dollars in American money.

"For your trouble *and* your silence. Tell the Vopos you were robbed and stuffed in the trunk. Do not tell them I took your vehicle; it will be returned to you unharmed. If you agree, I will let you live. If not . . ." Apparite made a throat-slashing motion with his knife.

"Yes, yes—anything you say."

"Good. Give me your wallet."

The man handed it to Apparite. He opened it and removed the frightened German's identity card.

"See this?" Apparite said, holding up the card. "I know where you live. If you tell *anyone* about me, your family will die." He threw the wallet and identity card back into the trunk. "Another car will stop soon, I am sure. Pound on the trunk when it does and you'll be let out."

He closed the trunk door (leaving the keys in the lock), and walked away, ignoring the man's muffled cries. Apparite had escaped the KGB thanks to the Russian obsession with making cheap vodka, but there were still two more tasks to perform before the day was done. First, he would kill Lohmann, whom Apparite guessed was still celebrating his coup at *Der Geisterkeller*. Apparite had a particular disgust for traitors and betrayers, and he planned to dispatch the treacherous East German by as cruel a means as possible. After that dirty business was done, he would go to Christiane and take her into the West.

He was relieved that he had never mentioned her name to Lohmann, and that her identity and situation remained unknown to the Russians. For him to succeed in her defection, the maintenance of secrecy was essential. It would be a tricky business, but as long as the vehicle D had procured for this part of the mission was still where Apparite had left it—about a block down the street from the *Geisterkeller*—he thought he just might be able to pull it off.

It was, after all, a *very* special sort of car.

Sixteen:
A New Alliance

Apparite drove at a rapid rate of speed toward the center of Berlin, though not *too* rapidly given that he did not wish to attract the attention of any Vopos or Soviets along the way. To his relief, he did not pass any cars traveling in the opposite direction for many miles—cars that would eventually stumble onto the dead KGB agents' vehicle—but not wishing to remain on this particular road any longer than necessary, he made a few turns to get onto one of the main highways which led back to the city.

After thirty minutes he was on the *Frankfurt Allee*. He made another few turns, drove the truck past the *Alexanderplatz,* and turned southwest: his plan was to stop a few blocks from the *Geisterkeller,* get a weapon from his own car parked nearby, and meet up with Lohmann at the East German's favorite haunt. With any luck he'd catch the unfaithful German by surprise, allowing Apparite to kill him quickly and without complications. His only worry would then be Christiane.

He pulled the truck onto the *Leipzigerstrasse* as twilight faded into darkness. He drove on a bit, made a turn, and parked the stolen truck in an alley just a short walk from the basement beer-hall at *Friedelstrasse 24.* He wiped down the steering wheel, gear-shift, and door handles to obscure any fingerprints, and climbed out of the truck. He jogged to where he had parked his own car earlier in the day, and was relieved to find it still locked and intact.

He opened the trunk and removed his Colt Super Automatic with silencer. He slipped it into an inside pocket of his overcoat. All he had to do now was find Lohmann.

A few minutes of walking and he was at the entrance to the *Geisterkeller*. He descended the stairs, opened the door, and carefully poked his head into the smoky room. He did not want Lohmann to see him, but in truth had little to worry about: the East German had been celebrating his successful five-thousand-dollar KGB deal with many glasses of the finest black-market champagne, and he was quite drunk. As if that weren't enough, he had two attractive blondes on his arm to further distract him.

Apparite motioned a gaunt but pretty blonde waitress over to him.

"See that fat man with the two women?" he asked her in German.

"Yes—he is having *some* party tonight!"

"I see that. Tell him an old friend is waiting outside to make a deal. A deal that would mean for him more than ten thousand West-marks." Apparite gave the waitress one hundred dollars in cash. She nearly jumped in surprise.

"Oh, yes—thank you, sir. I will hurry!"

She leapt into action a bit more quickly than Apparite expected, forcing him to dash up the cellar stairs and onto the walk. He took a few steps down the street and leaned against a dimly lit lamp-post with his back facing the stairwell. He removed his pistol from his coat and made himself ready. A few seconds later, he heard the sound of heavy footsteps coming from the direction of the cellar stairs—somewhat random and irregular footsteps, like those of a drunken man—which he then heard coming down the walk in his direction.

"Who wants to see me?" slurred Lohmann in German. "I'm always ready to make a good deal!"

Apparite turned around the lamp-post and held his pistol out in front of him. Lohmann put his hand to his mouth in shock and vomited on the walk.

"Surprised to see me, eh, *Herr* Lohmann?" Apparite said pointedly in English. "Lost your appetite for champagne, I see?"

Without a word, Lohmann raced down the street and turned into an alley. Apparite ran after him, divining the German's intent: the check-point at the *Zimmerstrasse* was only a block or two away. He hoped to outrun Apparite to it.

But Lohmann was drunk and his footing was lost when he awkwardly stepped on a stone. He hit the ground with arms outstretched, taking the skin off his palms, leaving them bloody and stippled with grit and small pebbles. He staggered to his feet and clumsily lurched forward.

Pheewt! went Apparite's silenced pistol as it spat out a bullet. The German fell onto the pavement as if pulled down by an invisible rope attached to the waist. He clutched the back of his left thigh, but the sound Apparite heard coming from him wasn't a cry of pain. Instead, it was the pathetic, drunken weeping of a man who knew he was about to die.

Lohmann stood unsteadily. He planted himself onto his good right leg and limped spastically down the alley. He fell again but with great effort raised himself up against the brick wall of a nearby building. Crying, he continued to stumble down the alley, his body turning around and around as he leaned and rolled against the building for support, his hands splaying against it in loud *smacks!* His ruddy, sweating face was contorted with fear.

Pheewt! Lohmann clutched his left arm with his right, and cried out in pain. He panted for a few seconds and lurched onward.

Apparite walked purposefully toward Lohmann, the distance between them shrinking as he slowly though steadily accelerated his pace. And as he did, his anger rose—more than anything, John Apparite despised a betrayal of trust and duty. He ran his tongue around his mouth to bring up saliva for use at the opportune moment. He took aim and squeezed the Super Automatic's trigger once more.

Pheewt! Lohmann staggered forward one more step and collapsed onto the ground, his other thigh struck with a slug. His weeping could be heard echoing throughout the alley, but pity was not stirred in Apparite's heart; not after nearly meeting his own end from the man's filthy, measureless greed.

"This is what men like you deserve," said Apparite. He spat in Lohmann's pain-contorted face, and with a final *pheewt!* put a bullet into the East German's heart. He returned his pistol to his coat.

"Greedy son of a bitch." He dragged the lifeless Lohmann to a cellar stairwell and threw him over the edge. The darkness enveloped the dead body like a man being pulled under a mass of still, black water.

"Hmm—I did not see that in you," said a calm, Slav-inflected voice. To Apparite's surprise, the words had been spoken in English.

Apparite pulled his pistol in a single quick motion and turned. He found himself standing not just face to face but gun-barrel to gun-barrel with Konstantin Zhdanovich, the KGB agent.

"Do not shoot," said the Russian. "Let us talk. *In English,* thank you. I know you are American, so please not waste time pretending."

The Russian motioned at the base of the alley's brick wall with his pistol.

"Please, sit."

Apparite complied. He sat down with his back against one side of the alley while Zhdanovich did the same against the other. But though each man remained cooperative and calm, neither seemed willing to put down his pistol. The barrel of each stayed pointed at the other's heart.

Zhdanovich laughed. "Much like our countries, eh? United States and Soviet Union—guns out, ready to shoot. We are in perfect *balance!*"

"I won't shoot if you won't," said Apparite.

"Let us try something," Zhdanovich said with amusement. "I count three; we put pistols on ground same time."

"Okay."

"One—two—*three.*"

But neither man moved a muscle. Both weapons remained aimed and steady.

There were two seconds of tense silence and then both men laughed aloud. Each slowly laid his pistol onto the ground, watching the other do the same.

"Why did you kill him?" Zhdanovich asked.

"He betrayed me."

"Why would he do that?"

"Why do people do anything?" Apparite said. "He did it for what he believed in."

"And what was that? Tell me—what would a man like Lohmann believe in?"

"Money."

Zhdanovich laughed. "Yes—we *all* believe in that! I think you are agent of American CIA, so I have curious to know: for what do *you* believe?"

"I believe in my duty," Apparite responded. "Fortunately for you, my duty at this moment does not include killing you. Instead, I think it is to talk to you, find out what you know. And you?"

"It is same." Zhdanovich paused in thought. "But is more," he added.

"There always is, with people like us."

"I am going to speak—how you Americans say—*frankly?* Straight scoop, eh?"

"Alright," said Apparite. "Let me have it."

"This is what I know. You are CIA. You come to East Berlin to kill KGB who kill defectors. You kill many men yesterday, but do not kill man you most want."

"Go on," said Apparite. "I'm listening."

"I will say something that surprise you: I, too, wish kill that man. You know who I speak."

Apparite concealed his astonishment as best he could. "Yes, I think I know."

"His name is Viktor. He is SMERSH, as are men you kill yesterday. Like you, I am sent to kill him."

"Why?" asked Apparite. "Why would you kill him? Aren't you on the same side?"

Zhdanovich shook his head. "You Americans do not know Soviet way! Three months past, First Secretary Khrushchev make speech; big speech denounce Stalin. Since then, much fighting in Moscow, *many* fights. Viktor was big Stalinist; when he heard speech, he go mad. My people think he will kill Khrushchev, maybe soon. Maybe when Khrushchev travel into Germany on way back to Russia. Prime Minister Bulganin, he tells me to find Viktor, to kill Viktor before this may happen. Viktor is threat to *us* as much threat to you. I wait in Berlin three month for him—but I wait also for you."

"For me?" Apparite asked. He wondered how much Zhdanovich knew, recognizing this moment as the most critical in their conversation so far. If the Russian knew too much about him or his agency, Apparite would have to make a lunge for his pistol. If so, both of them would likely end up dead.

"Yes—for you," said Zhdanovich, "or someone like you. I knew Americans would send assassin to kill him. They try in London last year, but Viktor escape and American assassin is

poisoned and die. I have other reason to kill Viktor, but before I
tell, I will give you my gun so there is no, hmm, *misunderstanding.*"

The Russian placed his pistol onto the ground. With his foot,
he pushed it away until it was close to Apparite. He held up his
hands where Apparite could see them.

"Yesterday, you kill my cousin."

Apparite remained silent.

"He was tall, have hair like mine, eyes very blue—like a German. You remember?"

Apparite nodded *yes.*

"Do you know reason I give you weapon?" the Russian
continued. "Is to show I will not kill you for this. But you ask
yourself why, yes?"

"Yes," said Apparite. "Why would you let me live? You
could've easily killed me earlier. Why didn't you?"

Zhdanovich rested his back a little further onto the alley's
brick wall; it was a gesture that hinted at a relaxation in his tension, followed by the smile of one remembering happier times.

"I love my cousin; we play as children in Moscow. We go
Dynamo football match, hunt in forest. He was very amusing as
child—make good joke so adult even laugh. But after war, he
changes; he is SMERSH. He serve only Viktor; he does not
make joke.

"I do not blame you for his death, my friend," he went on.
"You do your duty—like lion who kills to feed cubs. Is what lion
is meant to do—is what lion *must* do. So, I do not blame you."
He stopped to wipe the sweat from his face and resumed speaking, though very slowly and with emphasis.

"For his death, I . . . blame . . . *Viktor.*"

"I'm sorry," Apparite said. "I didn't know."

"Would it have made difference? I think not. You do as you
are told. I do as I am told."

"Yes," answered Apparite. "That's the way it is. If my duty was to kill him, then I would do it. If your duty was to kill me, then you would do that, too." After Zhdanovich nodded in understanding, Apparite stuck out his leg and pushed the Russian's pistol back to its owner with his foot.

"Thank you," Zhdanovich said. He picked up his weapon. "But you wonder why I not kill Viktor myself, do you not?"

"It crossed my mind."

"You see, we Soviets are not good at secrets. Perhaps that surprise you! If SMERSH discover I kill Viktor, there will be 'big smell,' as you Americans say."

"Big *stink*," said Apparite. "But I know what you mean."

"I need to avoid such a thing. After 'big stink' comes purge, and purge is no good. I need help by someone like you so no one find out. We work together to do this—like comrades, eh?"

Apparite laughed. "If anyone ever told me I'd be comrades with a Russian agent in the field, I'd have had them put away."

"Same for me with CIA!"

"I have a plan to kill Viktor," said Apparite. "But I need your promise not to interfere with one part of it. It involves a girl. If we kill Viktor, then you leave the girl alone."

Zhdanovich scratched an itch on his face with the silencer-tipped barrel of his Makarov pistol—obviously, thought Apparite, he has a high degree of confidence in its safety mechanism!—and grunted in agreement.

"Best not to say too much," the Russian said. "Less I know is better. But I tell you: if you kill Viktor, I not kill you for cousin, and I not care about girl. That is promise—*that* is how much I want kill Viktor." Zhdanovich pulled his tin cup and flask of vodka from his coat. He poured a measure of it and handed the cup to Apparite.

"We drink on deal, eh?" Zhdanovich rose from his sitting position.

"Sure," said Apparite, standing. "We'll drink on it."

They raised their drinks and interlocked elbows in the traditional gesture of goodwill and fellowship. Each then drained his vodka in a single swallow: Apparite from the cup, Zhdanovich directly from the flask.

As Apparite drove to Christiane's apartment to take her into the West, he pondered the Russian's final point in their unlikely conversation. To Zhdanovich, as long as Viktor ended up dead, little else seemed to matter, and Apparite knew that it was imperative he feel the same. He would do his best to save Christiane, but if it came down to saving her or killing Viktor, Apparite knew which one would have to come first. On this mission, there could be no stopping to stanch the bleeding of any unfortunate bystanders.

Seventeen:
Into the West

Apparite drove his new automobile, which D had nicknamed the "VS-VW" (for "Very Special Volkswagen"), to Christiane's apartment. The success of this part of his mission would depend as much on the car as it would the persons involved, and he was careful not to attract any unwanted attention, nor put himself or his invaluable vehicle in harm's way. While he suspected the Soviets remained unaware of Christiane's intentions, he could not be sure of it; he would have to thoroughly scout the area around her building before ascending the stairs which led to her apartment. And once the two of them had left it, there could be no turning back.

He parked the "VS-VW" around the corner from her building. Taking his silencer-tipped pistol, he quietly shut the car's door and began his careful reconnaissance. He circled her building at a distance to scan the area for anyone or anything that raised his suspicions.

A few persons were taking an evening stroll, but looked innocuous enough: couples on dates, a mother leading a child by the hand, an elderly man walking a small, mangy-appearing dog. But Apparite turned a corner and saw what he had been dreading. Standing in an alley a short distance from Christiane's building was a man smoking a cigarette, and though this in itself did not alarm Apparite, the way the man smoked it was of extreme concern: although his head moved from side to side as he took puffs from the cigarette, his eyes never left the door which led to her apartment.

Apparite walked around the block to the other side of Christiane's building, only to find yet another man whom he pegged as an enemy agent. This man was leaning against the wall of a nearby alley, but instead of smoking a cigarette, as was his colleague, he was drinking from a half-empty bottle. And though his head tipped upwards as he drank from his liquor bottle, his gaze also never left Christiane's building.

How much did they know? Was this a routine surveillance of a worker with access to confidential Karlshorst information, or did they have real suspicions of what she was about to do? But the presence of these men did reassure Apparite of one important thing: Christiane was alive and well. No one performs two-man surveillance on a dead person.

Unless they were waiting for *him*, he realized. He positioned himself so he could see Christiane's window from the street. It was illuminated, thank God; in fact, he could see the graceful curve of her silhouette through the flimsy, makeshift curtains. She was most definitely alive—but how much longer would she stay that way?

He retreated into the shadows. He situated his weapons so they were exactly how he wanted them, and approached the man smoking the cigarette. The smoker would be target number one; the drinker, number two.

Apparite took a cigarette out of his pocket. "May I have a light?" he asked in German.

"No," the man said sharply. "Go away."

"Please—I'll give you one for a light." Apparite held up a pack of Lucky Strikes so the Soviet could see them. "*American cigarettes—I'll even give you two!*"

The East German cigarettes that most Soviets got tasted like mothballs and smelled like truck exhaust, and the temptation proved too strong for the man to resist, regardless of his other duties at hand.

"American cigarettes?" he said. He looked around suspiciously, as if he feared his supervisor might be watching and what he was doing was breaking some rule, and then held out a match. "For two." He struck the match against the side of his shoe.

At the peak moment of the Soviet's distraction with the match, Apparite struck. He brought his free hand around, in which he held his switch-blade knife. He whipped the blade across the Soviet's throat, expertly slicing through the larynx, depriving the man of his voice. From now on, the killing would be done in near-silence. Apparite dropped the cigarettes he had been holding and whipped his silencer-tipped pistol from his coat. He put a bullet into the Soviet's blood-covered chest with a soft, muffled *pheewt!* and the KGB man crumpled to the ground, lifeless.

Apparite removed the dead man's pistol from his over-coat and tossed it into a street drain. With some effort he dragged the body down the alley, hiding it behind a group of overflowing trash bins. He retrieved his cigarettes, lit one with another of the Soviet's matches, and placed it in his mouth. He then moved onto his next target, slipping a small object from his coat into his left hand as he walked.

The drinking man was now leaning against the wall in a more relaxed posture, though his eyes remained locked onto Christiane's building. Apparite adopted a drunken stagger and approached the man, the lit cigarette dangling precariously from his mouth.

"Say *kamrade,* can you spare a drink for a fellow Leningrader?" he said, slurring his Russian.

"Go away, drunken fool. I'm busy." The Russian made a shooing gesture with his hand.

"Oh!" said Apparite, raising his voice in pitch, staggering

within two feet of the Russian. "You must be from Kiev—I hear the people there are very irritable! Something about the water!"

"If you don't want to get hurt, then go away, you drunken ass!" The angry Russian stood and Apparite went into action.

He dropped to the ground and foot-swept the Russian's leg, throwing him backward onto the pavement. The rear of the Russian's head struck the cement, stunning him; but before he could cry out, Apparite had his garrote-wire wrapped around his enemy's throat. A few tugs on it and the Russian was dead, his head nearly severed from his body.

Apparite pocketed the weapon and hid the dead man down a flight of cellar stairs. He performed one last reconnaissance of the area, but there was no longer anything suspicious. He crossed the street to the entrance of Christiane's building, stopped briefly to sweep the immediate area with his gaze—again, nothing—and opened the door. He entered the building and bounded up the steps to her apartment.

"Christiane!" he whispered, knocking lightly on her door. "Christiane!" He heard footsteps and the door opened.

"Hans!" she cried. She threw her arms around him. They kissed briefly and she ushered him into her apartment.

"We have no time," said Apparite. "Come with me."

"I mailed my things to the address you gave me," she said. "And I brought you this." She handed Apparite a parcel wrapped loosely in brown paper. He undid the string and opened it. "I don't think they noticed," she continued, "but they were acting very strange today. Aren't you proud of me?" She was beaming.

Apparite counted the sheets that she had stolen from the telephone directory. He had hoped that she could take five or ten pages of the most-used numbers, but when he counted past twenty-five, thirty, and then thirty-five, he could hardly contain himself. He reached the final page and spoke.

"Forty-two?" he said, incredulous. "How many pages are in the entire thing?"

She laughed aloud. "Forty-*three!* I left them page one and replaced the others with the same kind of paper. I even tricked the attendant into letting me put it in the lock-box so he couldn't inspect it—it was perfect! They won't discover anything is wrong until tomorrow morning."

Perfect from her perspective, thought Apparite. But someone on the other side had been suspicious enough of her behavior to have her watched, and he had been forced to kill two men because of it. And yet he knew it was worth the trouble: forty-two pages of classified telephone connections and identities would be a treasure trove of intelligence.

"You're incredible," he said to her. Seeing the pride in her face brought forth all of the emotions he was trying to suppress. He embraced her, kissing her deeply and with feeling until he snapped back suddenly into the reality of their situation: he could not afford any further displays; he *had* to maintain his distance. He let her go from his embrace, keeping her at arm's length in an effort to defuse his emotions.

"Come with me," he said. He led her out of the apartment. He had expected a show of emotion or perhaps even weeping as she forever left her home behind her, but she did not shed any tears, nor betray any signs of sadness. If anything, she seemed to be manifesting a quiet elation that showed only in the lightness of her steps and in the wide smile on her face.

He stopped at the front door of her building but did not discern anything out of the ordinary—good. With luck it might be an hour before the Soviet agents' bodies were discovered, so if he got her to the border in the next fifteen to thirty minutes, they would almost certainly be home-free.

He took her to the dark brown "VS-VW." To outward appearances, it looked to be identical to the thousands of other Volkswagens in Berlin, but Apparite knew better: it had been specially adapted for a job like this one. He drove the two of them to a deserted alley a few blocks away.

"I need to hide you before we reach the check-point," he said. He let her out of the car. "Men were watching you today. If the Soviets catch us, we will be killed."

"Where can I hide? It's such a small car."

Apparite took her hand and brought her around to the driver's-side door.

"This is a special automobile I've borrowed just for tonight. You can hide in here." He pulled back a hidden flap in the driver's seat, which had cleverly been enlarged and redesigned so that a person could fit within a special cavity inside it. "You're small-framed, so you should be able to squeeze yourself in."

Christiane whipped her head upwards at Apparite in a gesture of shock: no one could possibly fit *inside* the front seat of a Volkswagen. It seemed insane to even try! And yet the expression on her face remained unaffected—she continued to smile and her eyes were unblinking. He had never seen such strength in a woman.

"Yes," she said without emotion, "I should fit just fine."

Apparite fully opened the flap and removed a large, contoured piece of foam from inside the wood-framed, felt-lined cavity. The seat was an impressive feat of engineering. The hidden compartment began in the back-rest of the driver's seat, which had been deepened to accommodate the human head and torso. It continued on down even into the chassis, which the engineers had lowered in specific locations to increase the cavity's capacity. The front passenger's seat had no cavity within it, but had been enlarged in the same proportion as that on the driver's side to keep the interior to scale. This preserved the illusion of symmetry, so that even a person experienced in the appearance of Volkswagens would not likely notice the alterations.

D hadn't been kidding when he'd said it was a very special car, thought Apparite. He took the foam insert and hid it behind a pile of rubble in the alley. By the time he returned to the car, Christiane had nearly contorted herself into the tiny compartment, though she had torn her dress in the process. She looked up at him with an odd little grin and laughed.

"I need to bend my knees *just* so," she said, "and then turn my head all the way to the left, with my arms at my sides. But I think I'm going to fit—it's incredible. I feel like I'm in some sort of magician's trick!"

"In a way you are," Apparite said. "You'll disappear in the East only to magically reappear in the West."

She wriggled her svelte frame into place.

"You know, for once I'm glad we never get enough to eat!" She looked up at him and smiled.

Apparite bent over and kissed her, defying his internal directive to distance himself from her. He then knelt and held her hand as he spoke.

"This is going to be tough, Christiane. It may not hurt much now, but the longer you stay twisted around like that, the more pain you'll have. But you cannot make any noise, no matter how uncomfortable it might get. Breathe slow and deep—the material in the seat was specially made so you can get air through it. In fifteen minutes, we should be across the border."

"I'll be alright," she told him. "Don't hurry on my account. Better to go slow than give us away!"

Apparite securely closed and concealed the flap, sealing her in. He climbed in the car and carefully leaned back against the seat. There was a little *oomph!* of discomfort from Christiane when he put his full weight against it, but the only sound afterward was the barely detectable noise of his hidden passenger breathing evenly and quietly behind him.

He took a small packet from the glove compartment and

opened it. It contained yet another disguise, though different than the one he'd used for the event the night before. He removed the false goatee and squat moustache from the packet, and, using the rest of his supply of theater glue, carefully attached them to his face. He put on a pair of brown neutral-lens glasses and a similarly colored fedora, and adjusted them in the rear-view mirror until he had attained the look he desired.

He started the car and drove down the street toward the nearest acceptable check-point: the Brandenburg Gate. The symbolic Gate had been nearly as oppressed and misused as the people of East Berlin, so it only seemed fitting that this would be the place where Christiane would cross into freedom.

When he saw the check-point on the famous *Unter den Linden* come into view, he took his identity papers in hand. He soon found himself in a line of cars waiting to cross into the West, but there seemed to be an unusual number of Soviet soldiers and Vopos checking them, and it worried him. Apparite counted ten cars in front of him, and then a few minutes later there were eight, and then six, and then four. Any moment now the game would begin.

"Your papers," said an approaching Vopo. Apparite smiled at him, handing them over when he reached the car.

"Your purpose in going to the West?" the Vopo asked in an officious tone.

"I live there. Look at the address on the form."

"An address on a form can be falsified," the Vopo said, acting as if *he* was the one being annoyed with obtuse questions. "Your work permit, please."

"I already gave it to you," answered Apparite. "It's the one—"

"I have it—I have it," he said, irritated at some perceived slight—this Vopo seemed an unusually sensitive sort. He turned and waved a machine-gun carrying Soviet soldier over to him.

There were two important rules about crossing check-points,

and Apparite consciously reminded himself of them: he had to remain calm, and he had to remain in the car. If the threats got too hot, or the questions too probing, he'd have to drive away and chance getting shot. Anything was better than getting out of the car and subjecting it to search.

The soldier reached the Volkswagen. He looked intently at Apparite's face and took a photograph from his pocket. It was grainy and blurred, with evidence of air-brushing around the eyes and upper lip. Despite its poor quality, Apparite immediately recognized the man's face:

It was his.

Obviously, they *had* gotten a picture of him at the event—though only of his disguised face, thank God. He hoped his new disguise would be as effective as the old one.

"You seen man?" the Russian asked in very poor German.

Apparite leaned toward the photograph, adjusting his glasses for effect.

"Hmm, no—he looks a bit like my cousin, but he lives in Bremen."

"You sure? Is important. I have other picture of him with moustache and glasses." He showed Apparite the un-doctored version of the picture.

Apparite readjusted his glasses and held out his hand. "Let me take a closer look." The soldier handed him the photographs. "No—no, I'm afraid I don't know him. Who is he?"

"He is murderer, criminal," the soldier said. He took the photographs back from Apparite. "He sometimes use disguise—but we will catch him. Is only matter of time."

The soldier turned and spoke in lowered tones with the Vopo. They approached the car together.

"Your work permit says you sell electrical supplies," the Vopo said. "Are you carrying any at the moment?"

"No," Apparite said. "I was at a meeting."

"And where *was* this meeting?"

This was getting uncomfortable. Two cars that were behind him in line had already been waved through the check-point, so it was disconcerting to see the attention his little VW was beginning to attract: other Vopos were now staring at him, and more Soviet soldiers seemed to be mustering nearby. He hated being the focus of attention, particularly when each of the men he saw probably carried a copy of those blurry but incriminating photographs.

"Near '*Alex*,' " answered Apparite. "But we got nowhere. You're in the civil service—you know what meetings are like!" He tried to embellish his joke with a laugh but managed only a meek smirk instead.

The Vopo turned to the soldier and spoke to him in German.

"Maybe we should do a search," Apparite overhead him saying. "Electrical supplies were stolen yesterday in Friedrichshain, and the day before in Pankow."

"Black-marketeers—I have heard this," answered the Russian in his broken-German. "But this is *small* car—where would they hide? If *I* steal electrical supplies, I bring back in big, big truck. Not little German constipated s--t car."

For goodness' sake, thought Apparite, *that's what this is about?* If he made it through the check-point and got back to the safehouse, he thought he might throttle D for (albeit unknowingly) suggesting the alias of an electrical supplier in the midst of an apparent epidemic of East Berlin electrical supply heists! He adjusted his coat to bring the handle of his Colt pistol within reach, and took the switch-blade from his belt. If asked to leave the car, he would need to kill his interrogators as quickly as possible. After that, he would have to rely on the strength and speed of his little German "constipated s--t car" to escape. In other words, he and Christiane would probably get killed.

"I am hungry as bear," said the Soviet. "If we search this s--t car we be here all night. Pass him through with warning." The Vopo nodded and turned to Apparite.

"You may pass," he said. Apparite let loose his knife and removed his now-empty hand from inside his coat. "But I am giving you a warning."

"A warning—for what?" asked Apparite, unable to resist a jab: the Vopo was just the kind of autocrat every American naturally despised.

"Just—just a warning!" the Vopo said. "And don't do it again!" he added awkwardly. He motioned the little VW through the check-point as Apparite laughed aloud, joining, he could hear, the many Soviet soldiers who had also enjoyed watching the Vopo squirm.

Apparite drove as quickly as he could down the *Strasse de 17 Juni,* turning onto a side-street and then an alley a quarter-mile past the check-point. He jumped out of the car, opened the flap in the side of the seat, and helped Christiane from her hiding place.

Her face was flushed and sweaty, and numerous deep, red indentations were present on her limbs where she had been compressed by the weight of Apparite's body. And yet despite the torn dress, mussed hair, and general dishevelment she had suffered on her journey, she looked almost impossibly beautiful to Apparite—especially in the look of happiness on her face as she set foot onto the soil of West Berlin, and freedom.

"I feel like I've come home again, even though I've never lived here before." She threw her arms around Apparite. "Thank you, oh thank you," she said, dissolving into tears. Apparite held her tight, feeling the unbridled joy of her new-found freedom, but the moment was bittersweet. For even as he held her, he wondered how he was going to push her away, as he knew eventually he must.

EIGHTEEN:
A DYNAMO FAN

"That photograph—do you know how they got it?" asked D.

Apparite and the liaison were sitting in the safe-house kitchen discussing the situation over tea and coffee. Christiane, exhausted from the earlier events and stresses of the evening, had been put to bed shortly after her arrival in the modified VW.

"They must've had other cameras than just the one in the ceiling," answered Apparite. "Luckily it's a terrible picture. I don't think they've been able to put the whole story together."

"Yet," added D. "But they will. When they find the two dead KGB in the car and the others by the apartment, everything will come clear. And then they'll be absolutely mad to get you. When that happens, can we really trust Zhdanovich? Won't he want to kill you as much as Viktor, given the havoc you've wreaked on the KGB since you've been here?"

Apparite thought on the gregarious Russian, running their previous conversations through his mind. "We can trust him," he concluded. "His focus is Viktor and *only* Viktor at this point. But I see what you're driving at."

"I hope you're right, because you're on your own for the event tomorrow. For security reasons, I cannot be involved or even in the area. It'll just be you, the Russian, and the girl."

"As long as everything goes to plan," said Apparite, "I won't need anyone else. If Zhdanovich passed along what I told him to, then all Viktor will think is that we're exchanging the girl to move her to a new safe-house. For something like that, he won't bring more than another agent or two. And then we'll have him."

"And what if it goes wrong?" asked D. "You cannot be taken."

"I'd have to kill myself to erase the trail. I'm prepared for that."

"And the girl?"

"She doesn't know anything," Apparite said defensively. "Leave her out of it."

"If she's taken she'll be tortured."

Apparite gave the only sensible answer to the liaison's statement.

"You're right: I'd have to kill her, too."

"Yes, you would. I therefore suggest you put all of your energies into *not* failing."

"I'm meeting Zhdanovich in an hour to finalize the plan," said Apparite. "The event will begin at twenty-one hundred tomorrow. If I'm not back thirty minutes later, you can assume I'm dead."

"If you're not back in *fifteen* I think it's safe to assume you're dead."

"I know what you mean," Apparite replied. "And I agree— whatever happens will happen quickly."

"You're in a tight spot, Apparite. I hope you appreciate that. You've got this girl you're in love with, and you're not just going to have to put her in harm's way to trap Viktor, you'll eventually have to leave her behind at the end. To top it off, you're going to have to trust a known KGB agent to help you do it—despite the fact you're the Soviets' most wanted man in Europe at the moment.

"But what worries me most is this girl of yours," continued D. "You've *got* to stop seeing her; every time you do, it makes it harder for you to leave her. I blame myself for not being more aggressive in this matter, for letting you get too close to her." He put down his cup of tea, a gesture that hinted at the importance of what he was about to say.

"I've had to make a decision."

"What decision?" asked Apparite in a sharp tone. "What have you done?"

"Your immediate emotional reaction only reinforces the necessity of my actions. The girl is gone. I've already moved her to another safe-house."

Apparite put down his cup of coffee and ran up the stairs. Christiane was no longer lying on the bed.

"I'm sorry, Apparite," D called up to him. "It had to be done. When you were changing, I slipped her out of the house."

Apparite turned and walked slowly back down the stairs. His flushed face showed his anger.

"It's for the best," the liaison continued. "I told the girl you would take her to the airport tomorrow night, but that you could not stay with her, for fear of her safety. She understood."

Apparite sat at the dining room table and put his head in his hands. He took a few deep breaths to calm himself. "Just tell me what to do," he said. "Until I met her, all I wanted was to do my job. I never thought . . ." His voice trailed away but soon found its strength. "I'm sorry—I know you're right. We were doomed from the start. I don't know what the hell I was thinking."

Apparite raised his head, his expression one of disbelief.

"She still thinks my name is *Hans!*" he went on. "Can you believe it? But damn it, it's not like it would make a difference, anyway. As soon as she learns who I really am—or who you *tell* her I am—she'll hate me for it. And I can't blame her."

"Maybe at first," D said gently, "but sooner or later she might want you back, and you'd want to be with her. Where would that leave us? We'd probably have to eliminate you." He paused to take another sip of tea and then spoke with unusual firmness.

"After the mission, you can never see her again."

Apparite nodded: he knew it was true. But as much as he dreaded the pain that awaited him at the end of his mission, the fact that he could not possibly avoid it was even worse. He felt totally helpless—it *was* going to happen, as certain as a man's mortality. It was a feeling he despised.

"There's only one thing you can do," said D. "And that's to kill Viktor, complete your mission, and let her go. In the end, she'll be better off, anyway. We'll set her up someplace where she'll never have to worry about the Soviets again, and where she'll be comfortable."

Apparite spoke almost at a whisper. "I guess I'll have to settle for that. Who knows? Maybe killing Viktor will be enough for me. A month ago it certainly would have."

"*That's* the idea," said D. "Concentrate on the mission. Think of how you'll feel when Viktor is dead. Don't think about the girl! I have a hunch that when you see Viktor up close, nothing else will matter but killing him."

"Maybe you're right." Apparite tried to picture the SMERSH agent in his mind so he could redirect his anger and pain. "Maybe you're right."

"You look unhappy, my friend!" said Zhdanovich.

He climbed into Apparite's new car, a black Mercedes. Apparite was a wanted man, so his rendezvous with the Russian would necessarily be confined to the automobile—even in West Berlin it would be unwise to have him out on the streets. But there were advantages to that as well, for this afforded both privacy and mobility. Privacy was always an important consideration for men like them, and the mobility allowed them to scout the location for the event the next evening: a small café a few blocks off of the *Kurfürstendamm* (or the *"Ku'damm,"* as Berliners called it).

"The death of our enemy is coming," the Russian continued. "You should have smile."

Apparite put the car in gear and pulled away from the *Reinickdorferstrasse U-bahn* station where Zhdanovich had been awaiting him. The Russian lit two cigarettes and held one out for Apparite.

"I don't smoke," Apparite said. "Sorry."

Zhdanovich laughed. "More for *me* then!" He balanced the lit cigarette on the edge of the car's ash-tray.

"I have something to ask you," Apparite said. "Did you take my picture? I saw one at a check-point. I need to know if there are others."

"No, my friend. But I have seen picture, and you look awful! Even *with* moustache!" Zhdanovich grinned. "Not look like you; is very bad picture. Almost worthless! Best not to talk about. We must *trust* each other. But I ask you—did *you* take picture, too? Of me in alley, maybe?"

"No," responded Apparite in annoyance. "No, I didn't."

"Why so unhappy?" asked Zhdanovich. "So—what is word— *irritable?* Did your football club lose today or something? When Dynamo lose football match, I do not sleep!"

"Football?" Apparite said. "Oh, *soccer*—we don't have much of that in America. I'm a baseball fan." He wished Zhdanovich would quit fooling around and get to the mechanics of the mission; he was in no mood for games. He pulled the Mercedes to a halt at a stop-light and turned south toward the *Tiergarten.*

"Baseball—yes," the Russian said, intrigued. "That is what Americans like so much. Have you ever been to baseball match?"

"Baseball *game*—yeah, plenty," Apparite answered. His mood brightened some as he recalled the Senators game he'd just seen in New York. Thinking about baseball had always been a panacea for him in troubled times, and it was proving to be so again.

"Who is your team?" Zhdanovich asked with interest. "Tell me about them."

"The Senators—in Washington," Apparite answered, not really caring at this point if the KGB knew which baseball team he followed. "But they're usually terrible, even though they have great players. You should see Mickey Vernon hit a line drive— it's just a blur. You can even *hear* it go by—*woosh!* And fielding! Watching Yost stop a hard liner is something else." He broke a smile. "I can show you something interesting about the Senators. Would you like to see it?"

Zhdanovich nodded *yes.*

Apparite pulled the car to a stop at the curb. He reached into his coat and took out his wallet. He removed a small card from it, handing it to the Russian.

"*John-son—Washing-ton,*" Zhdanovich carefully intoned. He looked over at Apparite. "This Johnson—he is famous for baseball?"

"The most important person on a baseball team is the pitcher, and Walter Johnson was the best pitcher ever. He played for the Senators."

"He has signed this card—you know this man? This *Wal-ter John-son?*"

"No," said Apparite. "Right after my father died, someone sent it to me. I still don't know who. But I always carry it with me. It's like a lucky charm, I guess."

"I hope this *Wal-ter John-son* brings luck for you tomorrow," Zhdanovich said. He returned the card to Apparite. "Someday *I* would like to go to baseball match. I have seen in newsreel, but always the voice ruins: 'Capitalist American baseball players live like king while starving working man sit in cold! Ticket to Yankee match more than loaf of bread! Decadent Americans spend useless day at baseball field while poor suffer in street!' But I would like to see someday. Maybe *you* go to Russian football match someday, heh?"

"Tell me about that," Apparite said. He was enjoying the camaraderie of a fellow sports fan; no matter the sport or the country, they were the same everywhere. "The 'Dynamo'? Is that what you called them?" He put away his wallet and pulled the car back onto the road.

The Russian's face became very animated at Apparite's question. "Yes—the Dynamo of Moscow! Oh, too bad for your Senators to be terrible, because Dynamo are *best* football team in Russia! Number one! Russian Football Champion last year *and* year before—plus winner of Russian Cup, nineteen hundred fifty-three. If war with our countries end, I take you to see Dynamo, and you take me to see Senators. Even if they lose! Okay? I would like very much."

By golly, thought Apparite, this guy really is a kindred spirit, even if the team he follows sounds more like the Russian version of the Yankees than the Nats. He circled the Mercedes around the *Siegessäule,* the one hundred ninety-four foot-tall "Victory Column" in the middle of the *Tiergarten,* and continued driving southward.

"Yeah, let's do that," Apparite said. "Providing neither of us gets killed in the next twenty years and the Senators don't leave Washington. I've been worried about that happening recently."

"Your club leave Washington?" the Russian cried out. "How can you take? If Dynamo leave Moscow, I defect." Zhdanovich punctuated the statement with a laugh to show he was only joking (at least, Apparite *thought* he was only joking!), and took his flask from his over-coat. He poured a little vodka into his tincup and handed it to Apparite.

"We drink to Senators and Dynamo, and we drink to mission. And then talk about tomorrow, okay?" He snuffed his spent cigarette into the ashtray; leaning forward, he retrieved the one Apparite had declined and began puffing on it.

"Good," said Apparite. He balanced his drink in one hand while driving with the other. "I'll drink to all of that—but not until I've stopped the car!"

"Of course! You Americans never drink when you drive, so my advice for you is this: *never* drive in Moscow. You will be at disadvantage!"

Apparite laughed and pulled the car again to the curb. The two men locked elbows as they had done in the alley the night before, and downed their drinks. Apparite shook his head and coughed—he remained unused to hard liquor and had inhaled some of its vapors—and put the car into gear, pulling back onto the road.

"That had better be my only one," he said. "We've got laws against that back in the States, you know!"

"I think one is enough, too," Zhdanovich exclaimed. "You are bad enough driver *already!*" He took a moment to take another drink from his flask before returning it to its home in his coat. "I tell Karlshorst contact about girl who defect with you," he went on. "Their plan is for Viktor to intercept with two men. That is all I know; that is all they know. Now, please tell me rest of plan." He puffed on his cigarette, bringing its length down a full half-inch as its lit end flared bright red.

"I will take the girl to a small café near the *Ku'damm* at twenty-one hundred," answered Apparite. "I'm driving there now so we can check it out. It'll be closed by the 'health inspector' earlier in the day, so there won't be any civilians in it, but I'll unlock it ahead of time. If we aren't ambushed outside, then the girl and I will sit inside and wait for Viktor."

"And where I will be?" Zhdanovich said. He took another puff on his cigarette.

"You'll be positioned outside the café. I'll kill Viktor—he'll probably be in front, leading the way—and you kill the men with him. Is that possible?"

"Yes, is possible," the Russian answered. "But not *easy* kind of possible. Viktor come with SMERSH, and they are like cobra—strike quick; very deadly. We must have surprise."

"That is why the girl and I must seem unprotected and exposed. No disguises; no escorts or back-up—except you, and you'll stay hidden until the last possible moment. You must also kill them as silently as possible. No guns unless you have a silencer. No screams or warnings."

Zhdanovich sat in mute thought, smoking his cigarette until it nearly disappeared into his nicotine-stained fingers, leaving only the red tip visible. It was a wonder to Apparite that he did not continually burn his fingertips.

"Yes," Zhdanovich finally said, "it can be done. And I *like* kill in silence—is challenge, and I like challenge. But if I have injury and not escape, you must kill me. I must not be taken by SMERSH."

"It's good to hear you say that," said Apparite. "Because I was going to ask the same of you." He stopped the car. They had reached their destination, the *Café Schwarz,* which was located near the *Olivaerplatz.*

It was the only lit building on the dead-end street—the rest were offices or shops that had closed earlier in the evening—and through its large front picture-window Apparite could see people eating and drinking inside it. A large, sturdy-looking bar stood in the back of the café while a series of silver Art-Deco booths lined the sides; in the middle were about a dozen round café tables. Situated as it was in one of the most glamorous (and newly rebuilt) parts of West Berlin, the café was much more upper-class than the *Geisterkeller* or *Café Falke* had been in the East: the wait-staff were dressed in smart, new clothes; the majority of the clientele in elegant evening wear.

"How does it look?" Apparite asked.

"Very nice—I like go inside and have drink!"

"Not with me, I'm afraid. Maybe tomorrow night—afterwards."

"Yes, if we are alive, we have drink after," said Zhdanovich. "Is good place to meet Viktor. Can see everything good, but still places to hide." He pointed to two alleys near the café: each was about thirty feet from its front entrance, one on the left and one on the right. "I go there and wait," he said, indicating the alley to the left. "They will drive car to front—to kidnap you and girl, I think, will be their plan. I kill them when they leave car, and take car if need."

"Good," said Apparite. "It's better if they try and kidnap us—it will get them closer, and they'll be less likely to shoot at us. The girl and I will arrive at twenty-one hundred. By twenty-one thirty, it should all be over."

"That is good." The Russian opened the car door. "I think I have drink now in café. I will have one for you, too, my friend, since you cannot come with me!" Zhdanovich got out of the car and turned toward Apparite.

"Maybe someday, we meet again. Have drink, talk about Senators and Dynamo." He finished his cigarette and threw the butt onto the ground.

"I'd like that, Konnie," said Apparite. "But wait—I have something for you." He fiddled with the car's rear-view mirror and pulled out a small roll of film, only about four millimeters in width. "I thought you might like this—for a keepsake. I don't know if you have any recent pictures of yourself."

Zhdanovich let out a loud laugh after he realized what Apparite had done.

"And I have something for *you*." He tugged at the top-most button on his over-coat and a small roll of similar film dropped onto the walk. He picked it up and handed it to Apparite. "Since you look so handsome tonight," the Russian said, smiling, "I think you will want picture of yourself, too. *Das Vadanya, kamrade.*"

As Apparite drove away, he looked in the rear-view mirror: Zhdanovich laughed as he put the film into his pocket, lit yet another cigarette, and strolled into the café to get his drink. Of all the millions of Americans and Russians in this world, it seemed to Apparite that he and Zhdanovich were the only ones who really understood and trusted each other. The only use of it, however, would be to kill a SMERSH agent named Viktor— nothing more. There was something sad in that, he decided.

NINETEEN:
THE BREAK

The next twenty-four hours were uneasy ones for Apparite. Alone and with little to do except think, he soon became frustrated, for he could not control his thoughts as he wanted. Rather than concentrating on the mechanics of the evening's event, which he knew would be best, he instead had spent much of it re-enacting in his mind conversations he had had with Christiane, or picturing her face as she laughed, or trying to recall the sound of her lovely contralto voice.

He attempted to substitute this inability to control his thoughts with an excess of physical activity. He performed hours of calisthenics and stretching, broken only by the occasional meal or cup of coffee, during which he concentrated solely on the actions of eating or drinking. This effort to avoid conscious thought was almost as tiring as his exercises, and yet when he tried to take a nap in the late afternoon the sleep would not come.

Once evening approached, however, it became easier to keep his mind off of Christiane as the real preparatory work came upon him. His car had to be prepped, plus there were numerous maps of the café and immediate area to be reviewed as well. Lastly, Apparite had to carefully prepare his weapons for the event, a critical area to which he would have to pay particular attention.

For the first time in his experience, he did not have concerns of being searched by his enemies, so he could really be decked-out for it: "Dressed to the nines" was how D had termed it. Apparite would, of course, carry his Colt Super Automatic in his coat, but he would also have the miniature M1911 strapped to the inside of his right leg. The Super Automatic's clip would be filled with standard ammunition, while the small M1911's would contain two tetrodotoxin-filled rubber bullets followed by hollow-tipped rounds. As for knives, he would have the switchblade in his belt, and, as always, the all-metal throwing-knives in the soles of his shoes. Lastly, he would be equipped with hollow-shafted knives designed to inject deadly tetrodotoxin upon use. If deployed correctly, even a superficial puncture wound would prove fatal.

If it seemed an excessive arsenal for the killing of one man, it was only due to the uncertainties of the impending event. Apparite would not know which weapon would be best to use until the moment was upon him. He might have to kill Viktor from a distance or so close that he could smell his breath. He might have to kill in the presence of witnesses, where a quiet death from poison would be best, or in a back-alley, the two of them locked in solitary, deadly combat.

Apparite knew that killing Viktor would be enough of a challenge as it was, but approached impossibility if he had to dispatch two other SMERSH agents as well. For that part of it, he had to assume Zhdanovich would do the job. In a profession where trust was scarce, Apparite would have to place all of his in the hands of a former enemy. He might have worried about that under ordinary circumstances, but it was pointless now: the event had been set into motion. There was no room for second-guessing.

At 1900, Apparite ate a small meal. He had heard it was best to under-eat before an event in case one got "gut-shot" or stabbed in the abdominal cavity—it was easier for the surgeons to patch you up, with less chance of an infection—but his appetite was poor anyway, so after only a few bites of *wurst* and an old plate of *sauerbraten* he put his fork down for good. Overeating would have been the bigger challenge.

He drove to the café at 2000. There was but a single lit streetlamp on the darkened lane, and the café was dark. Only a couple of small nearby businesses remained open (and which would, he knew, close in just a few more minutes), and as this was a side-street that led to nowhere, there were no pedestrians in sight. D had picked the location for the event and had chosen well: a small riot could break out on this little street and it was doubtful anyone would even notice it.

Taking from his pocket the key D had given him, Apparite quickly exited the car, crossed the walk, and unlocked the café. He had planned on doing a brief walk-through, but had to hastily jump back into his car when he heard another vehicle approach. Worried that it could be the Soviets, he pulled the car away from the curb and slowly drove down the street, keeping his eyes locked onto his rear-view mirror. From behind him, a delivery truck pulled onto the street. It slowed, drove another fifty feet toward him, and stopped. A light came on in the cab—Apparite assumed its driver was lost and looking at a map—and the truck made an awkward 180-degree turn in the middle of the street, and drove away in the direction from whence it came. Probably not the enemy, thought Apparite.

Probably—but best not to linger, regardless.

He turned his own car around and drove back to the safehouse: Christiane was going to be dropped off at 2050 and the event would begin. But he was worried about those first few moments together: What would they talk about? What would she be thinking after having been taken from him so abruptly the day before?

No answers were forthcoming, nor would they be until she got in the car and they left for the event. But Apparite had decided on one thing for certain: he could not leave her believing he was a heartless German named "Hans Müller." If he could muster the courage to do it, he was going to tell her at least some measure of the truth about him: he was an American agent of Central Intelligence, and most importantly, that he had truly loved her. He could not leave her thinking anything else, regardless of his directives.

Apparite returned to the safe-house and waited. At 2049, a car pulled up to his door and sat at the curb, idling. The horn rang out once—pause—and sounded again. Apparite slipped on his dark brown over-coat and hat, and left the safe-house, briskly walking to the car. He opened the passenger's-side door. Christiane was sitting in the seat, wearing a long black dress covered by an unbuttoned, unbelted trench-coat. With the fashionable white hat she wore upon her head, she was dressed as sharply as a woman going to the *Staatsöper* on the *Unter den Linden*.

"I've missed you," she said in German.

"I've missed you, too." Apparite took her hand as she exited the car. "I wish we had more time, but I have to take you right away."

Her hand quivered in his and she shivered.

"Here," he said, buttoning her coat, "it's gotten quite cold."

They walked to his car; he opened the door for her.

"Thank you," she said. She climbed in, although her face showed a look of bewilderment as she did so.

Apparite entered the car from the driver's side, started it, and drove down the street. But he was far from comfortable, for he sensed that Christiane was on the edge of an outburst—questions, insinuations—and it alarmed him. Even her posture was significant: she was sitting bolt upright with her arms at her sides. Importantly, she was not looking at him.

"Where are you taking me?" she asked in an emotionless monotone, still looking straight ahead.

"We need to find you another place to stay—where it is safe. And then we'll get you out of Berlin. Probably tomorrow."

"Why can't you come with me?" She finally turned her head to look at him.

"I need to arrange for your airplane flight," answered Apparite. "The Soviets are looking for you—even in West Berlin it is not safe. I'll join you in a few days." She stirred in her seat, letting Apparite know that his answers were unsatisfactory.

"Hans, why don't I believe you? Tell me. Why don't I *believe* you?" Apparite had hardly driven three blocks and she was already becoming panicked and suspicious. This was precisely what he did not want to happen.

"It's—it's hard to explain." He would have to lie to her and he hated himself for it. He did not mind a deception against his enemies in the line of duty, but lying to this innocent girl was something else entirely. "I'm telling the truth, Christiane. It's just so hard to explain. You'll fly out of Berlin tomorrow and I'll join you later. You'll have to trust me."

How he hated abusing the word "trust" like that! He felt dirty saying it, as if he'd fallen into a deep cesspool and his efforts to climb out were only sinking him further into its filth.

She began to cry. Apparite was only a couple of blocks from the site of the event and he was losing her. He had to keep her calm until it had begun, but for what came after, he still had no firm plan. Best not to think about that: just figure out how to control Christiane before everything goes to hell. That was task number one at the moment.

"Christiane," he said gently, "I'm just trying to make sure you are safe. Please don't make a fuss right now. It might ruin everything, all of our plans to get you out of Berlin alive."

Her eyes widened at the sound of one word: *Our.*

"*Our*—yes, that is what I want to know, Hans," she said, rushing her words. "*Our* plans—whose are they? The Americans?

West German *Gehlen?* Who *are* you? I don't even know what you do!"

"You know me, Christiane—we've talked for hours! We've made love for hours!"

"Yes, we've talked—you've told me about your father; your hunting; your funny games as a child. But you haven't told me about *you!*" She shook her head in frustration. "I don't *know* you. I don't even know where you're *from!*" Tears fell freely from her face.

"Christiane, you've got to calm yourself!" Apparite said urgently. "Please—you'll get yourself killed."

"Killed? How can I get killed being driven from *here* to *there* to *here?* I'm spending all of my time in automobiles. It's ridiculous! *You're* ridiculous!"

Apparite was just one block from the café; he would be there in under a minute. Less than one block to go.

"Why aren't you *saying* anything?" she asked. "Why? We're in love—aren't lovers supposed to talk? When they dropped me off, you didn't even give me a kiss! You didn't want to hold my hand—I could tell."

Apparite sped up to reach the café as soon as possible; another half a block and he would be there. Without slowing he made the final turn, but then it happened: she opened the car door.

"Stop the car!" she said. "Stop it! I'm getting out! I need to get out!"

Wind rushed into the car through the open door; the sound of wheels grinding pebbles into the pavement became audible.

"Christiane, close the door! Now!"

But she was no longer listening to the man she thought was named "Hans Müller"; the man she thought she loved. She needed to get out of this car and think. She was willing to leap out of it, if that was the only way.

"I'm getting out." She prepared to jump but Apparite brought the car to a sudden, lurching halt. He reached over and grabbed her arm, but she had already positioned herself to exit the car and his grasp failed. Before he knew it she was gone, running down the street in the direction of the café.

"Stop, Christiane!" He leaped out of the car.

Apparite ran past the alley on the left of the café, but did not see Zhdanovich. Where the hell was he? Wasn't he supposed to be in the alley on the left side? Had he misjudged the man? But his thoughts soon turned to Christiane. She had run past the café, stopping about fifteen feet from the alley on the other side.

"Let's talk," said Apparite. "Stop and let's talk—I'll tell you everything." The street ended blindly, so he slowed to a walk. No matter how much of a lead Christiane had on him, he would eventually catch up to her. She had nowhere else to go.

She looked in his direction, put her head in her hands, and wept. Nearing her, Apparite reached into his over-coat's right inside pocket and gripped his pistol. It was after 2100 and something might happen at any moment. But listening as he walked, he heard no sounds other than her soft sobs and the skids and tramps of his own feet on the pavement.

"Please, Christiane," he said. "I have a key to the café. We can go inside and I can get you a drink."

She raised her head from her hands, nodded, and wiped the tears from her cheeks. She took a step toward Apparite but stopped, having heard a noise from the alley behind her. She unconsciously turned her head ever so slightly toward it.

It was a subtle gesture on her part, but it spoke volumes to Apparite: he knew that they were not alone.

"Christiane—get in the café!"

She turned her head back in Apparite's direction. The intense anxiety in his eyes told her that this was one command she needed to obey. Just as she took another step toward the café, a man stepped out of the alley holding a pistol. He aimed it at Christiane and fired.

TWENTY:
THE BLACK CAFÉ

Pheewt!

The Makarov pistol fired a silenced bullet and Apparite heard the all-too-familiar sound of metal piercing human flesh. Such a strange little noise, he'd always thought, like that of a boot stuck in deep mud that is suddenly pulled free. He had heard that sound many times in the past from his own body being penetrated by a slug, but this time it had originated from another's.

The body that had been struck was not Christiane's, however. Just as Viktor had raised his pistol, a man had leapt out of a deep doorway between her and the SMERSH agent, and it was this person who had taken the bullet, which had buried itself somewhere in the man's chest. The wounded man had struck the walk, rolled over the curb, and now lay motionless in the gutter.

It was Zhdanovich.

Christiane dove into the doorway from whence Zhdanovich came, and Apparite fired a shot at Viktor from his Super Automatic. The SMERSH agent flinched as the bullet hit him in the right chest, but he did not fall nor utter a sound. This was no surprise to Apparite. He knew from prior experience that Viktor never cried out in pain, no matter the wound.

Two SMERSH agents followed Viktor out of the alley. They ran down the street toward Apparite, for whom the battle slowed as his concentration intensified. Apparite ducked into the café's entryway, simultaneously taking an un-aimed shot at the Russian agents, praying that Christiane was not peeking out from her hiding place and putting herself in the line of fire. He heard the shot hit home with that odd, familiar sound, and discerned the noise of a body falling to the ground. He could not tell, however, to whom it belonged.

Apparite's blind shot had been a lucky one, for it had struck one of Viktor's SMERSH lackeys in the thigh, dropping him to the pavement. Apparite stepped out of the doorway with his pistol raised, ready to finish off whomever he had hit, but what he saw astonished him: Zhdanovich had somehow gotten to his feet and was fighting the remaining, unwounded SMERSH agent. Viktor had disappeared, along with the man whom Apparite had just wounded. Apparite guessed that they had slipped into another entryway to take cover.

Zhdanovich and the SMERSH agent were engaged in a fierce battle, trading karate blows and slashing at each other with knives. Apparite aimed his pistol but could not get a clear shot at the SMERSH agent for fear of hitting Zhdanovich, so he took a second course: as the way was clear (though not for long, he assumed, knowing Viktor's strength and resilience), he ran down the walk and quickly ducked into Christiane's hiding spot.

Despite his chest wound Zhdanovich brought a karate kick into his opponent's flank, and when the SMERSH agent clutched his side it provided an opening: Zhdanovich thrust his knife into his enemy's back, piercing the chest cavity. The wounded SMERSH man fell to the ground, gasping.

Zhdanovich suddenly jolted back at the left shoulder, taking a bullet after momentarily putting himself in Viktor's line of fire. But before Viktor could withdraw his exposed arm, Apparite quickly aimed his pistol and fired. An instant later, Viktor's weapon and two of his fingers were blown from his hand in a spray of red.

Having fallen to the ground, Zhdanovich had become locked in a death-grip with his opponent. He twisted the SMERSH man's head upwards and to the right while his enemy buried a knife into his flank. A low groan like the growl of an animal began to emanate from Zhdanovich's mouth as the SMERSH agent thrust the knife to the hilt inside him. It was an unnatural sound for a human, its pitch and intensity rising until it seemed to be coming from a supernatural being such as a ghost or demon when, with one final gasp, it stopped. And there was silence.

Zhdanovich let loose his grip and fell onto his back, but it was the SMERSH agent who was dead: with one final exertion, Zhdanovich had snapped his neck. The Russian crawled to the curb and threw himself under a nearby car, panting. Apparite felt pity for his courageous friend. He was going to die in the gutter, alone.

A voice cried out in broken English.

"Give us woman, American."

It was Viktor. He sounded as strong and intimidating as ever, apparently unaffected by his wounds.

"Go to hell," said Apparite, with an unmistakably American intonation. "*Ti u menea budesh' plakat' kak zjershina,* Viktor." *I will make you weep like a woman,* he added, repeating the words the SMERSH agent had said to him last year in the Reading Room.

"You're an *American?*" Christiane screamed in German at Apparite. "Who are you?" She was becoming increasingly hysterical. "Who *are* you?"

"Quiet!" Apparite yelled in English. "Be quiet!" He raised his outstretched palm to slap her, but when she saw it she became still. Apparite grabbed her by the arm and the two of them fled down the street and into the entryway of the café. "This is between you and me, Viktor," Apparite shouted. "Let the girl go and we'll have it out."

Viktor laughed loudly. The arrogance of it rankled Apparite.

"Let girl *go?*" the Russian said. "No. We take back to Karlshorst, and have our fun." Apparite heard rapid footsteps— the Russians were again on the move.

"You're not leaving here alive," said Apparite. "Not you or your *kamrade.*" He looked at Christiane and made a "one-two-three" gesture. At the count of "three," they slipped inside the café.

A moment later, a bullet shattered the front window, bringing all of its glass onto the floor and front walk with a loud crash. Apparite and Christiane ran to the back of the café and ducked behind the bar. A liquor bottle exploded above them after being hit with a slug; Apparite could taste brandy from the spray. He heard the sound of men shouting in Russian and decided to take a chance before they rushed him. If he could fell one of them with this shot, it would immediately even the odds. But if he could not . . .

Apparite leapt to his feet. Viktor's SMERSH colleague was standing on the walk with blood streaming down his wounded thigh, readying himself to fire another shot into the café.

Time stretched and slowed, until it seemed like a minute was passing between each of Apparite's pounding heartbeats. He raised his gun in front of him, the white reflection from the light of the street-lamp outside moving down the barrel like the slow overflow of milk over the lip of a tall glass. Brandy dripped from the tip of the Super Automatic in slow, tear-like drops; they clung to the end of the barrel, elongating gradually until the pull of gravity exceeded the molecular grip of the drop's base, and then fell to the floor.

The lids of the SMERSH agent's eyes narrowed, like shades being lowered by the pull of a cord as he concentrated the ambient light to better see his enemy in the shadows of the café, the barrel of his pistol elevating as he took aim. But Apparite's finger had been squeezing the trigger from the instant he had stood, and it was this that would make the difference.

Apparite felt the initial resistance of the trigger mechanism; that tug of tension and friction that the muscles of his forefinger were just beginning to overcome. Then a loosening of the tension was perceptible and the trigger began to move, his forefinger and thumb striving to meet the other in opposition. He felt a slight recurrence of tension at the point where the firing-pin briefly resisted release, but the resistance soon dissipated and the pistol fired.

Much of the force of the bullet was sent into the silencer baffles, and some of it turned into the recoil Apparite felt in his hand, arm, and shoulder as the powder ignited and the bullet left the pistol faster than the speed of sound; but most of the force remained with the bullet, and as it sped toward its target, racing ahead of the sound-waves that would follow it to its destination, the Russian's fingers were also about to meet in opposition, just as Apparite's had done the millisecond before.

The bullet rent the air. The force of it caused a vapor trail imperceptible to the human eye to form behind it and transient amounts of condensation to form at its tip, only to be vaporized by friction and force. The tip of the bullet hit the Russian's over-coat, tearing it, even burning it around the edges, as it passed through the thick fabric. It penetrated the man's shirt underneath and pierced the skin, singeing it on its deadly journey.

Boring through muscle and bone, the bullet split a rib, flattening its tip; a shock-wave spread from the blast, and the skin and muscles beneath the surface rippled like waves from a stone dropped into a body of water. Pieces of shirt fabric and rib fragments were thrown into the path of the projectile, which carried them through the pleura—the lining of the chest cavity—and into the thick muscle of the SMERSH agent's heart. As the blunt-ended invader drilled its way into the left ventricle of the man's vulnerable heart, the shock-wave increased four-fold, interrupting the electrical current that told the heart when to beat and when not to, causing it to fibrillate.

The bullet entered the cavity of the left ventricle, vaporizing blood in its path until it exited through the opposite side, finally coming to a halt against a rib in the man's back. The SMERSH agent collapsed onto the ground as blood leaked out of his heart, soaking his shirt and then his over-coat.

But the Russian managed to fire his pistol before he died, the un-aimed shot striking a metal post in the rear of the café. It ricocheted off it, burning away enough of its velocity so that when the *pheewt!* from the Russian's gun had reached Apparite's ears, he simultaneously heard that familiar sound of a bullet meeting flesh. He reflexively threw himself down behind the bar.

"Ohh!" cried Christiane. She fell prone onto the floor with blood streaming from her thigh. She reached down and clutched her leg, moaning in pain.

But Apparite could not stop to help her: Viktor, he knew, would be right on the heels of his fallen comrade. Apparite leapt up again and saw Viktor enter the café through the broken front picture-window. He held a throwing knife and was searching for his comrade's gun, unaware that it had become trapped under the man's body when Apparite had killed him.

Apparite had his chance and he took it. He squeezed the trigger but the silencer on the barrel had been bent when he dove behind the bar after his last shot. The gun misfired, the misdirected recoil nearly wrenching it from Apparite's hand. He dropped the unusable weapon and reached for the miniature Colt strapped to his right leg.

Viktor was nearly upon him, and though the SMERSH assassin did not have a gun, Apparite knew he was just as deadly without one. Apparite bent over, raised his pant-leg, and ripped the Colt from its small holster. But before he could aim and fire, he was hit in the right upper arm with a throwing-knife.

Ignoring the pain, Apparite fired one of the little Colt's poison-tipped rubber bullets. It hit Viktor in the mouth, violently snapping the Russian's head back. But the shot would not prove to be fatal. Viktor's head was turned and his mouth opened when the bullet had hit him. It had struck two of his teeth, wrenching them loose from their sockets, causing the needle mechanism to malfunction—it had not been designed to penetrate a tooth—and the poison had not taken effect. Viktor spat out his dislodged teeth along with the bullet and a mouthful of blood and saliva, but he did not waver nor did he fall. He kept coming.

Apparite fired the second of his rubber bullets, but Viktor had grabbed a metal café table and was holding it as a shield; the round glanced off it and struck a wooden beam. The Russian suddenly rushed Apparite, who realized he no longer had a shot. The fatal targets of Viktor's chest and head were blocked by the table, and the café's tall walnut bar did not allow him to depress his pistol enough to hit the Russian in the gut or legs. His hiding place had become a liability.

He stepped over the wounded Christiane and met Viktor at the end of the bar. But Apparite had not expected the quickness or strength that the thrice-wounded Viktor displayed. Before Apparite could get off another shot, Viktor swung the café table and knocked the gun from Apparite's hand. In the same motion, he brought his left leg around—Apparite marveled at the injured man's agility and strength—and gave a forceful blow to the right side of Apparite's chest, slamming him against the bar.

Apparite grabbed a corkscrew and in a single motion opened

it and drove it into Viktor's gut, which had been exposed by the karate kick. A liquor bottle came crashing onto Apparite's head; on the upstroke its jagged edge sliced open Apparite's neck above the clavicle. Blood poured down his chest in torrents.

Apparite thrust a powerful thumb-on-top *Isshin-Ryu* fist into Viktor's chest, lifting the Russian off his feet. Tumbling to the floor, Viktor drew the second of his throwing-knives and launched it at Apparite. The defenseless Apparite picked up the first object within reach—a hardcover copy of *Peyton Place,* of all things—and tossed it in the path of the blade. The knife embedded itself into the book, saving Apparite's life.

Both men had been wounded—Viktor in the mouth, chest, and hand, and Apparite in the shoulder and neck—and yet neither would ever submit, nor allow fatigue to overtake him. That would come later, perhaps, but only to the survivor. They rushed at each other again.

Viktor was fast, but his forte was in the deadly holds and grips of death-SAMBO, so Apparite kept his distance, using short little bursts of thrusts and the downward, maiming kicks he loved so well. Apparite connected with a thrust to the shoulder; Viktor countered with his own to the knife stuck in Apparite's right deltoid. The blade was twisted and driven further into Apparite's arm, causing him to grimace. He immediately responded with a kick to Viktor's knee, grazing it and bringing a flash of pain to the Russian's face as a ligament was stretched.

The Russian whipped another kick around and Apparite dropped to the ground in his signature move, a leg-sweep at his enemy's full kick-extension, but Viktor was no ordinary opponent. Instead of holding his plant-leg firm on the ground at his kick's termination, the Russian somehow brought it off the ground before Apparite could make contact. He instantly reaffirmed his footing with the other and Apparite's move hit only empty air. For a moment, Apparite lay supine on the floor, defenseless.

Viktor dropped onto Apparite's torso and grasped him by the throat. Apparite's hands shot up to protect his airway, but Viktor's bloody three-fingered grip was strong and unrelenting. His trachea compressed, Apparite's breaths started coming in bursts of short little whistles. Viktor thrust his other hand under Apparite's jaw and began pushing with all his strength, forcing Apparite's head ever upwards and back. If Apparite could not stop it, his cervical spine would soon be fractured, killing him.

But from somewhere in the back of Apparite's mind, the picture of a dying man came to him: a man lying helpless on the ground with bright, unblinking eyes. He let loose one hand from Viktor's right arm, redoubling the effort of the other, and sought out one of the knives at his side.

Apparite's hand crawled down his flank as the two men strained and grunted in their death-struggle until it found what he needed. Removing the small knife from its steel holder, he stuck it deeply into Viktor's buttock, squeezing its rubber base to discharge its deadly cargo. Apparite's larynx was now completely closed and his face had turned blue. The world faded to black, the strain on his neck nearly at the point where the vertebral process would snap and his spinal cord would be severed. Another few seconds and he would be dead.

And then there was a twitch; Apparite felt a minute twitch from Viktor's hand. A second later, the muscles of Viktor's fingers relaxed and his arm became limp. Apparite extricated himself from under the Russian and rolled him onto his back.

Viktor was staring up at him, but other than the slow rising and falling of his chest as he breathed he was unmoving. Up, down, up, down, it went, though after a few moments of silent observation Apparite could see the rhythm gradually slowing. Inevitably, he knew it would stop.

Apparite pulled the still-embedded knife from his arm, wincing in pain until it came free. He took a slow breath and looked into the SMERSH man's eyes. They were still unnaturally bright but the intensity in them was fading fast; as Viktor's life ebbed, so did the power of his unforgettable eyes. And although the SMERSH man was paralyzed, Apparite divined that his dying enemy was looking at him, even *wondering* about him: *Who are you?* Viktor seemed to be thinking. *How have you done this thing to me?*

But there was one more question his enemy seemed to be asking, though Apparite did not want to acknowledge it:

"Aren't we more than a little alike, you and I?"

Apparite leaned over his fallen opponent. He was at the peak of his revenge, the time when he had his enemy dying and helpless before him, but looking at Viktor's eyes as they became dimmer and dimmer, he was surprised when nothing but pity was stirred in his heart.

"My name is John Apparite," he said to his dying enemy. "You've killed many men and now I've killed you." But then Apparite stopped. Something was holding him back, keeping him from speaking what he'd wanted to say for so long to his now-vanquished foe: *You bastard! You killed my friend! You slashed the throat of an innocent boy!*

He couldn't do it. Not now; not with Viktor lying helpless and paralyzed on the floor, his life leaking out like sand from an hour-glass that was fast emptying. He had hated this man for months, had dreamt of the day he would spit in his face and take pleasure in watching him die, but no longer.

"I'm sorry," was all he could think of saying. "I'm sorry." Viktor's eyes moved in a minute, barely perceptible gesture—a gesture that Apparite would always believe showed understanding in response to what he had said—and then he died.

It was many months before Apparite noted the striking

similarities in how his friend J had died in London and how his enemy Viktor had died in Berlin—each giving up their lives from poison, each dying quietly in his arms—but even when he had, he had not understood the most perplexing thing of all: although J had been his friend and Viktor his enemy, he had felt a strange sense of regret and sadness for each when they had died.

A long time would pass before he fully knew why, but by then, after having looked into the eyes of many a dying man, he had experienced that peculiar feeling more times than he could count—and in some ways, he felt, the lesson had come too late.

Twenty-One:
"The Girl"

Christiane cried out in pain. Though the bullet had not hit any major arteries, she had lost a significant amount of blood and was in a weak and frightened state. Apparite cradled her head in his hands and spoke to her. In a bold though honest gesture, he decided to do so in English. The time had come to end his long lie.

"Do you speak English?"

Through her silent tears, she nodded *yes*.

"You'll be okay," he said. He ran his hand gently across the back of her head. "You've been shot in the thigh and lost some blood, but I'll take you to a hospital."

She nodded again, too weak and stunned by the frenetic events of the evening to speak. Apparite lifted her gently from the floor and carried her from the ruins of the café. The street outside remained quiet, but to his surprise, the car that had been parked near the café was gone, as was Zhdanovich. Despite the Russian's apparently fatal wounds, he somehow had pulled himself into the vehicle and driven away.

Apparite hoped that someday he would be reunited with the enemy agent who had become a most unlikely friend and ally; and that when they did, it would be in a time of peace. The first, events later showed, would happen sooner than he expected (though not in the year 1956), but the second would prove to have been put off indefinitely. This was not by the choice of the two men, who had found common ground in the chaos of the world around them, but instead by the anger and paranoia of two nations fighting an undeclared war—a conflict that the two agents were powerless to resolve on their own.

Apparite carried Christiane to his car. He placed her on the rear seat and spoke.

"Lie here and rest. I'm taking you to the American compound on the *Clayallee*. They have a hospital there."

She closed her eyes and fell asleep as Apparite drove southwest toward the U.S. military compound in Zehlendorf. He opened the windows of the car, concentrating on the sounds and sights of the Berlin evening, but did not hear or see any ambulances, nor cars of the West German *polizei* rushing in the direction of the café. He sighed in relief. The last thing he wanted was to be involved in another high-speed car chase in a major European city—the one he had in London the year before had ended badly.

Twenty minutes later, Apparite pulled up to the entrance of the American compound. An unsmiling guard was standing behind the tall, barbed wire–topped gates holding a submachine-gun. He had been specially stationed there this night, though all he had been told was that someone important might be arriving after dark. The beefy, square-jawed captain was not in an affable mood. Soldiers of lower ranks usually manned the main gate, so he had been quite annoyed by the assignment.

Apparite took out his "Hans Müller" identity card as the captain approached.

"Chattanooga," said Apparite.

It was only a single word but it meant something important to the guard. He ran to Apparite and took his German identity card in hand. After a quick glance at it, he picked up the guardhouse telephone and spoke hastily into it. He took a few steps away from the car to rouse a half-asleep corporal from the sentry-box, ordering him to open the gates. The imposing gates slowly parted and Apparite drove into the compound and parked the car. The captain rushed to him.

"What aid do you need, sir?"

Apparite motioned with his head toward Christiane in the back seat.

"Take her to the infirmary; she's taken a small caliber bullet in the thigh. I don't think it's life-threatening."

"Right." The captain shouted at the corporal: "Bring a jeep and stretcher right away!" The young corporal ran into a nearby building and returned driving a standard military jeep. A stretcher bridged the rear seat.

"We can take it from here, sir," the captain said to Apparite. He lifted Christiane from the car and placed her onto the stretcher. He smacked the rear fender of the jeep twice with his hand and the corporal drove away.

Apparite stood, watching in silence as the jeep disappeared into the distance. He walked slowly back to his car and addressed the waiting captain.

"Make sure she's well taken care of, soldier."

"Yes sir," the captain replied with a crisp salute.

Apparite got in the car, backed it out of the compound, and drove back up the *Clayallee* toward central Berlin. His injured arm throbbed and his neck wound stung, but though he, like Christiane, had lost a lot of blood at the café, his own health was of no concern to him. All he wanted to do was sleep, to sleep for as long as humanly possible, so that when he awoke he could try and make some sense out of his life. In his current state, he almost couldn't have cared less whether a SMERSH agent suddenly ran up to the car and blew his brains out.

Returning to the safe-house he took three "sleepers" and fell into a deep, unconscious state; free from any memories or thoughts that might trouble him until he awoke. He didn't believe that taking three of the little green pills would harm him

(one was the usual dose to provide twelve hours of uninter-
rupted slumber), but even if he had, he would have done it
anyway, so desperate was he to remove himself from his cares
and confusion.

"The girl is asking about you. I thought you might want to
know."

Apparite opened his eyes. He had been unconscious nearly
twenty hours and his joints were achy and stiff from lack of
movement. Despite his nearly day-long repose he had not
dreamt, of which he was mighty pleased—dreams after an event
like this were invariably unpleasant and disturbing.

He looked upwards. D was standing over him, holding a pipe
filled with fresh black-market tobacco in his mouth. His face
bore no expression and he held both of his arms behind his
back, much as if he were viewing an exhibition in a museum:
"Superagent—Wounded, Exhausted, Burned-Out Type."

"You look like hell," he said. He placed his pipe on the night-
stand next to Apparite's bed. He then leaned over and took the
young agent's injured arm in his hand. "Your arm should be
dressed, and you need an injection of penicillin. Fortunately,
your neck wound is not too deep; it's also low enough so a buttoned shirt collar or turtle-neck should cover it. But I think it
might require suturing."

"It's nothing," answered Apparite. He ran his hand along the
laceration above his clavicle. "What time is it?"

"It's eighteen hundred. You've slept nearly the whole day
away. Tell me about the event—I've only picked up fragments
from the West German *polizei* and what I heard wasn't good."

"She panicked," said Apparite. "She panicked and left the car
when I was almost to the café. If it hadn't been for Zhdanovich,
we'd probably both be dead."

"You could have just shot her. It might've been better to have eliminated her than put the mission at risk."

Apparite glowered at D. "I don't think this is something we should discuss right now. I might do something I'd regret."

The liaison opened the night-stand drawer and removed a pistol from it. "I thought there might be trouble—there can be, at times like this. Please don't make me use this."

"Don't make me take it from you and kill you," Apparite said with menace. "And you know I could, too."

Surprisingly, D laughed.

"My God, Apparite, both of us know we'd never kill each other, so let's not even talk like it. Did you think I really expected you to have shot the girl?"

"I don't know—*you* said it," said Apparite, confused by the change in the conversation's tone.

"I was just sussing you out." D held up the pistol. "It's not even loaded, though I suspect you could beat me to death with it if you wanted. No matter. It's obvious from your reaction that you're not ready to move on yet, and certainly not ready for another mission. No, I hadn't expected you to kill the girl, not unless she'd been a threat to you. In the end, you got the job done."

"And that's all that matters—*right?*" There was a hint of facetiousness in Apparite's answer that was not lost on the liaison.

"Yes, Apparite, that's all that bloody matters—for today, at least. Viktor is dead and we have the Karlshorst telephone exchange list. It's a miracle she was able to take forty-two pages without getting caught. But the information—it's like winning the Derby! Secret telephone numbers, the names of agents and the locations of others. It's all in Soviet code, of course, but we'll be finished translating it within a few days. You have a lot to be proud of."

"Thanks," Apparite said, though without much enthusiasm.

"It's going to upset every apple-cart they've got. The Soviets will have to reassign dozens of operatives who are now at risk of exposure, and they'll have to go to the trouble of changing all of their telephone connections—"

"Listen," interrupted Apparite, "I hope you understand why I'm not exactly jumping for joy."

"Why not?" said D. "You've killed Viktor. Just a fortnight ago you were sitting at Jack Dempsey's getting 'pissed' on lager about not having the chance to do that—and now it's done. You've obsessed over it for months and months, and now he's dead and you're alive and that's *still* not enough for you? Think about it: you've gotten revenge over your greatest, strongest enemy. That's a feeling few people ever experience."

"Revenge? Do you call what I did to Viktor *revenge?*"

"I'd figure it that way."

"You can call it anything you want, but don't call it revenge," said Apparite. "Since I was the one who let Viktor get away in the first place, the fact he's dead doesn't mean much. Hell, it barely makes us even. What Heydrich told me before he died was right: I can't take revenge on a man who was only doing his duty. There's no pleasure in that; there's no redemption in that."

"I don't follow you."

"Don't you see?" Apparite replied, his voice rising. "I certainly do now. Viktor didn't wrong J, or Clive, or even that kid outside the Reading Room. He simply did what he was *supposed* to do, just like me when I killed Zhdanovich's cousin. Viktor, and me, and maybe even Heydrich—I don't see much difference between us."

"But Viktor and Heydrich are dead, and you're alive. That's difference enough for the present, don't you think?"

"I don't know what to think anymore. Sure, Viktor's dead, and maybe that evens us for J, but because of him I've lost something I'll never get back. Christ, she was the only girl I ever—"

D stopped Apparite in mid-sentence. "Don't say any more. Don't try and figure things out. There's no purpose in it; you'll only hate yourself if you try. And don't worry about the girl. She'll be fine; she's in the infirmary at the U.S. compound where you left her. But there is one complication to be addressed, and it involves her."

"What's that?"

D picked up his pipe and took a couple of puffs before answering. The pleasant, sweet smell of the burning tobacco reminded Apparite of his father, who had a habit of smoking Amphora every evening after supper. For some reason, the memory softened his irritation and anger.

"She can't stop asking about you," D then said. "She wants to talk with you, and she's becoming a risk. I need you to speak with her."

"Are you sure that's a good idea?" Apparite asked quietly. "Isn't that a security risk?"

"I don't think so. Not if it serves to quiet her about you. But it's going to be tough for you to, um—"

"What is it?" Apparite asked impatiently, rushing his words. "Tell me."

"We need you to tell her you never loved her."

"I can't do that. I can't. After all that's happened, please leave her with *something*."

"You must!" exclaimed D. "It'll be worse for her if you *don't!* Send her on her way hating you and she'll do everything in her power to forget you. Send her on her way still in love with you and it will lead to trouble. We're going to have to monitor her as it is, and if we see the wrong signs—you know what I'm driving at, don't you?"

Yes, Apparite knew exactly what D meant. If the girl talked, even after she'd been relocated into the West, she would die.

"Her best chance of staying alive is for you to do this," continued D. "You'd be saving her—not destroying her. You *must* do it."

Apparite rubbed his eyes in frustration: there was no way out.

"I'll do it," he said. "But only because she'll stand a better chance by it." What Apparite left unsaid was how much he truly hated himself, his agency, and even the Director and his liaison at the moment.

"Tomorrow, we'll take you someplace where you can relax," said D. "There's nothing else brewing for you right now, so you can take your time to get over her."

Take my time to get over her? thought Apparite. *Is there enough time in a man's life to get over the only woman he'd ever loved, and then lost?*

"Sure," Apparite said. "I'll be fine." But his eyes were downcast and his voice filled with melancholy.

"That's the spirit. I've got something in mind that I know will make you feel better." D took one last puff on his pipe. "But first, the girl."

"First, the girl," echoed Apparite. *"The girl,"* he repeated softly to himself. He hated objectifying her with those patronizing, unfeeling words, but also knew that by doing so, it would help him to someday forget her.

"The girl," he whispered again as they left the safe-house, and the echo of those words played in his mind as D drove him to the U.S. military compound, right up until he walked into her hospital room and saw her for the last time.

"The girl, the girl, the girl, the girl . . ."

TWENTY-TWO:
Auf Wiedersehen, BERLIN

D drove Apparite to the infirmary, which was, in Christiane's case, a private Quonset-style hut in the middle of the American military compound. As a "special guest" of the U.S. Government she warranted such extreme individual attention (meaning that no one wanted her to escape or have access to outside civilians), though the "guest" herself would remain ignorant of her essential imprisonment in the small, aluminum building.

"You have about five minutes and then I'll poke my head in," D said to Apparite, unlocking the door. "I've sent the guards away so you'll have complete privacy. This may be the most important conversation of her life, so you need to be at the top of your game."

"I know," said Apparite. "I know what I have to do."

"Good."

D opened the door, locking it again after Apparite had entered. The liaison whistled and two uniformed guards appeared from around the corner of the small building.

"Make sure no one either enters or leaves," he told them. "I'll stay here by the door; you stand by the windows."

The guards acknowledged the order and positioned themselves by the windows at the rear and right-hand sides of the small hut. As for D, he remained standing just outside the front door. He removed a small pair of headphones from an inside pocket of his coat and put them on. He then took a small receiver from another pocket and tuned in the "bug" that had

255

surreptitiously been placed in the room earlier that day. Although he had faith in young John Apparite to do what had to be done, he was experienced enough to know that situations like this sometimes ended badly, if not tragically. No one was taking any chances.

After the door closed behind him, Apparite surveyed the hut's single, nearly bare room. Christiane lay on a standard military hospital bed; an intravenous line was in her arm and she was sipping from a small paper cup. Her bed was positioned in the exact geographical center of the room, directly under a slowly turning ceiling fan, and a bed-side stand rested over her lap. He walked toward her, taking notice of the objects sitting on the metallic stand: a small pitcher of water, a toothbrush, some tissues, and a copy of *Stars and Stripes.* The scene had a distinct other-worldly quality to it.

But Christiane looked beautiful; just as striking as when he had first seen her on the train. Her blonde hair had, as usual, fallen across the sides of her face and down onto her shoulders in random disorder, but her bright blue eyes radiated clarity and intelligence, locking onto him as soon as he had entered the room.

Apparite felt an impulse to rush to her and take her in his arms—but he knew he could not. He wanted to tell her how much he loved her; how she had awakened feelings in him that he had never had before—but he knew he could not. His duties no longer included being her lover, or protecting her from the Soviets. Right now, his only duty was to get her to hate him. He thought it the hardest he had ever been asked to perform.

He walked steadily closer, keeping his gaze firmly on her face. To complete this daunting task he had to show strength and conviction. He could not waver or falter; he had to be firm and certain in all that he would say.

"How are you?" he asked.

"I am okay, thank you," she answered in English, though with a slight (and undeniably charming) German inflection. "They say my leg is not a problem."

"Good." Apparite was pleased that she was so calm, that she was showing such strength, even as he worried his own might not be up to the task. "They tell me you'll be on a flight out of Berlin tomorrow."

"Yes. But they do not tell me where I shall go."

"Wherever it is, you'll be comfortable—they'll take care of everything. You'll have nothing to worry about." He smiled at her.

"I know," she said. "They are very kind for me."

Apparite noted how they were dancing around the one subject that neither wanted to broach, a subject that was, she had indeed guessed, the sole reason for Apparite's unexpected visit.

He tried to move closer to the target. "They are pleased with the information you gave them. It's going to give us an advantage, right where we need one."

She did not answer. For the first time she averted her gaze, looking downward before speaking.

"I loved you," she said with unusual feeling. She turned her face up to him; she was beginning to cry. "I would have done *anything* for you." Apparite held her gaze; he would not avert his eyes from it. Not now; not when the time had come.

"I know. I was only doing my duty."

Tears fell from her face, landing on the white hospital sheet in little round spots, though Apparite sensed no hatred or bitterness in her eyes. Her lack of anger made it all the harder for him.

"I was told to find a defector who had information," he continued. "I found you." It was killing him to treat her this way; he thought it the cruelest thing he had ever done.

"And the Soviets you killed?" she asked, still looking directly into his face. "Was that some of it, too?"

"Yes. We used you to draw them out." He desperately wanted to say he was sorry; he needed to tell her how wrong they were to have used her so. But he could not: it *had* to be this way.

She did not speak, but finally released Apparite's eyes from her discomforting gaze. She took a sip of water from the small paper cup and dried her eyes with a tissue, letting it fall upon the bed. To Apparite's surprise, she then reached out and took his hand. He wanted to pull it away—he *had* to pull it away—but could not. Her touch had seemingly paralyzed him.

Christiane looked him directly in the eyes once more, and the conviction he saw in her face exceeded any that he had yet been able to muster. Her hands stayed steady and her voice did not quaver when finally she spoke.

"You may say what you want: I *know* you love me, and always will. I do not know your name—but I do not care. I do not know who you work for—but I do not care. And I know I will never see you again, but I want you to know this one thing: I will not forget you. And you, I think, will not forget me. That is the only thing that matters. It is a curse, but also a blessing."

She closed her eyes and let her head fall back onto her pillow. The gesture told Apparite their conversation had ended, and he had failed in his duty to make her hate him. And yet his purpose had been served. In her final words he divined that she would remain forever silent about him, although she would, as she said, never forget him—nor would he, her.

Perhaps that was all she really needed, he thought: just a chance to tell him she loved him and to find the reassurance that he loved her, too. And when she had, she had been satisfied, knowing that the memories of their days together would sustain her, even as she lived a lifetime without him someplace else, and likely with someone else.

Just as Apparite had once memorized her face as they made

love, so had she memorized his on this day. The face of the other would remain indelibly printed in each of their minds, and as is true with much of a person's memories, this one would indeed be a blessing and occasionally a curse. But the memory would always be there—that was the important thing.

Apparite knocked on the door; it opened and he stepped outside into the muted light of dusk. D closed and relocked the door before speaking.

"How did she take it?"

"She did okay. She won't say anything; you can count on that."

"Good—I thought so." D lit his pipe; fortunately, he, too, had been satisfied of Christiane's continued silence in the future. "And you? I've been quite concerned about you since the event."

"I'll be alright. I just need some time away from all of this."

D smiled. "I agree—and I've got just the tonic for you. How does Brussels sound?"

"Sounds okay, but what's in Brussels?"

"Well," said D, "they've got a lovely city square and cathedral, not to mention the *Manneken Pis.*"

"Never heard of it," said Apparite. "What in the hell is that?"

"A fountain of a boy having a piss. It's really quite a famous attraction."

Apparite bristled.

"Want some advice, D? Don't quit your day job to become a salesman. Because frankly, your pitch stinks."

D put his arm around Apparite and led him toward their car.

"Hold your water—I'm not finished. There are two other things you might be interested to know. For one, the Belgians brew the best beer in the world; and for another, Dr. Hoevenaers is there, probably pouring one for you this very moment. He's just recently arrived from London."

Apparite stopped walking. Hoevenaers—of course! Apparite had been hoping the Doctor was up and around by now, though having an amputation at sixty-five years of age couldn't be easy under any circumstance. He was terribly anxious to see him again; he thought a reunion might be therapeutic for them both.

"When can I go?"

"I'm driving you to the airport now," responded D. "I've already packed an over-night bag for you, and I'll send the rest of your belongings to Brussels tomorrow. You can stay there for at least a month without much worry of being disturbed."

D drove Apparite to Tempelhof Airport. Though the ride was a silent one, both men sensed a welcome decrease in the tension between them. D in particular was pleased by it. Apparite had yet to form the close, automatic bond with him that had come so easily with J, and D knew it, even if Apparite did not. In some ways, it was no easier being the liaison in the Director's agency than it was to be a Superagent, and D wanted to do his best to insure that Apparite left Berlin on an emotional upswing. And so far, everything had gone to plan: the girl had been satisfactorily taken care of, and Apparite was on his way to visit Hoevenaers.

But the expression on D's face fell when he saw the plane that was to take Apparite to his first stop in Frankfurt. He had been promised the latest-model airliner for Apparite's journey, but instead, a World War Two–era C-47 Dakota was sitting in the middle of the tarmac. The liaison climbed out of the car with Apparite close behind, both men staring at the aircraft as its engines idled roughly and un-encouragingly.

As he stood looking at the plane, D's mouth slowly opened in astonishment at this seemingly horrible turn of events: he was going to have to put an exhausted and depressed Superagent with a known fear of flying on this relic! His lit pipe dropped from his mouth. Its full bowl hit the concrete tarmac and exploded into sparks and smoke.

"*Bloody* amateurs!" he cried out. "All I ask is for one decent bleeding aircraft—" But then he stopped: a loud, unfamiliar sound was coming from Apparite, who until a moment before had been standing silently next to him.

He was laughing without reserve. To Apparite, the sight of the urbane, professorial D dropping his pipe and flying into a rage was the funniest thing he'd seen since Donald O'Connor's voice had come out of Jean Hagen's mouth at the end of *Singing in the Rain!* D smiled, pleased to see his charge enjoying himself for a change, and patted Apparite good-naturedly on the back.

"C'mon, let's get you up in the air." He retrieved his pipe and gestured toward a green overall-clad mechanic standing nearby. "Say, you there—are you *sure* this is the right airplane? This man is going to Frankfurt."

The mechanic moved the chaw of tobacco he had in his mouth from one side to the other, spat, and spoke in a slow, profane, west Texas drawl.

"She sure as f--- is, and it's a *God* damn privilege to ride in her; you betcha'."

"Why's that?" asked Apparite. Like the liaison, he, too, was concerned that his fear of flying might make a dramatic recurrence in such an old, worn aircraft. "Because she was in the airlift of 'forty-eight?"

The mechanic spat on the ground before answering.

"Naw, about every f----n' plane on the hot-damn field was in *that!* This sum'bitch was one of them D-Day paratroop' models. C'mon over and I'll show ya." He led them in his bow-legged walk to the plane. "See that—on the underside of them wings?" The paint, while a uniform olive drab throughout, was thicker beneath the plane's wings in a discernible striped pattern. "Used to be black and white there—them's the *oh*-riginal 'invasion stripes' from June-the-God-damn-fifth, nineteen forty-four."

"I thought D-Day was June sixth," said D.

The mechanic bent at the waist in laughter, pointing at the liaison.

"*Gotcha,* mister! The invasion of Normandy was June the sixth on the ground, but June the f----n' *fifth* in the air. This here plane dropped off them pathfinders the God damn night *before!* Follow me and I'll show ya the damn holes from them sum'bitchen' Kraut eighty-eights."

"Um, thanks, but no, I must be going," said Apparite. He was certain he did *not* want a detailed outlining of the battle-scarred plane's structural damage.

"It's your loss. Say, Hank!" the mechanic yelled, getting the attention of a man down the tarmac. "Show this guy into the aero-plane, will ya? I gotta take a dump as big as Dallas."

D leaned toward Apparite and gestured at their coarse-mannered guide. "I think I remember him from Oxford—we rowed 'eights' together, if I recall," he whispered.

Apparite laughed. He and the liaison walked slowly to the aircraft together, discussing a few final matters for Apparite's journey along the way. A wiry sergeant met them by the plane. Though neither Apparite nor D was wearing a uniform of any kind, the man gave them a quick salute.

"We're ready to go, sir."

D nodded. He held out his hand for Apparite.

"See you back in the States. Give the Doctor my regards."

Apparite shook the liaison's hand. "I will—thanks."

Following the sergeant, Apparite ascended the small ladder into the side of the C-47. Looking around its interior, his first thought was, *Well, no one's gonna mistake* this *place for the Waldorf-Astoria!*

The aircraft's floor was covered in a pastiche of dirt, hay, and a particularly malodorous dark material that Apparite surmised was dung, which he still somehow managed to step in. There were numerous, knotty wooden crates anchored to the floor of the craft, between which he recognized the form of a rat darting about in search of food. Despite the fact that the war had ended over ten years ago, the worn paratrooper benches were still in place, providing the only means of resting one's legs. Apparite looked down at the long bench.

"Where's the best place to sit in this thing?" he asked the sergeant, who was busy making final adjustments to the rusty chains holding down the crates. The engines were idling much faster and louder than before, and Apparite had been forced to raise his voice to a shout to be heard.

"Take a seat back there," the sergeant yelled. He pointed to the port side of the rear of the craft. "There's a seat-belt to fasten during take-off and landing, so put it on."

"Right." Apparite walked to the far end of the paratrooper bench and sat down. He found the lap-belts and fastened them into place.

"Why do I have to sit way back here?" he asked. "I'd rather be up front."

"The tail's the safest part of the plane. If we crash, it'll probably break off and stop on its own. Usually the guys up front all get killed!"

"Great!" said Apparite. It was as if the sergeant expected it to happen.

"And when we're in the air, don't spend too much time on the starboard side. Sometimes the paratroop' door opens on its own during flight—something about the change in air pressure."

"Great!" said Apparite again. "Maybe I should put on a parachute—just in case!"

The sergeant shook his head.

"Can't. Used the last one a week ago."

Apparite prayed the man was putting him on.

The plane's engines revved for take-off, and if Apparite had thought a Boeing Stratocruiser made a lot of noise, it was nothing compared to the din of the Dakota's 1,200 horsepower eardrum-shattering pair of Pratt and Whitney engines. The plane shook and rattled in jarring up-and-down and left-and-right motions, and then sped down the runway with a deafening roar.

Apparite had no window by which he could gauge their speed, but he felt the shaking of the craft increase until his neck ached and his teeth clacked together. The whine of the engines continued to rise, reaching a pitch so high and abrasive that Apparite had to plug his ears, when suddenly they were airborne, the plane in an attitude that was surprisingly steep. The shaking soon ceased, the angle of the plane leveled out, and the roar of the engines reduced itself to a loud though not uncomfortable hum, like a tractor heard from a short distance.

And yet, Apparite had remained calm. Last year, he'd panicked in the most comfortable and up-to-date passenger plane in the skies, and now he had weathered with complete aplomb the take-off of a decrepit, unstable, rat-infested, dung-laden C-47 that might plummet to earth at any moment.

He smiled. Sometimes the little victories mean the most— especially when a victory is so desperately needed.

Aside from the pilots, the rat, and some birds he heard chirping from one of the wooden crates (why birds were being flown out of Berlin he could not guess), Apparite was alone on the flight and fell asleep from fatigue and boredom shortly after take-off. He therefore did not register the bumps and dips of turbulence as the plane plowed through a brief thunderstorm, nor the jolts and lurches of the craft as it landed. He awoke only when he heard the noise of the stevedores unloading the cargo, thinking it the easiest flight he'd ever taken. After deplaning, he took an awaiting cab to the Frankfurt rail-station.

Stepping onto the train only saddened him, however, for it understandably brought back memories of his first meeting with Christiane: their comparing of childhoods and fathers, her dramatic removal from the carriage by the Soviets, and finally the joy at seeing her message written on his newspaper, telling him she did not want their relationship to end on the train. And though he remained melancholy at the denouement of the events in Berlin, he had some satisfaction in knowing that he was leaving her alive, and that she, like he, would forever remember their time together.

In fact, all things considered, his mission had been significantly more successful than the one in London the year before. For starters, no one on their side had died and Apparite had escaped with relatively minor injuries, which was a rarity for him. Viktor had been killed (along with quite a few of his SMERSH colleagues), Apparite had come to some sort of reconciliation with J's death (and, once again, the difficult nature of his duties), and the telephone exchange book was providing a wealth of information.

And yet there would always be that business about "the girl." It would forever mark Berlin for him the way the Statue of Liberty marks New York City or the Eiffel Tower marks Paris for others. To John Apparite, Berlin would always mean Christiane, regardless of East or West, *Ossis* or *Wessis*, or even the erection of a twenty-six-mile-long concrete wall to divide it.

Twenty-Three:
A la Mort Subite

Apparite arrived in the Brussels city center in late afternoon. After his trips to London and Berlin, he had become rather immune to the previously awe-evoking architecture and sights of classic European cities. However, even he was forced to admit that the Belgian capital was remarkably handsome, its denizens unusually healthy and contented-looking compared to what he was used to back in Berlin.

And also in contrast to Berlin, color was all around him. The people were dressed in bright, casual outfits, and the buildings decorated with colorful awnings, flags, and signs, all of which served to improve his recently tenuous mood. Leaving Berlin for a city like Brussels had been a good idea.

Apparite stepped out of the *Gare Centrale* metro station. He asked the proprietor of a nearby *frites*-stand for directions to the place he was to meet Hoevenaers: the café *A la Mort Subite*. When Apparite had been told the title of the café by D, he had thought it possibly a weak attempt at a joke. It seemed bizarrely apropos, if not macabre, that a secret agent who had killed over a dozen men in the past two weeks would be sent to an establishment whose name translated-out as "To the Sudden Death." He had been reassured, however, that this was not only the true title of the café, but that naming it in that manner was quite consistent with the character of the Belgian people, who were notorious for their irreverence. Regardless, if Dr. Hoevenaers was indeed waiting for him there, Apparite didn't care what it was called.

He received the directions to the café, giving the man a franc for his trouble, and continued on his way. Passing the *Cathédral de St. Michel,* he turned onto the *rue Montagnes des Herbes aux Potagéres.* After a short walk, he saw the words *"A la Mort Subite"* spelled out in cherry-red letters announcing the café's location. He accelerated his pace and was soon within fifty feet of the building, close enough to see through its large front picture-window, on which were written the words *"Gueuze et Kriek"* and *"Mort Subite"* to announce its well-known beers. The sight of the people drinking and laughing inside the café gave it the appearance of being an unusually cheerful and welcoming place.

Reaching the front door, he entered the café with anticipation. It was larger than it seemed from the street, and yet it retained a sort of friendly intimacy he'd noticed and appreciated in the London pubs he'd frequented the previous autumn. Apparite instantly liked the place, regardless of its strange name.

Just inside the doorway to the right, he spied a wheelchair, a sight that told him Hoevenaers was, indeed, inside the café. He rapidly scanned the room, starting at the bar on the right, working his way through the long, wooden tables that provided most of the seating. But his probing gaze did not lock onto Hoevenaers as he had expected. Instead, his eyes found another man in the rear of the café, and they stopped and focused on him even as Apparite tried to understand why they were doing so. The action seemed automatic, beyond his conscious control, as if done solely on instinct.

The man in question was dark-complected and had jet-black hair; to Apparite, something felt vaguely familiar about him. His manner and posture were particularly arresting: he was drinking clear liquid from a small glass (vodka?) but never looked at it, even as he brought it to his lips. His back was ram-rod straight, his eyes fixed on a point to the left of the front door, well across the room from where he was sitting. The man had no companions, but Apparite noted that he had brought a cane, which was leaning against the table. His demeanor radiated intrigue and Apparite immediately suspected a dark motive for his presence.

Apparite followed the direction of the man's gaze. It was focused upon an elderly, silver-haired man sitting at a table to Apparite's far left, directly under a large mirror on which was written the café's drink selections. This man's back was to the door; his face hidden from view from where Apparite stood. He was alone and sipping a red-colored beer from a tumbler, but there were two other aspects about him that Apparite thought were more significant. For one, he appeared to be waiting for someone, for he looked out of the front window from time to time to scan the street outside. For another, only one of his feet was visible under his chair—the other could not be seen, or was, perhaps, *missing.* In a flash, Apparite realized that this was Dr. Hoevenaers, and the person the Doctor was waiting for was, of course, him.

But Apparite did not move. Something about this picture was not at all right. He glanced back at the dark-complected man, noting once again the cane, the rigid posture, and the unwavering gaze at Hoevenaers, and Apparite finally remembered: although he had seen this man for but a few seconds at the Red Lion pub, he realized that the Doctor's assassin had returned. He guessed the SMERSH agent had been sent on to Brussels when the Doctor had been transferred from University College Hospital in London, and had been waiting ever since, quietly biding his time until Hoevenaers went out in public and he would have another chance to eliminate him. He had found his man and was now closing in for the kill.

And what better reason for Hoevenaers to finally get out of the house than to meet his old friend John Apparite at *A la Mort Subite*? Surely that was the good Doctor's thinking. D would have told him how depressed the young agent was after losing Christiane; how he would need comfort and advice from the wise and experienced physician, with whom he already had an excellent rapport. Hoevenaers would not have let anything or anyone stop him from their happy reunion—and now, perhaps, he was going to die for it.

But not if I can help it, thought Apparite. Scanning the room again, he took a seat where Hoevenaers could not see him, but where he could still keep his eyes on the Doctor and his assassin. He figured the Russian was waiting until the Doctor either left the café or perhaps went to the toilet, and then it would be the cane-gun for him. It would probably be a quick death with a fast-acting poison this time around, leaving no time to apply a tourniquet nor administer any antidote—if there would even be one, which Apparite felt certain there would not.

This was going to be dicey. Since his varied devices and pistols would not arrive in Belgium until the next morning, the only weapons Apparite had on him at the moment were the throwing-knives and garrote-wire hidden in his shoes. None of them could be used in this public, well-lit setting, except as a desperate, last resort.

Allies? No help there, either. He knew no one in Brussels other than the Doctor, and had little knowledge of the Belgian secret service or of local police procedures. At any rate, he could not involve others for fear of compromising his agency. He would have to act alone.

What *did* he have, then? He had plenty of money in his little over-night satchel; there were rolls of French francs, German West-marks, and plenty of American dollars at the ready. Money *always* came in handy, particularly when one knew how to use it. But all the money in the world could not buy the answer to his most pressing question: *How does one kill a SMERSH assassin in a public place without arousing suspicion?* Was there anything else he could use? Anything at all?

He smiled—he had an L-pill in his sock; it had almost slipped his mind.

Damn it, that's it. He had a highly lethal, silently-killing, practically untraceable poison, and all he had to do was get it into the Russian's mouth.

He smiled again—now, how do you get a lethal poison-pill into a SMERSH agent's mouth? *You get him to put it there himself, that's how!*

A waiter stopped to take his order.

"*Monsieur,* I have a special request," Apparite said to the man in French. "Today is a *wonderful* day for me: I have a son!" He managed a wide grin to lend authenticity to his statement.

"A son—congratulations!" the waiter said with enthusiasm. "Are you here to celebrate? What may we bring you?"

"Do you have champagne? I always celebrate with champagne."

"Yes—a little. This place is for beer, *Monsieur,* but we have a little."

"Good! Bring me a glass of champagne and I will tell you what I want." Apparite handed the man fifty francs. "It will prove to be very rewarding for you."

"Oh, *Monsieur!* Thank you very much!" The waiter hurried to the bar and spoke excitedly to the other staff. A moment later he returned, bringing with him every other waiter in the café.

"This is the closest thing we have to a champagne flute," he said. He handed Apparite a tall, thin beer glass half-filled with champagne.

"It will do well," said Apparite. "First, I need to write a note to somcone—a friend is here and I am going to surprise him."

"Quick, quick," said the waiter, "someone fetch a pen and paper!" Another waiter walked rapidly to the bar and returned with the required items.

Apparite jotted a quick note in French: *"I am here. Do not move. Act like you do not know me. Your life is in danger. J. Judge."* He handed the waiter the note.

"Now, take this to the man who came here in the wheelchair; he is sitting under the mirror. Do it without a fuss, if you can. I need to go to the toilet, but when I get back, if you have three bottles of champagne and enough glasses to serve every person in this room, I will give you one hundred-fifty francs more!"

He laughed at the gasps of pleasure amongst the wait-staff.

"A hundred-fifty! Oh, you are too kind; thank you, *Monsieur;* this is such a happy occasion!" they cried, scurrying to prepare the order.

Apparite drank all but an ounce of the champagne and rose from the table. Still holding his glass, he entered the restroom and sat down on the toilet. Leaning over, he carefully removed the L-pill from his sock. He took the throwing-knives from his shoes and ground the tiny pill into a fine powder between them. When he was satisfied with the result, he dumped the powder into his glass. Using one of the knives, he stirred it into the remaining champagne until the powder disappeared. He put the knives back into their hiding place in his shoes and re-entered the café.

He quickly glanced at the Russian: the man was in precisely the same bolt-upright position as before, staring at his target. Though he had likely seen Hoevenaers being handed the note, he had apparently not given it much thought or significance, as far as Apparite could tell. As for the Doctor, he was still quietly drinking his glass of beer, but had obviously read the message and understood its meaning. His hands were restless and his lone foot tapped nervously on the floor. All that remained was for Apparite to play out his little ruse, and it would all be over—if everything went according to his hastily improvised plan.

He returned to his seat where four of the café's attentive staff awaited him. They had brought two metal serving trays, three bottles of champagne, and an assortment of tall, thin glasses identical to his own.

"We have everything ready!" they all chimed at once. They were a young group and unusually eager to please, for each man's cut would make a very welcome bonus.

"Good," said Apparite, "but first I'm going to make a little speech." He glanced over at the Russian. "I want *everyone* to share my joy."

Apparite stood on the table. This was the proverbial moment of truth, like when New York Giant Bobby Thomson faced Dodger pitcher Ralph Branca at the climax of that playoff game back in 'fifty-one. Thomson hit the ball into the Polo Grounds' short left-field stands to capture the pennant that day, and, just like the Giant third baseman, Apparite could *not* afford to strike out: he, too, had to hit a homer. If the Russian recognized him from the Red Lion, or if Apparite was unconvincing in his performance as the joyous new father, then there was going to be a murderous brawl the likes of which Brussels had never seen, and God help any man who got caught between Apparite and the SMERSH assassin during their fight. But if not—well, if not, then this was going to make one helluva story to tell the Director, that was for sure.

"Hello, hello everyone!" Apparite said in his best French, attracting the attention of all in the café. "Today, I have become the father of a beautiful son!"

There were fifteen patrons in the bar and all smiled and applauded save one: the SMERSH agent, naturally, who continued to rigidly sit and sip his drink while keeping his eyes on Hoevenaers. A heavy-set man at a table near Apparite, however, seemed very happy to hear the news: he stood and handed Apparite a cigar, which the young agent took in hand and sniffed

in appreciation.

"My father celebrated my birth with champagne in this café twenty-six years ago, and I will celebrate my son's the same. I would like each of you to drink with me in joy!"

There was more clapping and shouting as Apparite stepped down off of the table. He was pleased with the results so far. The Russian obviously had not recognized him from the Red Lion, and no one appeared to doubt his story. Even Hoevenaers appeared amused by Apparite's performance. His nervousness looked somewhat lessened, though he avoided directly looking at Apparite for fear of catching his eye and giving anything away. Apparite placed one bottle of champagne and a number of glasses on each of the three trays, and then gave the waiters his instructions.

"There are fifteen people in the café, not counting us. Give each one a glass of champagne, and at the end, I will buy all of you a drink and give you your well-earned reward! I'll start over there," he said, indicating the section where the Russian was sitting, "you go over there," he said to one of the waiters, indicating where Hoevenaers was seated, "and you do the rest," he said to another.

Another round of "thank yous" and handshakes, and they were ready to go. Apparite took his tray, which carried six full glasses of champagne—one for each of the persons he would serve, with the last glass reserved for himself—and walked to the first two patrons in his section; a young couple who were clearly quite madly in love.

"Thank you," the two lovers said in unison, each taking their glass. Like many young couples, they spoke, drank, and, it seemed to Apparite, even *breathed* simultaneously, as if they were physically connected. It reminded him of the way he and Christiane had once been, but he had no time to reflect on that now.

"You're welcome—thank you for celebrating with me!" he answered, and stepped to the next table. At this one sat two men, obviously brothers from their nearly identical facial features and rotund body types. Though it was but late afternoon, they seemed to be bursting with the expansive effects of alcohol.

"Hey, here's the champagne man!" said one of the two men, in a drunken mish-mash of syllables that Apparite deciphered as a form of French. "I don't like to mix my drinks, but I'll make an exception when the price is right!" His brother laughed and took a drag from a Gauloise cigarette. "Don't mind him," he said to Apparite, "he *loves* a sip of champagne after five glasses of *faro!*"

"And a *kriek*—don't forget that!" the brother added.

Apparite handed each their glass. "Champagne is delicious at any time. Enjoy."

"Congratulations!" the two men said as one.

Apparite picked up the tray, on which there were now but two glasses remaining: one for the Russian and one for himself. He walked in slow, measured steps to the SMERSH man's table. The Russian was still quiet and unmoving, his mind completely focused on Hoevenaers. Apparite attempted to draw his attention.

"Hello! Thank you for sharing my happiness!" He placed the tray loudly on the table. "Have a glass of champagne, my friend."

The Russian looked up at him for just the briefest of moments.

"Leave on table," he said in very coarse French. "I drink later."

"Now, later—it doesn't matter to me!" Apparite said with a flourish. "Enjoy it whenever you wish!" He reached down to hand the Russian his glass.

But when Apparite had placed the tray onto the table the

glasses had shifted, and he was no longer certain which contained the L-pill and which contained only champagne. He stared at the glasses, trying to detect any cloudiness or residue in them, but he had done an unusually thorough job in grinding up the pill, and the liquid in each looked the same. He remembered having put the "death glass" nearest on the tray to keep an eye on it, but now they were equidistant from him.

Which had it been—nearest to the left, or nearest to the right? Like many left-handers, Apparite sometimes confused left with right (the world was a right-handed one, which put him at an automatic disadvantage in such things), and while he was reasonably sure the glass on the left would be the lethal one, a tiny part of his memory made him think it could also be the one on the right.

But he could not linger or the Russian would get suspicious. Back in college, Apparite had been told to mark down the first answer that came to mind on any test—don't screw up your head thinking too much about it!—so he placed the glass on the left in front of the Russian and hurried back to his table with the remaining glass on the tray. He considered spilling it, but decided that any such move at this critical juncture would only arouse suspicions and perhaps ruin the whole game. By God, he was going to have to drink the one he had and trust he didn't keel over dead.

He put the empty champagne bottle and tray on the table, and stood on it once again. Raising his glass in the air, though only after taking one last look to make sure he did not see any particulate matter in it (which he did not), Apparite spoke.

"Thank you all! Thank you. And now, let us all," he said, looking pointedly at the Russian, "let us *all* drink to the health of my new son!"

"*Santé!*" everyone cried, lifting their glasses to their lips.

Apparite drained his champagne in a single anxious gulp, and looked over at the Russian. The SMERSH agent glanced briefly at Apparite, took a very small sip of the champagne, and put the glass immediately back onto the table. He resumed staring in Hoevenaers' direction.

Apparite sat back down and called for his waiter. He was feeling no ill effects from the champagne, so his glass, he felt safe to assume, had not contained the L-pill. Still, he doubted that the Russian had taken a large enough sip to cause a fatal ingestion. He would have to wait it out and hope the SMERSH agent got thirstier.

When the waiter arrived, Apparite put his next plan into motion.

"Here is your money." He handed the smiling waiter the promised number of francs. "But I have one more thing to ask. Do you have sausages or cheese?"

"Oh yes," the waiter replied brightly. "Good sausages, and very good cheeses: Beauvoorde, Old Postel—many kinds."

"Please give everyone a plate, and if they want another drink, you may give them one from me!" Apparite looked at the happy faces of the wait-staff behind the bar. "In fact, give yourselves a plate as well, along with any drink you like, just as I promised! This is a great day and I want everyone to share in it!"

"Yes, *Monsieur!* Thank you, *Monsieur*—for everything!"

The waiter rushed off and once again the café's staff leapt into action. In a flash, overflowing plates of meats, cheeses, and bread had been placed on every table.

Apparite sat munching on a slice of sausage, and when he'd finished that he tried some of the cheese, which he ate with beer-mustard and bread. He was very hungry so it made a tasty and satisfying little meal; and, as he had hoped, it was also making him thirsty. Calling a waiter over, he asked what beer he would recommend.

"Oh, *Monsieur,* you must have *Mort Subite Kriek*. It has a wonderful cherry flavor and is delicious with the cheese."

"The *kriek* it is," said Apparite. He handed the waiter enough bank notes to settle his account and resumed his death-watch on the SMERSH agent. He hoped the Russian was as hungry—and now, perhaps, as thirsty—as he was.

The Russian continued to steadily eye Hoevenaers, but had begun to eat the sausages. Apparite guessed he had been here most of the day and was likely quite famished—and what starving man could resist the lure of sausage, cheese, and free champagne? After a few more pieces of sausage, and then some cheese on bread, and then some more sausage, the man picked up his champagne and took a sip, and this one was encouragingly *medium-sized.* He continued to eat, though his eyes never moved from Hoevenaers—another piece of sausage, another piece of cheese, a piece of sausage with mustard—when, to Apparite's mixed relief and horror, given that he knew it was going to kill the man, the Russian drained the champagne in a single gulp.

Apparite looked away and took a sip of his *kriek.* It was sour but very refreshing, reminding him of the *Berliner Weisse* beers he had shared with Christiane at the *Café Falke.* As his little game with the Russian appeared to be coming to an end, he allowed himself to relax and enjoy his drink. Given the circumstances, he also figured he could now chance a talk with Hoevenaers. To disguise his intentions he visited a few of the tables between himself and the Doctor, accepting "thank yous" and congratulations from a variety of persons. After about five minutes of glad-handing, he had worked his way to the Doctor.

"You can talk to me now," Apparite said in French. He walked around the table and sat across from Hoevenaers. "I've taken care of the problem."

"What was it?" the Doctor asked.

"Your assassin has returned—the same man as in London.

He's sitting at the other end of the café. But I've given him poison so he's not going anywhere." Apparite looked over at the Russian but nothing yet had changed. The man's stare was still directed at Hoevenaers' side of the table, although he had stopped eating his meal. Apparite wondered if the poison's effect had been delayed by the food the Russian had consumed; perhaps he'd have to wait a little longer to make sure it had worked. Apparite looked back at Hoevenaers to resume their conversation.

"How have you been? Please forgive me for your leg."

Hoevenaers answered in his typically gentle and reassuring manner.

"I'm well—but I should be thanking *you* for saving my life. They took quite good care of me in London, and your supervisor has called on me periodically to make certain everything is well. I'm getting around by wheelchair, but soon I'll have an artificial leg and it will be easier."

"I'm so sorry. It's not right you should have to get involved in such things."

"It is my choice," replied Hoevenaers. "It was quite easy to make—and I made it long ago, you know. I do not like this business of killing people, but I understand it is sometimes necessary."

Apparite looked across the room. The Russian was still staring at Hoevenaers as if nothing at all had occurred. *When in the hell is this guy going to die?* Apparite asked himself. He'd never imagined it would take this long.

"But what is going to happen to you?" Apparite queried the Doctor. "Where are you going to go now?"

"We will both go to my daughter's house tonight. She has traveled to the Mediterranean; she has a lung condition and likes the sea air. I will be safe there. I doubt the Soviets will try and kill me forever, heh?"

"No—probably not, now that Viktor is dead." Apparite glanced again at the SMERSH agent; no change yet. "I should take you there before anything else happens, and before it gets dark. But the Russian still isn't dead. You're a doctor—do you know anything about poisons?"

"Not so much!" Hoevenaers answered. "My job is to *cure* my patients, not kill them! But if you get him moving, it may take effect faster."

Not a bad idea, thought Apparite, as long as the Russian didn't get too close or make any sudden moves. The idea of defending a man in a wheelchair from a SMERSH assassin in the middle of a busy street did not have much appeal.

"Alright," responded Apparite, "let's get up to leave and see what happens. If he follows us, maybe it will speed up the poison, if you think that might help."

"Yes, perhaps that is a good idea."

Apparite finished his *kriek,* reminding himself to one day return and have another, and lifted Hoevenaers from the seat. He helped the Doctor to the wheelchair, made a few adjustments to it, and wheeled him out of the door. He paused briefly to listen for the sound of following footsteps, but heard nothing and his danger-sense remained still.

They reached the walk, and as Apparite pushed Hoevenaers down the street he turned his head to look into the café through its large front window. He could just make out the back of the room, where he saw the Russian still seated in front of his plate of sausage, cheese, and bread. But something definitely seemed amiss, and a quick glance back to where he and Hoevenaers had been conversing confirmed his suspicions. Although they had vacated their table, leaving it completely unoccupied, the unmoving Russian's eyes remained fixed on the point where the two of them had been sitting.

He had been dead the entire time. *Mort Subite,* indeed.

TWENTY-FOUR:
A WHITE CROSS IN THE
ARDENNES

"Where to?" Apparite increased his pace as he pushed the Doctor down the street and away from *A la Mort Subite*.

"First, we must contact my wife," said the Doctor. "She will meet us at my daughter's house."

Apparite wheeled him into a nearby bookshop. While Hoevenaers made the call, Apparite stepped outside to keep an eye out for the police or an ambulance. To his relief, neither appeared. Apparently, unmoving Russians in bars staring silently into space don't draw much attention, he thought.

A few moments later, Apparite retrieved the Doctor from the shop. They took a long, wandering taxi ride around Brussels, ending at a downtown movie theater. After suffering through a Swedish-made double-feature dubbed badly into French, they took another prolonged cab-ride to Hoevenaers' daughter's house in the district of Saint Jossé, located just a few blocks from the *Gare du Nord* train station.

The house looked remarkably like the one Hoevenaers had used in London. It was a quaint, three-story brick town-house with pleasing white wood trim and lace curtains in the windows, as had all the dwellings on this quiet street. Apparite was confident that Hoevenaers would be safe here for some time, assuming the Doctor kept a low profile and the Russians did not press the issue of killing him. But he could not, however, take any more trips to *A la Mort Subite*. He would have to remain in the little house until the Director deemed it safe for him to leave it. Apparite figured it would be at least a month before that was possible.

He pushed the Doctor over the threshold of the front door and into the sitting room. The old but well-maintained house was quite tastefully decorated. There were many pieces of fine walnut and cherry furniture, as well as a number of oil paintings and intricately patterned Oriental carpets. As Apparite stood admiring his elegant surroundings, he heard a rustle in the nearby kitchen and noted the scent of baking.

"I see that my wife has arrived," Hoevenaers said. "Does her cooking smell familiar to you?"

Apparite heard the oven-door close. A moment later, who should walk into the sitting room but his *"Oma"* from the safehouse in West Berlin!

"You're married to the *Doctor?*" Apparite blurted out in English.

"Yes, of course," she said, in surprisingly good English in return. She placed a plateful of *streusel* cake onto a small lace-covered table. "At least, I was when I last looked!" she added with a laugh. "I thought you might have guessed it back in Berlin, but I did not want to trouble you further."

"And you know English! Why didn't you speak it in Berlin?"

She laughed again. "Because you were supposed to be German and I was told to play along. I used to be an actress before the war, you know, so I know how to play a part!"

"It's just the damndest thing," Apparite said. "It amazes me."

"What is so strange about it?" asked Hoevenaers. "My wife and I can never repay your supervisor for what he has done for us; we are glad to help him." He motioned for his wife to push him into the small dining room. "Follow me and we shall talk. It has already been a long day and we have much to speak of."

Hoevenaers' wife pushed the Doctor into the adjoining dining room and Apparite followed, carrying the tray of cake. He placed it on the table and took a seat.

"I sense your sadness, Mr. Apparite," Hoevenaers said. "You hide it for my benefit, but I do not wish you to."

"Do you know what happened?" asked Apparite. "How much have you been told?" He took a bite of the warm, sugary cake. Tasting it brought back those initial days in Berlin; those times of discovery and happiness with Christiane.

"I know enough," Hoevenaers said kindly. His wife came back into the room, poured each of them a cup of dark, pungent coffee, and joined them at the table. "You fell in love, and now she is lost to you," he continued. "You have killed your enemy but you do not feel better for it, though I believe you feel less pain for the loss of your friend, the one called 'J.' "

"Yes," said Apparite. "That's about it." His eyes filled with tears and the young agent turned his head in embarrassment. "That's about it."

Hoevenaers' wife rose from her chair and walked over to him. She placed her arms around him, like a mother would do with her own son, and feeling the warmth of her embrace brought the tears coursing out of Apparite's eyes and down his face. He shook in little spasms as he choked out his sobs, but any shame he might have felt had been relieved by the kindness and understanding of his hosts. And somehow he felt natural doing it, as if this was the reason he had been sent here.

After a time the sobs and gasps ceased and Hoevenaers' wife released Apparite from her embrace. She handed him a handkerchief and he wiped his face.

"I'm sorry," he said. "I don't mean to burden you like this."

Hoevenaers reached across the table and took Apparite's hand.

"You must do it; if you do not, it will only make it worse. No man with a duty such as yours can keep these things inside. To let them out is to free yourself from them."

Apparite nodded. He wiped his eyes once again with the handkerchief.

"Maybe you're right—after all, you are a doctor."

"Sometimes," added Hoevenaers in jest.

Apparite took another bite of cake but swallowed it in quick fashion, for he had a question to ask.

"Are you going to tell me more about you?"

"Yes," answered the Doctor. "I have wanted to share my story with you for some time, and your supervisor has given me permission to do so." His wife sat down next to him and took his hand in hers. Hoevenaers spoke.

"Without your supervisor, my family would not be alive. Before the war, my wife was an actress in Berlin—you knew Marlene Dietrich, did you not, my dear?"

"Yes," answered Hoevenaers' wife. "She was very particular about her lighting! She drove us all mad about it: *Always* from above! *Always* from above, she used to say. *Ach*—such a woman!"

"My wife is a Jew," Hoevenaers said, "and after Hitler came to power, everything changed for us. First she had to register with the police, and her activities were monitored. But we were in love and we married. We had a baby girl—her name is El-freide—and we were happy." Hoevenaers' wife walked to a nearby hutch and took a yellowed photograph from a drawer.

"This is her," she said to Apparite. "When she was only six." The photograph was of a smiling little black-haired girl who seemed not to have a care in the world, but sewn onto her dress was something which made him shudder: the emblem of a Star of David, put there by German law at the time to identify her as a member of the "inferior" Jewish race.

"You see what they did to us," said Hoevenaers' wife. "You see what they did even to little girls."

"Thank God it is over," the Doctor said. "Thank God. As the years passed, it got worse for us, and we heard that people were being taken away. We thought the time to escape Germany had missed us, but then we met your supervisor. He took us out of the country in secret, saving the life of my wife and my daughter. Since that day, we have pledged to help him, to help him fight the kind of people who do not wish others to be free. I thought you would like to know this."

"I know so little about him," said Apparite, "except that he's the most incredible, unusual man I've ever met. At times he scares the hell out of me, but at others—"

"Yes," interrupted Hoevenaers, "he is, as you say, a most incredible man. I have never seen him show fear, or do what he does not think is right. Even when we were surrounded by German soldiers he was unafraid, though he knew we might die at any moment."

Hoevenaers' wife stirred in her chair. "Oh! I have forgotten something. I have a letter for you, Mr. Apparite." She went into the front room and returned with a brown envelope. "The man called 'D' sent it to Brussels by air; by some miracle it arrived ahead of you. He must think it very important to have sent it so quickly."

Apparite took the envelope in hand. It was made of rough, distinctly cheap-looking paper, had no return address or postmark, and was addressed to "Horst Köller." Apparite turned it over in his hand but the reverse was blank; there were no other clues as to who had sent it. It appeared to be unopened, but Apparite knew that this didn't mean anything—there were always ways to do it without detection.

"Where did it come from?"

"No one knows," answered Hoevenaers' wife.

Apparite opened it, expecting to find a note or letter inside, but the envelope contained only a small photograph. He held it up in his hand and audibly gasped.

It was a picture of Christiane.

"It's *her*," he said. "It's her photograph." He handed it to the Doctor.

"She is very beautiful," said Hoevenaers. "I see why you fell in love with such a woman."

The photograph was only of Christiane's head and shoulders; she was directly facing the camera as if posed. She appeared to be wearing a drab gray dress, but her blonde hair fell about her shoulders just as Apparite recalled it so often doing. Her face was unsmiling and her expression contained a look of boredom, but her eyes were alive and bright.

Apparite turned the photograph over. Two words were written in block-letters on the back: *"Fight Senators!"* Who in the world—?

And then it came to him.

It was from the Russian, Zhdanovich! It *had* to have been him.

Apparite laughed as he completed the puzzle. This was Christiane's official Karlshorst dossier photograph. Zhdanovich must have sent it to the American military compound, where it had eventually found its way to D. It was the Russian's way of thanking Apparite for all he'd done, a token of their unlikely friendship.

"It's like a miracle," Apparite said. He removed his wallet from his coat, exposing its secret compartment in order to place the photograph inside it. As he did so, Hoevenaers spied the Walter Johnson card in its hiding place.

"What else do you have in there?" the Doctor asked.

"Don't tell anyone, but that's my good luck charm. I take it with me everywhere I go." Apparite carefully removed the card and handed it to the Doctor.

Hoevenaers looked at it, his eyes widening in recognition.

"Where did you get this?" He handed the card back to Apparite.

"That's a strange story. After my father was killed in the Bulge, it arrived in the mail a few months later. I've never found out who sent it."

"Mon Dieu," said Hoevenaers. *My God.* He put his hand to his forehead in a gesture of shock. *"Mon Dieu, c'est impossible!"* *My God, that's impossible!* He sat back down again, his face showing absolute astonishment. "I . . . I must make a telephone call—immediately." He wheeled himself with some effort into the kitchen, closing the door behind him.

"What was that all about?" asked Apparite. "Hasn't he ever seen a baseball card before?"

Hoevenaers' wife took the card from Apparite and looked at it. "I don't know—but then again, he doesn't tell me everything." She handed it back to Apparite, who returned it, along with Christiane's photograph, to the secret compartment of his wallet. He sat quietly and sipped coffee until Hoevenaers returned a minute later.

"What's going on?" Apparite said. "Is there something I should know?"

"It's nothing—I just remembered another matter to attend to. But tomorrow, I am told, you need to make a journey to Neupre. Your supervisor wishes to meet with you."

"Tomorrow? I thought I'd be staying here for at least a week or two."

"You will," Hoevenaers said. "He wants to show you something, and then you may return to spend some time with myself and my wife. That is all I can say for now—you know how he is."

"Yes," replied Apparite. "I know how he is." A look of worry crossed his face. Meeting with the Director at a time like this was disconcerting. He feared it indicated trouble.

The next morning, Apparite boarded the train that would take him to Liége, where he would journey on to Neupre by taxi. He disliked having to travel again so soon, preferring to have stayed in Brussels with the Doctor and his wife. As D and the Director had hoped, they were already proving therapeutic to Apparite's spirits; in fact, having a respite from his duties and being around normal people for even a few hours was a comfort to him (all too often his only companions were spies, counter-spies, traitors, and dupes, and such types only worsened one's psychological defenses, not strengthened them).

The evening before had been a welcome and pleasant one for Apparite, although the events at *A la Mort Subite* and the Doctor's strange behavior after seeing the baseball card were not mentioned again after supper. Instead, Apparite had spent the rest of the evening sipping brandy while the Doctor and his wife regaled him with tales of pre-war Germany. As they had a number of them, and all were quite fascinating, the time had passed quickly.

His "*Oma,*" as Apparite still thought of Hoevenaers' wife, had been in some very famous German films such as *M* and *Pandora's Box,* and had the honor of personally knowing directors Fritz Lang and G.W. Pabst. Apparite had not heard of any of the films or directors she'd mentioned, but gathered they were among the most legendary in German cinema. Despite Apparite's calculation that she was well past sixty years of age, the former beauty of her youth was yet evident in the confident sprightliness of her step and in her lively, deep brown eyes. He wished that somehow he could have seen her in her prime, as Lang and Pabst, and another director (Lubitsch—had that been his name?) had when they had filmed her, but then remembered there was an easy way to do just that: all he had to do was catch one of her old movies. He made a mental note to do that someday.

The Doctor told Apparite many tales as well. Using the cover

287

of a café owner near the town of Malmédy, he had fought in the Belgian resistance in the Second World War, battling the Nazis even as his wife and daughter escaped to London (to the very safe-house in Chelsea where Apparite had been taken after the tragic conclusion of his mission last autumn). Hoevenaers did much work for the Director during that time, taking many risks though saving many lives, and yet his family, whom he would not see for three long years, always remained foremost in his thoughts. Other events followed—some tragic, others inspirational and filled with courage—and by the time Hoevenaers concluded his remarkable story, ending happily with his family's reunion in Paris after the German surrender, tears flowed freely from the eyes of all in the room.

At the end of this long evening of remembrances, Hoevenaers toasted to everyone's health and of those they loved—at this point, he looked at Apparite with empathy—and they all retired to bed. But Apparite's thoughts thwarted his efforts to rest, and it was hours before he'd removed enough memories of Christiane, Viktor, J, Lohmann, Heydrich, and the Director from his head to allow sleep to overtake him.

But finally and blessedly it had, so that when he boarded the train the next morning his mood was not, perhaps, as low as that of the day before, and his energy had been a bit rejuvenated as well. Still, he awoke with tears in his eyes, as he had so often done since the events the previous autumn, reminding him that although he had not remembered his dreams from the night before, they continued to distress him. He had a long way to go before he was "normal," though whatever that was he could hardly remember anymore, for *his* normalcy included killing people in cold blood, and lying, cheating, and stealing for his country. What was "normal" for him, he realized, would be considered quite pathological for anyone else—and would likely remain so, right up until the day he was finally released from

the Director's agency.

The train passed through the pretty Belgian countryside on its journey to Liége, and Apparite tried to relax and enjoy the trip as much as possible. But with each passing minute, as he was taken further and further from the comfort of the Hoevenaers' house in Brussels, he became increasingly morose. It was bad enough to be bothered by one's unconscious while sleeping, but his waking memories were now troubling him significantly as well, for he could not stop thinking about Christiane, and, oddly, of his father. Traveling in Belgium, the country where his father had been killed, was bringing him to mind, too.

A young woman approached Apparite's booth.

"Excuse me," she asked in French, "would you mind if I sat here?" She had black hair and was not terribly attractive, but the situation echoed the first meeting of Apparite and Christiane enough to bring memories of her flooding into his head.

"Non," Apparite said without emotion. *"Pas du tout."* No, not at all.

He closed his eyes and tried to picture Christiane as she'd looked when they'd first met on the train. Sometimes it was effortless and natural to do so, and he felt as if she were right next to him, her head resting on his shoulder as she slept. But at other times the outline of her visage remained blurred and indistinct; her eyes shifting between blue, then hazel, and then green; her hair blonde, then chestnut brown, and then the color of sand; and sometimes he could not recall her voice in either timbre or pitch, or any of the words she had spoken. And so it was with this current effort, in which he had been rebuffed completely. The picture simply wouldn't come, lost in a confusing haze of memory and pain.

He reproached himself for his weakness. He was thinking of taking her picture from its hiding place in his wallet when a remembrance from his childhood came to him. Apparite tried

to imagine his father's face, but as with Christiane's he found it frustratingly elusive. If only he had a photograph or even a letter to remember *him* by, he thought; anything at all that might serve to anchor the memory he sought.

But all of Apparite's possessions had been destroyed after the Director "sheep-dipped" him back in 1955, removing all traces that he had ever existed as F---- K------- back in Eckhart Springs. His only remaining personal possession was his mysterious Walter Johnson tobacco card, but as that had come to Apparite after his father's death, even this did not provide the needed connection.

But there were also times when Apparite was glad for it, glad that the physical reminders of his father's presence were gone, for it allowed Apparite to form whatever picture of him that he wanted at any given moment. Apparite knew that his father had been an unsuccessful salesman and too often absent, but in Apparite's mind he could invent another one to take his place: the father who'd hunted with him, hugging him when Apparite made a tough shot; and the father with whom he'd listened to the Nats, sharing Apparite's happiness when their team pulled out an all-too-infrequent win.

But in the end, he was always left with the same final vision of him—one that he could not forget or alter in any way to make it less painful: the sight of his father, dressed in his U.S. Army uniform, waving as the train left the Cumberland rail depot; the last memory of him Apparite would ever form.

Apparite had loved his father when he had been home, and had hated his father whenever he had left it, especially when he had gone off to fight in the war. Losing Christiane had wounded Apparite, too, but their final conversation in the military compound had left a lingering scent of sweetness to the affair, and though he did not know it riding this train from Brussels to Liége, it would aid him greatly in the coming months. But the

wound from his father's leaving had not yet healed; nor would it, guessed Apparite, when he thought of such things, unless he somehow could be gifted the same scent of sweetness to that parting as he had with Christiane's. Since his father had been dead these last ten years, he knew that was not going to happen now, short of a miracle.

He opened his eyes. The woman across the booth was reading a book; Apparite was relieved to note it was not *Peyton Place*. He was glad she seemed engrossed in it; given his mood, he did not feel like conversing with a stranger. And not only that, but he was tired of pretending to be other people like "Hans Müller" or "Horst Köller." He longed to speak English, to tell people to call him "John," and to have a place, even if it were only a smelly cot in a D.C. warehouse, to claim as his own.

He looked out of the window at the Belgian scenery, wondering what was in store for him when he arrived at his destination. *The American Cemetery of the Ardennes,* he said to himself, *that's where I'm going,* but the reason for it remained a mystery. His mind flitted about the possibilities: Was the Director going to show him the grave of someone he needed Apparite to investigate—someone who perhaps was not really dead? Or was there someone of importance who would meet them there? A cemetery such as this would make a fine place for a "chance" meeting: it was quiet and relatively private, yet supervised by the U.S. Army. Perhaps this was going to be the starting point of a new European mission.

Hungary—maybe *that* was it! The Director had mentioned a revolt in Hungary planned for the autumn, and had told Apparite that the other Superagent, Agent B, had been forced to leave the country or risk exposure. But would the Director send Apparite into the field in the unstable mental state the young agent presently was in? There was a necessary balance to be maintained if Apparite was to fully recover: work might be used as a way to avoid pain or might only serve to exacerbate it, and while idleness sometimes was the cause of despair (Apparite had experienced that in New York), it could also do wonders in relieving it.

Given the situation, Apparite knew which was best for him.

He was certain that all he needed was one month with the Hoevenaerses in Brussels and he'd be ready to go again. Just one month, that's all he wanted—and not only that, but it had been *promised* to him. Back in the war, the generals found that a week away from the shelling was usually enough to restore a man's spirits and make him battle-ready again—didn't the Director know this? Or maybe he just didn't *care.* The Director had admittedly been very kind and understanding when Apparite was recovering from his near-fatal poisoning last year, but that was then—and this was *now!* And he was getting upset at the prospect of it.

By the time the train pulled into Liége, Apparite had wound himself into quite a state. He was tense and apprehensive and his temper was on a hair-trigger. He hailed a taxi at the station, which took him through Neupre and then on to the cemetery. The entrance was guarded by uniformed members of the U.S. Army (the cemetery was considered American soil), and portions of it were still under construction, but it was a moving sight to behold. On the expanse of the green lawn ahead were rows upon rows of white crosses, many more than Apparite could count or his keen eyes could even estimate in number.

The markers all bore the same information in their inscriptions: *Name, Unit, Rank, State,* and *Date of Death.* Each one of them, Apparite realized, had been erected over a man much like himself: a man uprooted from his home to serve his country, taken overseas to fight for what he believed in most, which was freedom. Each had left a family behind, a family that would have felt the pain of their loss just as Apparite had, when he'd heard of his own father's death. Each cross represented a man who had fought selflessly for the lives of others, even as he gave up his own at the height of its worth.

Apparite's anger left him as he wandered amongst the graves. These brave men were dead and yet he was still alive and fighting—shouldn't that be enough to sustain him? The pain of losing Christiane, or J dying in London, or even his father having been killed was nothing compared to the collective suffering which so many untold others had experienced, as evidenced by the thousands of white crosses (and occasional Stars of David) he now saw around him. He was humbled by it; he suddenly felt small and insignificant.

A young soldier walked up to where Apparite stood. "Are you looking for someone in particular?" he asked. "I don't know the lay-out too well yet, but I can get you pointed in the right direction."

Apparite relayed the information he had been given by Hoevenaers: a letter and two numbers.

"Oh—that one's over here." The soldier led Apparite along a grass path between two large fields of markers. Apparite had assumed that the numbers represented a gravesite, but until now he hadn't been certain.

"Looks like someone's waiting for you there," the soldier said. He pointed to a middle-aged man wearing a black suit standing in the midst of the white crosses, but the man in question wasn't just "someone" to Apparite—it was the man he knew as the "Director."

The soldier led Apparite to the appropriate row. "There you go—you grab any one of us if you have any questions."

"Thank you," Apparite replied softly. He walked down the row, his slow steps showing his hesitation, but when he got to within ten feet of the Director, the severe-appearing man raised his hand to stop him.

"Before you reach me, let me tell you a story."

Apparite halted. "Why did you—?"

"Please," interrupted the Director, "just listen. Back in the war, Dr. Hoevenaers was working for the Belgian resistance and I was with the OSS. I had been operating undercover in Germany and had stolen important plans from the Nazis, plans for their atomic bomb program. But Hoevenaers and I got caught in the middle of the Bulge, and were in danger of capture. An American GI helped us—"

"I know," said Apparite, breaking in. "The Doctor told me about him."

"We escaped to the American lines alive because of that soldier. I found out later he'd been captured and taken with other prisoners near the town of Malmédy. Wilhelm Heydrich, the man you killed in Rhinbourg, commanded the soldiers who shot them."

"So I've been told. Is that the real reason you sent me to kill him? Heydrich thought so."

"No," said the Director. "We are in the espionage business, not the revenge business. It is best we do our duty without emotion, or motives other than those the mission requires. Heydrich was killed because of his SMERSH activities—nothing more. But there *is* more to the story than you know."

"Like what?" asked Apparite. *What the hell was going on here?*

"The world is an unexplainable place, Apparite. Things happen so often for no discernible reason at all—and then something happens for every possible reason, even if we cannot see it."

He paused and took a breath, trying to find the right words. This was the first time Apparite had ever seen the Director hesitant or even vaguely uncertain of himself; he found it jarring. Something very strange was occurring.

"Your father was among those killed by Heydrich's men at Malmédy," the Director continued. "I did not want you to know this before you went on your mission, for fear it would compromise it."

"He killed my father? Heydrich killed my father?"

"He did not pull the trigger, but he condoned what happened. It is the same thing; in my opinion, he bears more responsibility than the man who does the killing. But the story does not end there. I am going to ask you a question that may very well change your life:

"Do you carry a signed Walter Johnson tobacco card in your wallet?"

Apparite hesitated. Was all of this simply a pretense to dress him down for defying an order not to carry items other than those he had been issued? And what was going to come after it—the burning of Christiane's photograph, perhaps?

"Yes," answered Apparite. "Yes, I do." He took out his wallet and removed the card, holding it up for the Director to view.

"Do you know where that card came from?"

"No. My mother got it in the mail. She gave it to me for my birthday."

"Do you have any idea who sent it to her?" the Director asked. "Or who it belonged to, before you got it?"

"No. I've never had the slightest idea." *What in the world is he driving at?*

"That card came from the man that saved my life in the Bulge that December day in nineteen forty-four. And I am standing at his grave." He motioned for Apparite to approach.

Apparite walked slowly to where the Director stood. He turned to see what was engraved on the marker: *"Edwin K-------, Private, 291ˢᵗ Engineer Combat Battalion, Maryland, December 17 1944."* This white cross marked the final resting place of John Apparite's father.

Apparite could not speak; he could hardly find the energy to breathe. The significance of this discovery was beyond anything he had ever imagined. In his overwhelmed state he was having trouble putting it together.

"Are you saying that the man who saved you and the Doctor—was my *father?*" Apparite asked very deliberately.

"Yes."

"I . . . I . . . how come you never told me?"

"I thought you knew," the Director said in a kind voice. "I sent you a letter of condolence in nineteen forty-five, though under an assumed name. But when I spoke with Hoevenaers yesterday it became clear you didn't know anything about it."

Apparite smiled in bitter remembrance. "There was a letter but I never read it. I threw it in the fireplace."

"You deserve to know what your father did. If my position had allowed it, I would have nominated him for a commendation. Secrecy had to be maintained, however—which was unfortunate."

Tears fell silently from Apparite's face. He had spent all those years hating his father for leaving to serve his country, never knowing that he'd died a hero. Apparite felt ashamed at having done it, and yet the pride of a son in his father's greatest moment of sacrifice had already begun to heal him of his oldest and deepest wound.

"But—but what does that have to do with my baseball card?" asked Apparite. He wiped his eyes and took a deep breath. "Who sent it to me?"

"I did."

Apparite's face went blank.

"You? *You* sent it?" He felt weak at this discovery, the unlikely solution to the single greatest mystery in his life.

"I found the card in your father's wallet after he'd been killed. I took it to Walter, had him autograph it, and sent it anonymously to your mother. I imagined it would raise your spirits. For you to have placed it in your wallet in defiance of my orders proves its worth to you!" He gently gripped Apparite by the shoulder to let him know the offence had been forgiven.

"*You* sent it to me," said Apparite wistfully. "But did you know when you interviewed me that—"

"Of course," interrupted the Director. "Of course I knew—in some way, I'd always known. Ever since I first saw you in that picture, I knew it would happen. I knew we would meet."

"Picture? What picture?"

The Director reached into his suit and removed a small, yellowed photograph. He handed it to Apparite.

"My Lord," said Apparite: it was a picture of himself as a young boy. He was standing next to his parents, dressed in his best suit from Sears; the three of them were smiling. He remembered it like it was just an hour ago. It had been his tenth birthday and his family had made a special trip to Cumberland to have their photograph taken. "It's the picture my father carried in his wallet when he traveled. I just can't believe it, after all these years—"

"I kept it to preserve the memory of the man who saved my life," said the Director. "A foolish, selfish gesture, but not one without meaning. Now that you know the whole story, I'm giving it back to you. Keep it hidden with your baseball card and the picture of the girl—as long as you don't mind taking an L-pill if they're discovered."

"I'd probably take an L-pill if you told me to get rid of them!" said Apparite. "And to think that when you called me here, what I thought you were going to tell me—only to find out that you've known me all this time. And that my father was the one that saved you. . . ."

Overcome by the shock of his many discoveries, Apparite fell to his knees and bowed his head in silence, cupping it in his hands, hiding his soft sobs. He looked up at his father's grave marker, instantly renewing his dedication to fight for his country as selflessly as his father had, willing to die for it in an instant— just as his father had. Ten long years had passed since his father's death, but at this moment Apparite had never loved or missed him more.

The Director put a hand on Apparite's shoulder and rubbed it with affection. Roused from his thoughts, Apparite looked up at him, smiling through his tears. The Director was the toughest son of a bitch he had ever met, but the gesture betrayed the man's undeniable humanity—particularly where this orphaned young Superagent from Eckhart Springs, Maryland, was concerned.

By Memorial Day, everything will be better, Apparite remembered telling himself back in New York, *if only I can make it until then.* He smiled again as he thought it, knowing he'd beaten his estimation by three full weeks. It was barely May, but he knew his emotional recovery from the events in Berlin and London had already begun.

Not that the future had been made any easier by the revelations in the cemetery. His duties as a Superagent would remain as dangerous and deadly as ever, and it was only a matter of time and circumstance before the Director would put him back into harm's way. But for now, all Apparite had been charged to do was relax and heal, and as the Director drove him back to the Liége rail-station, the young agent continued to stare at his "magical" Walter Johnson baseball card, marveling at the fragile chain of circumstances that had led to this landmark day.

And yet one question still begged asking:

What if Hoevenaers hadn't seen the card?

Would he ever have discovered the secret to his father's past? To the origin of the mysterious card? Or to the fact that the Director had not only known his father, having been saved by him in the war, but that he had known of Apparite as well, though the Superagent had been but a boy at the time?

Thank God for Senators baseball, Apparite concluded. *The Nats might be the worst team in the league, but thank God for Washington Senators baseball all the same.*

A sudden believer in *kismet,* he gently returned the tobacco card to its hiding place in his wallet. A moment later, he was asleep.

ACKNOWLEDGMENTS

Books are not created in a vacuum, and as with any published tale, *A Matter of Revenge* was not entirely written by the author alone. In fact, as I suspect is true of most historical fiction, it was written with the aid of dozens of others, including (in my case) the many unknown and un-creditable authors and researchers whose informative internet Web sites gave me such information as the make-up and effects of the poison tetrodo-toxin; the detailed lay-out of post-war, pre-Wall Berlin; the varieties of trees that grow on the Vosges Mountains; the appearance of Yankee Stadium back in 1956 (yes, its exterior *was* brown at the time); and other essentials. Whoever you are—all of you—you have my everlasting thanks.

Among the known and creditable, there are many for me to acknowledge: Cherry Weiner, of the Cherry Weiner Literary Agency; my editor, Hugh Abramson; my local proof-readers and improvement-suggesters (especially my lovely wife, Jackie, plus Mike Berg, Jocelynn Knight, Annmarie Penvose, and T.J. Potts); plus all of the fine people at Five Star Publishing. Lastly, since I am basically unilingual (having forgotten much of the French and Spanish I once knew), I'd like to acknowledge my foreign language translators: Natalia Fishler (Russian), Isabelle Kirkendall (German), and Jennifer Giesen (French). *Graçias!*

In addition to the fine works I previously acknowledged in my first Apparite book, *Under Cloak of Darkness,* I need to add a couple more that any author wishing to write about Cold War

Berlin must read: *Battleground Berlin: CIA versus KGB in the Cold War* (by David Murphy, Sergei Kondrashev, and George Bailey), and *Spies Beneath Berlin* (by David Stafford). Without them, Apparite's revenge would likely have occurred someplace else, or not at all.

Lastly, I'd like to thank my two young daughters for being great kids. It has nothing to do with this book, but I believe that when you've got great kids, they should be thanked at every opportunity.

ABOUT THE AUTHOR

I. Michael Koontz was born in 1963 and is a physician living in the Midwest with his wife and two young daughters. His John Apparite novels *A Matter of Revenge* and *Under Cloak of Darkness* are the result of a lifelong interest in Cold War espionage and military history. Readers interested in learning more about Superagent John Apparite and Cold War espionage, or who have questions or comments regarding the book, are encouraged to visit the author's extensive Web site, www.im koontz.com.